a novel by

Dahn
Ben
Amotz

to
remember,
to
forget

translated
from the
Hebrew by

Zeva
Shapiro

The Jewish Publication Society
of America   PHILADELPHIA

to remember, to forget

1 | *general cargo*

In September of 1959 I set out for Germany. Though at first I had been reluctant to claim reparations, certain events in my life—the chance to acquire an abandoned Arab house near the border, the need for a car of my own, the influence of a childhood friend who was returning to Germany, the approaching deadline for presenting claims—these events conspired to effect a change of mind that was absolute and final.

The same rational scheme with which I had resisted the idea of reparations became the cornerstone upon which I now based my moral claim. This unpleasant transaction turned into a highly protracted matter, so that I finally decided to go to Frankfurt to demand my due. I was granted leave without pay by the firm that employed me, Brumberg-Avishai-Landau Engineers. As this was my first trip abroad since arriving in Israel at thirteen, I decided to spend three weeks in Italy as well and to visit San Castello, a village in the north, where I had found refuge during the last three years of the war. Had I known then, as I set out on this voyage into my past, what I now know, it is doubtful that I would have undertaken to pursue my reparations claim; it is equally doubtful that these words from which I now find no escape would ever have been written. Which would, perhaps, be for the best.

2 | *inspection*

After four days at sea we arrived in Genoa. I had been standing in the prow since seven that morning amid a horde of screeching gulls, my eyes tensely scanning the horizon, seeking my own Cape of Good Hope. It was two hours before we were close enough to the port to glimpse the pale and frozen city suspended midst murky waters and polluted sky.

Now, my passport duly stamped by an Italian policeman, I was waiting to pass through customs. Catching sight of myself in a mirror set in one of the columns, I could not repress a smile. Here I was, a young man in a black raincoat with turned-up collar, set for adventure; this young man about to conquer Europe was me. I tried to conceal my excitement, to assume the manner of a seasoned traveler accustomed to the procedures of arrival and departure. I was eager to get through customs, find my train, and be off to Siena, Florence, Rome, to find myself in a role I had played more than once— comparing the Tuscan landscape as it unfolded past the window to the clear, fertile hillsides in the golden frames of Giotto, Fra Angelico, Filippo Lippi and Piero della Francesca. ("No, *signorina*, I haven't been here before, but the scene is familiar.") I yearned to walk through the Uffizi Gallery, the Pinacoteca in Siena, the Roman Forum ("Pardon me, *signorina*, haven't we met before? Perhaps on the train from Genoa?"); to sip espresso in a small café, eat spaghetti by candlelight, watching the wax make patterns on the checkered tablecloth. ("Isn't it strange, Sofia—Francesca? Beatrice? Monica?—that we should meet again? *Cin-cin*, this wine is really splendid.") I longed to walk through the streets of Rome, guarding my secret jealously: the gentleman in the black raincoat, addressing himself in Hebrew, a tongue foreign to this region—this gentlemen is me, anonymous, known to no one. I longed to leave the port, to knock on Aunt Anna's door in San Castello, and shout, "It's me."

But the customs proceedings dragged on. Passengers scurried around among the luggage which was sorted alphabetically, seeking themselves on the tags. One of my suitcases had not arrived. Was it lost? Misplaced? After searching everywhere without success, I lifted the one suitcase to the counter, clutching its handle tight.

The customs officer stared at me. I glanced past the policeman in the doorway toward the city streets beyond the gate, surveying the scene apprehensively, as if it would vanish like some delirium should I turn away even for a moment. There, beyond the gate, Europe awaits me. Another Europe. Not the one I had left at thirteen with a throng of children, marching in threes, waving white handkerchiefs as we boarded the boat and set off for a warm, distant land, a land of golden beaches, palm trees, orange groves, whitewashed houses—far from the black pitch roofs of home, of family scenes with white tablecloths and the scent of raspberry jam. All this is long since gone. In its place another Europe: Rossellini, De Sica, *ciao, bambina.* ("You dance so well, you dance with feeling. Shall we go to the garden? Let's sit near the river . . . cross the bridge . . . watch the water in silence. Your hands, darling, are so warm.")

The customs official caught my eye again, followed my glance toward the door, stared at the suitcase I continued to clutch, looked me in the eye, and said, "What do you have to declare, sir?" In Italian that to my ears had a remarkably natural ring, I told him I was waiting for another suitcase. I lit a cigarette. Why is he staring at me like that? I am not smuggling anything—except myself.

Finally the other suitcase turned up. By the time I lifted it to the counter a couple with eight pieces of luggage had claimed the inspector's attention. He asked if they had any valuable gifts, accepted their answer without any further check, and let them through. They are charming, these Italians, and so gracious. Always a warm smile. So I thought as I handed him my declaration and my passport.

"Please wait here," he said.

"But I have my other suitcase," I explained.

"I know," he said. "Please have a seat while we check the remaining passengers. It won't be very long."

What's the meaning of this? Why is he making me wait? Do I look suspicious? No, not at all. Or somewhat pale? I had hoped to spend four days relaxing in a deck chair, but the sun didn't show its face. I had been up early and hadn't eaten anything. Naturally I was pale. What's he thinking, this pig of an inspector? Let him search me if he wants to. I don't mind that part. But the humiliation! ("You, my dear fellow, have the manner of a smuggler. We noted your anxious glances. Someone is waiting for you at the gate. You have a parcel for him. We know your sort.") He stamped eight suitcases without batting an eyelash; now mine is the one he means to check.

The last of the passengers filed through customs, whispering and glancing smugly in my direction. ("The rat! He makes such a good impression, but he turns out to be a smuggler.")

A second customs official, one I hadn't seen before, appeared from nowhere and stood beside my suitcase, glaring at me with menacing eyes.

"Now then, sir" he said, "what do you have to declare?"

I handed him my papers. He leafed through the passport, left to right, staring intently at the photograph. "A handsome mustache," he remarked. The photo was two years old; since then I had grown a mustache. So what?

"Cigarettes, cigars, brandy, camera, personal effects," he said. "Is that all? Is that all you have to declare?"

"That's all," I said sincerely.

"Are you sure, sir?"

What does he mean? Has some idiot been telling stories at my expense? The son-of-a-bitch I met on the boat, I bet—he was leaving Israel after having been rescued from Germany and provided with housing and work, all at the government's expense (my expense!). Now, after collecting blood money, the bastard is going back to Germany to invest it there. The damn fool . . . I had said my piece and I knew he was listening when I sounded off about him and his kind. No doubt he was the one who whispered something in someone's ear.

"I'm sure," I said firmly.

"And what's the purpose of your trip?" he asked. I can show him the papers now. I'm going to Germany for reparations. This is no mere pleasure trip. Is it a crime to demand my due? I have it all in writing. Proof of everything.

"A vacation," I said. "A three-week holiday in Italy: Rome, Florence, Siena, and San Castello."

"A vacation," he repeated, calling a porter to take my bags. "Be so kind as to follow me, sir," he said leading the way to an office at the opposite end of the passenger section, where a single window, set high in the wall, provided dim light. The porter placed the suitcases on a large table and left, closing the door softly behind him. The inspector switched on a strong light, dragged in a chair from the next room, and placed it near the table.

"Open your bags, please," he said, unfolding my customs declaration and placing his pen on the document, poised for action. I unlocked the suitcase with the key that dangled from it.

"Sit down," he said.

"Thanks," I said, making no move. I offered him an American cigarette, which he accepted as he began to empty the suitcase systematically: shirts, pants, underwear, socks, a wool scarf, dark suit, winter coat, two towels, handkerchiefs, toilet articles, the briefcase that held my papers, cigarettes, brandy, camera. He looked up and searched my face sternly. I smiled, a faint, bitter smile, already relishing the disappointment in store for him.

"Don't be angry, sir," he said. "I'm only doing my job."

"Angry?" I retorted, a little too loud. "Who's angry? I am delighted to have this opportunity to prove my innocence. I am delighted at the failure in store for you. This little fiasco will surely discredit your judgment, sir. You may learn that not every decent-looking person is necessarily a criminal or a smuggler. You may even begin to distrust the whispers of rats who revisit cemeteries to cash in on the dead. Yes, yes, go ahead, sir, and do your job."

I enjoyed my little speech, the opportunity to flex my

Italian . . . but he was offended. These Fascists aren't used to dealing with people who insist on their own dignity. They expect you to kiss their ass, beg, implore, degrade yourself just as they did. (There were exceptions, of course, like Uncle Michele.) He tried to evade my eyes and, turning his back to me, began a thorough check. He shook out the folded shirts, rifled the toilet articles, squeezed the toothpaste tube, scanned countless forms and certificates, all in German (pretending not to know that language!), opened each pack of cigarettes, and was dismayed not to find anything. Small beads of sweat began to appear along his thin mustache. He fingered the lining of a new winter coat, acquired for the trip, opened my camera, measured the depth of each suitcase inside and out. He was expecting, no doubt, to find a false bottom filled with hashish, cocaine, gold. I looked on with a nasty grin as he took a screwdriver from his drawer and plunged it into the bottom of the suitcase, splitting it in two.

"Go right ahead, sir," I said, "and do your job. Your performance is consistent with the highest traditions of your people."

He turned to me, his lower lip quivering.

"Are you quite through, sir?" I said. "May I pack my things?"

"Not yet," he shouted. "Take off your clothes." He pointed to a door marked GENTLEMEN.

"With pleasure," I said. "Somehow this hadn't occurred to me. Of course—I'm concealing something on my person, the natural place for a beginner. How clever of you, sir. Now you've got me."

I entered a small cubicle, hung my raincoat on a hook, and began to strip.

"I'm nearly ready," I called out, opening the door a crack. "Be patient, I won't be long—I do this every night. Should I take my shoes off?"

"That won't be necessary," said the inspector, entering the cubicle with averted eyes. He stuck his hands into the trouser pockets, then the coat pockets, checking them perfunctorily.

"How careless of you, sir," I said. "You forgot to check my wallet. Or is it the custom here to offer one's wallet at the start of the investigation?"

"That will be all," he mumbled, turning to go.

"What about the rectum?" I said, posting myself between him and the door. "You forgot to check my rectum. So sorry to disappoint you, but it happens to be empty," and, as luck would have it, I let out a splendid fart—rich and mellow with sentiments of national pride and independence. "Perfectly empty," I repeated.

He brushed me aside and slipped out of the cubicle, slamming the door behind. "Pig!" he managed to exclaim as the door swung closed. I laughed until there were tears in my eyes. I laughed while I pulled on my pants, I laughed while I put on my sweater and jacket. I couldn't stop. What luck to have produced a resounding blast at that precise moment!

When I emerged my bags were packed. The shirts were folded, the toilet articles were in their case, the papers in order. The inspector's eyes remained fixed on the form he was filling out in a neat hand that had a distinctly aristocratic flourish. Still smiling, I locked the suitcases and noted that they had been approved.

"Permit me to express my deep regret, sir," said the inspector, not meeting my gaze. "There has been an unfortunate mistake. You may present this voucher to the cashier at the customs office and you'll be compensated for the damaged suitcase. I hope you have a pleasant vacation and, again, I'm terribly sorry!"

He handed me the voucher. I tore it to shreds, scattering the pieces on the floor.

"Thanks," I said. "I'd like to keep this suitcase as a memento of Italy. Sorry I caused you so much frustration. And I do understand your position—an alert civil servant wishing to apprehend one more Jewish smuggler and report him to the authorities. I am very sorry, really very sorry."

Without waiting for me to finish, he called a porter to help with my bags. By the time I was finally outside the gate it was one o'clock in the afternoon. Being tired and hungry I saw no reason to go on to the train station. I wanted to wash up and eat, to recover from my reception in Europe. So I checked into the first hotel and took a room with a shower.

3 | *the three-dollar surprise*

I showered, lay down to rest, and fell asleep—finding myself in a place I had never seen before, on a hard mattress that rested on the ground. Grass from outside crept under the door and into the room, trailing across the mattress, onto my face. The walls were thin, and I could hear voices: Brumberg saying I was lost, it was too late to save me, the grass would soon cover me completely. I woke up in another room where faded flowers grew along the papered walls; I woke up in Genoa at 4:30 in the afternoon. My window overlooked a narrow, dim alley, so that when I stuck my head out I could see a murky strip of sea in the distance. The nagging rain had stopped and an array of street noises—merchants hawking wares in the nearby marketplace, the roar of traffic, car horns, trolley bells—filtered through the window and beckoned to me.

I put on my coat. Remembering the inspector brought a bitter taste to my mouth—if it hadn't been for that idiot, I'd be in Florence now.

Open your soul, please, and let's see what's inside. Forget it, I'm free to go anywhere—a good restaurant, a movie, nightclubs, sweet cinzano in some dark bar ("May I join you, *signorina?*)—Europe on a silver platter. I checked my wallet and went out onto a street bustling with crowded displays: sunglasses, picture postcards, newspapers, ashtrays, fountain pens, souvenirs of Genoa. An elegant young man in sunglasses, clean-shaven and impeccably groomed, approached me in an underground voice offering me his Parker 51, a gold watch, a ring, all for next to nothing, a steal. He had to raise some cash quickly so he could visit his sick mother in Sicily. He would exchange my dollars at a favorable rate, show me Genoa, introduce me to his sister. He spoke to me in rapid English. I told him, in Italian, that I needed nothing and walked on. He trailed me, glancing furtively in every direction, shifting from one side to the other, whispering tantalizing propositions. He turned away abruptly, almost in midsentence, and vanished. I noticed a policeman at the corner.

A row of green cabs were parked near the crosswalk. The idle drivers were eyeing me with interest. One of them called out, "Taxi?"

"No, *grazia*." I answered.

"Oh, you speak Italian," he said.

"Yes, like an Italian princess abducted by Indians—"

"Don't worry. I'm not about to offer you a glass ring that looks like a diamond. Do you want to see something truly beautiful, something unique?"

"What?" I asked with a smile. "Fountains? A museum?"

"No, something you'll never forget. An extraordinary experience. A once-in-a-lifetime adventure. Hop in and I'll take you there. You won't be sorry."

"Where to?" I asked.

"I can't tell you," he said with a chuckle. "It's a surprise. Only three dollars. I'll wait there if you like and you can ride back with me. It's a long trip. You won't be sorry."

A tourist ship had arrived, and the vultures were all there. I should have left my camera at the hotel. It's a dead giveaway. I walked on. A three-dollar surprise . . . why not? After all, I am looking for adventure, and here it is for only three dollars. I slowed down and retraced my steps. The driver smiled broadly and opened the cab door with a flourish. I tried to find out where he was taking me.

"A nightclub? A restaurant?" I asked.

He laughed, "You'll never guess. Never. Come with me and see for yourself. Come on!"

I bargained with him. We settled for two and a half dollars, and I got in.

"Don't worry," he said, starting the motor. "You can trust me. Take down my number if you want to. They call me Gino and you can always find me at this corner."

I lit a cigarette and caught a glimpse of myself in the front mirror. Here I was—I, who hadn't left Israel since arriving there almost fifteen years ago; I, who had dreamed so often of returning to Europe, transformed, a grown man—here I was, sitting in a cab, moving toward the unknown. A young man, twenty-eight years old; so many doors as yet unopened, so many mysteries undiscovered . . . A green taxi, gliding through the streets of Genoa with Uri Lam inside it. Uri, who left the kibbutz to study architecture at the Technion. You all know me. Here I am now, moving toward adventure.

But where is he taking me, this charming fellow? He did say it was a long trip. He'll take me to a darkened villa and wait outside. An unforgettable experience. A surprise. An elegant pleasure house. A whorehouse, deluxe, like the ones in books: large mirrors in gilded frames; velvet couches embroidered in silk. "Suzy, Gigi, Lola! Come here, girls, we have a visitor from Israel. Tell us the truth about your one-eyed general! We see him on TV. Lola, bring our guest a drink." Why not? If it doesn't appeal to me, I can go right back to town. No one will force me.

We passed through the old section of the city, a series of palaces built of massive stone, black with time. Farther on the sidewalk was sheltered by mighty arches, dark structures resting on mammoth columns—this, I thought, is how we ought to build at home, to deal with the sun and rain.

"Via Garibaldi," Gino offered, slowing down. "I met my wife here, at that very column. She was sitting with her aunt." We passed through a square cobbled with basalt blocks. Gino talked about the bronze statue of men on horseback set in its center and pointed out once-splendid palaces transformed into public buildings. We left the city and entered the newer outlying quarters, a flat vista of plain structures with no soul—developments a la Brumberg-Avishai-Landau, to meet the housing crisis. At Via Bobio we made a left turn and began to pick up speed. We followed the river road. Weeping willows lined its banks, trailing thin branches into the yellow water. Like the trees along the stream in San Castello.

"Is it far?" I asked.

"Not very far," he said. I began to speculate. A surprise that could cost me twenty dollars, maybe even more. Anything goes in that sort of establishment—an elegant palace with mirrors, crimson couches, drinks, soft music. Separate rooms to wait in. It wouldn't do for the mayor to run into his chief of police in such a setting. What a scene! Like the scandals in the papers. All-night orgies with young girls dancing in the nude. Get this: I set out to collect reparations from Germany and here I am, about to spend a night of pleasure in the company of Parliament members and captains of industry!

We passed through an endless avenue of giant elms, flanked by fertile fields and gentle hills. At the side of the road I noted narrow patches of carefully cultivated land and rows of silvery olive trees. There was a forest in the distance, opaque and dark; grapevines that twined themselves about the dark tree trunks and stirred my heart. We left the highway and took a side road that followed a row of marble work yards. Then we crossed a vaulted bridge on the other side of which was a huge park enclosed by a high steel fence. Gino stopped the car.

"Here we are!" he said, pointing toward the open gate.

"What is it?" I asked.

"Campo Santo," he said proudly, "the largest and most beautiful cemetery in Italy."

"So what?" I asked.

"This is it," he said. "This is where I was taking you."

I searched his face for the trace of a smile, but it was earnest. "You're kidding. You don't mean to say that you dragged me here to show me a cemetery?" I said.

"Why not?" he asked in an injured tone. "You won't find a more splendid one in all of Europe. Tourists from every corner of the world come here to see it."

"You're out of your mind!" I said. "You promised me a surprise, a once-in-a-lifetime experience. Something that never—"

"This is it," he said. "I brought two Englishmen here yesterday and they couldn't get over it. Look around and see for yourself. If you want to learn the meaning of life, you've come to the right place. You won't see such wealth anywhere."

Gino was utterly serious; he didn't even smile. I began to laugh. I had come to Italy to explore its past, to frolic in its nightspots, to drink champagne from Gigi's cup— what was I doing here in a cemetery? This is funny. Terribly funny.

The situation was so funny and absurd that there was no choice but to accept it. It wouldn't do to go back without seeing the place after I'd already lost two and a half dollars on the deal. I might as well come out of it with a good story to tell. ("So much for Florence and Rome. Everyone has been there. But how many of you have seen the cemetery in Genoa?") I handed Gino the money and got out of the cab.

"Is there a bus that goes back to town?" I asked.

"Every half hour," he said, pointing to the stop.

"I'll take the bus back," I said. Gino waved and faded into the distance. I was alone—and instantly regretted it. Why hadn't I gone back to town with him? Sheer madness.

I had been in a cemetery twice before, and both times I had fled. I had gone with my father once when I was about eight. To this day I remember: a forest, red with fallen leaves, a flock of white gravestones scattered over the grassy meadow, people in black standing beside an open pit, heads bowed, silent. I remember an older man with a torn lapel standing on a mound of soft earth, his sharp chin trembling, his frozen eyes filled with tears. I remember that my father placed a large, firm arm on his shoulder and nodded once or twice, his broad golden ring gleaming in the sunlight. Then they lowered something heavy, wrapped in a white sheet, into the pit, and a bleary-eyed old man lifted his head to the sky and recited something in a voice at once ornate and monotonous. A woman stood at a distance, sobbing softly into her black veil. Two bearded men seized a pair of spades and began flinging moist, heavy earth over the thing in the white sheet. I ran—through fields and streets—all the way home. Without a word my mother took off my new suit, which was soiled, washed my face, and put me at her side in the big warm bed.

Many other times I watched my father put on his black mourning suit and leave the house, preoccupied. We would wait for him at the window. He would come home hours later, his face grave, and my mother would knock on the door of the drawing room where my brother, Martin, was playing the piano. He would stop at once. On such days we ate in oppressive silence, broken only by my mother's deep sighs.

Years later, years that went up in smoke along with my blue diary, I went to the cemetery again, this time to see them bury a boy called Yosi, whom I had known in the war. One night I saw him climb onto a jeep and wrap himself in a blanket. The next day his body lay there in the truck with four others, wrapped in the same blanket. This cemetery, on the road to Jerusalem, was different. Everything was different: the people who stood around the open grave wore sweaty khaki clothes; their heads were covered with handkerchiefs and hats made of newspaper; their eyes were hard and dry. All the furnaces of summer seethed in that bare and arid cemetery. You could hardly tell the rock from the gravestones that seemed to grow through the dry thorns. When they began to fill the pit with brown earth, I slipped away and ran through fields and streets to Ruth's room, where I drank cognac from the bottle and fell asleep on the cold stone floor.

And now I was in a cemetery. There was no one here, not even at the gate. All around me was deep calm. Birds chirped loudly in the branches of black trees, and the sun, pale and distant, floated behind a thin curtain at the rim of the sky. My footsteps, grinding the gravel path, grated the eternal rest that prevailed in this garden-of-tears. Here is life's one certainty, I thought to myself, fixed and immutable, the immortal signature of mortal man, rich and grandiose in a style I had never seen before: granite monuments inscribed in solid gold, white marble walls intricately webbed with veins of black; names, dates, inscriptions, flaming rose-bushes, perpetual wreaths; green velvet moss, ancient oaks; mausoleums of pink and violet marble, Corinthian columns, Doric crowns. Black Gothic tombs and Renaissance cupolas, baroque angels frozen in flight and transformed into milky marble. A garden filled with the dead, their bodies crumbling under the earth, their souls fixed in monuments of eternal ice. *"Non avrei mai creduto—* I had not thought death had undone so many."*

I strolled through this forest of souls overwhelmed by its calm. I alone am alive, I thought, and all around me the dead. Those who once lived are now long dead, and I, alive but dying each day, am moving toward them. Chance, a miracle, that I alone walk through this eternal silence, that only I hear the frogs croaking in the pond, see the flaming flowers blanketing those-who-dwell-in-dust. Why is it that I alone, of all these here, can sense the moist fragrance of autumn, and be stirred by the gentle breeze that moves through this vale of stillness? Where in the forest of life can you find such peace? In nightmares I am thrust into the middle of roaring throngs, trapped in a blaze with no way out, swept along as a bomb explodes, turning thousands of orderly marchers into a charging mob. I, who freeze with terror in a crowd, am searching for meaning in this vast peace filled with monuments, flowers, graves, trees—and not one living soul. But wait, who is that?

Among the bare trees in the distance I discerned the form of a woman draped in black. She placed a handful

* [From Eliot's *The Waste Land*. See notes to l. 63 for the precise reference to *The Inferno*.—trans.]

of flowers on a low mound of earth, knelt down, crossed herself, then turned and disappeared among the trees. I am not alone! A living being stands there communing with the dead. As for me, I have no message for my dead, dead who lie unknown in foreign fields, with no monument. No trace of them remains but me. Neither remember nor remind. All is erased, long since wiped out of memory.

I headed for the exit, certain I could retrace my steps. But after a few minutes' walk along the twisting paths I didn't know which way to turn. I started in one direction, then another. I cut across lawns and rows of flowers. I began to run. I leapt over gravestones and across ornamental hedges. Then I saw a high fence and followed it, knowing it must lead to the main gate. I ran and ran, the damned camera swinging from side to side. Finally, in the distance, I saw a way out. Someone was pulling the gate closed from the outside. The gatekeeper? Of course—it was the gatekeeper locking up.

I shouted to him but he didn't hear. I tried again, but it was no use. I continued running, over bushes and gravestones, across paths. I reached the gate in time to see his figure receding around the bend of the road. Once more I shouted—without success. I leaned my head against the chilly steel gate and breathed heavily. Now for the surprise, the unforgettable experience. A night in the cemetery, a whole night in the company of the dead, a night with myself and the dead who rise up from the ashes that float on cursed waters. "Gatekeeper! Gatekeeper!" I shouted as loud as I could. Then I heard a high voice echoing my call. The woman in black, who was now waiting at the bus stop, had caught the gatekeeper's attention and he was coming to my rescue. I could hear voices, then the ringing music of keys.

"What are you doing here?" the gatekeeper snarled. "Don't you know we lock up promptly at five? It's lucky for you that you caught me. This is no place to spend the night. There really are ghosts here, let me tell you— I saw one myself, dancing and . . ."

I ignored the rest of his sentence and thanked the

woman in black. She nodded and turned toward the bus stop. I handed the gatekeeper some change and headed in that same direction, toward the bus.

4 | *the woman in black*

The gatekeeper made a few odd gestures, smiled a quizzical smile, and went on his way. We were alone at the bus stop, the woman in black and I. The day began to dim and the skies were covered with heavy clouds.

"It's going to rain," I said.

She looked up, then spoke softly, almost to herself. "My husband died a week ago. I came to put flowers on his grave."

I noted the furrows on her face, the swollen eyes, the shoulders constricted, as if to hide her ample breasts. Just what I need, I thought to myself. Now she'll talk about her husband. How good he was to her, how much he loved her . . . the memory of that Sunday morning when he came to ask her father for her hand. She'll reminisce about the wedding and her eyes will fill with tears. I'll listen as she sobs and nod sympathetically. After all, I should be grateful. If she hadn't run after the gatekeeper, I'd still be stuck in the graveyard.

The wind whistled through the trees. The road to the cemetery stretched lifeless. What was I doing here? Just this morning I'd arrived in Genoa with fantasies of the train to Florence, museums, dim bars, night spots—and here was my Europe: a graveyard, an empty road, a gloomy sky, and a mourning woman. Thank God she's silent. But why *is* she silent, anyway?

A thin veil covers her head. Her face is pale. She left home suddenly, without a coat, to place flowers on his grave, flaming ones from her own garden like those near Aunt Anna's house—and ran to catch the bus. Now she is waiting for a bus to take her home to her empty bed.

A heavy rain began to fall, and she sought shelter under a leafy tree. I took off my coat and made an umbrella out of it, which I invited her to share. She started to refuse but the rain grew heavier. We stood very close. A fresh fragrance wafted from her hair. Two large raindrops streamed down her forehead, along her cheeks, across the line of her lips.

"I forgot my umbrella," she said, biting her lip apologetically. A fleeting smile lit up her face, making it seem softer and younger. I smiled, and she looked into my eyes—a long, earnest look. The rain subsided, but she made no move. Strange, only a minute ago I was oppressed by her presence, seeing only wrinkles of grief in her face, and dry mournful lips. Now, suddenly, the wrinkles were gone and her lips were close and vibrant. She looked into my eyes, my arm touching her shoulder, under the coat, the two of us silent.

"The bus is here," she said. Only when I took the coat back did I realize it was no longer raining.

"I am glad he's late," I said, noting a warm glow in her eyes. In the distance, we heard thunder.

The bus was almost empty: two drowsy old men, a woman with a basket in her lap, a well-groomed young man, another woman, with a sleeping child. She waited beside me while I paid the fare. Though there were empty seats in front, she chose to sit near the back window so she could look toward the cemetery, which was fading out of sight. I put my hand on the back of her seat and pressed her trembling shoulder.

"Are you cold?" I asked. She nodded. "We'll soon be back in town," I said, clasping her arm with my other hand.

And when we get to town? I asked myself, rejecting easy answers. Though I saw her at my side in the hotel elevator, I didn't dare hope for more. After all, that wasn't what I wanted from her. Not that. Oh hell, that too, but not just that! Absolutely not. I wanted to be more to her. A knight in a black raincoat, appearing when all seems lost and utterly hopeless. True, it was chance that brought me to her side, chance that I should have a coat when the rain began to fall. Yet there was no escape from this event. Having appeared, by chance, I wished to offer every lovely word of consolation, to be the sun shining for her alone, the birds resuming their song. I wanted to assume the role assigned to me by chance. I wanted to be her new day, to draw back the heavy curtains of mourning, to flood her room with light. I wished to restore some rhyme and reason to her life, to restore her wide bed to its proper dimensions. Not only *that* but . . . but (why pretend?) that too.

I wrapped my arm around her and drew her close. She continued to stare at the window, watching my reflection in the glass. I leaned toward her and began to whisper in her ear.

I don't remember what I whispered. Only that she listened, in silence, pressing her head to my lips from time to time. Was she straining to hear my words over the roar of the bus and the whirr of its tires on the wet road—or did she simply wish I'd be silent? I whispered all sorts of drivel to her. I told her, if I am not mistaken, about the sage Heraclites, how he was convinced that all things pass, that nothing is fixed, neither pain, sorrow, torment, grief, for all these pass. I remember that she nodded in agreement when I said she must push aside the curtains of mourning and shook her head in protest when I said she must stay in town with me. I remember pressing my lips to the soft shawl on her warm neck and whispering yes, yes, yes, asking her not to close the door in my face.

"What door? What are you talking about?" she asked in alarm, trying to disengage herself from me.

I explained that it was only a figure of speech, that I didn't mean what she thought, that all I wanted was company, to sit with her in a small café with time to talk and listen. She was reassured. I may have meant what I said. Yet, as I spoke, I saw myself tiptoeing down a long empty corridor, like the one in my hotel, finding one door slightly ajar, seeing her black dress draped over a chair, her white body languid in the bed. I told her she must not go home . . . that she must venture into other worlds, open new doors, discover that she is not alone, that the stream flows on into the distance, that she must find courage and cast her wilted flowers into the waters.

As I whispered these words, or words to this effect, my heart pounded wildly. But she seemed to relax. The cemetery now far behind, we rode on into town in silence. I sat beside her, a knight in a black raincoat, scheming darkly.

"I could eat something," she said as we stood on the corner, not knowing which way to turn.

"Me too. There's a good restaurant near my hotel. Let's go there." She made no response.

In the taxi she untied her veil, shook her hair loose, and sank into my arms. We were twined together, breathing heavily. She whispered, "No, no," lacing her fingers in my hair.

I whispered, "Yes!" drinking in her fragrance as my hands wandered over her body. She unbuttoned my shirt and placed her cold hand on my heart.

"You're so excited," she said, her teeth gleaming in the dark.

"And your heart, my love, says nothing?"

"That's enough," she whispered, pushing me away. "That's really enough. Please . . . We're going to eat soon."

"I'd like to eat you up right now," I said, biting the back of her neck. Her laughter tinkled like a gentle bell as she placed her hand on my mouth. I kissed it and kissed it again.

"My hands may be cold," she said, "but my heart—"

"Yes," I laughed, "I can feel it."

"Don't laugh," she said. "I'll probably get a chill. I'm soaked. Feel my dress. My *dress*, I said. Here we are, thank God! The Carlotta? I've heard it's good."

The restaurant was crowded. The owner, a fat woman with a downy mustache, was warm and welcoming. She led us to a small corner table that had just been vacated. The waiter cleared it quickly and brought on a flask of white wine, two glasses, a basket of warm rolls and biscuits. I realized I hadn't eaten lunch.

"Have you ever been here before?" I asked, pouring the wine.

"No," she said, touching her glass to mine.

"Here's to you," I whispered. "This wine is good. Does she know you? She said, 'Good evening, *signora.*' "

"No," she said, "I've never been here before. They treat all their customers like old friends here. Now, do you want to start with spaghetti? I see they have *pesto.* Then, if you like fish, let's order *burida* for two—that is, if you want . . .

"I want," I said. "I want whatever you want."

"But I'm not sure I want what you want," she said with another display of gleaming teeth. She caught the waiter's eye and summoned him to me with a regal gesture. I ordered all the things she had suggested.

"I am so hungry," she apologized.

The meal took too long. It was quite a while before the waiter brought on the first course, or so it seemed to me. I was very hungry, and the white wine, Quintoterri of Genoa, went to my head. I can't remember the flavor of the food. All I recall is anticipation, suspense stretched as taut as the skin of a drum. Instead of what was served, we consumed each other. My eyes were fixed on her, her eyes on me. Every move of her hand suggested other moves to me, in other situations. She bit into the roll; my heart throbbed. She drew a long noodle into her mouth, swallowing it slowly; my face flushed. She sipped the wine; I imagined her drinking from my lips. She smoothed the white tablecloth and I saw her smooth the bedsheets with that very same gesture.

Noting the intent gaze with which I read mysteries in her every simple move, she grew serious and seemed to sink into my eyes, as if to say, "I know you know what I mean when I say nothing." I thought this tormenting meal would never end. But finally, when I felt exhausted and drowsy, the check arrived. We left in a shower of good wishes and profuse thank-yous, our ample hostess escorting us into the rainy night.

My hotel was very close but it took at least an hour for us to cover this short distance. Just as we left the restaurant she suddenly said she would rather go home. I drew her into a doorway and started from the beginning: torrid whispers, sunshine, birds—whatever occurred to me. We would walk a few paces and stop. Talk, whispers, pleas, demands, again a few steps forward.

"I want to go home," she repeated. I stared at her in silence, not knowing what to say. I had already said everything. I was beginning to accept the idea that she was slipping away when she said, "I'd go right now, if there was another bus." A tentative step in my direction. I decided not to press her, lest I frighten her away.

"Then take a taxi," I said, holding my breath.

"You're kidding," she said.

"I'm not kidding. If you insist on going, if you choose to run away from yourself—take a taxi."

"You're crazy," she said, laughing. "Do you know what a taxi would cost? I live an hour from here. I only brought enough money for bus fare and a bite to eat."

I was relieved. I knew she'd stay with me and that made me take a further risk. So she wouldn't think I wanted only *that* of her. (That too, but not just that.) She must trust me, she must believe that I want her companionship, that I want to talk to her, that I want to help her. She mustn't see what she saw in my eyes at the restaurant. Better watch my step.

"Is that the problem?" I said, feigning relief. "I'll give you the money." She shook her head. "Then I'll give you my address and you can mail it back. Here, take it." I took out my wallet and stuffed ten dollars into her reluctant hands.

"All right," she said. "I'm going. Good night. Thanks for everything."

I held my breath. She took a few steps, then came back to me, laughing, her voice full and warm.

"I give in," she said. "I'll stay." I lifted her into the air and whirled her around.

"But on one condition," she added. "Separate rooms. I won't share a room with a stranger, a tourist at that."

"Separate rooms," I agreed.

She asked what floor I was on, then gave brief but precise instructions. She would go in first and get a room. I would come in while she was registering and eavesdrop to learn her room number. Then I would go to my room and she to hers. A little later I could come to her. She asked me to repeat these instructions.

"You go in first," I said. "Then I come in with, 'How nice to see you, darling.' By the way, what's your name?"

"Idiot," she said, smiling. "Maria. Maria Cristina. And you'll be sorry if you make a false move."

We ran through the rain toward the hotel. She went in and I watched from the entrance as the clerk nodded, then handed her paper and pen. When she finished writing I went in.

"*Buona sera*," said the clerk with professional good cheer. "Back so early? It's only eleven. Didn't you go to the cabaret I suggested?"

"I went there but I left," I said. "It was too gloomy— not one lively soul in the entire place."

I took my room key and followed her. The elevator boy closed the door and pressed the button marked three. I wanted to touch the soft veil around her neck, the small drops of rain glistening in her hair. I wanted to touch her, but he was watching.

"*Buona notte*," I said to the boy, following her out of the elevator. The hall was deserted. "May I help you, *signora*?" I asked, taking her key. "Thank you very much," she said, linking her arm in mine.

What sort of night was it? This night that began in the shelter of my raincoat and mellowed on the way back to town, this night that almost ended abruptly, first in the cab, then in the restaurant, is more difficult to recall in detail than any other aspect of my adventure with Maria. To tell the truth it was a disappointing night. Maybe because I expected so much, maybe because I had already foreseen its most minute details in her eyes back in that small restaurant. In any case, by contrast with my great expectations, it was dull and disappointing.

The outer signs of passion were certainly there. The key trembled in my hand, the lock refused to yield, the light switched on for a moment and burned out. My hands explored her body feverishly, her hands explored mine. A few drunken paces, then we were on the bed—sinking into cool pillows, tearing at clothes. Noisy sighs, shoes falling, a blanket flung on the floor, moans, whispers, everything. All the ingredients of seething passion. Passion without warmth. Loud demonstrations of love without a speck of truth. The devil knows why. For me, at least, this was all a repetition of what had already happened, before anything actually occurred. At the very moment of abandon she thought to purify her body. This may be the reason. But not the whole reason. Even after these ill-timed rituals, even after she was back in bed, damp and chilly, soaring again toward the peaks of excitement—I knew that I was not with her. Nor she with me. I was in the graveyard, I was dozing in the Technion library, I was lying under the grass in some familiar spot. I climbed a high turret, fell off a galloping horse, embraced another woman who grunted "*yoy*" in Hungarian. I dove into an empty pool, and performed. We both performed—what a show! One long scene, a noisy succession of entrances and exits—a dry, mechanical performance, without an ounce of inspiration, without a single true perception, without focus. Nothing more than a fast frolic, a rehash of a thin, hackneyed text: "Wonderful. Don't stop! More, more, more . . . That's enough. . . . I want to sleep now." And that was it. A maze of insipid words, then the curtain, and silence in the theater.

I lay on the empty stage, my back to her, my eyes closed. I heard her get up—again the ritual of soap and water, the bidet. Then the squeak of a chair, the rustle of silk underwear. When she came back to bed, I told myself I was asleep and, breathing deeply for effect, I did fall asleep.

I was awakened by a bell, a trolley bell. Pale light in the window—morning! Six-ten. Where am I? A gentle snore . . . she's asleep, her mouth is open. Silver fillings, yellowed teeth, hairy stubble in her armpits. To think that I took her for thirty! She's thirty-eight, at least. Maybe forty. The wrinkles around her eyes, the decaying teeth, the stench from her mouth . . .

I slipped out of bed and dressed quickly, quietly, lest she wake up all of a sudden and fling her long, lascivious arms in my direction.

Having savored the nectar of life, pushed aside the damned curtains, and opened the door to sunlight and birds, she might demand that I stay with her, quoting me word for word.

I grabbed my coat and camera. After a long, nerve-wracking struggle, I managed to open the door and tip-toe out. I rushed to my own room, and with bated breath I flung the toilet articles into their case, packed the camera, closed the suitcase, and left. Rather than wait for the elevator, I raced down the steps.

"Good morning, sir!" the clerk called. "Leaving so early? It's only six-thirty." I stuffed some coins into his hand (I had paid my bill the day before) and slipped out. At the corner I saw Gino, the cab driver. He had already spotted me.

"*Buon giorno,* sir," he said with a warm smile. "Where to?"

"To the cemetery," I retorted.

He laughed.

"To the train station," I said.

5 | *the 8:05 express*

"How was it?" Gino asked gleefully as soon as we got moving.

"How was what? The cemetery?"

He turned and looked at me in dismay. "You didn't meet a lady in mourning?"

"A lady in mourning?" I asked in astonishment.

"You didn't meet even one lady in mourning?" he repeated, fixing his large eyes searchingly on me.

"No," I said.

"Impossible!" he replied, offended. "It can't be! Are you sure you didn't see any such lady in the cemetery? You didn't see a woman in black placing a wreath on one of the graves? Didn't you see a woman going in or out of the cemetery?"

"I didn't see anyone," I said faintly.

"It's just not possible—it couldn't be!" he repeated. "They're always there. Do you mean to tell me there was no one there yesterday? How could that be? Do you think I simply took you to a cemetery?"

"What do you mean?" I asked, not wanting to hear the answer.

"Girls!" he cried, seeking my eyes in the rearview mirror. "Streetwalkers! Whores! Prostitutes! Tarts! Haven't you ever heard of the mourning ladies of Genoa? You must be the only person in the whole world who doesn't know about them."

"No," I said, grasping the whole picture all too clearly. Of course! How could I have missed it? The old gate-keeper waggling his finger and smiling lecherously, the warm reception in the restaurant, the money for cab fare (which she never returned), the noisy technique in bed, the shaved armpits, the elaborate procedures with the bidet, the yellowed teeth, the peeling nail polish. How could I have been so innocent? Gino had said this world-famous cemetery was popular with English and American tourists. Where there are tourists there are whores. It made sense—instead of accosting the wary tourist on street corners or in bars, instead of competing with younger, more attractive girls, they set their traps in the cemetery, where a guy's defenses are down.

"It's hard to believe," Gino said, shaking his head. "I was convinced you knew the minute I stopped at the cemetery. I never had this happen before."

Still incredulous, he searched my eyes in the mirror. He couldn't believe I had never seen the French-Italian film on this subject, a film that won worldwide publicity when the Catholic Church got it banned. This whole brilliant scheme, Gino informed me, had sprung from the head of a whore named Anna about five years back. Anna-Giuseppa, the mourning lady—to this day the First Lady of the Cemetery. She appeared in the cemetery one day in a black dress and black veil and in no time had an Englishman in tow; she told him she had buried her husband that very day and was destitute. The Englishman drove her around in his car, courted her, comforted her, bought her a new dress—and a new enterprise was launched in Genoa. Sunday afternoons the cemetery is jammed with mourning ladies. Last year, Gino went on, one of these ladies married an American millionaire and now sent generous gifts to the Church of San Giuseppe.

I couldn't choke back my laughter, and Gino's eyes sparkled with mischief and pride at the wisdom and craft of these women. An ingenious idea; simple, yet ingenious. Professional wailers make way for ladies in mourning, mourning becomes a respected trade among the whores. Theirs is an exclusive guild with strict regulations, Gino explained. They are forbidden to seduce or solicit visitors and they can't demand any kind of payment. The customer has to make the first move, and the ladies must earn their pay by assuming some role: I have no money . . . I can't afford a marble gravestone . . . my child is sick . . . my child can't go to school because I can't pay the fees . . . and similarly moving tales. Violations are punished severely, for the livelihood of everyone could be jeopardized by improper conduct.

"They have a head on their shoulders," Gino said, tapping his own head. "What man can resist a grieving woman? Who wouldn't fall for the idea that he alone can bring the love of life back to the sad eyes of a lady in mourning? I have yet to see a tourist return from the cemetery disappointed. They all bring back unforgettable memories. Except you. My first failure! I can't imagine what happened yesterday. Now that the tourist season is over they usually take turns. Every day a different one is posted at the cemetery. Something must have happened yesterday."

"A death in the family," I offered.

"That's good!" Gino laughed wildly. "The lady in mourning was really mourning yesterday! Great!"

When we stopped at the train station he was still roaring with laughter and slapping his thighs. I reached into my pocket, but Gino stopped me.

"This ride is on me," he insisted. "I won't take another penny from you—you paid enough yesterday. Usually a trip to the cemetery doesn't run more than two dollars, but I took two and a half because of the surprise. No, not a penny. A cigarette maybe, but money, no. Absolutely not."

I handed him the whole pack and he shook my hand warmly.

"I'm terribly sorry," he said. "I really am sorry. Nothing like that ever happened before. *Buon viaggio*, sir. Have a good trip and come back again. The mourning lady didn't show up because of a death in the family! That's really funny!" He was still laughing and waving as the cab pulled away.

I stood there on the sidewalk in the crowd, a foolish grin on my face. What should I do? Cry? Laugh? It really was funny. I couldn't have invented it. (Get this: Her husband died. We were waiting for the bus at the cemetery. We started talking. We stopped to eat. I comforted her. In the morning the cab driver says, "Did you meet the mourning lady?") Extraordinary. Only in real life would such a thing happen. For the moment, let's forget I was the victim. What do you mean, forget you were the victim? The whole joke of it is that you in particular, you with your refined soul, were the victim. OK. That's enough. Let's drop the subject. Forget the whole episode: the customs fiasco, the cemetery, the entire night. Wrap it all up in old newspaper and throw it in the trash to be forgotten, I said to myself. Wipe out these last twenty-four hours as if they were invented in a fit of depression; deny them the way I've denied the first thirteen years of my life. Thirteen times twelve months—let's see; ten times thirteen is one hundred and thirty, two times thirteen is twenty-six, add them together—one hundred and fifty-six months, times fifty-two weeks is . . . I had changed fifty dollars that morning. Times six hundred. Thirty thousand lire. Enough to get to Florence. From there on we'll see. Maybe Venice. Or San Castello. Your *coniglio* is back!

A porter offered his services. "Rome?" he asked. "No, thanks," I said; my suitcases were light. I joined the throng milling about in last-minute chaos, looking anxiously toward the giant clocks whose huge hands lurched forward every minute. The schedule of arrivals and departures stretched across an entire wall: Rome, Milan, Vienna, Geneva, Frankfurt, Paris. White letters on a mournful board of black. (The Union of Mourning Ladies extends its deep sympathy to its member-in-mourning, Maria Cristina, of unblessed memory.)

I ordered a large *cappuccino* and two buns and sat down at an empty table near the espresso machine. My eyes lit on the broken handle. I told myself that if I were to buy a new suitcase I wouldn't have to remember what I wished to forget. How many years is it since I was at the railway station? How old was I then? Enormous engines puffed away peacefully, giant wheels of steel glistened in the dimness that filtered through the sooty skylight. My hand was enclosed in my father's warm clasp. My mother stood on the platform, dressed in a fur coat, her chin trembling. When I tried to join the other children who were crowded together in the train, my father wouldn't let go of my hand. He kept turning my head toward the window and saying, "Look, look, there's mama." My father's breath, or perhaps it was smoke, was dense. When the train began to pull out, my mother was biting her knuckles. I never saw her again. How old was I?

I lit a cigarette and took a sip of coffee. Where to? Here I am at the railway station, a crossroads, not knowing which route to choose. Florence, Siena, Rome? I know

—to San Castello! To Uncle Michele and Aunt Anna. First a train to Venice and from there a bus. Suddenly, after fifteen years, "*Zia Anna! Sono io—coniglio!* Your rabbit is back." For three years they were mother and father to me. This was after the trip to the border with my father—we will all join you soon, he promised—and many nights at the refugee hostel in Zagreb, where the other refugees spoke German and sighed constantly. Who was the man in the hunter's cap who drove me to San Castello? Why did he sell me to Uncle Michele? How much did they pay for me? Are they still alive? And their baby, Tonio, how old is he? Eighteen, nineteen? Knock three times on the kitchen door—*Buon giorno, Zia Anna.* Remember me? It's me, your *coniglio*.

"Help, fire!" someone shouted in my ear in Hebrew. Turning around I saw three young Israelis who had been on the boat with me. They dissolved in laughter because I hadn't responded to their prank. Why were they laughing? Everything amused them. They had laughed savagely during the whole four-day crossing. They laughed on the Sabbath eve when the wine was blessed by the rabbi. They covered their heads with their hands during the blessing and combed their hair with forks. They laughed at the Greek songstress who sang "Hava Nagila" in the Altneuland bar. They woke up a frightened couple in the middle of the night, telling them the boat was sinking and directing them to go out on deck immediately in life jackets—and then roared with laughter when the couple appeared dressed in pajamas and speckled life jackets.

"Say, what did they want from you in customs?" Uzi asked. "Why were you the last one through?"

"Nothing," I said. "They searched my luggage."

"Where did they take you?" the blond one called Danni-boy asked innocently.

"It was nothing," I said. "Just a routine check."

"Cut the crap. They don't take you to a private room for a routine check," said the third guy, whose name I didn't know. I drank my coffee and said nothing.

"Did they make you strip?" Uzi asked with a twinkle

in his eye, and all three burst into laughter. "We played a trick like that in Haifa once, pretending to know someone was smuggling diamonds in his ass. The guy sure was pale when he came out of customs."

"But satisfied," laughed Danni. "He enjoyed every minute of it, the old faggot. He probably goes from port to port now, asking inspectors to check his ass for diamonds."

"Too bad we can't make peace with the Arabs," one of the others added, "he could have a ball in Nablus. Let's sit down, boys. Three *cappuccinos*. It's on Danni. And don't forget you owe me six dollars from yesterday. No lip, either. You should have come with us."

They pulled up some extra chairs and began to review the previous night's escapades, each one trying to top the others' stories. A waiter had taken them for Arabs—the memory of this scene set off peals of laughter. Uzi was constantly tugging at my sleeve. I stared at them, unable to believe we had anything in common. Are they incapable of quiet, civilized conversation? Must they tell the world they are from Israel? Everything is funny to them and they indulge in their silly schemes no matter what the price.

"What's the name of that wild spot behind the Piazza Ferrari?" Uzi shouted in his shrillest tones. "Boaz, you dragged us there. Piccolo something."

"Piccolo Mondo, you dope," replied Boaz.

"That's it!" called Uzi. "Piccolo Mondo. What a show! A bombshell. Too bad you weren't with us. Adam and Eve in the Garden of Eden. Wow! That dancer really had it! Never see anything like that back home. And that other dancer, the snake, poking around down there between her legs—that was something, wasn't it? Say, your broad was all right, too. Yeah, the dark one you picked up at the bar. A terrific dancer. She nearly bit my tongue off!"

I stood up and called the waiter.

"Where are you off to?" Danni asked. "Why don't you come with us? We're going to Siena, Florence, Rome. We'll take you to a museum in Florence that's out of this

world—I've been there. It's sensational, full of broads—
Swedish, English, German—all yours for the asking!"

I told them my train was leaving soon, that I was
going in another direction, that I was in a hurry. Giving
the waiter my remaining change I headed toward the
ticket office.

There was a long line for Milan. Propping my bags
against the wall I got in line. Fly away, get out of here
as fast as possible. How could I consider spending three
weeks in Italy? I want to combine business with pleasure, but it turns out the pleasure is revolting and there's
no getting away from business. I have to go to Frankfurt
on the first train and finish my business there. How can
I enjoy a holiday here with that long and tedious chapter ahead? I've got to take care of my affairs there once
and for all, cover the graves, lock the drawer, shut the
door behind me.

So many years of silent data, yellow with age,
clouded with dust, all but forgotten. Suddenly, on the
heels of my rash decision, what was long dormant begins to stir. Scenes I had managed to forget I was now
required to dredge up for the questionnaires and papers.
I had to show proof, to swear that I spoke the truth, to
present evidence. The evidence began to assume a life
of its own, to revive other things I had struggled to keep
out of mind.

So, on to Frankfurt! Sign the papers, seal the case,
close the chapter—and only then, maybe on my way
home, with my mind clear, my soul composed, would I
have the courage to come back and spend a week or
two in Italy. I'd visit Aunt Anna (is she still alive?) and
after that seek out the Italy you find in books and
movies. Frankfurt, here I come. I'd relax in the train,
read a newspaper, look out the window for Giotto and
Filippo Lippi, stand in the corridor smoking a cigarette,
zealously guarding my secret: that the young man in
the black raincoat with a turned-up collar is me, Uri
Lam of Jerusalem, architect, en route to settle accounts
with the past. To hell with them all, customs officials,
whores with whimpering displays of lust, my raucous

compatriots. I wanted to be left alone. Alone in a train, darting into the night.

Finally, it was my turn. "Frankfurt," I said to the clerk. He shook his head. No direct connection between Genoa and Frankfurt. The train to Frankfurt was supposed to leave Milan at 11:58 and the express to Milan was leaving in twelve minutes. I took out my wallet and opened it to pay for my ticket. Empty! I had the dollars hidden in a back pocket, but all my Italian money was gone. Maria Cristina. There could be no doubt. It wasn't the rustle of underwear I'd heard when I was feigning sleep, it was Maria Cristina searching my pockets. Five dollars for the hotel, eight for supper, two and a half for a cab, the ten dollars I had stuffed in her hand—altogether she had cost me about twenty-five dollars. What should I do? Inform the police? Miss the train? I didn't even know her last name. (Check the schedule: which mourning lady was on duty that day?) To hell with the money. Just clear out fast. I asked the clerk if he could exchange my dollars.

"Only privately," he said in a furtive voice, smiling nervously. At the rate of five hundred fifty to a dollar—he has expenses too, the bank deducts a service charge, otherwise it doesn't pay . . . But if I went to the bank I'd miss the train. By now the people behind me were beginning to grumble, so I exchanged thirty dollars, got my ticket, gathered up my change, and hurried toward the gate.

The train to Milan was at gate 7. I heard a whistle in the distance and began to run. I checked my watch against the big wall clock. Nine minutes to go. No need to run, I told myself, I can make it. All the compartments were taken and people were standing in the corridors. Leaving one bag in the doorway, I pushed my way through the crowd, trying to find room for my luggage. The overhead racks were jammed. In a compartment in the middle of the car I spied space for a suitcase, but it wasn't quite wide enough. Two suitcases were stacked one atop the other. When I asked whose they were, someone muttered a reply. I took out a paper I'd snatched from the news-

stand at the last minute and spread it out on the upholstered seat. I climbed up and arranged the two suitcases in an upright position. The owner stared at me
with hate. A round cardboard box slipped out of my
grasp and fell on a woman in a feather hat. I begged
her pardon and restored the box to its place. I squeezed
my suitcase into the empty spot and thanked the man
sarcastically for his generosity.

When I went back to the corridor again I saw a mob
of people rushing along the platform and peering anxiously through the windows. I tried to edge toward the
suitcase I'd left in the doorway. The corridor was filling
up, a mass of humanity crowding in on me from all
directions. I was stuck where I was, about three compartments from the doorway, with no possibility of
moving. No one in the crush was carrying luggage—
the 8:05 express to Milan was, apparently, a commuter
train. Whistles blew, doors slammed, but the flow of
people wasn't staunched. About ten passengers trying to
get up the steps shouted to the straphangers, "Step in,
move back!" as they forced their way through, climbing
over people's feet.

I don't know how the conductor managed to get all
the passengers on board and close the door. But when
the train departed at exactly 8:05 not a soul remained
on the platform. I found myself in the very center of the
corridor, surrounded by people pressing in on me from
all sides. I expected some of the passengers to move into
other cars as soon as the train left the station, but as
we picked up speed no one made a move. I had a spot
no bigger than the soles of my shoes—I couldn't even
shift my legs. A cold sweat covered my forehead, but I
couldn't get my hand up to wipe it away when the sweat
began to sting my eyes.

And I was looking for peace, I reflected bitterly. Oh,
to be alone on the train reading a newspaper. Instead,
this nightmare. Here I am, captive in a crowd with no
exit, no way out. What if someone were to suddenly shout
"Fire!"? Push, shove, climb on your neighbor's back,
trample him! The wails and groans of the injured,

feeble shouts for help, fragments of wood, twisted metal, splintered glass in that old man's face, a puddle of congealed blood along his neck; bodies, scores of bodies heaped on top of me, my breath giving out, the way it did in school when I was pinned at the bottom of a heap of squealing children. How do you get out of here? Why didn't I stay in Genoa? Didn't I see the train filling up? Why didn't I try first class? There at least the aisles are clear. I'd give all my money to be alone. Well, not all of it, but I'd gladly pay the difference between first and second class. I should have tried the toilet. One lucky stiff is no doubt installed there, legs outstretched, reading the newspaper with all the comforts of home: an open window and running water. A little kingdom— throne and all! I should have stayed at the door with both my bags. I could at least sit on them. Someone else is probably sitting on my suitcase right now, maybe three people. It has burst open and everything is scattered on the floor. My new shirts are being trampled, my jacket and corduroy pants . . . Why is everyone so quiet?

The people around me, sullen-faced and mute, were accustomed to this nightmare. It was routine—you could tell from their positions. Folded newspapers and eyes fixed on newsprint just as if this wasn't a ride of terror, a horror trip along the brink of disaster. The alert riders who had been able to grab a position near the open windows faced a cool and sooty panorama, their backs to the crush, the tumult, the crowd jammed together, the madhouse in the aisle. It was no concern of theirs—they were in another world.

A foggy gray landscape flashed by outside. Factories, industrial plants, black oil tanks, red brick structures with smokestacks. A long whistle from the engine and the wheels roared a chorus of messages that I refused to listen to. Violent, lashing rain began to fall suddenly. Someone shouted, "Close it! Close the window!" Newspapers flew, hands reached out to snatch them. Once again silence and the muted whirr of wheels. With all the windows closed the heat grew more intense. A bead of sweat dripped slowly down my nose. Hunching one shoulder up, with great effort I managed to wipe half my face. I wiped the other half on someone's sleeve, but my face was soon covered with sweat again. The heat was getting worse—all around there were shouts of "Open it! Open the window!" And the cries of a child from somewhere. The windows were opened a crack and the breeze wafted through. Cold sweat began to sting my eyes.

I could just barely see into the nearest compartment. People were standing in the aisle there too, but the crowd wasn't so dense. Oh, to be in there, I thought. To be able to bend a knee and lean on something solid. Will I ever wake out of this nightmare? It was just a bad dream. Have a drink, my boy. It will soon be over. Where does this train go, Father? To the border, my son. You will go on from there alone, and we will all join you soon. Why, father? Why doesn't Miri come with me? Why did Martin stay home? Why am I going alone, father? Why are you so quiet—why? We were standing in the empty aisle of the train. Father turned away and remained silent. Have a drink, my boy. It was just a bad dream. I am here beside you. Don't be afraid. Sleep, my son. Sleep. Have some water. From the faucet, the pump, the ice cubes in the refrigerator. It would have been better to go to Florence with those three idiots who run their fathers' businesses from a swimming pool. Very funny, really. Strip. A beard in her armpits. Teeth, yellow with decay.

My collar was drenched with sweat. A man whose face was very close to mine was gulping air in shallow, rasping breaths that sounded asthmatic. The sweat dripped down his scarred face. A breeze cooled my damp shirt.

"Get a load of this," someone whispered through discolored teeth and a mustache streaked by age. Nearby a man in glasses, finding himself close to a young woman, was pressing tight against her behind and swaying rhythmically. His eyes were partly closed, his nostrils trembled lustfully. The woman was struggling to shift her position. A soldier standing in front of her, greedily consuming a thick sausage sandwich, laughed as he watched her. The woman closed her eyes and bit her lip. The slow, insistent movements continued as the audience looked on in silence. Only the soldier laughed.

The train went into a tunnel, and there was darkness and a choking smell of smoke. Someone began to cough. The man with the scar complained, "I can't breathe." Smoke suffused everything as the train wheels continued to rumble through the tunnel. The cold shirt clung to my back; my mouth was filled with the salty taste of sweat. "Cut it out!" I heard the woman say, then the soldier's grating laugh. "There's no air," someone shouted from the far end of the corridor.

When the train emerged, the corridor was flooded with dim light. Wet grime dripped down the passengers' sooty faces. The man in glasses was swaying more intensely. His eyes were closed, his mouth gaping. A child cried, more urgently now, and was joined by two other children and an infant. The stench of sweat and urine was overwhelming.

"Look!" the guy near me whispered again through his rotted teeth. The man with glasses, finally still, was leaning against the wall, his head turned to the side. The soldier, having finished eating, smiled and let out an ostentatious burp. A tremor passed through the young woman's body. Her face was flooded with sweat and soot. With a sudden jerk she leaned toward the soldier and discharged a torrent of vomit. He gasped as the vomit streamed down his starched uniform. He looked around, offended, then stared impassively at the mess. He turned toward the woman, trying to wipe the vomit on her ample bosom. The entire train was overwhelmed by the stench. There were shouts from all directions. "Shut off the heat! Shut off the heat! Open the windows, we're choking!" Curious faces peered out of the compartments. I was on the brink of hysteria. Two windows that had been closed in the tunnel were opened again and a torrent of violent rain sprayed inside. The shouts were silenced; only the children continued their monotonous wail.

The train began to slow down. In the distance I could see the industrial area on the outskirts of Milan. Oil tanks, factories, warehouses, smokestacks, more smokestacks, sm-oke-sta-cks, s-moke-stack-s, smoke-stacks and rain.

Swift, gray rain.

6 | *routine check*

Waiting for the mob to leave the train, I sank into an empty seat and closed my eyes, saying to myself: when I look again, the car will be empty and I can wake up. I heard the steady shuffle of footsteps in the corridor, like an endless transport of refugees. I heard children crying, the wail of an engine, train whistles, the calls of porters. I breathed through my mouth to filter out the stench of sour vomit mixed with the pungent odor of urine.

Finally, silence. When I opened my eyes the car was empty. I was alone. Taking my suitcase from the rack in the compartment—now filled with papers, cigarette butts, magazines—I headed for the exit. But my other suitcase was not where I had left it. I checked the bathrooms, retraced my steps, peered into every compartment. It was gone. Stolen—no doubt about it. Nothing could be simpler. Someone obviously had just walked off with it. I went up to a porter and asked him what I should do.

"Try the lost and found," he said. "Someone may have found your bag."

But the suitcase was not at the lost and found desk. The clerk, adrift in a sea of suitcases, parcels, and boxes, said that four umbrellas, two coats and a walking stick from the Genoa train had been turned in, but no suitcase. He suggested that I wait, and if the suitcase didn't turn up, that I report the loss to the police. Ten minutes went by. Someone appeared with a bundle of papers and handed them to the clerk. Remembering my own papers, I opened my suitcase in terror. The papers were there right on top—thank God! What was in the stolen one then? My camera, my coat, toilet articles, and clothes. But the folder with the papers was intact. Without it there would be no point to the whole journey. My ethically correct demands, my life, were contained therein in triplicate.

Leaving the remaining suitcase at the checkroom, I slipped the ticket into my wallet, buttoned my pocket, and headed for the police station. I should have set out for Europe just like this, I thought to myself. Empty-handed. Free!

The police clerk listened to my tale indifferently without bothering to write anything down. He nodded as if he had heard it all before and gestured toward a bench where two other people were sitting. "Have a seat, sir."

"My train is leaving in an hour," I protested.

"You'll make it," he said. "It won't take very long. See, there's only one person ahead of you."

One man had gone inside and closed the door behind him. I sat down to wait. It was 10:25. I was thirsty. My feet were aching and cold. My shirt was still damp. I buttoned my jacket and lit a cigarette. It tasted bitter. Oh, what I wouldn't give for some sleep now, I thought. No, not the bed of shrouds in Genoa. A feather-soft blanket, a chance to wash, shave, put on pajamas and climb into bed, pull the sheet over my head, and sleep. Sleep, then wake up in a little room beside the azure sea, stroll out on the sunny porch, stretch, fill my lungs with fresh air and shout. Italy! Another Italy . . . the Italy of sun, fishermen, songs—sad and pure. Italy minus the blundering officials, idiot Israelis, shabby whores and thieves. But I won't be silent. I'm going to file complaints about everything: first, the customs department, then the graveyard bandit who took my money, and finally the stolen suitcase. This time I won't make any allowances. Yes, I'll even expose the deplorable conditions on the 8:05 express. They ought to know what's going on, those self-righteous Catholics.

The door to the office opened and the man ahead of me went in.

It might still make sense to forget the whole thing and run to buy my ticket for Frankfurt. No, civil indifference promotes crime. No one is willing to waste time in police stations and courts. Even though many people witness assaults, see a criminal's face, can describe the whore who stole the money (brownish hair, sagging breasts, a scar across her forehead at the hairline, yellowed teeth, coarse fingers), all are reluctant to testify. Why get involved? Why waste time? Life is short and the world won't be changed by one more scrap of evidence. Too bad I hadn't called Mati. Signor Mati Artzi. Export-import, in bold letters. Why was he so charming to me? Was it because I was with that high government official when we met?

It's 11:05. What's going on in there? He killed his mother-in-law and he's turning himself in, I suppose. The door opened, and the murderer emerged bareheaded. He is free.

The policeman, seated behind a giant typewriter in a cold, high-ceilinged room, was dressed in civilian clothes. A black scarf was draped around his neck. He had a cold.

He offered me a chair. I began to speak agitatedly, to relate the tale of Maria Cristina, the money she stole, the suitcase that disappeared, the crush in the train. But the policeman placed his hand on his forehead and shook his head.

"Wait a minute!" he proclaimed, readying his typewriter for action. He straightened the page and pounded a few keys before beginning. "Name, please." He stared intently at the lineup of letters, then picked at the keys slowly. "Uri!" he exclaimed, contemplating his creation with pleasure. "Family name?" I spelled it and he typed at the same slow pace. "Father's name?" he asked.

"Is that essential?" I said. "I'm in a hurry. I'd like to file my complaint and go."

"My dear sir," he said, his nose full, "I am not sitting here for my health. I have a cold and fever—I should be home in bed. I didn't make up this form, you know. I have to supply all the required facts before I can register the complaint. The law demands it. The law!" he repeated respectfully.

I gave him my father's first and last names. He wanted to know why he was Lampel if I was Lam. I told him I preferred the shorter name.

"Why Lam?" he asked suspiciously. "Why not Lampel, like your father?"

"Because," I said firmly, "that's how I wanted it." I explained to him that in my country it's common to change your family name.

"You are a foreigner?" he asked. "How do you happen to speak such good Italian?"

I told him that I had lived in Italy for three years. In San Castello. Until the age of thirteen. I also told him that I used to go to evening classes at the Dante Alighieri Club in Jerusalem.

"Jerusalem!" he said, sneezing. I noted a flicker of excitement in his eyes. Taking out a handkerchief he blew his nose and sighed, "The Holy City. The Holy City of our martyred Lord Jesus. Let me see your passport, please."

He scrutinized the passport, turning it this way and that. Then he began to read aloud and copy the information it contained. Occupation: architect (three years —housing developments). Birthplace: Frankfurt on the Main. (What remains of the city I was born in? Will I recognize it? My lawyer says the house wasn't destroyed. It still stands. What about the garden? And the apple tree and the berry bushes?) Date of birth April 29, 1931. (Two years before Hitler: The almond buds are new/ Hitler has the flu/on every rooftop birds now sing/welcome to the season spring. . . . It becomes obvious that Dr. Lampel is Jewish, so there are no more patients. . . . Hitler's dead—his wife is sick/a German submarine/a

bomb just fell—on his goddamn prick/a German submarine.) Height: six feet two. (Someone once said,
"You will be as tall as your father." Where was this?
When?) Eyes: blue. (Uri, look at me, Uri. Why do you
close your eyes? I love you, Uri. Don't pretend. I know
you're not asleep.) Hair: brown (but the mustache is
lighter. Almost blond). Special markings: scar on the
right arm. (A stray shell that flew in and out, splattering
blood on my shirt. "He's been hit. Careful—tie it tight
from the shoulder. And you shut up. No one is asking
you. Lie down and shut up.") It was 11:20.

"Some important details are missing," he said. "Your
mother's maiden name, her place and date of birth."

"I'm going to miss the train," I said, trying to hold
back my anger.

"I'm very sorry," the policeman said with exasperating patience. "Mother's name."

I told him I didn't know my mother's family name or
her precise birthplace. He eyed me with suspicion—how
could that be?

"Try to remember," he said derisively.

I explained to him that . . . I told him in a few
jumbled fragments that I lost her when I was ten, that
we were separated by the war. She stayed behind and I
was smuggled across the border. An Italian family
adopted me. I have no idea what happened to my
mother. Hell, why does he need all these irrelevant details? I came to report the facts: my suitcase and my
money were stolen. What does this have to do with my
mother's birthplace? Will she be called to testify? I came
to file a complaint, not to be interrogated as though I
were the offender. Will they ask for my fingerprints
next?

It was my turn to speak. "Never mind about the suitcase and the complaint," I said. "Thanks very much for
the goodwill. Thanks for your attempts to pursue the
guilty. I'm going. I haven't got time to waste on your
bureaucracy."

"Sit down!" the clerk ordered. "Sit down and answer
my questions. You are *not* free to leave. You have in-

formation regarding a criminal act which it is your duty
to deliver to the police. The law requires this!"

"But my train," I pleaded. "I've got to get to Frankfurt today. The train leaves at 11:58 and it's already
11:43. Forget my complaint. Give me my passport—
please—and let me go."

"Sorry," said the policeman, "I can't do it. Anyone
with information pertaining to a criminal act is required
to present full testimony to the police; anyone who
withholds such information is subject to arrest." I made
no reply. He studied my face and his eyes softened.

"But because you're a foreigner and speak such fine
Italian, here's what I'll do. I will write your testimony in
longhand, OK? I'll never learn to type. Not because I
don't try. You saw for yourself. I've been taking testimony by hand for twenty years, and suddenly the higher-
ups demand that I type on this damned machine."

He pushed the machine aside. "It'll go faster now," he
said, trying to be gentle. "Where were we? Oh, yes.
When did you arrive in Italy?"

"Yesterday morning," I said in despair.

"By plane?"

"No, by boat—the *Theodor Herzl* to Genoa."

"And so," the policeman said, dipping his pen in a
small inkstand, "on the ninth of September you arrived
in Genoa. What time?"

"Eight-thirty," I said. "But what difference does it
make?"

"At eight-thirty in the morning," the policeman repeated. "As soon as you left the pier you took a room in
a hotel. What was the name of the hotel?"

"Please," I implored. "At this rate we'll never get to
the suitcase."

"But you've already told me that a prostitute stole
your money in Genoa," he protested in an injured tone.
"It's our duty to protect tourists—tourism plays a big
part in Italy's economy. I'll forward your complaint to
the police in Genoa. They'll send a man to the hotel to
question the desk clerk—the prostitute who stole your
money must have filled out a form, the clerk must have

seen her identification card. We'll find her and you will have your money back, sir."

"Forget it," I said. But the policeman insisted on full details. I already knew I'd miss the train. I told him what happened in Genoa and in his painstaking manner he wrote it all down. A description of Maria Cristina. The name of the driver who took me to the cemetery, the number on his cab. The name of the restaurant we ate in. The number of her room. Exactly how much money was in my wallet. And so on, endlessly.

When he finished filling in the second sheet and finally got to the part about the suitcase—demanding a detailed description of the missing articles—it was quarter to one. With an operatic flourish he read me the completed form and ordered me to sign my full name in the margin of each sheet and initial every correction. I did.

"Now what?" I asked.

"That's it," he said. "We're through."

"What about the suitcase?" I asked.

"The suitcase," he said, shrugging, "was stolen. Without a doubt it was stolen."

"And what if you find it?" I asked.

"Just between us," he said, candidly, "I don't believe we'll recover it. I would consider it lost, if I were you. And there's almost no chance of our finding the thief."

"If that's the case, why did you insist on such elaborate testimony?"

"For the record," he said. "It's on file now, so we can investigate. That's the law. If we catch a suitcase-snatcher at that station we'll have charges on which to proceed. We'll surely find your whore in Genoa—I can promise that. Even if she didn't give her real name at the hotel, we can establish which of them was at the cemetery yesterday."

"But the suitcase is lost?" I asked, returning the passport to my pocket.

"I'm afraid so," he said. "Unless—" he began, then stopped. What now? Does he know where the suitcase is? Does he mean for me to drop two or three thousand lire on his desk in exchange for information? Are the thieves and the police in cahoots? Anything is possible.

"Unless—?" I echoed.

"Unless you go to the thieves' market on Via Vittorio and search the stalls," he said. "You might find your coat there or your shirt. You might even spot your camera."

"Then what?" I asked.

"Buy the article and bring it back here."

"What for?"

"See," he said, lowering his voice to a confidential whisper, "we're eager to learn who sells stolen goods. After you point out the culprit, we'll question him here until he discloses the source from which the coat or shirt were obtained."

"What about the other things?" I asked.

The policeman shrugged. "If the thief didn't sell everything, we'll find the rest in his house. But I don't think we'll find a thing. They generally go directly to the market and sell everything there."

"Thanks a lot," I said.

"It was nothing," he replied earnestly. "Be more careful in the future. Never leave your suitcase unattended. When you're with a lady, always put your wallet under your pillow or leave it in the hotel safe."

I thanked him for the advice and left.

My heart was heavy and my pace slow as I went to inquire about the next train to Frankfurt. The rain had stopped. The black sky was beginning to turn gray. On the way to the ticket office I stopped at an espresso stand and ordered hot tea with lemon, a medicinal brew. I felt feverish.

I won't go to Frankfurt now, I thought. I don't have the strength to set out on another trip, to be herded into a crowded train, like cattle. I can hardly keep my eyes open. I've got to get some sleep. Why is your father's name Lampel and yours Lam? Hirsch Lam. Hirsch, which became Zvi. And Zvi, wishing to escape even further from himself, became Uri. Do we look alike? I can't even remember my father's face. I used to have some photographs. In one faded snapshot he was lying on a couch in flowery silk pajamas, his small eyes smiling. Mother sat beside him, an ample woman with a high forehead and large gray eyes. His hand rested on her arm; he wore a wide ring. The repose of a Sabbath afternoon. There was another photo—of the small garden that surrounded our house in Frankfurt, with Mother standing near a table, pouring something into thin china cups. Miri, my sister, is near her (Miri's bangs are cut in a straight line across her forehead), and my big, handsome brother is lifting a cup to his lips. The small boy off to one side—a child of five or six—is me.

I burned all this stuff on my fifteenth birthday: the six photographs and four letters I had taken with me to Palestine. I made a small bonfire in the empty lot behind the Youth Center and burned it all—including the diary I kept from the time I was ten. I changed my name from Lampel to Lam, and when anybody asked where I was born I would answer defiantly, "Tel Aviv." A simple answer that avoided unpleasant issues. "Frankfurt? Then where are your parents? What do you mean, you don't know? How did you get here? You have no one here? Really, no one? Poor thing." What brings this to mind now? Issues I have tried to avoid. This train station perhaps; I haven't seen it since I was a kid. Or the fumes from the engine. Maybe because I'm just plain sick. Not gravely ill, merely in need of a few simple attentions: a properly smoothed pillow, a thermometer, a glass of hot tea—with sugar and lemon.

Now that I was sick, I didn't want to be alone in this strange city. I found a telephone booth and called Mati Artzi. At first he didn't remember me. When he did remember, he was glad to hear from me and asked how long I planned to stay. I told him I was on my way to Frankfurt to . . . to write a series of articles on Israelis in Germany. This was the story I'd invented when someone on the boat asked about the purpose of my trip. I told my acquaintances at home that I was taking a vacation in Europe. Even after changing my own position, after convincing myself of the moral justice of my claim, I didn't have the courage to admit that I was going to demand reparations from Germany. Day after day I told myself that I was demanding only what was due to me, just a small portion of what was owed as compensation for interrupted studies, damage to health, denial of freedom, loss of property, destruction of family, and similar items listed neatly by my lawyer in reviewing the first thirteen years of my life. I knew that justice was on my side, yet I couldn't acknowledge it. I refused to grant the premise that crime can be expiated by money. I refused to admit that I, determined as I was to forget and erase everything that had happened before I reached Palestine, had agreed to convert my nightmare into German marks, to tally the horror on an adding machine. More than once I saw myself as a whore, conscious and deliberate, ashamed of the guilt feelings induced by the moment of payment.

I told Mati that I missed my train. He invited me to lunch and promised to get me a seat on the night train to Frankfurt. "I'll take care of everything," he said. "Find a cab and come right over." I checked my suitcase and went to Artzi's house, at 15 Via Canzone.

7 | *tea with lemon*

Now when I try to remember the visit with Mati Artzi I realize once again how many details, the sort of details I normally recall quite clearly, have been completely blurred and confused in my mind—pushed aside, perhaps, by the odd events that occurred later in Germany, crucial events that altered the entire course of my life. It may be that these details were forgotten because I was sick that day. I'm still not sure what really did happen. It's as if I was attempting to reconstruct a chess game, though most of the key pieces are no longer in my hand. I remember the beginning and end of the game and its principal moves, but the board, faded by time, consists entirely of white squares. Among the few remaining pieces I find two white queens, one black king, three knights, a crumbling castle, and a motley band of pawns.

I remember well the sense of rest and relaxation that engulfed me as soon as I entered the house, relief such as a fugitive feels when he finds a haven. A white-gloved servant ushered me in, leading me down a white marble hall to a spacious room, its walls lined with impressive leather-bound volumes. There was a fire in the fireplace; above it a long-necked Modigliani hung captive in a heavy gold frame. The servant disappeared and I sank into a deep armchair, closed my eyes and listened to the crackling fire.

What a place to be sick! I could pamper myself and no one would notice. After dinner I would rest. I might even tell Mati I had a fever, that I caught a chill on the train. A clean soft bed would be made up for me at once in a corner room overlooking the garden. The servant girl would flutter about the room in her white uniform, bringing tea with a slice of golden lemon. She would sit beside me, steadying my hand as I drank the hot brew. A pink-faced doctor with graying hair, a doctor like my father, would place his black bag on my bed and feel my pulse, studying me with concern. Pronouncing me gravely ill, he would prescribe rest, attention, quiet. Everyone would tiptoe about. In a distant room someone would play Scarlatti, even as I lay in bed with scarlet fever, moaning softly. Poor guy. Such a young man. En route to Germany to collect reparations. Yes, his whole family—parents, brother, sister, all of them gone. He is alone. Caught a chill on the train from Genoa. It turned into pneumonia in Milan and he died. I knew him quite well. A great guy. Excellent student. Superb architect. Such scope and imagination. He would have gone far. Yet suddenly, an ordinary cold and that's it. Pity.

I heard voices in the next room, a conversation in Italian, someone mentioning my name, saying it was hard to believe I would do such a thing. Someone else insisting it was a fact. He had learned from reliable sources that I was on the way to collect 150 marks a month in return for my parents' ashes. "How does he know they were liquidated in the camp?" voice one asked derisively. Someone answered that I had a folder filled with evidence, that I knew more than I was willing to say. "And for 120 Israeli pounds he is willing to forget what was done to his parents!" the same voice remarked with disappointment. Not so, a second voice countered; for 120 pounds I would remember them every month—when the check arrived. The voices merged in laughter, fading into the distance as the sound of footsteps coming toward me grew louder.

I sprang from the armchair to open the door, but the hall was deserted. I listened a long moment but now I could hear neither the laughter nor the footsteps. I closed the door quietly and heard someone playing Ravel's "Concerto for the Left Hand." I was certain the pianist was Perlmutter, but it was my brother that was seated at the black grand piano playing, an empty sleeve tucked in his right pocket. I closed the door and sat down in the armchair again. I did not wish to interrupt. I'll wait for him to finish, I thought.

Mati Artzi stood near the fireplace talking in whispers to a woman whose back was turned. He was leaning on a black wooden stick with an ivory handle. The fire sparkled in his eyeglasses. He pointed to me and made some remark. The woman turned her head . . . and she was my mother in a summer dress printed with roses. They came toward me, the two of them. Mati said, "Good morning."

I opened my eyes and found Mati standing beside me, beaming. He clutched my hand warmly and introduced me to his wife, who held out her soft fingers, saying, "Laura (or Flora). So pleased to meet you." He spoke Italian to her, calling her Maminka—a name that suited her perfectly. She was small, plump, dressed in soft silk. Her bare arms were full like my mother's arms in that photograph. Little Mama from the Italian melodramas. Mama, serenaded by Neapolitan tenors, fingers locked over their hearts, eyebrows knit with empathy and love. Mati asked me to sit down and make myself at home. After his wife was settled in the armchair I let Mati take my arm and lead me to the broad sofa in front of the fireplace. His wife gazed at me with moist eyes, a smile of pleasure fixed on her face. Mati loosened his silk tie, unbuttoned his collar, slapped my arm lightly, and said, "So goes it."

"So goes it," I said.

He asked a few polite questions. When did I arrive in Italy, how was the crossing, how are things at home, how did I like Italy? I answered politely. All is well at home, the crossing was pleasant, I am enjoying Italy, and so forth. I didn't have the strength to tell him everything that had happened since I arrived in Genoa. My tongue was heavy and dry. I was struggling to keep my eyes open. The maid brought in a silver tray with salted almonds and long-stemmed crystal. Mati poured some tawny Spanish sherry and toasted, "*L'chayim*," Maminka and I clinked glasses and she said, "*L'chayim*," mispronouncing it. My mother was there, standing at a table, its white cloth scattered with rose petals that dripped from a vase. She was holding a slim goblet and saying, "*L'chayim*."

My eyes were half closed. I soon realized Mati was talking about Germany, leading me into the trap I had foolishly set for myself. He seemed to accept my story—that I was writing a series of articles on Israelis in Germany—and took it upon himself to brief me on this "painful question." He had canceled his appointments for the day so he could visit with me and recount his role in rescuing the Jewish people. I felt the noose tightening.

His tale, like all those I wished to avoid, began in 1938. After two or three sentences he asked why I wasn't taking notes. I said I had a good memory but he insisted on my jotting down key words, dates, persons, place-names—something. "Get some paper," he said to Maminka in Italian. She rose dutifully and went to the desk. My head was buzzing, and despite the central heating and the crackling fire I was chilled. All the lovely images—cozy bed, tea with lemon, the doctor, peace—went up in flames. My host would now relate the story of his life, and I, his captive, would listen and take notes: how and what he did, when and where. He would cite dates, emphasize place-names, repeat the names of witnesses who could verify his account. I would have to sit there and nod from time to time in understanding and appreciation.

About a year ago, together with other scraps of paper pertaining to this trip, I found some notes which were the remnants of this conversation with Mati Artzi. In 1939 he escaped from Poland, I had written. ("Our house was gradually emptied of its furnishings. My brother and I slept in the same bed, and one morning I asked him why his thing was so big. He slapped me and turned toward the wall.") His parents remained there. (Where all the parents remained. Perhaps in the very same hut, in the same sewer. Skeletons in striped pajamas like the ones in the photographs that fill commemorative issues of the newspaper.) A kibbutz, then Italy with the British army. (Was he the one who tied an SS officer to an army truck and dragged him through the streets of Mannheim at 50 miles an hour so that first his uniform, then his skin, were torn by the black basalt while soldiers, drunk with victory, clapped in rhythm and sang "We bring you peace"?) In '45 he deserted. Refugees. Illegal immigration. Breaking through the blockade with boatloads of refugees from southern Italy.

Some of the words convey nothing to me now: "Gaeta," "Saul," "to '48," "*Exodus*," "Famagusta," "40,000," and "sleep"—traces of Mati Artzi's endless monologue on the sofa in front of the crackling fire. I remember watching his thin lips move endlessly. Maminka, who understood not one word, gazed at him with large adoring eyes, nodding agreement. She had undoubtedly heard his tales more than once, tales of rescue five minutes before the zero hour. Her smile was replaced by a suitable expression when he said "Dachau."

I had no wish to hear his stories. I had tales of my own that I didn't want to recall. Hiding my face in my hands to feign emotion, I stuffed a finger in each ear and closed my eyes. I wanted to sleep, to rest my head on a pillow and doze off just as I was, on the couch by the fire.

This is fitting punishment for my trivial lies, I told myself. So, you're writing articles on Germany—well, go ahead and write. In bold letters: "port of Bari," so he will see that you're with him. "Dachau," framed in black, "European exodus." What does he want from me? Having suffered for years from the chronic constipation of underground life, it's his turn to crap on me.

I should have told him the truth: that I was going to Germany to collect reparations. Then maybe I would have been spared this nightmare. At most he would have shaken his head with irritating pity, and instead of telling me what I didn't want to hear, he would speak of Rosselini, the Italian Renaissance, Etruscan tombs— any topic but that one: ashes deposited in lakes whose water will never be clear again.

I cannot remember the extent of this exhausting lecture. At any rate, it didn't end even when a servant appeared to announce dinner in a loud, festive voice. Mati took my arm and talked incessantly as he led me down a thickly carpeted hall to the dining room. We took our places at the gleaming white table, the waiter poured the wine and served the food from sparkling silver trays, and still Mati talked on. In his endless word album I once more saw nostalgic pictures like the ones that are shown around after dinner by collectors of the past. "There I am with a group of survivors. The guy next to me was the captain of the *Exodus*; here are the ovens of Auschwitz; that leg on the right is mine."

My water glass was empty. The servant, who stood in the background following our every move, filled my glass with ice water instantly. I gulped it down, and he quickly refilled my glass. Maminka, observing my untouched plate with concern, signaled with her eyes as if to say, "Eat, eat."

Mati suddenly remembered that he hadn't been able to get a reservation for me on the night train to Frankfurt—the trains were filled with Germans returning from vacation in southern Europe—but he had a second-class reservation on the 11:58 the next morning. "After lunch we can take a drive," he said. "I'll show you Milan. Tonight we can go to La Scala—you shouldn't miss it. You can spend the night here, rest, have a good sleep, and about 11:30 tomorrow my driver will take you to the station." Maminka finished her veal steak. The servant was waiting for me to push my dish aside so he could clear the table.

"You're not eating anything," Maminka said reproachfully.

"Leave him alone, Maminka, he's a big boy," Mati said, getting up and taking my arm again. "Let's have coffee in the living room. Where was I? Oh, yes. The train from Germany was two hours late . . ."

In the living room, where there really was a grand piano, I sat down in a leather chair, a Mies van der Rohe. The maid poured coffee from a silver swan-shaped urn. The sheets of notes I had left by the fireplace were now on my lap and Mati's lips moved constantly. I no longer heard what he was saying. Even though he gesticulated and spoke with great intensity, his voice didn't get through to me. I tried to suppress the tremor that flashed through my body. Although there was no one at the piano, I could hear the finale of the "Concerto for the Left Hand." My lids began to droop. Maminka looked at me anxiously, and suddenly Mati's voice came through again, as if someone had pushed a button on a stereo. He was at some train station in Italy, greeting a group of gaunt children, twelve- or fourteen-year-olds marching hand in hand in rows of three, wide-eyed, staring fearfully at the policemen and customs officials. The scene was familiar—was this the group that Maxie and I had marched with? Max Herman, who had

been in my class, who had insisted on carrying me on
his back when that wild ball ripped the flesh off my
right arm. Max Herman, my good friend the Arabist,
who went back to Germany with Edna, back to our
Frankfurt. What does this man want of us?

"Do you understand?" Mati charged. "When I remember what it took to get those children to Palestine; when
I think of all the efforts invested by teachers and educa-
tors once they arrived, what it took to transform these
poor creatures into more or less normal people, young
men who could work the land, study at the university,
serve in the army; when I remember those boys who
fought and were wounded in the War of Independence,
many of them killed—and then I hear that some of
those very same youngsters are returning to Germany
to collect reparations and spend their money in the
nightspots of Hamburg, Munich, and Berlin, I . . . I
don't know where to bury my shame. You'll see them
in Frankfurt, too, and you won't want to believe your
eyes. It's ghastly." He stared at me obstinately, and I
quickly nodded in agreement. I pictured myself dancing
with Edna in one of Max's bars, and it was true—I
couldn't believe my eyes. A sour, burning taste rose in
my throat.

"Me, too!" Mati went on excitedly. "I could have collected reparations. Thousands of dollars. Loss of freedom and property, interrupted studies. I was orphaned
too. I certainly have a right to reparations. But I
won't touch that sort of money. I will never forget. I will never forgive. I can't bring myself to buy
anything made by Volkswagen, Leica, or Telefunken.
Everything you see here was earned with my own hands
and my own head, even though I had to work fourteen
hours a day to do it. There's not enough money in the
world to compensate for what was done—What is it,
Uri? What's the matter? Don't you feel well?"

"No, I don't feel very well," I admitted. "Could I step
outside for a minute?"

He looked worried and showed me to the bathroom.
Behind the closed door I vomited, spewing my soul into

the toilet. I turned on the gilded faucets to drown out my awful noises. I washed my blazing face with cold water and took a couple of deep breaths before returning to the living room. They both came toward me anxiously.

"You're very pale," Mati said.

"I think I have fever," I said. "I seem to have caught a cold."

"Why didn't you say so?" Mati was clearly annoyed. "Maminka, he feels sick. Let's take his temperature."

"It's nothing much," I said. "I must have caught a cold on the way from Genoa. I'll be all right. Go on, Mati, I'm listening." But he ignored me. The commander, the organizer came to life. He ordered the maid to make up the bed in the guest room. He ordered his wife to bring me a thermometer and an aspirin. "You keep out of this," he said to me, even though I hadn't uttered a word. "Just do as you're told. Get into bed. We'll take your temperature and decide what to do."

Everything that followed is foggy. I don't know how I got to bed. I remember the softness of Mati's wife as she knelt over me, thermometer in hand. I had fever, 102 degrees. Through the window the sky was already dim. I lay there in Mati's pajamas, shivering. I fell asleep as Mati was telephoning. When I awoke later I found a short plump man looking into my eyes, his black leather bag on the bed. He clutched my hand, keeping his eye on his watch, and then handed me two pills to swallow with a glass of water. I asked for tea with lemon and closed my eyes again. My father was standing at my bedside saying, "Drink some water, boy. You'll soon be better."

Nearby I heard footsteps and the voice of Aunt Anna. "Sleep, sleep, my darling. If you need something ring the bell. The doctor says it's flu. It will be over soon. You need to rest. Sleep." Sleep my bunny, my little *coniglio*. Someone is ill/it's our little bunny/he caught a chill/and his nose is runny.

When I opened my eyes again, a small night light glowed in the room. On the table beside the bed was the tea, already cold. Even after I drank it all I was still thirsty. I was drenched with sweat. I wiped my face and neck with the sheet and got out of bed. The door in my room opened into a dark hallway. Back in my room, I urinated in the sink, then rinsed it out and got back into bed, trembling. I pressed the bell beside my bed. It was a quarter to eleven. The house was silent. Closing my eyes I saw a young servant girl come into the room and sit beside me . . . on the grass. The fragrant smell of apples wafted from her neck, red ripe apples at the foot of a tree in tall grass. "Don't climb that tree," my mother said from the kitchen window, shaking a menacing finger. She disappeared suddenly, and, in the crowd at the train station waving white handkerchiefs at me, a crowd that shrieked like the gulls in the blue sea, I couldn't find her face. The maid placed her cool hand on my forehead and said, "What is it, dear? Do you want something?" I opened my eyes and saw my mother, Maminka, kneeling over me in a soft, glistening robe, her cool hand brushing my blazing forehead.

"Can I get you something?" she asked.

"I'm thirsty."

"I'll bring you some tea," she said.

"Water, water from the canteen. It's my turn now. A can of water from the barrel on Mamilla Road in Jerusalem. How many days will that water last?"

"What? What is it you want?" Mother asked. "Tell me what you want, poor child."

"*Acqua fresca, acqua corrente,*" I mumbled. Footsteps, then water flowing from the faucet.

"Have some water," I heard Mother's voice say. "Pick your head up. Take a drink, dear. You'll feel better."

Maminka supported my head as I drank all the cold water.

"*Mama, sono tanto felice,*" I murmured and her full face broadened into a smile. She wiped my face with a towel.

"I'll bring you tea," she said.

"Where's Mati?" I asked.

"Asleep," she replied. "He works very hard."

"Yes," I said, "he worked very hard today. He talked five hours straight. He doesn't want reparations—OK, so he doesn't need it! He has plenty of money. He stayed here in Italy and used his underground connections to good advantage. He sent gifts to your ministers and they didn't forget him. Export-import. Engraved calling cards. Industrial enterprises: plastics, washing machines, nylons. He didn't give the best years of his life for nothing."

"Are you talking Hebrew to me?" Maminka asked. "I don't understand a word. Speak Italian, my treasure."

"I said that Mati is all right," I went on in Hebrew. "He is one hundred percent all right. A great man. Saved many lives and his own, too, at the last minute. He kept a place of honor for himself in the lifeboat. I didn't want to go alone, I wanted to stay home. Father said they would come, but they didn't. At the border he disappeared. Then strangers who spoke no German came and gave me black bread. One of them said, in a funny dialect, 'You here. You. Papers, so you can travel on. Now here.' Then one day a hunter came and seized me along with two other children, a pale girl with a red pigtail and a boy who licked his snot. It wasn't my fault. I was just a child and father said I had to; there wasn't any choice. Later, in the village with Aunt Anna, they all used to cross themselves before tasting the potato soup. I too, my Santa Maria, crossed myself like the rest, and before closing my eyes I would say, '*Padre, padre nostro.*'"

"You're delirious, dear," Mother said, stroking my moist hair with her soft hand. "You have a high fever. Try to sleep. I'll bring some tea. Keep the covers on. I'll be right back."

The hand on my forehead vanished . . . I saw the wide gold band on my father's finger. Sleep, my boy. Sleep. You're going on a long trip. Say good-bye to our house. You won't see it again. Wagner-Gasse 9, Frankfurt. I fell asleep in the train, my head on my father's lap. . . . When I woke up in Milan it was nine in the morning. The room was flooded with sunlight. My fever was gone.

I went down to breakfast. Mati had already gone. I drank coffee and ate fresh rolls and two eggs in a cup. Maminka, sitting opposite me, looked on with satisfaction. After I convinced her I was healthy she gave me my train ticket. I phoned Mati at his office to thank him for his hospitality and for the enlightening conversation. When I left, Maminka, standing on tiptoes, kissed me on both cheeks and smoothed my hair with her soft fingers.

8 | *Germans on the train*

I arrived at the station with almost an hour to kill. I had already eaten breakfast, the ticket for a reserved seat in a second-class compartment was in my pocket. What was there to do? Go to the police station and ask if by any chance my suitcase had been found? Better not risk it, I thought.

The sky was clear, with a herd of downy white clouds grazing at its fringe. A cloud of white pigeons rested on the square, a circle of women and children swarming around them. I sat on a stone bench and watched the crowd, in constant motion, headed somewhere: toward trains, buses, cabs, stopping for a moment and speeding on again. A man in a heavy black coat, with a gray woolen scarf wound about his neck, caught my eye. He stood in the middle of the crowd, scanning the scene indifferently, turning to check the great clock. He was simply there, without destination, an unfathomable riddle, someone who forgot why he came, who doesn't know where he is going. Withdrawn from the world.

I remembered my big brother. When I last saw him I was ten years old and he was nineteen. One day, many years later, a man came up to me at the Technion

Library in Haifa and asked if my name was Lampel, and if I had a brother Martin. I didn't know this man—he was a childhood friend of my brother's, he said. When he was sent to Teresienstadt he found Martin there, and fell on his neck. But my brother had stared at him vacantly. He called Martin by name, but though Martin's eyes had filled with tears he made no sign of recognition. Martin's empty sleeve was tucked into his jacket pocket and his lips trembled. "He was withdrawn from the world," his friend recalled.

The man stirred and shifted his glance toward the swarm of pecking pigeons. He bought a bag of pigeon feed from an old woman, scooped up some seeds with his hand and moved toward the pigeons, but not one would light on his hand. He kneeled and tried to attract them, but they flew away, preferring to respond to the children's activity. He flung the seeds into the air. Flapping their wings noisily, the birds soared upward, toward the glass roof of the terminal. . . .

Collecting my suitcase from the checkroom, I bought two English newspapers, sipped coffee at a counter, and then headed for platform 3. The front car had a sign: ROME-MILAN-BASEL-FRANKFURT.

Mati was right. The train *was* full of Germans. Red-faced Germans, returning home from summer vacations in southern Europe. They leaned out the windows, exchanging pleasantries with people on the platform who handed them sandwiches, beer, soft drinks, and wine.

These were the first Germans I had seen since childhood. The Germans that I remembered, dimly, were like the ones in the war movies. They were in uniform, carried machine guns and barked curt phrases. Like the soldier who ate lunch at Aunt Anna's house once. I remember Uncle Michele standing silent in the kitchen as Aunt Anna served the soup. I sneaked out of my room, though I had been told to stay there until I was called, and stood at the kitchen door. It was open slightly, and through the crack I could see the soldier eating in oppressive silence. I heard his noisy gulps, every squeak of the chair. Once he looked up from his plate and stared directly at me. I froze, not daring to move. After a long moment he looked back at the plate. I tiptoed to my room, and waited for the sound of his boots on the wooden floor. Aunt Anna appeared finally, her eyes moist and filled with concern. She embraced me, buried my head in her warm bosom fragrant with garlic, and said simply, "He's gone." I was kept inside the house a whole year. You mustn't go out, my *coniglio!* Away from the window! Shut the door. Go to your room and don't come out until I call! There are Germans in the village!

Now here I was in the train compartment, besieged by Germans. They spoke that same language, the same curt, sharp phrases I had heard in movies and in my own nightmares. The two opposite me, men of about fifty, were surely SS officers. It couldn't have been otherwise. The moment I took my seat I clothed them in black uniforms, adorned their necks with iron crosses, exchanged one man's spectacles for a Prussian monocle, the other's camera for a pistol. The flat-faced woman with a cigarette was no doubt the camp supervisor I had seen in a documentary. The poodle at her feet was a black German shepherd. The gentleman on my right, a handsome young man of about thirty with soft lips, was an interrogating officer who paced the floor in gleaming leather boots, issuing shrill commands. And I? I was in the underground, trying to cross the border with a forged passport. Soon one of those Nazis would inform the policeman on the platform, I would run the length of the corridor, climb atop the car, leap from roof to roof. There would be a rapid volley and then the soft-lipped officer would nod, satisfied that order had been restored, and light his gold-tipped cigarette.

I tried to brush away these fantasies and to see my fellow passengers as ordinary tourists: a bank clerk dreaming of his pension in a sun-drenched cove on the southern shore of Spain; a housewife, already imagining herself at home, opening windows and wiping dust off the sills; a music teacher thinking about the students back home; a saleswoman in some large shoe store.

But their language was oppressive. As were their possessions: mementoes and gifts acquired on their holiday—a Spanish guitar, a large drawing framed in gold that rested on one of the suitcases, a colorful rug from Greece, Chianti bottles of braided straw, a salami, a smoked provolone swinging on a string—these innocent articles were the spoils of war, plundered from houses, pillaged from display cases shattered by bayonets. Even the smoke from chimneys I saw through the window assumed a terrifying significance.

I opened one of my newspapers and hid behind it. I tried to read an article on anesthesia but I couldn't absorb even the opening sentence. The young man on my right was staring at me. I tried to avoid his gaze, but our eyes met by accident. I turned away quickly and looked out the window at the shedding trees.

I was unprepared for this first encounter with Germans. It took me by surprise. I expected to meet them in their own country and failed to foresee that the German language, coming from real Germans—not elderly waiters, doctors, clerks who speak Hebrew as if it were a foreign tongue—would arouse my suppressed wish to hide. There was no doubt about it: I did want to hide. I didn't want my fellow passengers to know I understood German, I didn't want them to know I was Jewish. The thought that they might guess the reason for my trip to Germany filled me with horror.

My eyes were riveted to my newspaper, while I strained to digest the notion that the sea of chatter that surrounded me (on the price of Italian shoes, the weather, the exchange rate in Athens) was an element in the confrontation—between the victim and his murderer—an encounter to which I was drawn these many years, much as I dreaded it.

I'm going to demand reparations from these people, I reflected bitterly. To *request* reparations, not demand them. To request in a vigorous and proud voice, that's true. Still . . . request, not demand. For where in the world is a victim required by the culprit to fill out questionnaires, present credentials, provide evidence that the goods are really his? Where is the precedent for this procedure? I should have addressed myself to the victors, to the powers that vanquished this scarecrow, demanded that they force the thief to return what was stolen, to sentence the offenders to hard labor to compensate me for interrupted studies, impaired health, loss of freedom, premeditated murder. I demand a just verdict, rather than crumbs from the brimming table of the murderers. But if this were true I wouldn't be consumed by shame, I wouldn't feel the need to conceal my face lest they guess that I'm the victim, delivered into their generous hands, awaiting a sentence. I would go off, head high, to receive what's coming to me, though it can never compensate for what was done. Now that they are offering symbolic restitution, they declare themselves abused if one is disinclined to forgive and forget. Who was the Christian of refined sensibility who said, "Forgive? Yes. Forget? Never." I spit in his face. Forgive? Never! But one must forget. That is the only answer. One must forget!

"Time to eat, gentlemen. It's one o'clock on the dot," one of the passengers declared. There was a rush of activity. One man went to wash his hands. The women opened plastic bags and took out bottles of beer. I folded my newspaper and put it on my lap. The young man was still waiting for me to look his way. I took out a cigarette and a lighter appeared; the hand that held it for me was delicate and well cared for. The young man smiled.

"May I look at your newspaper, sir?" he asked in English with only the slightest trace of an accent. I nodded. Even before I could hand it to him he had claimed it. His eyes searched mine. I turned away. The bespectacled Nazi was back in his place opposite me.

"Let's get down to business," he said, displaying well-scrubbed hands for all to see.

"Johann, get the table down," the camp commander lady said. Her hands were busy with a roast chicken wrapped in papers drenched with fat. Johann spread a clean handkerchief on the upholstered seat and stood on it. He took down the gold-framed picture and placed it face down on a companion's lap. The other woman quickly spread a plastic cloth over the picture. The flat-faced woman placed the chicken on the "table," folded the greasy papers carefully, and stuffed them into a bag. She emptied out a checkered cotton bag: rolls, tomatoes, pickles, a thick sausage, a large wheel of yellow cheese. "Stop dreaming, Friedrich dear," she said to the man who was holding the table on his knees. "Serve it up."

There was silence. All eyes were fixed on Friedrich.

First he removed the wings of the bird and placed them side by side on the tablecloth. Then he plucked off the legs and divided each leg in half, inserting three firm fingers in each joint. He added these four pieces to the row. With a single swift twist he removed the neck and then, placing two fingers under the white meat, ripped off the breast with an experienced motion. Peeling the skin off the breast he spread it in front of him, arranging the liver, gizzard, and heart, which he had extracted from the depths of the bird, on the skin. The breast meat, which he divided into four parts, was lined up with the other sections. Only the back remained. He split it in two. Now that the bird was dismembered and its parts neatly arranged, he looked at the two women proudly. Popping the liver and heart into his mouth, he laughed heartily.

"Friedrich Baum, you are a pig," the camp commander lady scolded.

"I worked hard; I deserve it," Friedrich said, munching away. "And you know how much I love the heart."

"I know," she laughed. "If you have no heart, eat the hearts of others. Johann, you slice the sausage and the cheese. Greta, pass the rolls around. We'll soon be home, eating good rye bread. The Italians will never learn to bake decent bread."

The young man beside me pretended to be reading the newspaper, but even without looking at him I knew his eyes were studying me. The train entered a grove of pine trees.

"Won't you join us?" Herr Baum said, wiping his fingers on a paper napkin and shifting his gaze back and forth between me and the young man and then back to the chicken parts in front of him.

"No, thank you," said the young man from behind the newspaper.

"No, thanks," I said in English, closing my eyes.

Was this the relief I had yearned for? If I hadn't reserved a seat I could have chosen more congenial company. The whole train couldn't be filled with Germans. There must be some Italians going to the mountains, Swiss traveling to Basel (the site of the First Zionist Congress), a girl studying simultaneous translation in Geneva. But here I am stuck in the midst of this noisy, gross bunch. A reserved seat, first row center, among murderous sadists who tear off legs and pluck out wings. She issues orders, that camp commander lady. Pass the bread, open the bottle, let me have the wing. I closed my eyes, but sleep was out of the question. I went out to the corridor—thank God it was empty—and opened a window. A sunlit lake gleamed in the distance.

You've got to forget, I told myself again. In order to live without losing your sanity you must strain to forget. Scratch out what's engraved in your head, erase what is written there. Make a small bonfire in back of the Youth Center and burn the memories, the letters, the pictures. Scatter the ashes upon the water and that's that. Forget. If you want to live, to work and make something of life. The alternative is madness.

Madness! A perpetual striptease of the soul; waiting in ambush for fugitives of the holocaust, offering them replicas of one's own nightmare at bargain prices; beating the drums of hell on every holiday, raising the roof, disturbing the peace of those who sleep; a continuous performance! See what they did to me. Come one, come all; the show is beginning. First the number on my arm, but that's nothing. Pay attention, gentlemen, to my soul, to my heart, fluttering sixty hells a minute. And now for this evening's featured attraction. A contest of grotesque memories! Anyone who can prove he has suffered more than I, can recall memories more horrible (to be determined by a special gauge that measures and records the intensity of sighs and groans), this man, ladies and gentlemen, will win a free tour of the concentration camps, including air fare to Bergen-Belsen and back.

Enough of this garbage—a whore-in-mourning! If you mean to forget, you must forget it all. No point in compiling a new list of things to forget and checking daily for omissions. Forget, goddamn it! Forget everything. Or else go back into that compartment—and break their necks, peel their flesh, pluck out their hearts. Sweep through the streets of Frankfurt with a machine gun, striking down old people, women, and children; poison the reservoir; destroy, destroy, destroy without distinction. But not all of them are guilty. There is a new generation, confronted with photographs of Daddy in a tattered army shirt, letters from Warsaw and Paris; young men who wash their hands with soap and ask the pale reflection in the mirror, "What about my father? Could it be that he didn't know?" There is another Germany. It must be so. Lord God, help me, help me find it.

The compartment door opened and swung closed. My heart began to rattle with the wheels. I sought refuge in the smooth green fields beyond the window, but the wheels began to repeat relentlessly "Sm-oke-sta-cks, s-moke-stacks-smokestacks!" The young man stood near me, silent, resting his hand delicately on the windowsill.

"What a beautiful day," he began, filling his lungs with air. I said nothing.

"The Germans are going home," he said, "and the sun will shine again over Italy."

Still I didn't answer.

The train was following the course of a broad river. Here is the true Europe, I reflected, green fields and abundant water. What a waste of God's blood, Exupéry, my saint! One such river would solve many problems in my own arid land. Trees, so many trees! Not the kind that are planted by aging laborers in a public works program, but trees that grow wild, with no irrigation, no weeding. An intricate forest of senseless trees planted by streams of wasted water. I remembered a sign I had seen long ago on the road to Jerusalem: CAUTION, SAPLINGS. I must have smiled, for the young man smiled too.

The train slowed down and started to cross a long steel bridge. In my mind I saw a thin canal threading its way through the alfalfa field back home, its locks barely opened, sprinklers squeaking in the tomato patch.

Loud voices echoed from the compartment. The camp commander lady was singing, her dear Friedrich at her side. The other couple, swaying in rhythm, tapped their bottles, flung their heads back, and took long swigs of beer.

"Ghastly," said the young man, following my glance. "I saw you watching them. I know that look. You were trying to hide behind your newspaper. Are you angry that I followed you?"

I shook my head.

"Your eyes tell all," he said. "I often see that expression in kids' eyes when they first encounter our raucous tourists. An expression of wonder. This generation of Germans, forty years old or over, are these really the ones in the movies? The soldiers that marched through the streets of our city, the ones that did thus-and-so. You know what I mean?"

I nodded.

"Are you familiar with Germany?" he asked.

I shook my head.

He was silent for a moment. "Do you mind my being here?" he asked finally with a trace of bitterness. "Would you prefer that I didn't speak to you?"

"No," I said. "But you do surprise me. Aren't you . . . German?"

"Yes, I'm German," he said sadly, "but with a difference, I hope. Do you smoke? Oh, excuse me. Of course you smoke. I lit your cigarette in there." He opened a silver case and offered me one of his black color-tipped cigarettes.

"I'm used to my own brand," I said, taking one and passing the rest to him. He gazed into my eyes, searching for deeper meaning in these words. I lit a match. When he bent down for a light his hand grazed mine ever so lightly. He looked into my eyes with an open question. Again I looked out the window.

"Our tourists are a ghastly bunch," he said after a pause. "Why can't they talk quietly like anyone else? The entire world must know they're Germans."

"Tourists from . . . from America are just as noisy," I said.

He began to sketch the German tourist in the blackest, most devastating strokes, a la George Grosz. I couldn't decide if these were his real thoughts or if he was guessing at mine. He spoke with emotion, glancing inside from time to time at the Germans, who were still singing and drinking, as if to feed his contempt.

"Believe me," he said, placing his hand on my shoulder with sudden intimacy, "they are intolerable." I looked at him reproachfully. The hand slipped away. He continued to chatter about restaurants, camping grounds, tourist spots swarming with Germans. Then, when he began to describe a fashion show he had seen in Rome, he realized that he still hadn't introduced himself.

"My name is Martin," he said. My heart leaped. My brother, Martin, the musician, stood before me in the train station, his eyes lost in the sea of people. "Martin Schiller," the man beside me said, extending his hand. I told him my name and he trembled when he heard I was from Jerusalem. Now it was his turn to elude my gaze.

He stood there withdrawn, staring out the window, seeing nothing. His fine lips, having moved incessantly from the moment he entered the corridor, were now still. An odd shudder, the meaning of which I couldn't guess, flashed across his sharp chin.

What is this all about? I asked myself. Why the

hush the minute I disclosed my identity? Anti-Semitism? Impossible. If that was it he would have offered a polite sentence or two and disappeared. But there he was, staring out the window, waiting. What was he waiting for? Did he expect me to question him? (What did your father do in the war?) He was surely aware of the gulf between us. I would have to show willingness to listen, or at least indicate that a hand extended in my direction would not be rejected. He must feel how impossible it is for us to communicate. What can a murderer's son say to the son of the victim? "I'm so sorry that my father killed your father"? What a strange situation.

I tried to humor him, but his responses were brusque and discouraging. He was my age: twenty-eight (he was thirteen when the war was over). A fashion designer— naturally. Born in Berlin, he had been living in Frankfurt for some years. Without being asked I told him I was born in Tel Aviv, that my brother played the cello in the Philharmonic, that my sister was married and had two grown children, one in the army; that my mother lived alone on a pension left by my father, who had been a doctor in Jerusalem during the war. My mother listens to records and plays solitaire, I added.

For a moment I believed the picture I was sketching for him. He listened, politely detached, and asked no questions. I told him I was writing a series of articles on "The Other Germany." He reacted to this information with a slight tremor. Our conversation dwindled to nothing. I expressed my pleasure at having met him, excused myself, and sought refuge in the dining car.

The rest of the trip was uneventful. The Swiss border police were businesslike. The German customs man smiled generously and didn't even check suitcases. After a lavish dinner in the dining car, which included a bottle of Alsatian wine, I found myself a seat in another compartment and fell asleep. After a while someone woke me, saying I was in his seat. I returned to my own compartment, now dark. My SS officers slept the sleep of the righteous in their girl friends' arms.

Martin's seat was empty. Closing my eyes I saw the other Martin, my brother, walking through a huge empty square, his one arm extended. The sky was blanketed with black pigeons. I felt the sweet, revolting smell of smoke. The pigeons suddenly dispersed in all directions and a blinding beacon shone in my face.

I opened my eyes—the light was on in the compartment. The passengers were already shoving their way down the corridor, suitcases in hand. Martin stood opposite me, impassive, smoking a black cigarette.

"Frankfurt," he said.

The train slowed down. I could see tall buildings with sloped roofs through the window and a succession of sparkling lights. The train wheels repeated their message with slow persistence. Martin, tucking in his shirt and adjusting his soft red tie, gave me a long look. The camp commander lady, standing at the door, nudged Herr Friedrich Baum with her elbow and glanced knowingly at us. He stared at us disapprovingly and uttered a single word, which struck with the force of lightning: "*Goyim* —gentiles!" So—my SS officer and my camp commander lady were both Jews! I realized this with horror and immediately I began to correct the picture I had created. German Jews!

"Where are you staying?" Martin asked as the train pulled into the station. I told him I had a room. He handed me a card and said, "Call me if you need anything. I'll be glad to help you if I can. Frankfurt is an awful place, but I can show you 'the other Frankfurt,' if you want to see it."

I thanked him and stuck the card in my pocket. Jews, after all. Martin and I shook hands. I took my suitcase and followed the stream of passengers to the end of the platform. Outside it was raining. I grabbed a cab and asked the driver to find me a clean, inexpensive hotel.

9 | *a new day*

That night in Frankfurt, my birthplace, I slept soundly, undisturbed by street noises, a dripping faucet, footsteps in the hall, conversation on the other side of the thin wall. Resting on the soft mattress, I sank into dreamless sleep, a deep pool into which the scenes and conversations of the past few days were all neatly submerged.

I woke up at ten minutes to ten. A sunny strip of daylight crept through a crevice in the blinds, lighting the polished wooden floors and touching the edge of the bed. I lay with my eyes open, relaxed, drinking in deep tranquillity. The events of these days became distant, as if someone else, someone close to me, was recounting them. When had all this happened? To whom? A certain figure in a black raincoat with a turned-up collar. . . . Was this simply the delicious sensation of coming home after many years of wandering in strange lands, a sensation that severed the remaining webs of sleep? I leaped out of bed and showered.

Wrapping myself in a huge towel, I phoned down to order breakfast—in English. Yes, the works: omelet, coffee, jam, everything. I was hungry and dressed quickly. The grave face that confronted me in the mirror over the sink was adorned with a two-day growth of beard. My toilet articles having been in the stolen suitcase, I brushed my teeth with a soapy finger and made a mental note of what I had to buy: toilet articles, a shirt, pants. Maybe I could get by without a winter coat. When I pulled back the heavy blinds the room was flooded with bright sunlight. There was a rap at the door and a slender young chambermaid set the tray, laden with silverware and china, on the table. With a smile, radiant and childlike, she bade me "Good morning," in German. I asked for an English newspaper. She looked at me, uncomprehending, then in a flash of understanding she opened the desk drawer and produced notepaper and a pen.

"Paper," she exclaimed with a satisfied smile.

I tried to explain that what I had in mind was a newspaper—to no avail. I finally relented and said, "*Zeitung.*" The Herald Tribune *Zeitung* or any other English *Zeitung.* "*Jawohl, mein Herr,*" she said, and flew out of the room.

I sat down with my back to the window and surveyed the tray with relish. A large coffee urn, a pot of warm milk, a pitcher of sweet cream, a bowl brimming with fresh butter, poppyseed rolls, croissants, a dish of clear red jam, sugar in a shiny silver bowl, an omelet in a covered oval platter, gleaming silverware, napkins, one rose in a clear vase—what a magnificent morning. I poured myself some coffee.

I don't know what was so singular about this breakfast, but immediately, with the first bite of roll, remote yet familiar tastes came back to me. Had I eaten rolls like these in this very city, in my parents' home? Or was it the special taste of coffee in a thin china cup? What was my mother pouring in the photograph I destroyed? Was it coffee like this? I was expecting the breakfast I used to have as a child—that's why even the omelet seemed so unique. An ordinary omelet. . . . And preserves like these—I hadn't tasted anything like them. Jam from the fruit of those prickly bushes whose branches had scratched my arms when I was a child in Frankfurt. A servant in a white apron had stood over me in the sun, her body sending forth the sweet fragrance of raspberries like the jam in that small dish.

A rap on the door.

The chambermaid appeared smiling mischievously, an English newspaper in one hand, the other hand hidden behind her back. I thanked her in English, but she made no move to leave. I watched her quizzically, wondering why she was standing there with a grin on her face. I was about to hand her some coins when she showed me what was in her other hand: an electric razor.

"*Ja?*" she asked playfully, lest I take offense.

"*Ja,*" I said, rubbing the stubble on my face.

She connected the razor to the outlet above the mirror in the bathroom.

"This, too?" she asked in another German, a softer one, passing a finger across her upper lip. "The mustache—*ja?*"

I shook my head. She wrinkled her nose playfully and waited. A moment of infinite suspense. To seize her swiftly, sweep her off her feet, fling her fluttering body on the bed, peel off the white apron and the dress, drown in the raspberry fragrance of her body, swallow up her tiny breasts, grip her trembling, white thighs, pierce her blazing body with the "scepter of my desire"? Instead, I fished a few coins out of my jacket and handed them to her. She bowed, smiled, said, "*Guten Tag, mein Herr,*" and was off, leaving her playful smile to toy with me.

I poured another cup of coffee and set it on the glass shelf under the mirror. "*Ja,*" I said to myself as I shaved. How charming of the little maid, how discreet, to offer me the razor as if she thought I had forgotten my own. This coffee really *is* different—a different smell, a different taste. What was she pouring there in the garden? What was in the cup that Martin pressed to his lips? Coffee? The very brew I was now drinking after twenty-one, twenty-two years? How old was I in that picture? Five—six at the most.

Back in the bedroom, clean-shaven and younger, I glanced with regret at the havoc I had wreaked on the breakfast tray. One crystal glass was still clean. What was it for? Wait, I hadn't checked the slender pitcher. Fresh, strained orange juice! Oranges from home, maybe. Jaffa oranges.

I scanned the newspaper. Nothing. Not one word about my country. The world ignores us, occupying itself with remote wars. A miners' strike in Wales. Ex-fireman kills wife and sets house on fire. Bank robbery in Edinburgh. Old woman who tends eighteen stray cats wins eight thousand pounds sterling in Irish Sweepstakes. Actor, name not disclosed, is arrested in London for approaching young boys in the public park. Queen will tour Bahamas. Max Beerbohm once said of Bernard Shaw . . . call Max, immediately!

I picked up the phone and asked for Max Herman's number. A gracious voice promised to call me right back. I put down the receiver and lit a cigarette.

He'll certainly be surprised, I thought with satisfaction. I hadn't written to say when I'd arrive. I didn't even answer his last letter, the one inviting me to stay with him in Frankfurt. He'll be very surprised. Max Herman? Golan speaking—Commander Golan, of the Israeli police. Could I see you on important business? No, I'm sorry, it isn't a matter that can be discussed on the phone. Herman, it's in your interest that there be no delay. Or: Golan speaking, from the Income Tax Division. Herman, we'd like some information regarding your dealings with certain Israeli citizens who have given us your name. Or better still: Golan, of the Foreign Office. It's my pleasure to inform you that the government of Israel has awarded you the Recovery Medal. Yes, that's right—a new award granted to foreign citizens who contribute to the economic advancement of Israel. Just when he begins to believe it, to get really excited, I'll laugh and say, "Come on, Maxie, come on." He'll be wild. "It's Uri. Yes, yes, Uri Lam. Where am I speaking from? Jerusalem, of course. I can hear you very well, too. A better connection than the one with Tel Aviv. I decided to come to Frankfurt. When? I'll be at your place in fifteen minutes. I'm already in Frankfurt, you nut. Yes, yes. Hirshof Hotel, or something like that."

Max Herman: small, thin, smooth blond hair, spindly legs. Chasing the ball across the basketball court in khaki shorts as we all shout, "Maxie, Maxie, come on, Maxie!" We walked to the station hand in hand and left the train together at the Italian port. (That suntanned man in the white shirt open at the neck, the one with tightly curled hair who handed out bags of fruit, could that have been Mati Artzi?) Hand in hand we went up the gangplank and hand in hand we landed in Haifa.

Maxie, so good and so sad, who used to wake us at night with his terror-filled shrieks. What is it, Maxie? You can tell me. It's me, Uri. What were you dreaming? I won't tell anyone. OK, Maxie. It's not important, go to sleep. I'll sit here. Sleep . . . The phone is ringing.

"Hello, hello, may I speak to Max Herman?" I spoke into the receiver without paying any attention to the voice at the other end of the line. "Mr. Lam, here is your party." Someone answered in a strange voice: "Herman residence."

I asked, in English, to speak to Mr. Herman. The voice responded, in brusque German, that Mr. Herman was out. I asked for the lady of the house and gave my name. Footsteps, then silence.

Max Herman three or four years later: all at once he had outgrown the khaki pants, which were always too short. Max, the grave one in our yearbook: arms folded across his chest, some dark little girl staring up at his blond mop. Later Max, in dark-rimmed glasses, a bunch of books under his arm, sunning himself on the university steps. (This snapshot was inscribed: "To Uri from Max, with true friendship. No kidding!") No. This was much later. First there was the war . . .

Quick footsteps at the other end of the line, and a cry of surprise. "Uri!"

"Hello, Edna," I said. "How are you?"

"Uri!" she trilled again. "Uri, are you here? Really here? When did you arrive? Where are you? Max won't believe it. He's in Munich today. Why didn't you let us know you were on the way? I'll pick you up, right away."

"No," I said. I didn't want to be alone with her. I said I had an important engagement that couldn't possibly be put off.

"Then come for supper," she said. "Say yes. No excuses. Everything else can wait. Max will be stunned. He won't believe you're finally here. How are you, dear Uri?"

"OK." I thanked her, told her everything was fine, I was getting by—all the things you say when you don't know what to say. I promised to come at eight. A tense, unnerving silence followed.

"Edna," I said.

"What? What is it, Uri?"

Another long silence. "Don't tell him I'm here. Let's surprise him."

"Terrific! Marvelous idea," she cried mischievously. "I'll tell him my uncle arrived unexpectedly from Haifa and I invited him to dinner. He can't bear my uncle— he gets on his nerves with all his Zionism. Then you'll come in and Max will pretend he knew all along. You know how he is. He hasn't changed a bit. To the world he's Max Herman, but inside he's little Maxie. Uri, Uri, so you're really here. I want so much to see you and . . . to hear all the news from home."

We chattered a few minutes more. I told her everything was fine at home, and found myself opening the door of her room on the roof. She was sitting on the bed barefoot, in pants and a man's shirt, her knees drawn up under her chin, as Segovia strummed his guitar for her from a speaker hidden among the books. I told her one of her girl friends had married, another had had a baby. She squealed with glee. Again I opened the door to her room. This time she was sitting on the bed with Max, who was explaining a complex formula; there was a sudden hush when I came in. I told her two students now lived in her room on the roof, that it had changed entirely. Bright posters on the wall, green bottles with thistles in them, straw mats on the floor. She asked about our old café, who went there now, which couples were still sleeping together, which were not.

"Leave something for tonight," I said.

"All right, all right, but I'm dying of curiosity. Don't be late. I'm cooking dinner for you. One more question, Uri. What happened to that fellow . . ."

Another question and another, the pauses becoming more and more uneasy; we both began to say, "Yes, that's how it goes. Yes, indeed." Then she hung up and I was holding a dead line.

It was 11:30. I'm glad I could put off meeting Edna, I thought. Her questions would carry me back to Jerusalem and now I needed to be in Frankfurt, alone with myself; to walk through the streets, step into a real beer hall and listen to the people; to sit alone at a heavy wooden table and watch, without letting anyone know that Uri Lam, who escaped from this city at the age of ten, is watching them. I wanted to test my feelings on the streets of Frankfurt. I probably ought to go to the lawyer's office right away and settle my accounts. But it's Sunday. Everything is closed. Stores too—my purchases will have to wait.

I went down and gave the desk clerk my key. On the couch in the lobby a young woman in a silvery fur sat watching me. A small dog snuggled in her bosom. He was watching me too with his black button eyes. ("What a cute dog, madam. May I pet your soft fur too?")

"Good morning, sir," the clerk said in German. "I hope you slept well."

"Yes, thanks," I replied in English, and asked him for a map of Frankfurt.

He took a colorful leaflet from the drawer and spread it out, marking our spot. "Would you like to take a tour of the city, sir?" he asked in English. "There's a bus of English-speaking tourists leaving at two. A most interesting tour."

I thanked him again, adding that I'd prefer to take a walk.

"A fine day for walking," he said, handing me the leaflet. "It's been raining all week. It just began to clear up yesterday, for Sunday, I presume."

I stood in front of the hotel, not knowing which way to turn. The city, new and at the same time dead, lay before me, its broad streets of inhuman scale flanked by giant masses of glass and cement. Those who stepped out of the endless flow of traffic were swallowed by electric-eye doors, others were disgorged from buildings, only to be swallowed by cars. There were no leisurely strollers, nothing on this new street, not a single display window. Only glass walls, cold and transparent, exposing banks and travel bureaus in well-appointed cross-section.

So this is the new Frankfurt risen from the ruins, I thought. The Frankfurt of my childhood? I passed a black glass sign: BEER HALL, in gold lettering. A car discharged two passengers. I followed them in through the glass door, and found myself in a bustling crowd. Neapolitan pizza, Bolognese spaghetti, Turkish shashlik were served at the counter; small groups huddled together at Formica-topped tables. The giant hall was lit with fluorescent fixtures hung close to the ceiling, a large mural in shades of gray covering the long wall on the right. A classic scene: the traditional beer hall with wooden tables, a waitress in native costume, accordion players in Bavarian shorts and hats, mammoth beer kegs, mouths brimming with song, frothy mugs floating like banners in the air.

I had to cross the whole room before I found an empty table. The waiters were scurrying about, and it was a while before one of them noticed me. I ordered beer, in German, and asked what there was to eat. No point in continuing the language game, I thought. He'll simply ignore me. The waiter produced a menu and reeled off a few dishes with Italian, English, and French names. I ordered knockwurst with sauerkraut.

"One number five," he said, "with a number sixteen and a pitcher of beer."

"Half a pitcher will be enough," I called after him.

Many people ate in silence. They seemed to be sharing tables with total strangers. A group of young men were arguing noisily about a soccer game. Someone put a coin in the jukebox, pressed the button, and—presto —the air was filled with Elvis Presley, accompanied by a full orchestra of guitars. Two older people at a nearby table looked on with open disapproval. I glanced toward the kitchen door, watching the waiters emerge with trays of food and drink, but my waiter was nowhere to be seen.

I took out the leaflet and spread it on the table. The Church of Saint Bartholomew, the bridge over the river

Main, the commercial center, the old Saxon quarter. Population: 700,000. A center of industry, culture, trade, and finance. Major products: pharmaceuticals, chemicals, electrical equipment. Father—pharmaceuticals, my mother and sister—chemicals. My brother got what he got with the help of electrical equipment. Frankfurt became a free city in 1372. And then what happened? Where was this freedom exactly five hundred sixty-six years later? What about the Rothschild family, born here in this very city? In 1866 Frankfurt was annexed by Prussia and in the Second World War, while I was feeding Aunt Anna's ducks under the elms, Frankfurt was destroyed. Demolished by the Allied Forces. Did the spirit of Goethe, a native son, rise up from the ruins? How is it that no one sings Goethe now, to the accompaniment of guitars?

An ascetic-looking man of about fifty was standing beside me, leaning on metal crutches. "May I sit down?" he asked. I nodded, but he was no longer looking at me. He leaned on the chair and sat down heavily, resting his crutches on the wall. His right trouser leg was folded neatly to the knee. I returned to my leaflet, hearing in my mind the whistle of a shell, seeing it strike a house and slice away this man's leg, seeing him, devastated, stare at the torn limb, aware that it would never stamp, kick, march again.

No, that would be too simple. A soldier in the rear lines, advancing through a snowstorm. The retreat has begun. Three days now he has been tramping through the Russian wilderness, his legs wrapped in a tattered, frozen blanket, only to realize that morning that there is no sensation left in the leg.

The company doctor amputates his leg with a kitchen knife on some peasant's table and flings it to the dogs yelping at the door. Or: a shell exploding at the front, two days out of Moscow. The leg is severed and falls in the snow before his very eyes. A black German boot with a leg in it, tangled in the barbed wire.

The waiter finally appeared, bringing lukewarm sausages and beer. Sipping my beer I watched the cripple, who ordered a number 32 and a pitcher of beer. His face was drawn. Two deep ridges extended from murky eyes to a protruding chin. The jaw of an officer. I could hear him instructing his lieutenant to take command. "Take over, sir. I . . . I won't . . . be there for the victory march."

Three youths stood near the jukebox, gyrating to the noisy wails of Elvis Presley. The two older men at the neighboring table shook their heads in disdain.

"What will become of this younger generation? They're a disgrace. A real disgrace," one of the onlookers commented.

The other agreed: today's youth is empty and vain. "We were never like that," his companion asserted. I didn't catch his response, but the shrug of the shoulders communicated despair. "They have no goals," he continued. "Money—that's their only interest. A new Mercedes, a racing boat, a four-room apartment by the time they're twenty-two—these are their ideals. In our day we knew that our life had significance, meaning. We had noble goals, we were striving for a better world, we had aspirations. Look at them now. Ye-ye—Elvis Presley and ye-ye."

"*Ja, ja,*" his companion nodded glumly. "The world isn't what it used to be. Everything has changed. Nothing is left of our Germany. It's hard to find a decent beer cellar these days. Even the beer isn't what it used to be."

I downed my beer and as I stretched contentedly my arm knocked over the crutches, which were propped against the wall. The cripple gaped at me as if his two feet were sprawled down there on the floor. I picked up the crutches and apologized.

"A mine?" I asked, pointing ruthlessly to the crutches.

He shook his head. I looked into his eyes and smiled. "A shell," he volunteered.

It was my turn to smile mechanically. I wanted to clear out but my waiter, having emerged briefly from the kitchen, disappeared through a side door. Exchanging nods with the cripple, I followed the waiter and discovered a smaller room filled with old men sitting at tables of real wood. Crystal chandeliers cast a festive light on their hoary heads and the oversized beer mugs. I heard peals of hearty laughter and hoarse singing. The first line of the song was familiar: "Who can afford to pay the price? Who has so much cash?"

The thought flashed through my mind: Why not? Why not take out my Carl Gustav and shower the entire assemblage with a round or two? A few shots from the hip that would prostrate all these veterans, fill the air with the crackle of shattering glass, the roars of terror, the whimpers of the injured. See them hurled to the floor, clutching tremulously at their guts as they spill out, the mutilated faces in thick, sticky puddles of blood. Why not? Siren, ambulances, police cars, a charge of murder. OK, I have murdered. So what? What can you do to me? Three years in prison, like the rest of your criminals.

Nonsense. Will that settle my account? What about all the others? Those who deported, imprisoned, violated, raped, fired, turned on switches, confirmed, signed, observed in silence? What about them? There is no end. For, having slaughtered, you shall be slaughtered; and in the end all your slaughterers shall be slaughtered.

The waiter finally noticed me. I paid the check, adding a coin beyond what was due; and he said "thank you" in a tone that matched the size of the coin and disappeared. To the accompaniment of wild guitars I left the beer hall.

By the time I got back to my hotel it was 1:45. A red tourist bus loaded with about a dozen passengers was waiting at the curb.

10 | *evening in the street*

I don't know what possessed me, but I decided to take the guided tour of Frankfurt. The minute I set eyes on

the American tourists and heard the practiced laugh
with which the German guide introduced his wisecracks,
I should have realized it was a mistake and turned
back.

At first I paid no attention. I sat near the window,
straining to see something familiar, while scene after
scene unfolded with irritating speed, as if someone were
showing old family photographs without allowing me to
stop and examine any of them. I had seen this forest of
black tree skeletons, that heap of fallen leaves flaming
in a garden, the same murky river, the mighty arches
under the bridge, the gabled towers of the dark cathedral.
But in every picture something was not right. Some details were missing, others had been added: the steel
bridge, the modern brick building, the new cars on
smooth asphalt roads. Like coming home one night and
finding a strange bed where my own should be, the table
from my parents' house balanced on my table, new
pictures on the wall, an unfamiliar coat draped over the
chair, the window that overlooked the street opening
onto a blue expanse of sea.

Once, when we passed through a quarter that had
hardly been touched by the war, I knew we were near a
large cobblestone square, with a statue I remembered
that was perched on a water fountain and surrounded
by an iron fence. Another time when we headed down a
narrow one-way street I was certain an upstairs window
would open and a toothless woman would shriek, "Jews!
There are Jews here!" The house was really there, but
the window remained closed; no one was hiding behind
the delicate draperies.

The guide was reciting the history of Frankfurt in a
dull, mechanical voice. Two old women with bleached
blue-blond hair exclaimed, "Really? Is that so?" at every
event that preceded the discovery of America. (Such as
the fact that in 1300 or so Frankfurt was declared a
free city.) It was difficult for them to grasp that even
before the *Mayflower*, a civilized world with refinements
such as plumbing and bank loans had existed. The

announcement that Frankfurt was the birthplace of the mighty Rothchilds evoked a chorus of: "Is that a fact?" Whereas the information that Gutenberg died in this city was dismissed with a noncommittal, "Oh."

A young man of about nineteen in an American Air Force uniform sat in front of me. A graying gentleman, apparently his father, sat beside him. They were trying to find some common ground, to relate man to man, but with little success.

The bus passed through a new quarter. The guide pointed out the modern buildings, the new streets, the broad highways that didn't exist ten years ago. He lamented the beauty of old Frankfurt, utterly demolished by enemy bombs—or rather, he was quick to correct himself, "bombs of the Allied Forces." With practiced emotion he remembered emerging from the air-raid shelter, only to find his parents' home destroyed and to discover, in the debris, a mangled doll that had belonged to his sister—who was killed by the very same bomb. A scene I knew from scores of war films. This guide must have seen those films too.

He turned away, as if overcome by emotion. There were gasps and sighs of sympathy from his audience, which he acknowledged with a valiant smile.

"Yes, yes," he offered gravely, "war is a terrible thing."

"Were you here during the occupation?" the young soldier asked.

"No," replied the father.

"The Germans are a great people," said the son. "The best soldiers in Europe. Brave, devoted, disciplined—first-class soldiers. And dependable."

The father nodded.

"I like Frankfurt," said the son. "I feel at home here. It's so much like America, don't you think? Bars, supermarkets, department stores, television—everything."

The guide paid tribute to the conduct of Frankfurt's people during the "catastrophe," the years following the war and preceding the great economic miracle. In his version Germany was the victim in World War II. These innocents, in whose name others waged war, were ruthlessly bombarded, their homes destroyed, their cities demolished. The shellings continued even after the city had been reduced to rubble—which was unfair and contrary to the rules of the game. But the diligent Germans did not despair. With enthusiasm and determination the ruins were rebuilt. Witness the new city, a testament to their tireless efforts.

He didn't say all this in so many words, but this was the implication of the numbers and dates he cited. In decrying the bombings he raged against war in general and its gross injustice: the plight of the postal clerk whose house was destroyed, the pharmacist whose aged mother was buried alive in debris, the teacher who was blinded, the old man whose dog expired before his eyes. Whether these good, simple folk are English, French, or German is unimportant. Nor does it matter who began the horror, for war is such an awful thing. But let's forget the past. He is willing to forgive. It won't happen again, he hopes—humanity has learned its lesson.

I couldn't take any more of this. When the passengers got off the bus to photograph the old clock above the church and the bell towers, I slipped away and walked until I was bathed in sweat. I stopped to rest and, feeling thirsty, I stepped into the nearest bar. It was close to five. The place was empty except for a waiter in a white starched jacket who was scouring glasses. The room was dimly lit. Only the bottles, crowded together on long shelves, glowed with bright yellow light.

I ordered a beer to quench my thirst and then switched to whiskey. The waiter brought some salted almonds and tried to make conversation. I was silent. He went back to scouring glasses but was quick with the refills whenever I tapped the counter. He asked if I would like music and pointed to a pile of records. I shook my head. With a shrug he turned on the TV, which was at the other end of the bar.

Why was I so enraged, I asked myself. From his point of view that guide was justified. To the pharmacist, the postal clerk, the teacher, it was hardly relevant who started the war. For them the horror was reduced to a single fact: one night after an all-clear signal they left the shelter and found themselves homeless. Searching the ruins they discovered the broken piano, fragments of the Biedermeier table (a family heirloom), the remains of a landscape in oil that used to hang in the living room, the mutilated torso of a quiet, well-mannered neighbor. You couldn't really say that these were the people who bombed Holland, Belgium, Poland. You couldn't claim that the lame postal clerk and the blinded painting teacher set up those camps to which peaceful citizens like themselves were sent. At most they were guilty of not acting to reverse the situation, of averting their eyes when neighbors were hauled away in trucks, of lacking the courage to protest, of wanting more than anything to remain alive. And who among us could swear that he would have behaved otherwise? Who can say with confidence that he would not have adjusted, gradually, to the horror, hoping and praying that one day the nightmare would end and life would resume a peaceful course? It was their right to be bitter about the bombs and destruction, even though history could justify these actions. Even a criminal has the right to complain of mice in his cell, the tightness of the handcuffs, the guards' brutality.

Then what was it that enraged me so? Was it the hypocrisy and pretense, the notion that the German people were unaware of these crimes and uninvolved in these events? Was it the standard remorse, the lip service, the flattering asides to Americans in the group and to all things American? What did I expect? How can a German today respond to the questions that confront him everywhere? It may be that silence is the one option. . . . Let them proclaim silence throughout the land, don sackcloth, place ashes on their heads, and transform Germany into a vast monastery of mutes. I have no answer. We all know the questions. No one knows the answers. It is necessary to forget. It is essential to forget. There is no other answer. One or two more whiskeys and all this will sink into billows of cotton.

The bartender, still occupied with the glassware, was watching a soccer game on TV as he worked. I had only to tap the counter and he would bring me another drink. I noticed that his right ear was deformed. Becoming aware of my stare he smiled and asked if I was an American.

"No," I said, too loudly. "I'm from Israel."

"You're from Israel?" he repeated with surprise. I nodded, expecting him to switch to Hebrew. In a Tel Aviv café I remember hearing someone say that the bars in Germany are filled with Israelis. You find them in every nightclub, in the bars, in the whorehouses, he had remarked.

"You know," the bartender said in English, "I was almost in Palestine. We were in Tobruk in '42. Sand, dust flies, and powerful sun all day. They told us we'd be moving and we'd soon be eating Jaffa oranges. We were anxious to get to Palestine, but we moved west instead. For two months we had been advancing toward the rising sun and suddenly we were moving in the other direction, toward the sunset. Is it true that in your country they drink fresh orange juice like we drink beer?"

"It's true," I said, imagining him in uniform, drinking orange juice from a pail. In '42—I was eleven—I didn't even know what an orange was. On Sundays in the summer when Aunt Anna came from church, wearing a black dress, her eyes moist, she would pour me some red wine and say, "Drink, little *coniglio*, drink." Uncle Michele would sit in the kitchen downing glass after glass, until his whiskers dripped wine and his eyes drooped with sleep. This was probably in '42, when my bartender was marching through scorching sandstorms to Tobruk, dreaming of orange juice. My first orange, shared with Max in Haifa harbor, reminded me of bitter medicine, of a white bed in my parents' home in Frankfurt. Max tried to eat it peel and all, and the kids all laughed at him.

Max: I see him in the dim shade of the carob tree, in the abandoned crate near the barn that reeked of cheese.

He sat cross-legged, digging out cookies, peanuts, and sourballs from the depths of his pocket. "Where did you get them, Maxie?" "Parents bring them," he said, meaning other children's parents who used to visit and leave packages. At suppertime, when the children were in the dining hall, Maxie would go from room to room searching the closets and the suitcases and filling his shirt with candy. He would take three or four candies, a handful of peanuts, a slice of cake. "Mustn't take it all," he would say, "they deserve something too." In the darkness of the crate we would sort out the loot. Maxie would hand me some cake and pretend. "I don't have the strength," he would say. "Every Saturday my mother comes with packages and says, 'Eat, Maxie, eat.'" After a while I began to treat him to cakes brought by "my mother" and left for me in other children's drawers. One day he appeared at the furniture crate with empty pockets. "What happened, Maxie?" I asked. "My mother didn't come today," he said. "She's dead." He began to laugh and sing at the top of his lungs. "My mother is burning up—up there on the roof." I laughed and sang with him. We rolled on the mat until the cookies in my shirt were all crushed.

My ice cube had melted, and the whiskey had a medicinal taste. My cigarette had a long ashen tail. If I raise it to my mouth holy ashes will drip into the glass. You can get drunk on ashes mixed with whiskey. Especially those ashes, floating on lake water. The warm ash, heaped in wheelbarrows and scattered by the wind. You need only look at it, breathe it in, and your head will begin to flutter. "Attention! This is my father," he said, pointing to a jar of ashes on the bookshelf near the radio. "A little memento," said the lunatic, smiling. "That's all that's left of him—ashes." That's all that's left of them all—ashes. If you place the contents of this jar in the palm of your hand and stick it out the window, there will be no further trace of your father. He will fly away with the wind, vanish.

Once when I went to have a paper verified at an

office dedicated to "immortalizing the holocaust," I overheard an odd exchange. "I'm very sorry, but we have no room," the clerk said, addressing an earnest couple. The man, holding a cardboard box in his hand, bowed his head and asked, "But what shall we do with it? We have kept it all these years. We thought that perhaps here there would be a suitable spot." The clerk shook his head. "We don't have room. I am terribly sorry, but we simply have no room. Bury it." When I came closer I could see what was in the box: a piece of soap nestled in cotton. Even museums dedicated to the memory of the holocaust are crowded. The horror brims over. One must forget, just as Max forgot.

He certainly did forget. What did he forget? I can't remember what he forgot. Too much to drink. If he hadn't forgotten he couldn't have come back to Germany. After school, after the war and the university, he came back to settle in Frankfurt, where he was born. He came with Edna and, in this city, he planted two children. Why did he come back? God only knows. He collected reparations, invested wisely, and wrote that I should come too—forget all my doubts, get what's coming to me! Because Frankfurt doesn't belong only to those who thrive there now—it's mine too, and I deserve all I can get. One more drink and that will be it.

"Bartender, another whiskey," I said.

"I don't drink whiskey." A young woman, pale and blond, was sitting next to me. She placed her black purse on the bar and said good evening to Willy, the bartender, in German. "Would you buy me a cognac?" she asked me in English.

"On the condition that you shut up," I said. "One cognac, please."

"Of course I'll shut up," she said. "I can be quiet. Some girls can't shut their mouths. A man likes silence sometimes. He likes to think. He's busy, worried. And it's important to know how to be quiet when you meet such a man. Thanks, Willy. To you, sir. To the night. To silence."

I nodded and gulped down the drink Willy brought

me. After a minute or so she invited me to come with
her.

"Where to?" I asked.

"Wherever you like," she said, smiling mechanically,
"your place or mine."

I shook my head.

"I have a room nearby," she said. "I'll make you coffee
and I'll be good to you. I know how to be good. I'll shut
up—just wait and see."

I shook my head again.

"Why not?"

"My parents died."

"Really?" she cried with sincere interest. "How?"

"Your parents killed them," I said.

She slapped my back and laughed. "You're drunk," she
said. "You need some sleep. I'll make you coffee and
then you can sleep. Next to me."

I called the bartender and asked for a check. He drew
eight slips from a cup and added up the bill.

I paid and left without a further glance at the little
tart.

Chimes and whistles welcomed me to the brightly lit
street. Once or twice I tried to clear my head, but it was
no use. The bells of all the churches in Frankfurt were
ringing, the way they used to on Sunday when I was a
kid. I stumbled along, not knowing where I was going.
Passersby made way for me muttering as I passed.
I stepped on someone's toe. He glared at me and exclaimed, "Damn it!" I fell on the sidewalk near a
grocery store littered with boxes. Someone tried to help
me up. I pushed him away and managed to get up myself. I leaned against a door. It flew open and once more
I lay sprawled on the ground, my face in a layer of
sawdust.

"Nazis!" I screamed, picking myself up again and
heading for the crowd of curious onlookers. "Damned
Nazis!" I shouted, wiping the sawdust from my lips.
Faces from horror photographs I had once seen gazed
back at me impassively. I lunged at them and they
quickly cleared a path. Before I knew it I was in the

middle of the street. Barely missing me, a car jolted to a stop with a clamor of screeching brakes and wailing horns. I made my way to the sidewalk, swaying from side to side. Pedestrians kept their distance and stared at me with revulsion, as if I were a leper, as if I were a Jew.

"Gestapo!" I shrieked. "Dirty Fascists! Murderers! Neo-Nazi bastards!" They ignored me, though they heard every word.

Suddenly I was circled by three hoodlums in leather jackets whom I'd noticed earlier. When I glared at them they slowed down but kept on trailing me. "Nazis!" I called, spitting in their direction. But the saliva trickled down my own chin.

I was fully conscious. I knew I was drunk. I knew I was spouting nonsense, that there was no rhyme or reason to my ridiculous cries. The scene I was creating wouldn't end well. But I went on shouting imprecations in every direction in curt, cruel German cadences familiar to me from war movies. As a matter of fact I *wanted* the drama to come to a violent head. I was hoping to provoke an attack, hoping someone would hit me. I wanted the Germans to be true to their assigned roles so I could play the role of victim. But despite my shrieks no one approached me. Even the three youths vanished.

I turned into a deserted alley that had a small public park at the end of it. I was urinating behind a tree when I heard footsteps. I turned around, glimpsed the three hoods in leather jackets before feeling their blow on my head. The bells of all the churches began to chime more vigorously than ever. I charged at the hood closest to me, aiming for his balls, but I was pulled back by my coat collar. My head hit the tree, one leg gave way, and my nostrils were filled with the smell of earth soaked in urine. As the thick fog melted away, I saw everything clearly: they would beat me to death. One of them would pull a knife. (Not in the belly. My guts would drip out and I would try to hold them in with my own two hands.) They were standing over me with their brass knuckles ready and waiting. I sprang up and struck one of them on the neck. The other two lit into me with their whole weight. They pinned my hands behind my back. The third one began to dance around me like a professional boxer, landing blows on my face, my chest, my stomach. I couldn't breathe, hammers were pounding in my head. Beyond the tree skeletons the skies seemed clear and vivid.

"What do you want from me?" I shrieked in German as soon as I regained my breath. They continued to belt me without a word. I struggled to free myself but again I was out of breath, sprawled on the ground, sinking into infinite darkness.

Suddenly, without knowing why, I cried out with all my might, "I am a Jew!" My attackers vanished in the darkness as swiftly as they had appeared. Their quiet footsteps receded. I whispered, "Nazis!" and lay at the foot of the tree gasping for breath. Gradually the hammers stopped pounding, the drums in my chest subsided. I was able to breathe again. I tested my leg and struggled to pull myself up, clutching at the tree trunk. As I stood there, drinking in the cool air, a light rain began to fall. I left the park and stumbled toward the distant light of the main street.

11 | *black coffee*

In the cab, on the way to Max's, I closed my eyes and dozed off. At the foot of a distant apple tree, I saw Martin. He was lying on the grass with the servant girl, her legs spread open, lying on top of him. My father stood with Aunt Anna, drinking wine from a bottle. The white clouds floated away as someone touched my leg.

"We're here," the driver said, looking at me with concern.

We are here. Where are we? Streetlamps. Rain. Cars parked sleepily at the sidewalk. We were at Max's house.

The driver offered to walk me up the steps, but I said I could make it and staggered into the dark building. My head was still throbbing. When I got out of the elevator at the fifth floor a little woman ran toward me on high heels.

"What happened?" Edna asked. "What happened to you?"

I mumbled an answer.

She looked at me in alarm. "*What* bells?"

I told her I was drunk and tried to force a smile, but the aching half of my face wouldn't oblige.

"You're dirty. Look at your jacket. Where *were* you?" Edna demanded, in my mother's voice. It was true—my clothes were covered with dirt and sawdust. I told her in German that I had been playing soccer with some children. Then, smiling uneasily, I tried to brush myself off.

Edna's eyes were red. It was already nine, she said. They had waited and waited for me until they could wait no longer. They had eaten, worried, called the hotel where no one had any idea . . . How could I do such a thing? She took my arm and led me to Max.

It all happened so swiftly I barely had time to digest the fact that this corseted little housewife with the bouffant hairdo and heavy gold earrings was Edna— Edna, who used to sit cross-legged on the bed in Jerusalem in jeans and a man's shirt, her hair clipped short. All at once I was embraced by an ample man in a dark suit—Maxie. The same little Maxie who used to climb to the top of the cherry tree overlooking the girls' shower. His face was stern. How could I do such a thing? Why hadn't I written to say I was coming? Why wasn't I there at eight? They had waited and waited, not knowing what to make of it.

I pleaded guilty, begged their pardon, and promised to repent. "I was drunk," I explained, pouring myself a drink, "but I'm perfectly all right now." Max smiled and stroked his thinning hair.

In the dining room their son, Yoav, a neatly groomed boy of ten in a suit and tie was seated at the table, which had not been cleared. How I would have loved to slap him on both cheeks. Edna prompted, "Say hello nicely," and the little shmuck said hello nicely, extending a hand as soft as Maxie's was way back then, on the train and on the boat. I asked if he spoke Hebrew and he mumbled a reply. "Of course he speaks Hebrew," Edna said. "We speak only Hebrew at home. Say something, Yoav."

"I don't want any pudding," Yoav said.

"See!" said Edna. "Of course my children speak Hebrew! Yoav, you can't go until you finish eating. And that's final."

The boy went back to the table and began to stir something brown and sticky. I said the pudding looked like shit and Max laughed. That was what we used to say about the pudding at our school.

"Uri!" Edna exclaimed, shocked. "Please . . ." The boy pushed his dish away.

Max asked me what had happened. When I began to relate my adventures Edna's eyes filled with alarm. She wanted to know how, where, who, when. Max insisted that we notify the police, that we shouldn't let a thing like that go unreported, and he went into the other room to phone. I turned to follow him—and walked into the door. When Max picked up the receiver I told him to hang up, that there was no point in calling the police— those bullies would never be found; it was a waste of time. He argued with me, but when I began to scream at him he put the receiver down. I sank into the armchair, spilling whiskey on my pants. Edna stood in the door- way clutching her frightened little darling. I told Max I had knocked cne of them down with a kick in the balls but had to admit that they had finally overwhelmed me, that two of them held me down while the third one beat the shit out of me. "But, really, it was my own fault," I said, "I had no business shouting 'Nazis' in the middle of the street." When Edna heard the word "Nazis" she decided it was bedtime. "Yoav, say good night to our guest."

Yoav kissed his mother and father, bowed to me, and

turned to go. I would have kicked him in the behind if I'd had the strength. I never could tolerate goody-goodies.

"Such a wonderful boy," Edna said. "An excellent student, a hard worker, and he plays the guitar too. But he has no appetite. It takes him forever to finish a meal."

I observed that no kid had died of starvation in Germany in recent years, or words to that effect. This was followed by silence. I said, "Excuse me, where can I . . . ?" Edna showed me the bathroom and turned on the light. To hell with them, I thought, dousing my face with cold water. A pain near my right eye, a pain at the edge of my jaw and under my ear, an ache in my back. I made a face in the mirror. My eye was swollen. To-morrow the swelling would be blue and lantern-shaped. With this lantern I would seek truth in the streets of Frankfurt. You're a nut, I told myself, peering into my own drowsy eyes. You're a big shit, I said. That's no way to behave with friends—you said you'd come at eight. Eight whiskeys! After one you get high, the second makes you sing. You want to be free, charming, gay. Now look at yourself—you pissed-up drunken puss. You're right, I said to my reflection, I really *am* nuts. I shouldn't have come here tonight, I should have called and said I was sick, I had a headache. And I really do have a headache. Damned Nazis. So this is the other Germany, the generation that can't be held responsible for what happened. "To hell with them!" I said aloud as I dropped my pants.

A slight swelling above the knee. Other than that I saw no sign of injury. The sink seemed to be in motion. I held my head in my hands and closed my eyes, but the motion persisted. A brief but heated exchange could be heard through the door. The voices were hushed so that only fragments of sentences could reach my ears. "I don't agree. Absolutely not," he said; then, "Honey, this is no time for a scene. Can't you talk quietly!"

She replied, "Only you could do such a thing." Then something else and, "I'm getting tired of the whole deal. You may as well know it."

He said, "Me too, I'm sick of it." Something else, whispered with venom and hate, and then, "Just what do you have in mind, anyway?"

She snarled at him but the only word I could make out was "hate."

"Thanks a lot," he replied.

"It's all the same to me," she retorted. "I'll say what I like in this house and if you don't like it, then please . . ." More words.

Then it was his turn: "OK. That's fine. I'll remember that."

I flushed the toilet noisily, pulled up my pants, and began to sing: "I know that day will come . . ." When I opened the door Max asked how I was feeling, Edna asked if I was hungry. Max wanted me to sit in the armchair beside him. Edna offered the sofa. They each smiled and spoke warmly to me ignoring each other. When I asked for black coffee, Edna suggested that I might want something to eat after all. "He wants coffee," Max asserted with exaggerated calm. Edna tried to tempt me by describing the roast duck she had prepared, the Persian rice, the eggplant salad—all of which were still on the table. I said I wasn't hungry, and Max repeated that I wasn't hungry. I asked for black coffee. "He wants black coffee," Max echoed pointedly. Edna left the room without a word.

"So, you're finally here," said Max just as the phone rang. "Excuse me, I'm expecting a call from Berlin." He picked up the phone and took it into the other room. I could hear just well enough to notice that he spoke good German. I sank back into the pillows that were scattered on the broad sofa and closed my eyes.

"It won't take more than two days," Max said. I was lying in the hospital; my bandaged arm, throbbing madly, rested on my chest, Max stood over me in a comical stocking cap; his ascetic face was sunburned, his nose peeling. He had brought me chocolate and a thick novel. He was saying, in German, that he wouldn't pay more than 4 percent, even if Wolf was offering 5. He bent over and whispered to me that he had found an apartment in the German quarter of Jerusalem. When I was out of the hospital we could move in and live it up. My bed was rusty. It creaked. Thinking Max was asleep, we tried to move as little as possible. She lay with her back to me, her knees folded. I sailed inside her in silence. I told her to be quiet, not to move. But she couldn't restrain herself, and when it was all over we saw Max sitting up in bed staring at us. We pretended to be asleep, and then we did fall asleep. I dreamed that Max came to our bed and lay there with us, his body rocking over hers. I awoke, only to drift off into the middle of another dream, this time about bombing. The shells were coming at me; I tried to reach the door but my legs wouldn't respond. Max shouted, "Move over. Can't you see you're in our way? Go back to your own bed." And she said, "Let him sleep here. He's dead. I'll bring a blanket and cover him."

A door opened and closed. When I opened my eyes I could see someone pacing back and forth across the thick carpet. A woman came in carrying a blanket. Herr Max, Frau Edna, and I, ten years later, in Frankfurt. What a torment!

"I fell asleep," I said apologetically.

"You're probably dead, poor thing," Edna said. "I was going to cover you up and let you stay there."

"When did you start drinking?" Max asked.

"I don't usually drink," I said. "I don't know what happened to me today."

"Why not go back to sleep?" Edna suggested.

"No. It's all right," I said. "I didn't come here to sleep."

"Make yourself at home," she said. "You're tired. We can talk tomorrow."

"I'm not sleepy anymore," I said.

"He's not sleepy," Max echoed.

"I have a headache," I said.

"I'll bring you something for it," Edna said mincing out of the room on her high heels. I took a sip of coffee. It was cold.

"The coffee must be cold," Max said. "Can I get you another cup?"

"No, it's fine," I said, touching the swelling under my eye.

"I think we should have reported it to the police," Max said. "It's not right to let an incident like that go unreported."

"Forget it," I said. "It's not that important. Why don't you tell me how things are with you. How are you, Max? You've put on some weight."

"I weigh two-oh-four," he said patting his stomach. "I eat like a pig, and the heaviest work I do all day is picking up the phone. I've developed good ear muscles." We both laughed. He sat down next to me. I slapped his knee and we laughed again.

Edna brought water and two pills. She sat in the armchair opposite us. Everyone was silent.

"More coffee?" she asked.

"No thanks." Again, silence.

"Yes," Max said, "time flies."

"What's new in Jerusalem?" Edna asked.

"Everything's fine," I answered.

"Then tell us something," she said.

"What is there to tell?"

"We heard you have a girl," Edna said.

"A girl?"

"Her father is a big contractor—at least that's what I heard." I dismissed this with a gesture.

"When are you going to straighten out?" she asked. I looked at her quizzically. "When are you going to marry and settle down? You ought to have a family. Oh, you must see our other boy, Dudik. I'm going to wake him up," she said.

"Leave him alone," Max said. "He's asleep."

"You'll see, he's great," she said as she left the room.

Max shrugged in despair. I slapped his knee again. We looked at each other, not knowing what to say. "How is your work going?" I asked.

"No complaints," he said. Max had become the head of a leading electrical appliance company. "And what about you? What will you do with the reparations money?" I made no reply.

Edna came back carrying a sleepy boy in blue pajamas. When she set him down on the rug he rubbed his eyes and turned away shyly.

"How old is he?" I asked.

"Dudik, tell Uncle Uri how old you are," Edna coaxed. He buried his face in her dress.

"Seven," Max said.

"Let him speak for himself," Edna countered.

"Do you want a cookie, son?" I asked. The boy squirmed.

"Juice," he said uneasily.

"Max, bring him some juice," Edna said. Max got up, sighing, and went for the juice. Edna bent over to whisper something in the child's ear. She was no doubt promising him everything: a trip to the moon, a real gun, a bicycle with a horn—concluding the deal with, "Now tell Uncle Uri, how much is a quarter times a quarter?" The boy squirmed awkwardly. When Max brought the juice the child clutched it in his small hands.

"Slowly," Edna said. "Now, say the poem." The child looked at me with big eyes. I nodded encouragement. Edna kneeled close to him, pulled the string as far as it would go, released it, and her toy was in motion.

Taking a small, stiff step forward the boy opened his mouth and then closed it again. "I forget how it starts," he said. "On a high hilly pass," Edna prompted.

"On a high hilly pass," the child recited, "all covered with grass/a gentle brown cow/empties its ass."

Edna burst into laughter and applauded. Max covered his eyes.

"On a high hilly pass/all covered with grass/a gentle brown cow/empties its ass."

"He has a fantastic memory," Edna said as the child recited the poem a third time.

"That's enough," said Max. "Go to sleep, Dudik, go on."

"What's the matter?" Edna asked. "What is it? Why are you so nervous?"

"I'm not nervous," Max said emphatically.

"You are so nervous," Edna insisted as the child prepared to recite again.

"That's enough," Max declared, raising his voice. "We've *heard* it!"

"Don't you like it?" Edna challenged. "What do you want him to recite? 'The Ancient Mariner'?"

"I don't want him to recite anything," Max said. "I want him to go to bed."

"On a high hilly pass/all covered with grass," the child began.

"Then put him to bed, if that's what you want," Edna said.

Max picked up the boy and left the room. I stared at Edna in disbelief. This was not the girl I used to know in the room on the roof. This one was never young; she never had had short, cropped hair or army pants. I saw her standing on the high hilly pass.

"He's cute, isn't he?" she said.

"Yes," I agreed, "he is cute."

"See what you're missing," she said. "You ought to marry and have children . . ."

"Edna," I said smiling, "forget it. It's enough that you got married and brought children into the world. It's enough that you're happy."

"Of course I'm happy," she said. "I have everything. What else is there? What do you have against domestic life?"

"I don't want a family," I said. "And I hate children. They irritate me, they nag, they repeat themselves endlessly. I can't stand good children from proper families. 'When will you settle down?' I feel like vomiting when I hear that question. Settle down? Bury yourself alive, wife and all, in a development with a mortgage, a refrigerator, a washing machine, modern furniture, all bought on time. I panic whenever a girl hints at marriage. I see myself under the canopy, the rabbi mumbling, her mother sobbing, the photographer scurrying about with endless demands. Then I have to study furniture displays and help her decide which sofa will adorn our suburban living room. She'll ask my opinion about a coffee table, a mattress, Danish chairs, artificial plants. She'll want a housewarming party, friends on the weekend so we can drink coffee on our porch and watch our neighbors drinking coffee on their porches. Then she'll get herself pregnant and begin to sigh and complain. She'll expect to go walking on Saturdays with me pushing the carriage, the squalling brat inside. And I'll have to carry her purse. Movies on Saturday night, like everyone else. Cyprus in the summer. The whole idea makes me vomit. I don't want to get married, I don't want to settle down, I don't want children. There are plenty of children in this world. Besides, not everyone should have children."

"You're not normal," Edna said, laughing nervously. She turned to Max, who was standing in the doorway, listening, and exploded: "Why are you grinning like an idiot?"

"I'm not grinning," he said, "I'm listening."

"He stands there grinning," she said derisively. "Did you see him?"

"I'm tired and I'm dying to go to sleep," I said.

"Stay with us," she said. "We have room."

"No thanks, really. I'll go back to the hotel."

"Why waste money on a hotel when you can stay with us? We've already talked it over, right, Muki? He could stay with us."

"Of course, Shnucki," Max said coldly.

"Thanks very much," I said. "But really, I'd rather stay in a hotel."

"Then at least stay with us tonight," she persisted. "I'll make you breakfast in the morning, and you can tell me what's new back home. Stay, Uri."

I insisted on going back to the hotel and she finally relented. I took Max's office number and promised to call. He suggested that we have lunch together.

"Good idea," Edna said. "We hardly touched the duck."

"I thought we'd get a bite downtown, near the office," Max interjected.

"Suit yourself," Edna said in a chilly tone.

I asked Max to call a cab and said good-bye to Edna. I asked her to forgive me for spoiling dinner. She nodded sourly, said good night and left the room.

"Don't mind her," Max said when he hung up. "She's in a bad mood. She was doing her best to irritate me. Don't think she wakes the boy up every night and makes him recite for company. She knows how much I despise that sort of thing. She can be nice when she wants to."

We shook hands. I promised to call him in the afternoon. He walked me to the elevator.

Outside it was still raining. My cab was waiting at the door.

12 | *meeting in the dark*

The next day I woke up late with a terrible headache, sharp pains in the back, a stiff neck, swollen eyes. It was raining hard. The sky was heavy and dark. I went back to bed, making room for the warm little chambermaid. I could almost hear her giggling under the blanket as I let my head sink into the pillow. I'll stay in bed, I thought, and when she brings breakfast I'll circle her hips, slip my hand under her starched apron, then over the blazing oven of her thighs. Ssh, don't even laugh. Quick. Right here beside me. Don't worry, I'm locking the door!

A knock on the door. A melancholy Italian waiter brought the breakfast tray and was off. The coffee was murky and bitter. Instead of fragrant raspberry jam, I found a thin jelly. I picked up the phone to call Max, but at the last minute I gave the operator the number of the German lawyer who was to handle my reparations claim.

My claim had some unusual aspects and required special handling. Had I been content with the categories of reparations which were automatic—for loss of freedom, interrupted studies, impaired health, and so on—the matter could have been concluded by my lawyers in Tel Aviv. But I was demanding reparations for my parents' house and property, which I was claiming as their sole heir. Hence the complications. My parents' house was in a good section of Frankfurt. It had been damaged by the war and renovated by a German family, its present occupants. More about them later.

It wasn't difficult to establish ownership of the house. My father's name, address, and phone number, 62582, were listed in an old phone book. Since the city's real estate records hadn't been damaged I was able to obtain a copy of the deed for the house, which had been confiscated by the authorities when my parents were expelled from Frankfurt in 1941.

The matter appeared to be simple but it wasn't. After the war a law had been enacted allowing refugees or their heirs to demand their property or appropriate compensation until a designated date in 1948, after which they forfeited their rights. The German government had then paid a symbolic sum to various Jewish organizations for the unclaimed property, and the chapter was thus concluded.

My case was exceptional. In 1948 I was seventeen years old, a student in high school. At that time it didn't occur to me to claim reparations at all. In those days I was totally occupied with the tormenting process of severing my links with the past. Every day I dug a new defensive system, masked myself with camouflage, planted mines of falsehood. I burned the letters and the pictures of my parents. I changed my name from Zvi (Hirsch) Lampel to Uri Lam. I refused to speak German and began to introduce Arabic words into my Hebrew conversation. By the time I left school that year I was saying I was born in Tel Aviv.

Later, after finishing the Technion, I decided to apply for reparations after all—only to learn that I had missed the deadline and wasn't likely to get anything for my parents' house and property. The clerk in the Tel Aviv law office had shaken his head mechanically and closed my folder. "I am very sorry," he had said without a trace of sorrow, "I can't do anything about the house. It's too late." When I told him I wanted to sue the organizations that had inherited my money, he discouraged me but nonetheless gave me the address of a lawyer in Frankfurt, a Dr. Ernst. Dr. Ernst, with whom I corresponded over a period of several months, finally agreed to take my case on the condition that I would provide him with all the papers and come to Frankfurt. He couldn't promise me success, but the special aspects of my situation interested him and he hoped to make a test case of it.

I spoke to Ernst's secretary on the phone. She found my folder and asked me to come to the office, which was downtown, in one of those concrete and glass buildings.

I found the lawyer's name on a polished brass directory in the lobby and stood at the elevator for a long while without going in. Something was preying on my mind. Smoking one cigarette after another, I went out into the driving rain, then came back into the building, struggling with the conflict that suddenly besieged me. There were flaws in those pillars on which my "just and ethical demands" were founded. Doubts I had already dismissed were circling my head like black birds of prey. What am I doing here? I asked myself this question again and again as I paced the marble lobby.

Why don't I go up and deposit the damned papers on Ernst's desk? Why not take the quickest course toward settling my accounts with the past once and for all? What in the world is troubling me so? He'll ask questions. Of course—there will always be questions. I've got to adjust to that. He'll demand reparations for all those ghastly things. Five marks for each day of forced labor by my brother. Five marks a day multiplied by father, mother, brother, sister. Three Israeli pounds plus seventy-five agorot a day for cold, hunger, tuberculosis, personal abuse. So many marks for parents who vanished in that camp, so many more for the wide eyes of my sister gazing up at me from every full ashtray. Still, I'm not sure . . . Do I have the right to ask anything for all these horrors that have no price? Compensation for a house with so many rooms, for an apple tree and berry bushes in the garden? Yes, absolutely. Reparations for the frozen, naked bodies of a man and woman who once carried me in their arms (loss of security?), for eyes clinging to barbed wire, bare feet tramping through the snow (loss of freedom?), reparations for a last brief moment in the shower before the gas was turned on (the final solution?). What diabolical calculation can determine this? Let's assume I agree to it. What if this settlement should open up other accounts in my soul, accounts that can never be resolved? What will be demanded of me in exchange for this money—money with which I can acquire a house, a car, records, vacations and rest? What's the implication of the required signature, signed in blood in triplicate? What manner of hell lurks at the end of this road to tranquillity? Where are you leading me, Herr Mephisto? How can I be sure that at the end of your tranquil avenue the very world I wish to bury does not await me? No, I am not prepared to sign. I must consider the matter further. I want to study every clause of this contract, decipher the fine print and learn what commitments are implied by the fateful signature. Let me consider it another day or two.

I went back to the hotel and, without taking off my coat, I flung myself on the bed and lay motionless, staring at the white desert that was the ceiling, at the shrieking birds of prey that circled my head. I fell asleep finally and found myself dead, being carried on a stretcher through a black cobblestoned square. I could hear many voices and the whistle of a speeding train. The stretcher was carried by my father and my brother, Martin, who set me down beside the apple tree on a heap of antique furniture. My father took a sharp scalpel from his black bag and began to cut into my shoulder. I felt no pain. I could see the flesh being cut away, the white bone, but no traces of blood. He severed my arm from my body as if it were the arm of a doll and handed it to my brother. My mother, sitting beside a heavy table, dripped tears of tallow on my sister's soft hair. The crowd cheered as my bother displayed my severed arm, crying: "One arm in good condition, very cheap! Five marks, that's all. Who will take it?" I was surprised that Martin, whose white sleeve flapped empty in the wind, didn't take it for himself. I wanted to tell him to keep the arm, but I couldn't get up. My heavy head was fastened to something. Opening my mouth to shout, I found I couldn't make a sound. I closed my eyes and woke up in the dark hotel room. I wanted to cling to the dream but all that remained of it was my brother's empty sleeve and the tallow tears of my mother. I undressed and went back to sleep.

I spent the next two days in the hotel. I closed the shutters, drew the blinds, and turned on the light. I lost all sense of time. Once when I called room service for lunch I got a drowsy response: "Lunch? At two in the morning?"

I vegetated these two days; I slept, dozed, lay awake in bed, choked Raymond Chandler's little sister, wrote airmail letters (which I flung in the wastebasket) to a student who had the key to my house. I read four detective stories, drank beer, paced the room. I ate standing up and drank more beer. I didn't shave, I didn't wash, I didn't turn on the radio. I talked to myself without hearing what I was saying. I called for the little chambermaid on several occasions, but each time an old woman appeared instead and I didn't know what to say. On the third day I opened the shutters—it was another gray morning—and decided.

I decided that I lacked the courage and strength to defer the reparations money. I couldn't afford to give it up. I need a car, I told myself turning away from my image in the mirror. I've got to pay off the mortgage on that house at the border. I have debts. After all, the money is mine. If all that had never happened the money would still be mine. Why give it up? I'll sign a paper saying that I received whatever sum they are kind enough to grant, but I will sign nothing more. They'll get nothing in return. They took their share long ago. I make no promise to forgive, to forget, or even to close the account. I retain the right to remind them of their deeds until the end of time, and even this doesn't exhaust my demands. I want more, more, more. More is coming to me! I will continue to demand, to pound on desks, to cause uproars, until I am paid in full for every day my father, mother, brother, sister worked in the camps. Why five marks a day, why not thirteen, the wage of a common German laborer? Why not more?

I'll get what I can by whatever means possible. Anything is legitimate. If I can deceive them, I'll go right ahead. I'll invent evidence that I suffered illnesses I never heard of. I'll forge papers and produce testimony about my parents' alleged wealth; a diamond necklace, a Renoir, three Paul Klees, and a little-known van Gogh.

On the third day I left a layer of filth behind me in the tub, shaved carefully (the swelling under my eye had disappeared and the blue spot was now dark purple), put on clean clothes and dark glasses, and set off for the lawyer's office. This time I was determined not to dawdle in front of the building; I was going to leave the shadowy doubts behind. I stopped for a moment to light a cigarette and review the aggressive opening sentence I had prepared, when I noticed a pretty girl walking past me into the elevator. The door began to close, but with three leaps I was in. The sunglasses slipped down my nose. When I tried to catch them the folder slipped out from under my arm and fell at the young woman's feet. The elevator door closed. Turning to pick up the folder I discovered that my coat was caught in the door. An absurd situation. I tugged at my coat and worked it loose. She smiled in amusement. I bent down to pick up the folder and stole a peek at her legs. The elevator began to move. I realized in a panic that I didn't know what floor Ernst's office was on. The young woman was carrying a black folder.

Filing clerk? Secretary? I asked her in English if by chance she knew which floor . . . suddenly the lights went out. The elevator stopped abruptly.

"Oh, no!" I heard her groan with annoyance, in German.

Many visions flashed through my head in the dark. Power failure! Here I am, caught between two floors behind a closed door! Lightning struck the power line. The hand of Providence. Time to reconsider, a last chance to retreat. People are sometimes stuck in elevators for hours. She and I, alone. There was a dimple in that smile. She is twenty or twenty-two. Suspended in space. . . . Do it right on the floor. There's room. Or on my coat. Then the lights will suddenly come on and the elevator will resume its course.

Her clothing rustled faintly. Two steps, nylon stockings rubbing against each other. Groping in the dark, I rattled the locked door. There should be some buttons on the right. A cool hand. Oh, excuse me. Smooth skin. I pressed one of the upper buttons—nothing. I lit a match. Its flame flickered in her eyes. She pressed the button for the main floor—no response. As I looked into her eyes the match went out.

"I'm afraid we're stuck," she said in German. I lit another match.

"English?" I asked, commenting to myself that this was no time for games. She shook her smooth, flowing hair, and the sweet fragrance of a familiar perfume wafted my way. She pressed the red alarm bell, but it didn't ring. Silence. I asked in English if by chance she spoke Italian. Though it was dark I could tell that her perfumed hair was swinging from side to side—no.

"German," she said, "only German."

I banged on the door and listened. Silence. I kicked the door and listened. In the distance I heard a typewriter tapping away.

"*Kaputt*," I said.

"Then you *do* speak German," she said brightly.

"*Nein*." I insisted. "*Kaputt*. Just *kaputt*."

I lit a match and glanced at my watch. It was 10:30. She held her watch up to the light and shook her head in annoyance. Pretty hands, I thought. Thin, strong fingers. Clever fingers that know how to do things. I pressed my ear to the cold door—now I couldn't hear the clatter of the typewriter. The dry rustle of nylon stockings made me shiver. A single footstep. She pounded on the door. Silence.

"What a predicament," she giggled. "Hey!" she shouted. "Is anyone there? We're stuck in the elevator!"

"Hey!" I yelled at the top of my lungs. "*Kaputt!*" "*Deutschland kaputt!*" She laughed. Then a long tense silence. I heard a gentle metallic tap and saw a lighter gleaming in her hand. I reached for my dark glasses. She lit a cigarette. I took one from my own pack, and she offered me a light. We both smiled faintly.

"This is wild," she said.

I didn't want to speak German to her. "No German," I said with finality, making a face in the dark. This was more than a game. One of the many things I had asked myself during my two days of seclusion in the hotel room was why I wouldn't speak German. The answer was clear and simple, an instinctive response easy to understand: since it was the Germans who perpetrated all those crimes, using German as a tool—"Thirty-five hundred" (people!), "I hereby certify receipt" (of the transport!), "Get a move on! Faster" (dig!)—I was possessed by the idea that the mere use of the language would implicate me, from a linguistic point of view at least, in those crimes. I knew this was absurd, that other things were said in this language, that since the war the regime of terror had been denounced in that very language with more courage than in any other, Hebrew included. Still, I could not overcome my need to build a barrier, to separate myself from people who spoke that language. I regarded German as the tool the crimes were committed with—a tool I was reluctant to handle.

She inhaled, illuminating her face for a second. There was no face like this one in those photographs, the intelligent face of a young woman who could be Danish,

Swedish, English—or even Israeli. A pleasant face with a trace of a smile. A face that can't be fathomed right away but nonetheless attracts attention and interest.

"I'm very sorry," I said, not knowing just what I was sorry about.

She shrugged, as if to say, "What can you do?" or perhaps, "What does he want from me?" I kicked the door, once, twice, three times. Pressing my ear to the wall I could hear voices in the distance, but they faded away. It's impossible, I thought, that they haven't noticed the elevator isn't working. Unless the electricity is out in the entire building. It couldn't take this long. What a pain.

Then the situation began to appeal to me. Two people trapped in an elevator, with no common language. A voyage in the dark to the brink of mystery. A decidedly pretty girl. Smooth hair. Natural. Purposeful fingers. And her legs, yes—her legs . . . My heart began to pound. I felt the sweet tension of this critical moment. In the darkness I could accidentally touch her hand for a moment, a long moment. At first she would take no notice. But her hand would remain in mine and everything would become clear. No, not that way, not by accident. She might be frightened. A strange character with a black eye—what's he after? I must have a better strategy. Next time she takes out a cigarette I'll offer her a light. No, wait. *I'll* take out a cigarette and when she offers me a light, I can brush her hand as I shield the flame. That would be more natural. I'll gaze into her eyes and establish contact. Maybe, maybe not. Some preliminaries are called for. To touch her suddenly, just like that . . . that won't do. If the mystical tension is there, anything goes. But if there's no spark, no previous contact, no meaningful glance, my touch will offend her. A more tentative approach is called for. Conversation. Two or three inane questions and then, "I'm completely bewildered by the intimacy imposed on us." Or "Here we are, suspended in space; we've lost contact with earth, yet we're still far from heaven."

Something in that vein. If I could only say it in English. Or in Italian. But *not* in German. "I'm completely bewildered by the intimacy imposed on us"—these could be the words of a proper German gentleman upon finding himself pressed against a strange woman in one of those transport trains. Was the black bag still in my father's hand when they pushed him into the cattle car? "*Schnell, Herr Doktor!* Hurry up, hurry, Doctor!" No, I couldn't bring myself to speak that violent language.

I kicked the door with all my strength and shouted, "Hey!" The light went on, but the elevator didn't budge. We pressed all the buttons—nothing happened. What could be the matter? Over and over I pressed the button, with no results. We began to shout and stamp. Her face, so close to mine, was rosy with effort. I smiled. She smiled. She tapped the door with her umbrella and stamped her feet in a charming manner. By degrees my stomps turned into a wild dance. I circled around her and began to emit wild sounds, savage wails, the roars of a jungle beast. Her grin blossomed into laughter.

"Help," she shouted, "wild animals! Help!"

"*Kaputt!*" I shrieked. "Help! *Aiuto! Gevalt!*" We couldn't stop laughing. My glasses slipped off my nose, but I kept right on prancing, leaping, stomping.

Then we heard someone call, "Quiet there! What's all that shouting?" We stopped abruptly.

"We're stuck in the elevator!" the young woman cried.

"*Padre nostro,*" I said, lifting my eyes piously to heaven and crossing myself.

"Stop," she said, trying to be serious. "The elevator isn't working. We're stuck!" she shouted.

"Yes, yes," the voice said, "we know. The repairmen are on the way. Please be patient."

"Thanks," she said and fell silent.

I handed her my cigarettes. With painstaking effort she said, "Tenk you." I nodded approval, like a teacher acknowledging a good student and lit her cigarette. My breathing was still heavy from the war dance. Making no attempt to conceal this, I panted in an exaggerated manner like a barbarian. Again she rewarded me with a smile that emphasized a slight frown in her eyes—they were gray, I discovered. I looked into them steadily, without shifting my gaze even when she became aware of it. Her face was grave; the frown drifted up to her forehead and became a question mark. She looked into my eyes, at my right eye mostly, a question still marring her brow.

I touched the bruise under my eye with my finger and explained: "Nazis." She strained to fathom the riddle. I clenched my fists and bestowed two mock blows on the black and blue spot.

"Nazi *Barbar*," I said, "Frankfurt Nazi. German *Barbar*."

She shook her head in disbelief. "*Nein*," she said incredulously.

"*Ja, ja*," I reiterated. "*Barbar*—barbarian."

She smiled, obviously relieved, and pointed to herself, saying, "Barbara."

I laughed. She laughed. I pointed to myself and said, "Uri."

"Stahl," she added. "Barbara Stahl."

"Uri," I said. "Uri Lam." We shook hands.

"How do you do," she said in German.

"How do you do," I repeated carefully in German, and she nodded acknowledging my success. Our eyes met for an instant. She tried to avoid my gaze, but I persisted. I hid my right eye behind my hand, but she shook her head and pulled my hand away, saying, "*Nein, nein*. OK, OK."

Suddenly we heard someone shouting from above. "Anybody there?"

"We stepped out for a minute," she answered. "We're back now." I choked back my laughter.

"What? What?" the voice called.

"Nothing!" she said. "We're here."

"In twenty minutes," the voice continued, "half an hour at the most, the elevator will be fixed. The repairman is on his way."

"Thanks very much," she said. Again silence. I asked, in English, what the man had said. She took my left hand and moved the large hand of my watch ahead from 11 to 11:30. Only half an hour had passed since the elevator broke down. I spread my coat on the floor and with a royal flourish invited her to sit down. I bowed deeply, repeating the elegant gesture. She smiled. I sat on the coat, and leaning back against the wall I invited her to join me. She put down her umbrella and curled up beside me.

13 | *a touch of silence*

In my favorite fantasies I find myself alone with a strange woman in a place or situation from which there is no escape: a train, a ship, a desert island, a boat—a broken elevator. In these sweet fantasies, invented with feverish lust, I see myself looking darkly into the eyes of a woman, her gaze melting slowly in mine, our hands clasped, our fingers whispering words such as are whispered in dark movie theaters, on buses, in darkened booths, on park benches, in dim hallways. Later, when all the words have been spoken, I follow her into a dim room which is all bed and, still without a word, watch as she slowly undresses. Her eyes cling to mine; footsteps lead the way to the bed and the rustle of cool sheets. All the while silence, not a word. Only rapid breathing.

Fantasies such as these have, in fact, been fulfilled two or three times in my life, beginning with the time I first kissed the faintly sour lips of a long-legged girl called Tammy in the dark furniture crate near the barn. To this day, on hot restless nights I seek refuge in these mute passions, as in some cool sanctuary.

I despise the endless conversation, the verbal hocus-pocus, the cold calculations that seem to be a necessary prelude to the moment of truth—a special fee demanded in advance, intellectual prostitution, the skeleton key with exclusive power to unlock bedroom doors. More than once I've responded to this transaction with deep revulsion. Pay attention, please, as I unfold my soul for you to see: how clever I am and how sensitive, how delicate and wise; flesh and blood flaming, spirit hovering over the waters. See how unique I am—a rare gem, a treasure of the sort that doesn't often come your way. Now that I've opened the private recesses of my heart, having paid ahead in the gold coin that is my soul— come to bed! Like any wholesaler, I know just what the customer will pay. Sometimes even in the heat of the chase I observe myself with irritating cynicism and whisper in my own ears reproaches that almost wipe out the victory. Now you tell her, I whisper to myself with contempt, that you never imagined . . . and so on and so forth . . . that this is too beautiful to tarnish with words, or some garbage like that. Now that her breath is heavy with excitement, whisper into her neck those same phrases, sweet and guaranteed, that you have whispered before, assuring her in a mumbled confession that nothing quite like this, so strange and wonderful, has ever happened. How well I know the text—it's enough to make me puke! Why all this verbal preamble when it's clear from the start that she didn't come to my room in the middle of the night just to drink coffee and hear Ray Charles. Why can't we do without all the chatter? How much more pure is the night when it's not offered up for sale. How much more virtue in open desire, true passion, naked lust, whose depths are plumbed in silence! Afterwards, yes. Afterward, when we rise up from the deep-sea dive, return breathless to the shore— then we can talk. The switch will be turned on and a special intimacy will follow: her bare shoulder, damp hair clinging to her back, a relaxed smile, the fresh smell of another body, beads of sweat between her breasts. Now we can really hear Ray Charles. This is the time to talk. The conversation is free, relaxed, honest, unmarred by the ring of the cash register. The cards are on the table. Two people, once distant, now close, are leafing through each other, opening locked drawers, passing candid snapshots to each other—a moment of truth. Sometimes.

I'm not sure these were my thoughts when I found myself trapped in the elevator with the girl, but there's no question that from the first moment I found elements in this situation that linked it to my pet fantasies. We sat on my coat waiting for an unseen hand to fix the elevator and save us from ourselves, not daring to look each other in the eye. We were silent. Without a language in which to phrase my advances, I was unable to shower her with flattering whispers, unable to construct a ring of charm and fasten it with metal links of logic. I saw myself at the gate of a magic garden, a gate that refused to yield to my fervent whispers.

Would nightfall find us in her room or in mine, I mused. (Why not here in the elevator, standing up or on the floor, with the coat spread under us? The door would open and suddenly, "What's going on here?") A sign that it's me she wants, just as I am, without intellectual calisthenics, without practiced maneuvers, without a display of my spiritual treasures. A sign it's my mouth, my hands, the magic key to her garden that she's after. Now for the test, I thought, touching not-touching her hand. Her eyes flashed and her hand slipped away. Short circuit. Bad connection. What now?

Her legs were curled under her. Good legs, I noted again, in taut nylon that rustled with every move. Full thighs captive in a tight skirt. When and if, I mused furtively, I could go there, between, over, without, straight, yes, yes and more; this way, with my head in the perfume of her neck. When and if. Meanwhile? Nothing. No contact. The key is not in my hand. Or my eyes—she refuses to meet my gaze. She looks straight ahead. Her eyes are glued to the ceiling. She glances at her watch. Time, which should pass quickly, is passing slowly. Nothing is happening. I can count her every breath—one every two seconds. My breathing is more rapid. The key is in her head, beyond her temples, beyond her smooth, soft hair, beyond her open brow. It can be reached only with words, soft whispers in her ear. Her eyes are closed—what does that mean? Now? Touch my hand. My fingers will tell what my eyes mean to say. I am not here, I am not connected. I don't know what is happening. I forget myself. Now . . . Or is she saying she's asleep, not to be disturbed until the elevator is fixed? She opened her eyes with a start, as if reading my thoughts. She looked at me suspiciously out of the corner of her eye. What did she expect to see? A diabolical gleam, a mask of intrigue? Vice or device— one or the other, certainly. Now, I'll close my eyes and inhale with a show of relaxation. Let her watch me as much as she likes. Like this—I opened my eyes suddenly and she was caught. She smiled like a naughty child—she had only meant to find out what was in that jar on the top shelf, not to taste it. I grinned back at her and the smile, which had begun to fade, shone again, lighting up her face.

"Hello, Barbara," I said.

"Hello, Uri," she said.

"OK?" I asked.

"OK," she said.

"Boom-boom," I suggested, pounding the door with my fist.

"Boom-boom," she echoed, patting the coat under her with her palm.

I got up, offered her my hand, and drew her toward me. She shook out her hair as if she had been in the water and smoothed her skirt, pulling it down over her soft thighs. She made no effort to free the other hand, which rested in mine. Her fingers seemed to be asleep. I let go of her hand, touching not-touching her fingertips. Squeezing my palm in playful rebuke, she withdrew her hand and began pounding on the door.

"Shhhh," I whispered. "*Nein* boom-boom."

"*Warum?*" she asked in surprise.

"Shhhhh," I hissed again. "*Jude,*" I whispered, pointing to my sleeve. She looked at me, bewildered, and frowned. I pointed past the elevator door and said,

"Nazi *Barbar*. Boom-boom *Jude*." She laughed and her white teeth glistened.

"*Amerikaner?*" she asked.

"*Nein*," I answered. "Israel. *Yerushalayim*."

"Ah, Jerusalem!" she cried.

"Jerusalem," I said. "Solomon. David."

"*Ja, ja*," she said and her eyes lit up. "Salomo *und* Bathseba. David *und* Jonathan."

"*Nein*," I said. "Smoked Salomon *und* David Ben-Gurion."

"*Ach, ja*, Ben-Gurion," she said, a question lingering in her eyes. Even in German I didn't know how I was going to extricate myself from the smoked salmon I had ascribed to Jerusalem.

"Cuckoo," I said, twirling a finger near my temple.

"Ben-Gurion?" she asked.

"*Nein*." I pointed to myself. "Uri. Uri cuckoo."

"Why cuckoo?" she asked, thoroughly confused.

How do I get myself out of this? A person can indulge in nonsense, chatter in gibberish that is of no importance, only if he's fluent in the language. The dozen international words that could be a bridge between us assume too much importance. Every word must say something. No wisecracks. I peered at my watch. It was 11:30. I kicked the door twice and the light went out.

"Oh, no," she said in a dejected tone.

"Oh, yes," I said, groping in the dark. My hand brushed her arm. I placed my hands on her shoulders, softly, gently, so she wouldn't be startled. She wasn't startled. She said nothing. She didn't stir. I clasped her shoulders. I could hear her breathing. I inhaled the fragrance of her hair and brushed her cheek and neck gently with my lips. The light went on.

"Oh, no," I said.

"Oh, yes," she said, laughing.

We heard pounding in the distance, and the elevator stirred ever so slightly. My hands, still on her shoulders, trembled. When she gazed into my eyes, I could see my shrunken image in her pupils. I drew her nearer but she pulled back. As I picked up my coat and handed her the umbrella a question flashed through my mind: Will the elevator simply go on up now? The lawyer, the papers. . . . But what about Barbara? OK, I said to myself, if the elevator goes up I'll see Ernst. But if it goes down I'll have time to reconsider. Leave it to fate. Heads or tails. Let it not go up, let it go down. No, I won't meddle. Another tremor of the elevator. They are working on it. More pounding. I put on my coat and lit a cigarette. She looked at me expectantly. I offered her a cigarette and struck a match. As she bent over the flame, her hand touching mine, we exchanged a long glance. In silence. The elevator began to move—downward. It was going down!

"Barbara," I said.

"*Ja?*"

"*Gut?*" I asked.

She nodded. The elevator stopped and the door was opened by a mechanic in white overalls. He shrugged as if to say, "What can you do? It happens," and got on as we got off. We were on one of the lower floors, the second or third. Through a window in the stairwell, I could see a glass building and the crowns of dark trees. Barbara headed for the stairs.

"Coffee?" I asked, grabbing her arm. She thought a moment before shaking her head.

"Tea?" Again she refused. "Beer?"

"*Nein,*" she said.

"How about champagne?" I suggested. Smiling, she shook her head once more. In that case, everything that had happened—the touch in the dark, my lips on her neck, my hand in hers—it was as if it had never been. A brief encounter in the elevator, then good-bye, good-bye. "Guess what happened to me this morning. I was stuck in an elevator with a real oddball, an Israeli from Jerusalem. He said something about Ben-Gurion and smoked Salomon. I couldn't understand what he was talking about—he spoke no German. What? Nothing, honestly. He touched my hand once, that's all. We were in the elevator a full hour and nothing happened. We couldn't even talk to each other. It was really bizarre."

"In that case—" I began in English.

"Cocoa," she said.

"Cocoa!" I repeated, jubilant. "*Gut!* Me too cocoa!"

We went to a small café down the street and sat in oppressive silence, drinking cocoa from tall, thick mugs. Time passed slowly. Our captive glances, at times forced, at times forbidden, sought relief in the crowd, the waitresses, the cakes in the window, the cars passing through a thin film of rain.

I sat beside her, but I was with her in my small hotel room, in the shower, in bed—and the chambermaid, no, the Italian waiter, brought us breakfast on trays. I was with her—between sips of cocoa—in her room, her apartment, her house in the country. We sat on a thick carpet with a fire crackling on the hearth. We lay on soft sheets, twined together, panting. We sat in another café, in Jerusalem, where someone at a neighboring table remarked, "Uri is back with a German girl and a Volkswagen." She popped a piece of cake into her mouth. My eyes were fixed on hers, but from time to time she allowed my gaze to slip away from her eyes and shift to her lips, to her long neck which seemed to sprout, from a small, tantalizing area of bare skin, to her breasts that swelled softly under her thin woolen blouse. Returning home to her eyes I received a playful rebuke: naughty boy, I know where you've been, don't tell me stories. I know what you're scheming. And what about you, my eyes questioned. I say nothing, was the message I read in her eyes—maybe yes, maybe no. It depends. These things aren't simple.

"*Wunderbar gut,*" she said. What is *wunderbar gut,* I asked with my eyes. When she pointed to the cocoa I twisted my lips in such extreme disapproval that she couldn't resist a giggle. Pointing to the cocoa I shook my head. Then I pointed to her and nodded yes.

"*Gut,*" I said. "Very *gut.*"

"Cuckoo," she said, twirling a finger close to her temple. Her mouth smiled, her eyes shone. I covered her hand, which was resting on the table, with my own and began to stroke it. Her eyes followed my fingers, then shifted to her watch.

"I have to run," she said in German. I pretended not to understand. "To go," she said, her fingers marching across the tablecloth.

"*Nein*," I said, coaxing.

"*Ja, ja*," she answered.

"*Warum*, Barbara?" I asked.

In answer she lifted her hands upward, appealing to those powers that required her to return to a task from which there was no escape.

"Restaurant," I said. "Frankfurter and chips. Schnitzel. Beer. Shashlik. *Ja?*"

She sighed deeply and placed her hand on her stomach. "Diet," she said, teasing.

"*Gut*," I said. "Salad."

She shook her head as if to convey, "What can I do with you?" and said, "At two," moving the hand of my watch to two o'clock.

"Two o'clock." I showed two fingers.

"Two o'clock," she repeated, pointing to the table, meaning here in this café at two.

"Got it," I said to her in Hebrew. "At two we'll meet here and go to my room. I'll tell you I left something important in the hotel—my money, let's say—and you'll come up with me for a minute and I'll kiss you all over."

"*Was, was?*" she asked, shaking off the shower of foreign words.

"I said that I would like to kiss your entire body," I repeated in Hebrew in the rhythm of dictation. "I—you. All of you. Your breasts, your long legs . . ."

"*Was zagst du?*" she asked again. "*Was ist das?*"

"*Das ist das*," I said to her. "*Das ist* blah blah blah."

"So, you *do* speak German," she said gleefully.

"*Ja*," I said in a deep mocking voice.

She got up and let me help her with her coat. I hugged her as she slipped her arms into the sleeves. Paying the waitress I led her out into the rain. She hailed a cab and as I opened the door I kissed her hand with an elegant flourish. I held up two fingers and she nodded. The cab drove off. It was 12:30. The rain began to let up.

I wandered through the streets aimlessly for an hour and a half, looking in the shop windows, at books, cameras, optical-equipment-at-bargain-prices, automobile showrooms, records, Spanish furniture, typewriters, more books and cameras. I browsed in a giant department store, covering every section of each of its five floors. I tried on a leather jacket and warm slippers. Finally I bought a small memo pad with attached pencil and a calendar. In the women's dress department I fingered the empty garments, touched the nylon stockings stretched taut on sawed-off display limbs. The saleslady, watching me with suspicion, approached and asked if she could be of some help. I told her I was looking for an Indian sari and gloves of *cimex lectularius*. She found a sari but I told her the color didn't suit me. Gloves of bedbug leather were no problem— she'd never heard of them.

At ten minutes to two I left the department store and started toward the café. Or so I thought. I was sure I'd come from the direction of the church tower that soared above the other buildings, but I began passing stores I had just seen and I suddenly found myself in front of the old opera house, destroyed by the war. In a mild panic, I realized I didn't even know the name of the café in which we were to meet. I began to retrace my steps at a quick pace that turned into a run. It was already five past two. She arrived on time, I thought with alarm as I ran. Germans are always prompt. She waited five minutes, thinking, What is this? Does he expect me to wait around until he shows up? The nerve. She'll put on her coat and leave, only to be swallowed up by the crowd. I'll never see her again.

I found myself in front of an enormous department store: Kaufhaus. Yes, I'd been browsing there. I had come from that direction . . . which direction was it, anyway? The clock in front of the building said 2:10. A lost cause. I won't find her. Then I almost kicked myself—why hadn't I thought of it sooner? Grabbing a cab I gave the driver the lawyer's address. He looked at me quizzically and was off. The cab turned off the main street, entered a side street, turned back to the main street, and stopped at the curb. I paid, and without waiting for change I ran down the street—at least I remembered the way from the office building to the café. It was exactly 2:15.

I burst into the café, huffing and puffing. She came toward me in a different coat and leather gloves, a small purse slung over her shoulder, her lips repressing a mysterious smile. As we left the café I begged her pardon for being late, asking her to forgive me in half a dozen languages. She said, in German, that it was quite all right, she'd been late too and hadn't been waiting more than two or three minutes. The rain, turning into a downpour, forced us into a cab. Where to? She directed the driver to a street with a name I didn't catch.

As soon as the cab began to move she took off her gloves and put them in her purse. Why, I asked myself —it's cold in the taxi, it's raining outside, and we'll soon be getting out again. Are her hands at my disposal now? Is that what she means to say? As if she were to kick off her shoes and perch on my bed? I placed my hand on hers tentatively. She looked into my eyes. As I gazed at her dimpled neck I saw myself in the bosom of Maria Cristina. The same thing all over again. No, this is *not* the same, I thought, feeling the warmth of her thigh through the thin skirt. She looked into my eyes, her nostrils quivering. Not at all the same. For one thing, we didn't meet in a cemetery. What then is that lawyer's office? The stacks of folders on his shelves? The entire city of Frankfurt, the very street we were now crossing —is it not built over graves? The buildings—these giant monuments—the bare trees, are all one huge cemetery. No, that isn't true, not at all, I whispered to myself, placing my hand cautiously on her waist.

The driver stopped the cab and turned around. "Where to?" he asked. "This is the end of the street." She looked into my eyes.

"Hirshof Hotel," I whispered in her ear. She shook her head firmly and took a breath as if to speak, but said nothing. The driver looked at us. It was still raining. The windshield wipers screeched obstinately from side to side. "Barbara," I whispered. She hesitated another minute before giving the driver an address: Something—Strasse 30. In two years, I thought, my age will match that address. Was that her address, I wondered, my heart pounding. The cab drove off.

"Restaurant?" I asked, just to make sure.

"Barbara Stahl Restaurant," she said tensely. My neck and face were flushed with color.

"Salad?" I asked, pointing to her. She nodded. "What about me?" I asked in English, pointing to myself.

"A la carte," she said, a faint smile flickering in her eyes and then fading.

"*Café pauvre*," I told her. Poor man's coffee. A proper French meal ends with coffee, and after coffee, bed. The poor in southern France, unable to afford the price of coffee after their meager meal, go right to bed. Their afternoon orgy is known as *café pauvre*—don't ask me which English travel guide included this tidbit in a footnote.

"Just coffee?" she asked with surprise.

"And you," I said, kissing her hair lightly.

We got out on a quiet residential street lined with two- and three-story houses, and my breath all but stopped as the street of my distant childhood flashed before my eyes. A street exactly like this one: a few leaves fluttering on black trees at the edge of the sidewalk, low fruit trees growing in front of the dark houses, thin rivulets of rain streaming down windowpanes as a black sound truck booms its piercing message: "*Achtung, achtung.*" I walked to the corner and peered at the sign: Apfelwein Strasse. Barbara was watching me in amusement, assuming, no doubt, that I wanted to learn her address. Apfelwein Strasse 30. I'll remember. A street of apple wine, three years before Hitler. We went in through a small iron gate. She opened the door with a key from her purse. One of the two nameplates said BARBARA STAHL in fancy type. Off a hall, pleasant with the aroma of cleanliness, polished wood steps led to the second floor. Barbara opened another door with a small key. Hanging our coats on gleaming brass pegs, she guided me into a spacious room with rugs, a deep sofa, shelves lined with books, a crystal chandelier above a heavy wooden desk, two easy chairs, and a basket heaped with newspapers.

Now what, I reflected. Wrap her in my arms and, groping with closed eyes, find the way to the sofa? Slip the shoes off those sleek legs and lose ourselves? No. Not yet. She invited me up to eat with her—that is the camouflage she chooses. Maybe the final goal is still not clear to her. She may not want to think of the outcome. I mustn't violate her mask. She would take offense. I must accept her terms: grace, good manners, composure. She is looking toward the door, eluding my gaze. What a mess, she's probably telling herself. Now he thinks I brought him here to sleep with me. Better not touch her now. Let her relax. Let her be surprised. Let her wonder.

"Want something to eat?" she asked. I pretended not to understand.

"Ham-ham?" she asked, making chewing motions.

"Sleep," I said. She frowned questioningly. I rested my head on my hands and closed my eyes. She shook her finger at me menacingly and laughed.

14 | *from passion's kitchen*

Sweet peace descended, a sense of being pampered. I was enveloped by the warmth of home. The couch was soft and comfortable, the room warm. A melancholy quartet by Telemann cast puddles of pleasure on the windowpanes. From the kitchen came the sound of dishes being wiped. I took a long sip of whiskey and saw Barbara lying on the couch, her head resting on my thigh. I saw her in the armchair, book in hand, her light hair falling over her eyes. I saw her on the white fur rug, her bare feet rubbing against each other. The fire began to lick the charred wood and thin strips of bluish smoke curled upward. The tranquillity and repose of a distant autumn day. Did I not once sit beside such a fire on such a couch, in small flowered pajamas, rain falling outside, as my brother played the piano in a far-off room? Did he play Telemann too? A door opened and closed. Footsteps.

Barbara brought in a small tray piled with sandwiches. Picking up a glass of white wine she settled herself in the far corner of the couch. "Well," she said, lifting her glass. I raised mine too. "Skoal."

"*L'chayim,*" she said to my surprise, wrinkling her nose.

"*L'chayim.*" I took another long sip. Helping myself to a cheese sandwich I passed her the tray. She kicked off her shoes and folded her shiny knees under her chin. The tiny triangular sandwiches—white bread, no crust—were arranged on a bed of fresh lettuce, a toothpick in each one.

"Very good," I said with my mouth full, and her eyes lit up. When the record was over she got up to choose another. Miss Barbara suddenly suited her much more than plain Barbara. There was something in her posture, so erect and confident against the gray light of the window, that put distance between us.

"Izaak, Schütz, Buxtehude?" she asked, showing me the three jackets. The woodcut on the Schutz attracted me.

"Schütz, Fraulein Von Stahl," I said.

"*Kein* 'Von,' " she said above the drone of the church choir. "Why 'Von'?" Just then the phone on the desk rang.

"Telephone," I said.

She picked it up. "Yes, yes," I heard her say several times. "I don't know, I'm not sure. Maybe. Call tomorrow or the next day. We'll see. Yes, I hope so." What doesn't she know? What is she unsure about? Me? Who's she speaking to? An aging admirer, elegant, with graying temples? A pinstriped lawyer with a Heidelberg scar the length of his cheek?

"Definitely not tonight," I heard her say. "I'm busy." Busy with me, with *me*, I thought, as she hung up the phone. I got up to tend the fire and when I sat down again she was settled in the corner of the couch. Sitting close to her, I placed my arm on the back of the couch, not knowing what else to do with it. The small distance between my hand and her head seemed infinite.

It's good there's some music, I thought. I can pretend to be listening. Otherwise I couldn't bear the silence. I was beginning to question my own theory of mute, wordless attraction. Why not speak? There really is no line between words and touch. The word is a beginning, and touch is an extension of words. The lines of intelligence that suddenly appear in your face are there because of what you say. Your eyes reflect your soul through the words you mouth. You can't bear a redundant phrase, but how about a touch and a glance? Don't they repeat each other? You have looked into many other women's eyes in this very same way. . . . caressed other women's hair just this softly. Your body, too, repeats itself, fingering the same instruments of delight time after time. So why not talk? OK, what shall I tell her? How pleasant it is to be with her, to watch the fire together, to hear the music. No, better let the silence be unbroken and learn what we can of each other without words.

"Hello, Barbara," I whispered.

She looked into my eyes without a word. Slipping my arm under her back I slid over to her corner of the couch. Her head rested on my shoulder and my hand was on her waist. *Achtung.* I didn't lift a finger. We sat in this position a very long moment and I could hear her even breathing over the church choir. Don't make a move. Not a word. If only I could slide my hand over the blinding top of her stocking and feel her soft warm flesh. *Achtung!* She is searching my eyes. She will notice that I'm staring at her legs and be shaken out of this sweet reverie.

I placed my lips on her forehead and inhaled the fragrance of her hair. I kissed her closed eyes ever so gently and moved my lips slowly over her nose, letting them come to rest on her mouth. Her shoulders seemed to quiver. As she turned her head sharply, I found myself kissing her neck.

"Cigarette," she said, suddenly straightening up.

"Barbara," I whispered in her ear.

"Cigarette, please," she repeated, utterly cool.

We lit cigarettes and a gulf seemed to appear between us. She needs time to collect herself, I thought. To take herself in hand while she still can. Now she is calm enough to think. She's looking at me. Let her look. I won't look at her, though. Too bad I lit a cigarette. I should have sat like this, at a distance, watching the fire, until she finished her cigarette. You can't kiss a mouth filled with smoke. This is ridiculous.

I crushed my cigarette in the ashtray in her lap, wondering if the heat would pass through to her belly.

"Why did you do that?" she asked in German, pointing to the crushed cigarette. I shrugged. She might as well know I'm annoyed. Suddenly, right in the middle of everything, when all is going so well, when we're almost—a cigarette! How long will it take her to finish it? I'll close my eyes to show my annoyance. Like this.

The choir continued to wail. I was aware of the fire crackling on the hearth, puffs, puffs of cigarette smoke, the faint rustle of legs scraping against each other. This ploy with the cigarette is old hat too, I thought bitterly. Why not climb right into bed and allow our bodies to whisper love to each other? Why does it have to be so complicated? A little yes, then a little no. Almost . . . almost . . . but not quite. What's the point of all these stratagems?

Her lips touched my hand. I opened my eyes. The ashtray was back on the table. Her head was bent over my hand and her eyes seemed to be saying, Forgive me, but try to understand. I'm not sure. I'm a little worried and I don't want my body to speak for me. Don't be angry. Wrapping my arm around her I drew her closer and buried my head in her breasts. Just then the damned record was over.

"Just a minute," she said slipping out of my hands. I rested my head on the arm of the couch and stretched my legs. I could hear the rustle of a record jacket, the click of the button, the record dropping to the turntable, then bare footsteps bringing her back to me.

"Buxtehude," she said lying down beside me.

We listened. We held our breath and listened to ourselves. Her head was resting on my arm. Though the rest of our bodies didn't touch, I felt her body heat passing through her clothes to me. Her eyes were closed. From time to time she held her breath and listened tensely, as if trying to determine my intentions. Her hands were folded on her chest, her legs were frozen, one on top of the other. I placed my hand lightly on her hip and buried my head in her hair.

I don't know how long we lay there without moving. Then her hip brushed against my hand and her whole body seemed to relent. She turned her head slightly so that her blazing cheek fluttered past my lips. She sighed gently; then her soft lips were on mine and her arms were wrapped around my back. Everything began to happen at once. My hand wandered feverishly under her blouse but she said no. I whispered into her neck, "Barbara, Barbara."

"What?"

I only repeated, "Barbara," and as I caught hold of her cheek, she bit my hand. I sensed that she was anxious as if overcome by the fragrance of forbidden dreams. My hand slid over her writhing legs, touched the soft blazing flesh above her stockings. She mumbled, "No, no." I continued to grope in the moist darkness of her legs, my mouth pressed against hers, and probed the bare flesh under her blouse. A button popped, and her breast was in my hand. She seemed tense. Her whole body began to writhe and in one swift motion she pulled away.

"That's enough!" she said in a low voice. "Stop!"

I tried to ignore her, but with a powerful thrust she was free of my grip and fell off the couch, pulling me after her. She picked herself up quickly, but I just sat there on the white fur rug. The absurdity of the whole situation was all too familiar. The disappointing curtain that concludes the second act. Is there more to the performance, or is that it? Time to go home? She stood there with her back to me, skirt askew, stockings loose, blouse crumpled and unbuttoned. She straightened the skirt, fastened her stockings, tucked in her blouse, and with a single shake of her head, set her smooth hair in place. Buxtehude pursued his own course as if nothing had happened. Ridiculous. Why couldn't it be simpler?

"Barbara," I said.

"*Barbar!*" she said, pointing to me. I smiled bitterly. "Israeli *barbar*," she repeated a little less vehemently. I sat up in one corner of the couch, she sat in the opposite corner. Without looking at me she lit a cigarette. I watched the fire in silence. I didn't know what to say. What does she want, I asked myself. Why can't she decide? How can you say this far and no farther? But maybe she's . . . ? Impossible. She's twenty or twenty-two. That wouldn't make sense. Not to judge by her kisses, which say all a body can say. But you never can tell. Some women remain virgins even after having children. Just a minute! Could it be because I'm . . . ? I did tell her "*Jude*" in the elevator. Couldn't be. If that were bothering her we would never have come this far. But who knows what lurks in the dark cellars of her charming head. To hug and kiss, maybe. But that? With a Jew? Who knows what dark fears were planted in her when she was a child. "If you don't finish your soup a Jew will snatch you." Or "Barbara, my child, remember that you're a German. I don't want to tell you what to do. You're a big girl and a clever one. I have nothing against Jews—some of them are charming people. They suffered a lot during the war. This boy you're seeing is nice enough and intelligent, but nonetheless . . . Do you understand?" Who knows what she absorbed at home, in school, from her friends. Oh, nonsense. There I go, acting like a Jew. A girl turns me down and I accuse her of anti-Semitism. Ridiculous. Still and all . . .

"*Jude*, eh?" I asked clearly, to see how she would react.

"Idiot!" she exclaimed in German. "Are you crazy? How could you even think such a thing?"

"Barbara, Barbara," I tried to calm her down. "I didn't mean it, I was only fooling," I said in English. "Ha-ha, *Jude. Jude* ha-ha. OK, OK, Barbara."

Her face softened perceptibly.

"Cuckoo," I said twirling a finger and pointing it at my temple.

"*Ja*, cuckoo," she agreed.

"*Gut*," I said. "Shhhh," I added, placing a finger on my lips and cupping my ear. "Music." She smiled faintly as I handed her the ashtray. She stubbed out her cigarette and put the ashtray back on the table. Slipping my arm behind her head I leaned my head on her shoulder. When she opened her mouth to speak, I pressed a finger to her lips and whispered, "Music."

We sat like this until the record was over. Still she did not stir. Her eyes were closed, her even breathing sent quiet ripples over her whole body. I kissed her shoulder gently. Suddenly she opened her eyes and scrutinized me for a long moment, tightening her lips decisively as she got up. Fool, I said to myself as she stood looking down at me, you've ruined everything. The rain had stopped. She turned off the record player.

The concert's over, I thought. That's that. Now she'll hand me my coat and tell me to go . . . she has an appointment, she's busy, it's been very pleasant. "No, don't call me. I'll call you in a few days. I'm *so* busy."

With three firm steps she was back, offering me her hand. I got up, my heart pounding wildly as she drew me after her. Stopping for a moment at a closed door, she held her breath then opened the door. In the dimness, delicate and perfumed, I saw a wide bed. Only a bed. There wasn't even a chair in the room.

To this day I don't understand what happened. I'd like to tell my story simply and calmly (after all, it's been years), but it's actually very complicated. I don't know how to explain it. Perhaps I had been preparing for something different. Not entirely different but somewhat different. It was the middle of the day, and that was disconcerting. . . . But no, it wasn't that. The minute we were in the bedroom she closed the curtains and heavy blinds so that day became night. So far, so good. Still, it might have been better to turn on a small light. Visual contact, the one link between strangers, is cut off by sudden darkness. I'm not sure this was it, but I do know it was disturbing. We undressed in the dark and this added a special quality. The tension of guessing. Again, the rustle of nylon stockings. I heard her skirt slide down her thighs and slip to the floor, the buttons of her blouse open one by one. The swish of another garment I couldn't identify. Seductive—but it did take too long. I trembled under the strange blanket; the sheets were cold. I never dreamed that anything would go wrong, but it did—and I'm consumed by shame. Shame that overwhelms me even now when I remember her flaming body, her groping hands, her excitement—and then that humiliating fact.

Nothing helped. I tried everything, knowing it was useless. What was the point of trying? Either it works or it doesn't. No amount of determination can salvage this kind of situation. You've got to accept it. But I couldn't accept it. As soon as she realized how it was, she tried to be helpful. First gently and discreetly, then firmly and with force. But it was no use. It was just not in the cards. A hangman's noose loomed over me. The old nightmare was haunting me and I couldn't wake up. There was nothing to do—a lost cause.

We lay there exhausted, depleted. The bedding was heavy and intolerably hot. I couldn't bear the touch of her fingers. They seared my flesh. I pulled away my hand which lay lifeless on her warm, tense belly and slid my arm out from under her damp back. "Uri," she whispered tenderly. "Shhhhhh," I answered harshly. I closed my eyes, wanting to wake up in another place, in some other bed, on some other night.

What should I do? What in the devil was there *to* do, I questioned myself over and over, my nails digging into my flesh. If I could at least explain it to her. But what was there to explain? Besides, what could I tell her? That it was her fault? Blame it on those long drawn-out games of hers? Say that I was tired, that she shouldn't have yielded so suddenly, that I was distraught, not ready, overinvolved, the devil-knows-what? And in what language should I convey all this? I couldn't let her know I speak German just to make excuses for this humiliating failure. The irony: this was the one language that could be a bridge between us. (And see, Barbara, there is another thing. I don't know how to say this. You are German, and I . . . you understand. After all that happened—not exactly to me, but . . . you understand, my parents and all. . . . It's not so simple, all of a sudden, like this. . . .) Liar! Imagine dragging the holocaust into bed to rationalize your own private holocaust. You know deep down that it isn't true, that none of that disturbed you until this very moment. You looked into her eyes without seeing your sister's eyes reflected. You saw the eyes of a young woman, and that's all. Now, after it didn't work, you suddenly remember she's German. The truth is that you were attracted to her not *just* because she's German, but *also* because she's German. Definitely. Screw them, all those Germans. Knock up their women, their wives and daughters. Make them all pregnant. Fill Germany with six million bastard Jews who will suck their blood and bring on them a holocaust from which they will never recover . . . Another grand performance—make the whole world pregnant, indeed! Let's see you perform once! If such a thought really did flash through your perverted mind, this is the punishment you deserve . . . cut out the foolish recriminations. Don't make a tragedy out of it. It's not the end of the world—it happens. You're a sensitive person, not a stud horse always ready for action. You have to be emotionally prepared. You talk a good game, now let's see a little action. I can do it. Of course I can. This happened once before, and I thought it was the end then too, that I was finished once and for all at the age of twenty-three. How well I remember the blend of pity and mockery on the lips of that woman whose name I can no longer recall, the terror, the triumph and relief two days later when everything worked the way it should. Total recovery. The nightmare became a distant childhood dream. Here it was again: the angel of death returning to me in midday and taking my soul in his cold hand. I trembled.

"Uri," she whispered.

Her hand touched my throbbing heart. I brushed it away. I opened my eyes and in the darkness I could see her, so close, looking at me. I covered her eyes with my fingers. Let her not talk, I thought. Let her not say anything. No matter what she says I will hear pity. Better not to imagine what she is thinking. Not that. "I'm so glad you called, darling. The entire episode was disappointing. He's simply not a man, and that's all there is to it. I know I should have taken your advice. What? No, I think you exaggerate. They're not all like that." Oh, I could die of shame. Bury my head in the pillow. Stop breathing. Suffocate. Think for a moment what it was like for her. She wanted to yet she didn't want to. There she was on the couch with a mute pawing at her clothes. What does she know about me? Only that I come from Israel. Do you suppose that for an instant she had the fleeting thought, What if he's one of those avengers? He might strangle me because of all the horrors that transpired? That's when she shouted, "That's enough!" Later, when she calmed down a bit, my foolish question, "*Jude*, eh?" was the slap in the face that pushed her to the wall, leaving her with no alternative. After grave doubts and deep inner turmoil she made the decision, surprised by her own courage. That's it—she's to blame. She had no business dragging me into this room and undressing in such a casual manner.

It should have developed naturally. There, on the couch. Without stopping for cigarettes, without changing records. "You know, Luisa dear, I was sure he was OK until we got into bed. It was awful." Of course—she's a Lesbian. I quickly seized the rope I had thrown myself. She's a Lesbian and that's why it didn't work.

Stop that. Why can't you admit defeat? Stop inventing excuses—she's a German, a Lesbian, an anti-Semite; you wanted her too much; she should have behaved this way instead of that. Next you'll blame it on the smell of the pillow. Admit you failed. It's not so terrible, nothing to be ashamed of. Just as there's no reason to pat yourself on the back when it works the way it should, to regard it as a victory (I screwed her!) and a proof of manhood (I fucked the life out of her!). You're a sensitive person and you don't have to show the world you're a man. You've proved it more than once. Remember that night in the room on the roof? And the creaking metal bed in the German quarter of Jerusalem? The couch in the living room with Cimarosa repeating himself over and over again? And behind the Engineering Building? She said she had never met a man like you, and she had obviously met all sorts.

I produced many testimonials: other nights, good nights, effortless nights. I fell asleep in the bosom of a woman called Lola. (Not beautiful; flat-chested, flat-assed—and it was only a drunken carnival that brought us together in a strange bed. Lola, contrary to every expectation, contrary to the accepted rules of esthetics, was beautiful in bed—and wildly stimulating. To this day I can't say why. Not beautiful, not clever, not experienced. Yet she had a quality no one else could match. It was not only her lips that whispered. Her entire body whispered.)

I saw Lola galloping over me in high grass, among ripe, red apple trees. I clutched her hips and woke up from this sweet dream to find myself inside Barbara.

15 | *a night, a day*

I will never fathom the mystery: how did it happen and when? Was I asleep or awake? When exactly was the switch from Lola, galloping on top of me with long black Rousseau braids, to my Barbara? How did it happen that I was, suddenly, cruising in her sea? When did the miracle occur? All at once everything was simple and oh-so-perfect. Now. This way and that. It's me! Yes, me! You thought all was lost. You thought I wouldn't make it. Now you can see. And feel. But this is nothing, just the beginning. No hurry. Slow. Slow, so it never ends, so it lasts, like this. Sail away. Sail the seas, then back to shore, touch her madly panting heart, her entire tingling body. Yes.

Her hand slipped away and groped in the darkness. She snapped on a small night light which cast a soft light on her flushed face and flashing eyes. I pulled the blanket over me and buried my head in her neck. Why the light? It could spoil everything. No. It's all right. Perfectly all right. No need to dwell on it. That was long ago, years back. In fact, I only imagined it. It was a dream and when I woke up everything was all right. Like now. I passed the test, a crucial test. I like her. She is important to me. Because she's German? Why that? What does that have to do with it! They're all the same. These hands holding her are simply hands, that's all. This neck under my lips is a woman's neck, that's all. No, that's not all. A rare woman. An attractive woman, intelligent eyes. (What color are her eyes? Gray. Gray eyes. I remember.) And what else? I don't know. Only that this is good. This way. Yes. And more. More. She is getting there.

Breathing wildly, she seized my head and pushed it into the light. Her eyes flickered, searching for mine; her nostrils quivered with passion. She bit her lower lip and panted. "Yes, yes, yes!" she cried suddenly, locking her arms around me. Then she turned her face to one side and with a single gasp her energy was spent.

I was overcome with foolish, irritating pride. She lay under me in a swoon, her eyes closed. I studied her face with concern. She is dead. Miss Barbara Stahl was found, without a breath of life, in the vicinity of . . . I turned her face toward me; she opened her eyes and stared at me absently.

"OK?" I asked.

She responded with a nod and a smile of well-being. Beads of dew glittered under her eyes, around her nose, and along her neck. A thick bluish vein throbbed in her neck. Slowly, steadily, quietly, I sailed onward, as she planted her firm fingers in my hair, her gaping mouth wide open. I saw a smooth summer sea and dove into its deep silence. Coming up for air I heard her whispered breath echo on the shore. Not yet, not yet, I said to myself, shifting my thoughts to other realms. I relaxed my body, which was stretched over her taut as a string, and thought: on a high hilly pass/a cow in the grass . . . a boy shaking the branch of a tree to make the red apples roll on the green. Not yet, I told myself. My head, having already begun to whirl away, reeled back into place. I want to see her bite her lip again. I want her to die here, to swoon, to expire, to be crushed in my hands, and only then, then only, at the very last moment, will I leap from the cliff and die, swoon, expire, be crushed inside her. Like this. And again and again. Now. Yes, that's it, without stopping. More, still more. She won't go away, she'll come back to me! With—opposite— against—like this—yes—yes—Yes! The end. Death.

My head took off and soared away. An instant of sweet death. An endless instant. Infinite. She too, she too is gone. Spasms of pleasure in her face. The end. The sun within her begins to sink and we sink with it in the soft twilight of slumber.

I don't know how long we slept. Once I opened my eyes and saw a little girl napping at my side, a dream-smile on her face. (The tip of her thumb was in her mouth, a finger was curled around her freckled nose.) Once I opened my eyes and saw Max sitting there watching us. Once I fell asleep and saw two children eating

squashed cakes on a mat in the dark furniture crate.
There were two children, but I was not one of them.
I opened my eyes in alarm. A child! What if . . . No,
I thought, resting my head near hers. She surely took
precautions. A diaphragm and the certainty of the
tenth day before or after. Otherwise she certainly would
have said something. She wouldn't have drawn me closer
at just that moment—when she knew it was now.
Martin. I'll call him Martin. "Now that I am about to
die, Martin, my son, I want you to know that your
mother wanted you from the moment we met. It was
raining that day when I first met your mother." Nonsense. Nothing to worry about. She's a smart girl. She
wouldn't risk it with a man she doesn't know at all.
"Farewell, Martin, my son. You were flushed down the
toilet. Your mother got up while I was asleep." Yes, I
remember. I heard the water distinctly through the door
and saw the open floodgate in the alfalfa field.

I kissed her cheek, then her eyes and forehead. She
opened her eyes. They were full of dismay—where am
I? what is this?—dismay that yielded to a smile I'd
never seen before. She drew me to her and again we
were asleep.

Now, when I dwell on that first night, asking myself
what was so singular about it and how it was different
from other nights, in other places, with other women,
I am at a loss. I have no single clear answer. I have
many vague ones. Still, even when I put these together
I don't understand how that chance encounter could
have altered the entire course of my life. Was it mere
chance? Is this the humiliating truth? If I had gone to
the lawyer's office the first day, if I hadn't dawdled at
the directory, if I'd left the hotel later or earlier, would
I have met Barbara anyway—in some other situation?
Would someone have said (at a coffeehouse or a party),
"Meet Barbara Stahl." Would we have connected? Would
a similar relationship have evolved if we had met somewhere else? Did the events simply unfold as in the
legend of an open book in which a divine hand inscribes
the fate of all things?

Though I couldn't see them then, I am aware now of some of the forces that paved the way for that singular night; tempests that raged in other times and places, distant tempests I couldn't avoid, which swept her into my arms and swept me into her life. What I saw then was incessant rain outside, warm peace inside when for the first time in very many years I awoke in a real home. A home to live in, not just occupy. A home with books, records, a fire on the hearth, a kitchen, a bed, a woman whose clever hands touch everything, whose fingers fill a wondrous clock that ticks forever. A home like my parents' home. I felt myself wanting to live in such a home; I felt that this is what I had always wanted. I saw myself reading in the yellow velvet armchair, sitting at a table and sketching a better world. I saw Barbara bringing me coffee in a thin china cup, going back to her book, to her knitting, to the mystery of her kitchen, to our wide bed. When did I feel all this —I don't know. Other things too. Little things, but nonetheless important. At least they seemed important to me that night.

Barbara taught me not to be ashamed of my body. It's strange. I was twenty-eight when I met her. I had been with other women, slept with them, lived with them. Yet I was always careful to turn off the light when I undressed, and it had never occurred to me to walk around naked in front of a woman. I have no blemishes (except for the scar on my arm, which is really not much). Still, I was always quick to pull on my pants before I got out of bed. I don't know why. This seems childish to me now, but before I met Barbara I felt uneasy if anyone looked at my naked body even for a minute. At first I was nervous with Barbara too. But there was a special quality about her that changed this attitude, a special quality that was conveyed in a look, for we exchanged few words.

I remember whispering "Good morning" in her ear as I emerged from one of my dreams. She peered at her watch and cried out in alarm, "Good evening, you mean!" It was seven or eight o'clock. When she threw off the covers and leaped out of bed I pulled the covers over me quickly, but she tore them away again. I sat up and she sat on the bed too, her eyes glowing. She looked at my body as if it were her own, as I look at myself when I am alone. I had never before seen a gaze so open, so intimate, so simple. She studied the pores of my skin, the freckles, the thin wrinkle above my stomach. Her fingertips glided over my legs. She fingered a vein in the hollow of my groin, she inspected my toes, which I vainly tried to bury under the blanket. She looked even *there* with innocent curiosity, and I was suddenly overcome with a peace I had never known before. She had said nothing, yet I understood for the first time that there is no "good" or "not-good" body, that when someone appeals to you (God knows why) his body becomes like your own. This simple discovery shocked me. It struck me as odd that I hadn't understood this until now, as I sat naked across from Barbara. She was looking at me as though I was not there, as if she was alone with my body, and gradually I began to regard her body that way, too. It was the first time I had seen a naked woman close up. Our eyes met and we smiled. I smiled with relief, but she just smiled. Because I smiled maybe.

It wasn't just this. That night and the next day other things struck me as new and different. Small things, trivial perhaps, but I was moved by their newness. We took a shower together, for example. Standing in the tub surrounded by a striped plastic curtain, we played under the water like children, like kids in the sprinkler on a hot day. We soaped ourselves, hugged, laughed, opened our mouths to gulp the spray from the shower, licked each other like cats. Afterward, when we were dry, we didn't get dressed, but sat on the couch in the warm room across from the fire, embracing, discovering our bodies all over again.

"Want something to eat?" she asked, opening and closing her lips rapidly like a fish. I nodded vigorously. I was very hungry. "And to drink," I said, lifting an imaginary glass to my mouth. She kissed my lips and

floated (naked!) out of the room. I added logs to the
fire and blew with the bellows until the wood began to
burn—a leather bellows with shiny brass nailheads, exactly like the one that hung near the fireplace in the
living room in my parents' house. I looked around. No,
the room was not like this one. Still, something here
evoked my distant childhood. The polished wooden desk,
the rugs on the parquet floor, the alien night beyond the
window, the glistening furniture, the soft velvet up-
holstery, the fragrant cleanliness—all of these wafted
toward me from far away. I saw our servant girl in her
white apron fluttering through the room, sweeping the
furniture with a colorful feather duster. In the kitchen
I heard the clatter of dishes, something poured from a
bottle, the tinkle of glass, a refrigerator door slamming.

Who is she, I thought. What does she do? How does
she live? What is she after? What did her father do
during the war and what does he do now? What things
interest her? What does she think about? Shelves filled
with books, all in German. I'd read many of them,
mostly in Hebrew, a few in English. Rabelais, Shake-
speare, Goethe, *The Brothers Karamazov, The Trial* and
The Castle, Sartre, Pascal, *Ship of Fools*—old friends I
used to take to my room from the library, wrapped in
brown paper. We do, in fact, have mutual friends. Does
she love Stavrogin as I do? Did she cry in bed at night
over De Amicis's *The Heart*? And Copperfield and Master Baum and *The Golden Ass* and *Pere Goriot*, Salinger,
The Story of San Michele, Madame Bovary, and Saki's
little liar? All these volumes that first passed through
my hands in school, on the kibbutz, at the Technion,
these volumes that awaited me in the house on the
border in Jerusalem—they were all right there, glaring
at me in German from her bookshelves.

"What are you doing?" she called from the kitchen.
I was just going to tell her about our mutual friends
when the phone rang. Coming in from the kitchen,
naked, she snatched up a yellow robe and slipped one
arm into a sleeve as she picked up the phone. I took a
copy of *Der Spiegel* from the pile of newspapers and

magazines, the smiling face of a Wehrmacht officer adorning its cover. She said, "Yes," then paused to listen. Then, "What does *that* mean? . . . I imagine so. . . . Of course." Another long pause and then in a very chilly voice, "It's really wonderful that you like Jews." She said "Jews" in a whisper, glancing at me furtively. "Be seeing you," she said and hung up. I walked past her and she said, *"Moment,"* brushing her lips across my shoulder. I got my shirt from the bedroom and put it on. What did that mean: it's wonderful that he likes Jews? To whom was she talking? And what about? When had she had a chance to inform the world that she'd met me? What did it mean—did she call all her friends and report she'd caught a Jew? Was she taking odds about the outcome? The whole thing annoyed me.

She appeared in the doorway with a full tray and motioned for help. I placed the tray on the low table in front of the couch, while she brought in another tray with plates, long-stemmed goblets, and a chilled bottle of wine. It must have been obvious that I was disturbed, for she ran her finger over my frowning forehead. Her eyes seemed to ask, "What's the matter?"

"Bon appetit," I said, taking a slice of toast spread with fresh white cheese and topped with smoked salmon. Swallowing this in two bites, I reached for another slice as she poured the wine and clinked her goblet against mine. To this day I am particularly fond of this wine. Its name—Liebfraumilch, inscribed in Gothic letters on the colorful label—appeals to me too: "Milk of my beloved," from the Rhine River. Putting down her sandwich suddenly as if she'd just remembered something, she excused herself and went to the phone, leafing through a small book before dialing. I filled my goblet with wine.

"It's Barbara again," I heard her say in a dry voice. "You know, I don't like you," she said. "People who make a cause out of loving blacks offend me as much as those who openly hate them. I can't stand simple-minded generalizations." As she listened she shook her head disapprovingly. "But . . . but . . . ," she repeated several times, without managing to cut into her partner's monologue. "But you don't need to love them *or* hate them. How can you say you love or hate all the any-things you know—all the newsdealers, all the people who tan in the summer, all the Zen Buddhists or metal-workers? No one expects you to love a whole group of people. What? What did you say? Society consists of individuals; you're free to like them or not. Now, that was really stupid. I know . . . I know you didn't mean it. That's what bothers me. I want you to mean what you say, to think. It worries me to see signs of a familiar disease. Philo-Semites are just as revolting as anti-Semites. Of course—sure I'm angry. No. I don't want to forget your slip of the tongue, and I don't want *you* to forget it. Yes, yes. Good. OK, see you."

When she came back to the couch I kissed her eyes and forehead, I buried my head in her bosom and kissed her under the robe. When she tried to fathom the mean-ing of my sudden excitement I drank a toast in her honor. "Did you overhear me?" she asked, worried, point-ing to the phone.

"I didn't hear a thing," I replied. She laughed and poured steaming, aromatic soup thick with crab, saffron, sherry, and cream into my bowl.

"You OK," I said, tasting the soup. Acknowledging the compliment, she lowered her head modestly. She's all right, I thought. The telephone conversation had opened a door to one of her inner rooms, and I was pleased with what I saw: a healthy, open mind. First of all, she wasn't referring to me—she was talking about some party where a Jew or some Jews would be present. Who in my own circle would have spoken out against a similar generalization? Not many people would have re-sponded as sharply to "I can't bear Germans" or "Listen, here, an Arab is always an Arab." Not one of them (my-self included, I'm sorry to say) would have spotted the hypocrisy in an innocent statement like, "I love the Spanish, the Arabs, the blacks." She was so right—that kind of generalized love for a people or an ethnic group seethes with venomous bigotry. She is a real person, my sort of person, I thought, and I kissed her hand. She made a face and shrugged her shoulders as though giving up on me.

"Cuckoo," she said.

"I like you, Miss Barbara," I said to her in Hebrew and we went back to eating that marvelous soup (I had a twinge of disappointment when I found an empty can of French crab soup in the kitchen the next day). After the soup, an omelet cooked in butter with sliced white mushrooms, accompanied by a salad of hearts of lettuce with a dressing of oil, lemon, and mustard, and a bottle of red Beaujolais; then fruit and coffee. We were hungry, we left our platters clean.

These were the things, perhaps trivial, perhaps not, which made that night with Barbara so special—I remember it even now with nostalgia. The meal, the books, the records (while we ate we heard the twelve *balletti* of Gastoldi), the magazines piled beside the chair, the phone conversation, which had transformed her from just any woman to a person, the fire, the fragrance of home, the infinite bed to which we returned in utter detachment from the world.

A night, a day, with no hours. We slept in snatches, waking to each other's touch, searching for ourselves in darkness and in light and found each other alike and other, close and discrete. I invaded her dreams and she was with me in a vineyard where I had never been. Dream and reality begin melting into each other and I'm not sure if we really did those things that recur in my reveries. Though it seemed that we wouldn't be able to move a muscle, after a bit of sleep we returned to those same delights, which shifted constantly and assumed new forms. As day dawned we stood at the window watching the sky begin to pale, the black trees, the damp, glistening street. She stood before me naked, my lips on her neck, mumbling words that were new to me. It all seemed wondrous. I remember asking myself over and over, How can it be? How could such a thing grow from a chance encounter?

We got a blanket and fell asleep on the couch in front

of the fire. When we awoke many hours later it was only ten o'clock, and I no longer marveled at anything. It seemed natural for me to be lying at Barbara's side as she whispered sweet nothings in my ear—intimacies she probably wouldn't have uttered if she knew I understood almost every word. It seemed as if we had known each other a long time, as if we had lived in this apartment in Frankfurt, my native city, many months, even years. The truth was hard to believe.

At breakfast—the kind of breakfast which seems unique to Frankfurt—as we drank coffee from delicate cups, I couldn't believe that I was Uri Lam, of this city, that Barbara's father was, possibly, the very man who had sent my father, mother, sister, and brother to . . . there. I couldn't believe they were no longer alive, that I had come back as their sole heir to demand reparations. For a moment I had the feeling that this was our usual pattern, that Barbara and I would soon get dressed, that she would go to work and I would be off to Brumberg-Avishai-Landau to deface the landscape with more housing developments.

But after breakfast we didn't get dressed. On the way to the bathroom I drew her onto the big bed. Again, "Barbara, Barbara," and "Uri, you lunatic. Beast, savage! I'll die. I can't—no more. I'm dying . . ." Nothing like this had ever happened to me. I hardly knew myself. I asked the same question over and over, arriving at the same answer—I'm not pretending. I want to, I really do. Good, great, marvelous . . . and more and more until we die.

Again we slept, again we showered, again we ate and drank, heard Bach and—back to bed. I remember in one of our awakenings, as we lay in bed like children tired of playing in the tent under the blanket, her beaming eyes all but convinced me to confess that I could speak German. I wanted to talk to her. Our hands, lips, eyes having whispered everything, it was now time to talk and to say the little things that needed to be said. "Barbara," I began, but she, apparently suspecting me of other intentions, ran to the bathroom and locked the door behind her, laughing.

"*Du bist cuckoo,*" she called through the door over the pitter-patter of the shower.

I dressed and went to the other room to browse among her books. A letter on her desk from the editor of a literary journal informed Miss Stahl that her three poems would appear in the Christmas issue. So, she writes poetry. Another door was opened. Over the desk hung a picture of a man no longer young. At first I just glanced at it, but on closer examination I noticed something odd about this yellowing photograph with crooked edges. It had been trimmed with a razor, leaving only the man's face, to his chin. He gazed out with eyes that were pale and watery. In the original photograph the man was no doubt in uniform. Whoever cropped the photo threw the hat in the trash and maybe along with it a military decoration that had adorned his neck. Who was this man? Her father? Did he serve in the army or in the Gestapo? Probably dead. If he was alive she'd hang a more recent photograph. No doubt this was one of the few remaining pictures of him. He must have been close to her; she must have loved him if she took the trouble to purge him of those signs and put him up over her desk. Hearing footsteps I got up quickly and picked out a book at random: a German-English dictionary.

"What are you looking for?" Barbara asked in German. She was wearing pants and a large white sailor sweater; her hair was parted, like a schoolgirl's. I leafed through the dictionary until I found the word I pretended to be looking for.

"*Sprechen,* Barbara. *Sprechen.* I vant *sprechen mit* you," I said. She took the dictionary from me and leafed through it.

"Me too," she said. "Iy conversayshun you. *Nu, ja. Conversatzion*—conversayshun." Her eyes lit up. "*Moment,*" she said, pointing to her head to show she had an idea. Hunting in her little book, she picked up the phone and dialed. She placed a finger on my lips to silence me. "Hello, Barbara speaking. Barbara Stahl. Yes, yes. It's me. How are you? . . . Thanks . . . yes, that's right. In the fall. I meant to call you . . . What? I wanted to see you. To hear what you're doing . . . Fine. Listen, Herman, I have a friend here. Can you have dinner with us? Yes. Today, definitely. Let's say at eight. All right? Very good. See you then."

"*Was ist das?*" I asked menacingly as I circled her throat with my fingers. She held her hands before me in a pleading gesture. When I released her she leafed through the dictionary and, finding her word, declared triumphantly, "Translator!" She had invited a translator to dinner. Absurd!

16 | *simultaneous translation*

What utter madness, trying to woo a woman through a translator—who could imagine anything so ridiculous? Is there any way out of it, I wondered. Should I tell her the truth now, before it's too late?

I was picturing the shock on her face if I were to say, in fluent German, "Can I help you set the table, my love?" or "You won't be angry with me, Barbara, if I confess I understand German?" I'd tell her why I came to Frankfurt and then I'd say, "Try to understand my natural revulsion against that bloodstained tool . . ." Or maybe, "Besides, Barbara, I didn't want to woo you with words. I prefer to avoid the power of verbal persuasion." Even as we embraced, my head on her shoulder, her head on mine, and she whispered in my ear, "It's exasperating, Uri, that we can't talk to each other," I withheld the truth. If I let on that I speak German, I thought, dinner with the translator becomes superfluous and we are in an awkward spot. Might as well keep the game going one more night. Besides, the situation promised to be amusing. I would understand them without their knowing it: the thrill of peeking through a keyhole.

At eight on the dot the translator appeared, with flowers and a bottle of wine. From the moment he took off his rubbers in the foyer, hung his coat carefully on a peg, shook the rain from his hat, and stopped at the mirror to comb his well-combed hair, I disliked him. He was neat and well groomed to the point of unpleasantness, his expensive suit spotless and meticulously pressed, a three-pointed handkerchief tucked elegantly in his pocket, his face tightly buttoned and expressionless. He looked as if he'd just stepped out of a fashion ad. When he tried to smile his thin lips contorted nervously. I shook his well-tended hand, as Barbara introduced us and then led the way to the living room.

The first sentences they exchanged weren't much of a clue to the nature of their relationship. He said he was about to complete his work at the university, that he was still working part time as a guide to government guests. She said she was doing some writing and the rest of her work was going along about the same as usual—no hint as to just what that work was. In response to his mumbled question she placed her hand on his shoulder and said, "Now really, Herman." From the looks he stole when he thought she wasn't looking, from his tone when he said, "I hope everything's OK, Barbara," it was easy to surmise how he felt about her.

I saw them sitting on the couch (no, no, not the couch!). I saw them in a café, a year ago, on a rainy day—that's better. She snuffs out a cigarette in the dregs of her cocoa. He clenches his teeth, his face pale and tense in anticipation of the crucial dialogue. "Look, Barbara. You know very well what I'm thinking . . . that is, how I really feel about you. You understand. This lack of . . . lack of certainty. You know what I mean. It's hard for me to . . . It's foolish, I know, but I'd like to know where we stand. Yes, where do we stand? That's what I want to know." And she says, "The rain won't stop today. We're in for a real flood." He stares out the window and replies, "Yes. It's raining." He looks at her again, his head drooping. Finally, she places her hand on his trembling arm, maybe even lifts his chin with her finger and says, "Herman, Herman. Look at me. Yes, like that. Now really, Herman. Why do you have to ask such difficult questions? If I knew the answer there would be no need for questions. I simply don't know, I really don't. I . . . I like you, Herman. And you know that I respect you, but I don't know. That means I don't feel it. Do you understand? I don't . . . How shall I say it? Why can't we remain friends—without complications, the way it's always been?" "I understand," he responds, his misery apparent in his face, and begins to clench his teeth again. "Perhaps it's better this way," he sighs, grimly decisive, and gets up. "Shall we go?" he says without looking at her. She tries to soothe him, begs him not to be so melodramatic, but he is silent, enclosed in the heavy armor of wounded self-esteem, having already decided never to see her again and believing that one day she would regret this dialogue. He would become a senior official in the government, maybe even an ambassador—why not? Ambassador to Paris, London, or Washington, and she'd be sorry then, but it would be too late. He would place his hand on her shoulder and say, "Why not, Barbara, why can't we just remain . . . friends?"

Maybe it wasn't like that at all, I thought. Perhaps the crucial conversation still hasn't occurred and he remains hopeful. Otherwise why would he have accepted this last-minute invitation to be part of a threesome? Apparently they are just friends. How old is he? A year or two older than she is, I guessed. He may have tried to tell her everything without quite daring. He may have tried to say how he felt about her (there's no doubt that he still feels it). You only need to see him lower his eyes when they meet hers to understand everything. He'd never raise his voice or lose his self-control. He does as he's told without asking questions. Chronic spiritual constipation—and not just the spirit: I'll bet he hasn't been to the toilet in two weeks, that this natural function inspires him with panic.

"Israel," I heard Barbara say, explaining that I was the friend of friends who visited Israel, that since I didn't speak German and she knew no other language except for a smattering of English, we'd need his help to carry on a conversation. He replied that he would be very glad to help out.

This is getting complicated, I thought. Now we have to pretend to be casual friends. Why didn't she tell him the truth? Naturally, that would be impossible. "Herman, this fellow was stuck in a broken elevator with me, and he's been in bed with me ever since. Now we'd like to talk too. Ask him if he likes me." Clearly, she couldn't say anything like this. He'd have a fit and shut himself in the toilet for two days. We'd have to play friends. I had no choice—I'd just have to stick to general information. That might be what she wants anyway, I reflected. She knows how much I like her, how much I like being with her. Is it true, dear Barbara, that you sense how happy I am with you? All she needs to find out is what I do, who I am, what I'm after. And these, more or less, are the same questions I want to ask her.

When we sat down to eat, Barbara asked for my impressions of Frankfurt. (Before Herman arrived we had set the table together and for a moment, taking places at opposite ends of the table, we had assumed the role of a couple engaged in polite chitchat. I had said, "*Bella-bella-bella* Barbara." She had replied, "Uri, *pit-pit-pit*.") Herman quickly translated her question. I answered that Frankfurt had a somewhat depressing effect on me, though I had found a few surprising bright spots. Again Herman translated rapidly, precisely, and impassively.

"For example?" Barbara asked.

"For example?" Herman asked in English.

"For example: you," I said. "You, for example, please me very much."

"He says that you please him," Herman said uneasily.

Barbara smiled. "Tell him, please," she said, "that he doesn't have to be so polite."

"She says," Herman repeated with obvious relish, "that you need not bestow your compliments so lavishly."

"But it's the truth," I said. "Tell her that I like her very much. Doesn't that make sense?"

"Absolutely," he said. "It makes absolute sense. To me, that is. It's the lady who doubts the sincerity of your impulsive declaration."

"Is that so?" I asked, lifting a spoonful of soup to my mouth.

"What are you discussing?" Barbara asked, looking from me to Herman and from Herman to me.

"The gentleman insists on repeating his original statement," he said grimacing. "He insists that he really likes you very much, and he wants to know if that seems illogical to me."

"And what did you say, Herman?" she asked coyly.

"I said it's quite logical to me, but I doubt if you regard such declarations seriously."

"Absolutely," she said. "I'm pleased that he's pleased. Is the soup good?"

"The lady would like to know if the soup is good," he translated.

"Very good," I said, looking into her eyes. She gave me a trace of a wink. Herman's eyes were fixed on the soup bowl. After a moment of silence during which only the clatter of spoons in bowls was heard over the Bach, I asked her eyes what was the matter with our translator. Her eyes answered, It's all right, there's nothing to worry about. I touched her leg under the table, she brushed her bare foot against my leg.

"*Gut?*" she asked with the innocence of an angel.

"Very *gut*," I said pushing my empty bowl aside.

"Tell him please," Barbara said hastily, "that I had a letter from my friends in Italy and they asked me to thank him for his marvelous hospitality and all the attention he gave them in Jerusalem." She winked ever so slightly in my direction.

Without looking at me Herman translated the sentence, saying something like "reception" instead of "hospitality."

"How *are* Freddi and Elsa?" I asked. "When will they be back in Frankfurt?"

"He asks when they will be back in Frankfurt," Herman said. "Do you mean Elsa Kramer?" he asked.

"No, no," she said. "Another Elsa—you don't know her. They'll be back in two weeks. Now, please excuse me for a moment," she said, getting up to collect the dishes. Herman stood up quickly. "Sit down," she said. "I'll be right back"—but Herman remained on his feet until she left the table. When I reached for a cigarette he immediately produced his gold lighter and offered me a light. His fingers were thin and delicate. He swept a crumb of bread from the cloth and brushed it into the ashtray, then asked a few polite questions about the situation in the Middle East without bothering to listen to my answers. When he spoke he avoided looking at me. When he listened, or pretended to listen, his eyes strayed all over the table. I asked him how long he had known Barbara and he said two years.

"Good friends?" I asked.

His lower lip trembled. He shook his head and said, "Acquaintances."

"A good-looking woman," I said, blowing smoke rings.

"Yes," he said, plucking a white thread off the table-cloth.

"I'll tell you a secret," I said, lowering my voice and motioning him closer. He moved his head a bit in my direction, his fingers toying with the thread in small, rapid movements. "It seems to me," I whispered, "that I'm in love with her."

"Oh!" he said drawing back in alarm. Then more soberly, clutching at straws, "You're joking."

"I'm not joking," I said, as earnestly as I could.

"But you hardly know her," he said.

"Right," I said. "I don't know her, I haven't talked with her. We have no common language. Still, I think I'm in love with her. It may be childish, but my instincts seldom mislead me. Even without talking to her, I sense that she is a clever woman, intelligent and unique. Am I mistaken?"

He didn't know how to answer.

"A very beautiful woman," I said, puffing smoke and following its trail with my eyes. "And you . . . aren't you in love with her?"

His lower lip trembled again. He mumbled something but Barbara appeared in time to rescue him. Again he stood up and remained standing until Barbara was seated.

"What were you talking about?" Barbara asked as she reached for the dishes.

"About you," he said with a guarded look.

"And what did you tell him?" she asked playfully.

"I told him nothing," Herman said in a subdued voice. "I only listened."

"Is that so?" she asked, marveling, and looked into my eyes. "What did he say?"

"He said you are beautiful," Herman answered with averted eyes.

"Yes?" she said, handing me a dish.

"Yes. He said you are clever and intelligent. He said you are unique," Herman answered. I nodded and she covered her mouth with her hand to hide her smile.

"And when did he find all this out? We haven't talked at all," she asked.

"That's just what I want to know," he burst out with a tinge of bitterness.

"Didn't you ask?" she asked handing him his dish and then serving herself from the brown earthen pot.

"The lady would like to know," Herman repeated in English, "how you discovered that she's clever, intelligent, and so on. You are not angry that I told her? After all, I am here as a translator."

"Of course, of course," I quickly reassured him, though his excuse was brimming with irony. "It's perfectly all right. Tell her it's a matter of instinct."

"Your guest claims he can tell instinctively," Herman reported with open mockery. I was tempted to kick him.

"You told her that I like her?" I asked.

"Yes, I told her that," he said.

"Please be so kind as to tell her I love her," I asked politely.

He raised the fork to his little mouth and remained silent. We both stared at him: she with curiosity, I with a wicked smile.

"Hmmm . . . beef stroganoff," Herman said. "Very tasty."

"And . . . ?" she said searching his eyes.

"And what?" he asked, playing dumb.

"What did he say?" she asked.

"Oh, him? He said that . . . that he is in love with you, or something like that," Herman said skeptically. I confirmed his words with a nod and tried to touch her leg, but I couldn't find it. A faint blush spread from her cheeks to her eyes, which sparkled with either contentment or ridicule.

"He's joking," she declared.

"The lady also says you are joking," Herman quickly complied.

"I don't understand it," I said. "What makes you think I'm joking? Barbara's a beautiful woman, though not by ordinary standards. Her beauty unfolds slowly. I love her eyes. They are wise and reflect her every mood even when she doesn't say a word. I love her smooth hair, tied back when she gets out of the shower. I love her full, round body. She is a woman, a real woman. And a human being."

He stared at me with large appalled eyes, his mouth slightly ajar in disbelief. For a moment it seemed to me that I had taken the words from his mouth, that it was I who was translating his thoughts.

"And you want me to translate *that*?" he asked in English.

"Absolutely," I said. "Absolutely."

"What? What did he say?" Barbara asked uneasily.

He hesitated a moment, shifting his gaze from me to Barbara and back to me again. He sought the ghost of a twinkle in my eyes, but finding innocence, a deliberate show of innocence, he began to translate. An entertaining play. At first the translation was fluent and in the third person. Suddenly, without realizing it, he shifted to the first person and began to stutter. Instead of "He says he loves your eyes," he said, "I love your eyes." Only when he noticed a quizzical look on her face did he quickly add, "So he said." When he got to her smooth hair he suddenly forgot about me, and the words that tumbled from his mouth were not all mine. The sentence about the moods reflected in her eyes was amended to include a reference to eyes sometimes suffused with gentle sadness—when listening to music or watching the rain through the window. I had noticed just such a look in her eyes toward morning, when we stood naked at the window. He left out the part about the shower, but he did say that her lips were vibrant even when they said nothing. As she heard Cyrano's mounting emotion she continued gazing into my eyes. Herman told her other things I'd never said and suddenly, odd as this may sound, I saw in him distinct proof of the existence of "another Germany."

Here before you is an average citizen, I thought, a young official who does as he is told. Having been asked to translate, he translates. It is irrelevant that every sentence he emits is a scourge and torment to his heart. Everyone must perform the task assigned to him: *Ordnung must zein*! To hell with it; if I were in his place I'd go crazy! Imagine translating someone else's words of love when you love her yourself! I'd throw the table at him, soup and all, smash the dishes, and make short shrift of this ugly game. But not Herman. Herman was an experienced man who did as he was told without questions. I thought he'd go on indefinitely in this fashion, but at last something snapped. He began to reject his role, stopped translating mechanically, and began to speak for himself. If such a thing could happen to Herman, my stereotype of the average functionary, of a small cog in the wheel, then there was hope for this whole nation.

"I love your round female body . . ." Herman concluded his great confession and held his breath.

"Herman!" Barbara cried in dismay.

"That's what he said," Herman quickly explained. "He said he loves your round body."

"Please tell him that I'm on a diet," she said. "Tell him that in the summer I'm not so fat."

I waited for Herman to finish translating before protesting. "She's not fat," I told him. "Her body is round and that's how I like it. She should give up her diet immediately. It wouldn't hurt for her to pick up two or three pounds. In the behind." When Herman conveyed my words, Barbara burst into ringing laughter. Herman didn't laugh, but I noticed a slight twitch in his lips.

"Tell her," I said, "that I refuse to accept an esthetic code dictated by fashion photographers and homosexual designers. Their beautiful women, those who rule the magazine covers and dominate the film scene—all those women look more like boys. They're flat-chested and narrow-hipped. Tell her I admire a woman who is round and curvy, with an ass like a ripe peach, hips soft and full, breasts one can drown in. Tell her a woman should look like a woman and be proud of it. Renoir's fat women mean more to me than Audrey Hepburn and. all those other skeletons. Tell Barbara she ought to be proud of her body."

Herman looked miserable. He didn't know where to begin or how to translate words he himself had never dared to utter. He conveyed the spirit of my words but avoided the details. The sentence about homosexual fashion designers came out in a jumble; her ass became buttocks and the other parts of her body were described like the anatomical sections of a corpse. Barbara shook her head at me in mild rebuke, attempting to rescue Herman.

"No need to translate word for word," she said. "I get the idea."

"Thank you," he said with obvious relief.

"Did you tell her I like an ass to be like two peaches?" I asked.

"He says you ought to be proud of your beautiful body," he reported.

"Ask how long he plans to stay in Frankfurt." Barbara offered, trying to change the subject.

I turned to Herman and waited for him to translate. I told him I wasn't sure, it would depend on many things. What sort of things, she wanted to know. My eyes said it would depend on her; my lips said it would depend on matters beyond my control. "If all goes well, I'll conclude my affairs in Germany in two or three weeks," I said. Barbara wanted to know the nature of my affairs.

Herman raised his eyebrows; her questions violated the rules of polite dinner conversation. So what? The situation must already be clear to him, I thought. Only an idiot would fail to put two and two together—and he's no idiot. The relations between us must be obvious. If I were actually a guest, merely a friend of friends, as she said when we were introduced, I wouldn't have greeted him at the door. I would have waited in the living room. He surely must have noticed a look, a smile, a wink. I poured the wine, as if I were the host. And what could be the meaning of: "I love her smooth hair, tied back when she comes out of the shower"? Everything must be clear to him. And why should it matter? What's the difference if he knows or not? He might as well!

He was repeating her question. What sort of business keeps me in Germany? What dealings do I have here? Very well, folks, I've come to collect reparations. Hell . . . that had all but left my mind! I came to demand reparations for loss of property (Wagner-Gasse 9), loss of freedom (transport number thus-and-so), orphanhood (Dr. Lampel and his wife, telephone number 62582), and similarly familiar items. When I met Barbara in the elevator I was on the way to the lawyer who is handling . . . No. That can wait. I don't need an intermediary to tell her the truth. He might decide to translate freely and I won't be in a position to correct his version. Too dangerous. Better invent something.

I came, I could tell her, to consult German scientists on the possibilities of perfecting an Israeli invention and exploiting it commercially—an invention, I said, of a young scientist from the Weizmann Institute who developed a method for exploiting the natural gases emitted by the human body and transforming them into a source of energy for daily use. Shocking? No. Did you know, for example, that in the course of twenty-four hours the average man nourished on an ordinary diet produces gases with the power to bring 31 gallons of water to the boiling point? By supplementing lunch with 2 ounces of canned kidney beans a much higher output can be achieved. One obstacle remains before this new source of energy can be exploited: the foul odor of the product. It's possible that German scientists, having acquired an international reputation in related areas, can successfully filter the smell or mask the product by introducing petro-chemical elements . . .

Despite its comic possibilities, I decided to forgo this tale about the ingenious invention at the Weizmann Institute and pulled something else out of my sleeve: the documentary material I was supposedly collecting as background for a fictionalized film on sex life in Germany. The aim of the film, I told Herman, was to establish sex hangups as the source of the characteristic violence of German males.

Even before Herman finished translating I began to elaborate on this theory, which seemed like a potentially sensational subject for some women's magazine. The white wine I'd been drinking throughout the meal (Herman, who probably had digestive difficulties, refused more than one glass) seemed to have gone to my head and I was no longer responsible for my words. I wasn't drunk, but I felt free of all restraint. I almost began to speak German.

The average German male, I argued, suffers from spiritual and physical constipation, the result of a rigorously Puritan education. This form of constipation, which the Germans rationalize as social grace, finds a sublimated outlet in dark reserves of physical force. Uniforms become a fetish, the reign of order approaches the level of sadism. I invoked evidence and support from Freud and Adler, taking pleasure in Herman's mounting confusion and the deep dismay in Barbara's eyes. I nudged her foot under the table several times, a signal for her to ignore Herman's words, but the dismay did not fade from her eyes. (Later, when we discussed this dinner, she told me it wasn't the theory that shocked her, but my sadistic abuse of poor Herman. The poor jerk was taking me at my word.)

Luckily, Barbara changed the subject before the situation became intolerable. We began to talk about the weather, the European Common Market, manned flights to the moon, De Sica's latest film. Toward the end of the evening, through direct questions as well as devious ones, I did succeed in learning some things about Barbara. It turned out she wasn't a secretary, as I had thought in the elevator, but a student at the university who wrote criticism and some poetry. She was from Düsseldorf, where her parents still lived. Her father manufactured optical equipment (submarine periscopes?), and her brother was studying mechanical engineering in Berlin. Having left home a year before, she was enjoying her independence.

Near midnight, when the silences were growing more frequent, Herman checked his watch and got up to go. He apologized, saying he had to get an early start the next day and hoped Barbara wouldn't be angry if he left so early. Dinner was magnificent, he continued, and he was very glad to have met me. Could he drop me at my hotel, he asked slyly. No, I'll stay a little longer, I retorted. As we shook hands he said again that it was very pleasant and promised to call soon.

I didn't see him to the door. Leaning my head back against the sofa I closed my eyes. I could hear him putting on his coat and rubbers, then the sound of their whispering. The outside door opened, there were footsteps on the stairs, the door closed. Now I'll tell her I speak German, I thought. I knew she was near me. I opened my eyes and shouted "Boo!" She wasn't frightened. She lay down beside me, her head on my shoulder, tapped my forehead and said, "Cuckoo."

17 | *first symptoms*

I was sitting on a tall chair near the ceiling in a room filled with pink and black feathers, while down below, on ordinary chairs, members of the collective reviewed my application for membership. One guy whose face I had never seen took off his stiff straw hat and placed it on his heart, explaining in German why a man who uses reparations money to acquire a whorehouse in Frankfurt rather than contribute it to the collective should be denied membership. Barbara, sitting with the women and knitting an endless sleeve, rose to my defense, only to be silenced by cries of "Get out! *Raus,* Frau Kraus!*"* Max, pale with rage, pounded the table with his right hand, which was in a cast; it snapped at the elbow and fell to the ground, shattered. I stood up on my tall chair and began to soar through the room over everybody's heads. They watched me with envy and respect. I steered toward an open window and found myself resting at the foot of an apple tree, gazing in terror at my sister, Miri, who had slipped from a high branch and was falling toward me, her thin, piercing shriek like a stuck car horn. When I got up to catch her I awoke in Barbara's big bed.

How long have I been here, I asked myself. Is it really only two days since I met Barbara in the elevator? Wasn't it two months ago or a year? I have always been here, and she has always slept at my side, breathing gently, her cheek pressed against her arm, her legs folded under. Herman is gone. Booo! Cuck-oo! The lights go off, one by one; we shed our clothes on the way to the bedroom. I left my shirt there on the table, I remember that. Afterward, under the covers, good night. I kiss her closed eyes. She turns her back to me with a relaxed sigh. I fold my knees under hers, wrap my arm around her, and suddenly, on the brink of sleep, one of her breaths becomes a hollow moan, her warm body clings to my skin, and again, as in the morning, like yesterday only different, we are drifting on tranquil waters toward the falls.

"My own sweet Barbara," I whispered in German. "Are you sleeping?" I listened tensely, my jaws tightly clenched. Her breathing was even and undisturbed. "Barbara, my love," I whispered into her neck in German again. "Wake up, my darling. I want to talk to you. Wake up, my sweet. I can't sleep." She sighed self-indulgently, straightened her legs, and turned over on her back. "I am speaking German, Barbara," I said somewhat louder. "I know German. Barbara, wake up."

"*Was?*" she said suddenly; then, in a voice filled with suspicion, "Uri?"

Even before I could answer yes, she pushed me aside and switched on the lamp. Her eyes were wide open.

"Was that you speaking German?" she asked. "Or was I dreaming?"

"You weren't dreaming," I said. "I spoke to you in German."

She sat up, in shock. "You . . . ," she began and then fell silent. "It can't be true. What does it mean? You . . ."

I tried to comfort her. I began to talk. She wouldn't believe that the stammering, in German, was really coming from my mouth. She shook her head from side to side in agitation, which gave way to deep injury. Her eyebrows were knit in anger. What was the meaning of it? How could I do such a thing to her? Why did I deceive her? Why this pretense? What sort of ugly game was I playing? Why didn't I say right off that I speak German? How could I do anything so vile? Why? Why? What was the point of this ghastly game?

I made no attempt to interrupt. She was consumed with rage. I tried to put my arm around her, but she pushed me away with disdain. I was waiting for the torrent of questions and charges to exhaust itself. I knew that in the end she would ask a question and pause for an answer. When this finally happened, I asked her to be patient and listen. In German that was halting at first but improved as I went on, I tried to explain my instinctive recoil from the language, realizing at once that I wouldn't succeed without revealing the whole truth to her—a truth which I myself had refused to hear.

I lit a cigarette that tasted as bitter as the words in my mouth. It was four in the morning.

"I see I have no choice, Barbara," I said. "I must begin at the beginning. I was born here. My parents were forced to leave Frankfurt when the war broke out. They are no longer. . . . What I mean is that I'm the only one left. But I don't want to talk about that. Not yet."

I didn't want to talk, still the words flowed. It was the first time I'd heard them spoken aloud. I listened to myself in a detached way, as if I were uninvolved. The words seemed distant and strange in German. I tried to avoid anything specific, but the terrible details slipped out in fragments, by implication, in jumbled phrases that had no relation to lack of skill with the language.

She listened, her eyes wide with wonder, and at various points when I searched for a simple word to express something awful, she turned away, her cigarette dripping ashes on the sheet. I remember clearly how much I appreciated her silence, how grateful I was that she didn't put her arm around me to show she understood. She didn't even look at me. Her eyes were distant—a kindness I will never forget. Again I explained to her my natural revulsion for the language that had been a tool for the execution of those deeds; she nodded once or twice in agreement. I went over the thoughts that had been in my mind when the elevator got stuck. I strayed from the subject of the broken elevator to doubts about collecting reparations; a faint "yes" escaped her lips. I fell silent. She handed me a cigarette and left the lighter beside me. I wanted to kiss her for not handing me a lighted cigarette, for her tact in avoiding the conventional gestures of sympathy and pity. Even at the beginning of the conversation, when the sentence about my sister—naked, with her hair cropped—had burst from my lips, she reached down and pulled up the sheet to cover her nakedness.

The silence began to oppress me. I drifted back to the elevator and the silence there. "That wasn't the only reason I pretended not to know German," I said. "I was glad we had no common language. I wanted you as a woman. I didn't know then what I know now; still, I wanted you. I heard the rustle of your stockings in the darkness and remembered the shape of your legs from my furtive glance when you bent down to pick up the papers. Your playful eyes, the smell of your hair . . . everything about you attracted me. I wanted it to happen without intellectual advances, without all the clever maneuvers."

She wrinkled her brow and looked at me with mild dismay. I tried to explain myself but I felt I was making excuses. "Those calculated moves, the phrases that repeat themselves, seem like a form of payment, which I find revolting. Displaying your soul at the bedroom door is enough to ruin one's finest dreams. I wanted it to happen just as it happened with us. Without talk, without coaxing, without the endless repetition of what has already been said."

"Silly," she said, ruffling my hair and smiling ever so slightly. "So what if the things we say have already been said?"

"It's important," I insisted.

"Everything has already been said," she continued. "Still, every word, every combination of words, has its moment of truth. Even the most tedious clichés can become ultimate truth. Sure we repeat ourselves. We're free and extravagant with grand words like 'love,' 'death,' 'loneliness,' 'friendship.' Only rarely, very rarely, do we sense their true significance. Everything repeats itself. Even a silent passion, which seems so pure to you, repeats itself. Everybody uses the same gestures to express feeling—yet these gestures become special and unique with every new combination of two."

I kissed her on both eyes, then on her mouth. She clung to me with her entire body, the laughter rattling in her throat.

"What?" I asked. "What, dear Barbara, is so funny?"

She threw her head back and laughed heartily. "Herman," she said, amid peals of laughter. "Herman," she repeated, rolling on the bed. I tried to imagine Herman naked, lying in bed between us and translating our whispered passion. His body was white and smooth; for some reason I couldn't get his long, striped underwear or his socks to come off. Ask her if she's happy. He asks if you are happy. Tell him I am happy. Yes, yes, it is marvelous. *Er sagt ja, ja, das ist wunderbar gut.* More. Tell him, more, more. She says more, more. I smiled a depraved smile.

"You are an actor," Barbara said. "Part actor and part louse. I never suspected you understood German. That simultaneous translation of Herman's! How could you bear to wait for him to translate? You understood everything. Your theory about the sources of German violence, that nonsense about sexual sublimation. . . . You were teasing him and you enjoyed every minute of it. 'Tell her I love her.' 'Tell her she pleases me.' 'Tell her I love her full body.' You could see he was perplexed."

"Those weren't lies," I protested. "I really do love you, Barbara. You really do please me."

"Come on, now. You don't have to pretend," she scolded.

"I'm *not* pretending," I argued fervently. "I really do— at least I'm almost certain I do. I've never had such a feeling before, and of course you're not the first woman in my life. I don't know what it is if it isn't love. I know this is different from ordinary passion. Clearly that's involved too, but it's not just that. Maybe at first it was, but now it's something entirely different. Don't interrupt me. I know what I'm saying. I love your body and it's good to be here with you in bed. (Herman, tell her it's good to be here in bed with her), but it's not just that. You're a real human being. Don't ask me how I know. It was enough to hear your telephone conversation and a sentence or two to Herman, to take a tour of your books and the records you love, your silence when I told you about my past. That's enough. Don't try to confuse me."

"It's you who confuses me," she said, burying her face in my neck. "You could be telling the truth. I believe you, I want to believe you. I have no reason to doubt you, even though you're a great actor. I don't want you to feel obliged to say all that. Do you understand? I wanted to be with you even before you said those wild things. When you told them to Herman, I was convinced you were kidding. You had the smile of a satyr in your eyes. If you were to say nothing, if you were to withdraw your impulsive declaration, we'd still be together. If you want to, that is. Now hush. As for me, let me say this: I'm certainly not indifferent to you. I'm not sure I can say much more. But I have the impression that you're OK. So far, so good. But who knows what lurks behind those eyes? And stop flashing those enchanting smiles at me! But I'm talking too seriously and too much; my mouth is dry. Want some coffee?"

We sat in the kitchen until dawn. The ashtray was filled with butts and the kettle had whistled three times. Drinking from large mugs, we held hands across the table, listened to each other, and talked endlessly. This morning conversation had all the magic of a first encounter. After two days of starvation and thirst, we indulged in this reckless orgy, wanting to know everything at once and lacking the patience to follow any thought to its end. It was a wild marathon, a lightning tour of our inner rooms. No, it was more like a polite first visit, each receiving the other in our living rooms. Two creatures discovering each other in a desert— utterly desolate until that very moment, studying each other curiously. We extended long, cautious feelers. Delighted to meet you. Tea or coffee? Bach or Tchaikovsky? Paul Klee, Cranach, or Jackson Pollack? East or West? A quick tour of the soul. For now, we showed only the most respectable pictures, exchanged keys only to our living rooms. We weren't ready to entrust each other with secret keys to inner rooms, to the locked private drawer, the most guarded hiding places. We were content with a brief guided tour, leading each other by the hand. What lurks behind that door? Hesitation, hope,

depression. What's hidden in that heavy chest? What do
you keep in the attic? What are you harboring in that
dark cellar? Turn on the light. I let you peek in my
cellar, I want to peek in yours. Just for a minute. Yes,
it's all right. Later. We'll get to it, we'll come back to this
cellar. Let's go on. You know your world is very much
like mine, yet different—totally different. I look deep
into you and see myself there, and you, and the world
that belongs to the two of us. I want to see more. I want
to know more, more, more. Talk to me, keep on talking.
I listen, even to things you don't say. We don't agree
about everything, thank goodness. But at least we have
a common language. We'll find each other in the maze.
Gradually, patiently, lovingly, we will find each other.

Pale sky filled the windows. The rain had stopped.
Barbara's eyes were red and tired. We went back to bed
and fell asleep, whispering like children in camp the
first night away from home.

I woke up at 2:30. The bed was empty. I called
Barbara's name but there was no answer. The apartment
was heavy with silence. I found a note in the bathroom,
stuck in the mirror over the sink: "Good morning, darling. I went out to do some errands. Be back soon." Suddenly I felt a burning sensation. As soon as I began to
urinate I knew something was not right. My heart filled
with terror. There it was: an alarming discharge, a
single, loathsome yellow drop, a burning sensation in
the urinary tract. Panic-stricken, I examined myself
carefully. It's not possible, I told myself, how could it
happen? Yet the symptoms were clear—a discharge and
a burning sensation. There could be no doubt—venereal
disease. As in all the books . . . the nightmare, the
haunting fear that wells up from every strange bed is
now fulfilled. Here it is in my hand. Still, maybe it's
just an innocuous discharge, a remnant of passion. No,
that's not it, the spot is distinctly yellow. A foul spot.
But how could it be? I didn't find her on the street. A
respectable office building. She isn't that sort. She
doesn't look it. Impossible. But come to think of it, why
not? It certainly is possible. That doesn't mean she's

promiscuous. It occurs in the best families. What's the difference? It can happen to anyone. Without knowing it, she could be carrying a communicable disease—it's hard to detect in a woman. He may not be aware of it either. He may have discovered it two or three days later, even a week later. He may have not had the nerve to call and tell her. Wait a minute! It's impossible. When did I meet her? Wednesday. Today is Friday. Two days in all. It takes a week or ten days for symptoms to appear. Maria Cristina! Oh, my God, Maria Cristina, the shabby whore from Genoa. That's it. Her infection has traveled with me from Genoa to Milan, from Milan to Frankfurt, and now everything is lost. Barbara, I have infected Barbara. What shall I do? Run away! Clear out fast before she gets back.

I collected my clothes and washed quickly. I was on my way out the door when I stopped and sank into an armchair. Stop, I said to myself. Not another escape. My whole life has been a series of escapes. I ran from Frankfurt, I ran from the village when I broke Aunt Anna's clay pitcher, I ran away from school to the war, from the kibbutz to the Technion. I ran from my name, my past—myself. Whenever it's time to confront myself and make a decision, I run away. Yesterday I ran from the reparations problem, today I want to run away from Barbara. I've got to drop this tactic and begin to assume responsibility like a mature person. I'll wait for her here, I won't stir from this spot; and when she gets back I'll tell her, "Barbara, I'm sick and I'm afraid I have infected you too. I just discovered the disease. It's not my fault—I was sure she was a lonely widow." I'll tell her about the cemetery, the mourning lady, that whole ghastly night . . . and she will decide. If she says nothing, I'll go. It would be cowardly to clear out now, even if I were to leave a note: "You are sick. It is my fault. Go to the doctor immediately—a specialist in diseases of the skin and gynecology. I love you. Forgive me." It was ghastly. Nothing like this had ever happened to me. Now, just when I really cared, after our first conversation, when it all seemed so good, now this had to happen. I had tramped through her scented parlor with my muddy shoes, littering it with trash and refuse. Was there no way out? Maybe it would pass by evening. I could be mistaken. Maybe it's already gone . . .

I checked. It wasn't gone. A foul tear-shaped drop filled me with disgust. When a door opened and closed on the ground floor, I got up and listened tensely. Three footsteps on a wooden floor, a door squeaking, then silence. That's not Barbara, thank God. I have to collect my thoughts. I have to think, to decide. I tried to compose a sentence that would tell her everything at once: What-who-when-how-where—in one sentence. After that, the doctor. I went to the phone, and dialed a number from my address book. A young woman said good morning. I asked for Max Herman. Who wants him? Uri. Uri what? Uri Lam. The nature of my business? A private matter. Does Mr. Herman know you, sir? I think so—ask him. Silence, then very graciously, I'll connect you.

Before I could say, "How are you, Max?" I was flooded with questions and recriminations. What had happened to me, why hadn't I called, where did I disappear to? After phoning the hotel and finding no trace of me, after learning that my things were still in my room unpacked, he had called the police. Yes, he'd left a photograph of me at the station and reported the mugging. I should have realized he and Edna would worry, especially after the attack that night. If I just didn't want to see him, if his domestic life had put me off, why hadn't I just called and said I'd be away for a few days? Why didn't I just invent some trivial lie? Where was I? Where had I spent those nights? Where was I calling from? What is the number there?

"Say!" I finally snarled into the phone after several futile efforts to get a word in, "what are you screaming about? Am I a kid who has to let his parents know what he's up to? Do I need permission to spend the night out? Listen for a minute and stop talking so I can get a word in. Thanks a lot. Do you hear me, Max? What was I saying? Good. All right. I am sorry I didn't call. I didn't think you'd worry. I wasn't thinking of you. I had other things on my mind. I was busy. What? Yes. Very simple. A girl. Right. I'm calling from her place. I'll tell you, Max, but not right now. Fine, but that's not the point. Just a minute. Listen. I have a serious problem, a very serious one. I need a doctor. No. Skin and urology. I don't know, I'm not sure. Yes, yes—I must have caught it in Genoa. It's a long story. Good. I'm waiting. Just a minute, Max. And listen, call the police and tell them not to worry. The prodigal son has returned. Yes. I'm waiting."

He gave me the name, address, and phone number of a Dr. Franz Mayer, a Jew who had lived in Haifa and then returned to Germany. Dr. Mayer speaks Hebrew, he's discreet, charming, and reasonable, Max told me. I thanked him and promised to call that evening or the next day. We concluded with an exchange of jokes, saying farewell-farewell-forever, and Max assured me the whole affair would go no further.

As soon as I hung up, I heard a door open, a dog's bark, then rapid footsteps on the stairs. Running back to the chair I grabbed a newspaper from the heap.

"Quiet, Pluto!" Barbara's voice commanded over the loud barks, and the dog began to quiet down. "Uri?"

"Here I am," I said, setting the dog off again. He bounded into the doorway, a large, black German shepherd, pulling Barbara after him by the leash.

"Quiet, quiet, Pluto. Quiet, dear," she calmed him removing the leash. "It's all right, Uri, he won't touch you. He was surprised to find someone here. How are you, darling? When did you get up?"

"About an hour ago," I said, not taking my eyes off the dog. Approaching me cautiously he began to sniff my shoes. "Charming dog," I said in my own most charming voice. "Yours?"

She put down two bags of groceries and bent over to kiss me. I brushed her cheek ever so lightly in return. When she sought my eyes, I looked out the window. The dog began to sniff my pants.

"Do you like him?" she asked. "He was a gift from

my father. He wanted to be sure I had someone to look after me here. Pluto's a very lovable creature. Yes, Pluto, you are lovable. Right, we're talking about you. Sit. Sit, Pluto."

Pluto settled down and looked at Barbara gravely.

"Where has he been?" I asked to make conversation.

"In quarantine. The poor thing was shut up for ten days. He was bitten behind the ear by a stray dog— nothing much. See, the sore is healed. I was afraid of rabies so the vet suggested I leave him for a few days. The incubation period is about a week. Without a shot he could suddenly have an attack, and then of course it's too late. I was supposed to pick him up three days ago, but that very day I was stuck in the elevator with a strange man. I only managed to slip out of his clutches today." Her eyes were laughing. I tried to smile but she noticed the effort. Picking up one of the bags she headed for the kitchen. As I lifted the other bag the dog began to sniff at my pants again, pointing his nose upward and sniffing at The Problem persistently. I tried to push him away, but he was obstinate. Barbara smiled.

"He knew me right through your smells. Come on, Pluto. Come!" The dog trailed her to the kitchen, I trailed him.

He senses it, I thought, he knows I have something. How can I tell her? What should I say? (Barbara, I have news for you, not very good news.) As I put the bag on the table, Barbara moved close to me. I slipped away and lit a cigarette. She stared at me, her eyes full of questions. Dodging her gaze I leaned down to pet the dog, but he drew his head back and began to sniff my hand. I didn't dare look at her for fear that she would read the truth in my eyes. I didn't want to touch her, I didn't want her to touch me. I am contaminated, contagious, I whispered silently. My hands are diseased, my lips, my entire self is infected. A poison snake lurks between my legs. Keep away, my love, I carry millions of germs. Don't touch, be careful. I must wash. Comb my flesh with iron brushes, dip it in Formalin, ammonia, alcohol to kill the germs that are feasting on my body.

"Barbara," I said.

"What, Uri?" she asked, searching my eyes.

"I . . . Can I take a shower?"

"Of course, darling," she said with concern. "You'll find shaving things in the cabinet. One of my lovers left them."

"Have you had many?" I asked, without looking at her. "Forgive me—you don't have to answer that. It just slipped out."

"I've had many," she said. "Three. And the first wasn't a lover—just passing through at the right moment. But that was some time ago. You look upset—do you really mind?"

"No, no," I replied quickly. "I was thinking of something else."

She took a bone from the bag and threw it to the dog. "Take it, Pluto," she said, and the dog carried it to a corner of the kitchen, where he eyed me with mistrust.

"Uri," she said. I paused in the doorway. "Has something happened?"

"No, nothing. Why do you ask?"

"When I came in, I noticed something strange about you," she said. "What's the matter?"

"Nothing, Barbara," I said. "Maybe I'm tired."

"I'm fixing something to eat," she called after me as I closed the bathroom door.

Later, as I sat at the table, washed and shaved, the sensation of filth was overwhelming. We ate in silence, my eyes on the dish, her eyes on me. I wasn't hungry. The dog crouched in his corner nibbling the bone. A ray of light sneaked into the kitchen and played on Barbara's hair. She looked at me searchingly. I opened my mouth to say something, but lifted the glass of wine to my lips instead.

"Uri," she said.

"What?" I asked.

"Something is bothering you."

"Yes," I said.

"And you don't want to tell me what it is."

"I want to," I said.

"Then why not?" she whispered.

"I don't know how to begin," I said. "It's hard."

She was silent.

"Here goes," I said. "About a week ago I arrived in Genoa and didn't know what to do with myself. I planned to go to Venice but it was too late. I walked around a bit, and then a cab driver offered me an unforgettable adventure for three dollars. He took me to the cemetery in Genoa. . . ."

18 | *Dr. Mayer*

I am not certain—in fact, I am far from certain—if I would react as Barbara did to the news about Maria Cristina's present to me. At first, as I described the cemetery episode, she followed my account attentively. In the cab, at the restaurant, outside Maria Cristina's door, Barbara was with us. She lay beside us in bed, tense and wrought up. She laughed heartily at my conversation with Gino, the cab driver. But when I finally arrived at the damned symptoms, her smile faded. I tried to hold her with a rapid shower of words, to win her, to convince her that this didn't have to be the end, to soften the verdict I expected to see in her eyes.

But she was far away, though her hand was still in mine—a cold hand with dead fingers. I stopped talking; she didn't acknowledge my silence. The dog, sprawled in the corner, gnawed at the heavy silence that engulfed us. Her hand slipped away. This is the end, I thought. She'll get up and go into the bedroom without a word, locking the door behind her. I would tiptoe across the room, open the front door noiselessly, and that would be it . . . the end.

What in hell would I have done in her place? What would I think if the roles were reversed and she informed me of such news? I'd run away too, no doubt about it. Slam the door, erect a wall, isolate myself. No point in making excuses and being defensive when she just doesn't want to listen. What was, was. Now she'll go, slip away, disappear from my life. What are you waiting for? I can't bear looking at you. I don't want to hear any more . . . Get out.

I have never understood why she didn't respond that way. I remember that her eyes focused on me, a long awful moment. I didn't dare look up. She moved close. Cautiously, as if I was balanced on a windowsill ten stories up, she began, with carefully phrased sentences and in simple, logical words, to extricate me from the grip of misery. "It's not so bad," she argued. "After all, it wasn't your fault. Anyone could have fallen into the trap. It may not even be what you think. It might be something else . . . an infection, a cold, something insignificant. Even if it is serious, there are new medications, shots, antibiotics. You look so pathetic."

That was the gist of what she said, and I didn't know how to thank her. If I had had any doubts left—if for a fraction of a second I had questioned my declarations of love—it was suddenly clear to me that I really did love her as I had never in my life loved a woman. There wasn't anything in the world I wouldn't have done for her at that moment. I would have willingly jumped out the window for her (second floor), run naked in the rain, destroyed myself on her behalf, converted. I would have even forgiven the Germans.

Not knowing what to say, I repeated what I had already said. I swore fervently that nothing like this had ever happened before, that I was ashamed and humiliated, that I didn't know how to express my regret, that I considered myself loathsome and revolting. She tried again and again to reassure me.

Later, on the way to the doctor, she put her arm around me and locked her fingers in mine. I felt relief, as if this simple gesture communicated that all was well, there was no need to worry, the tempest-tossed ship would return to shore. I wanted to say something generous.

"Poor girl," I ventured faintly. "Just your luck to get mixed up with me."

"That's right," she said softly.

"And now you don't know how to get out of it," I said.

"I know how," she said, "but I'm not sure I want to."

"I don't want you to want to," I said. She studied this sentence without a word.

"You're worried," I said.

"A little," she admitted.

Of course she's worried, I thought. She regrets the whole business now. She's been told so many times to be careful, and she wasn't careful. "Barbara, my child, you're a big girl now and a clever one. All sorts of experiences will be open to you in the big city. Watch your step. Frankfurt is full of strangers. Don't be impulsive. We trust you, my child." Now, having reassured me, she herself is feeling bewildered and questions that have no answers rear their heads again and again with irritating persistence. Why did she yield to me there on the couch? On the very first night? Why didn't she resist? Why did it have to happen at all? A stranger, a Jew, a liar—and to top it all off he's diseased and infected. He tells tales about the mourning lady of Genoa. (Why should she believe me?) An unscrupulous tramp who buys love in the whorehouses of Italy and can't pass up a bargain! (Herman, tell her that's not true.) She thinks I've been carrying this ghastly disease for years. She suspects I'm plotting to infect all of Germany in order to avenge my sister. (It's not true, Barbara, not true.)

I wanted to tell her it would pass and nothing like this would ever happen to us again. I caught myself. To us? Plural? Yes, us. Definitely—us. I wanted to whisper gentle words in her ear, but I couldn't mouth them. I breathed the scent of her hair. What more could I say in this impossible situation?

Even after we were alone in Dr. Franz Mayer's waiting room—the woman who had sat scrutinizing us with small, suspicious eyes had gone in to see the doctor—we still didn't talk. Leafing through old journals we sat like strangers who had met by chance in this depressing setting. The pendulum of the old wall clock swung to and fro, whispering relentlessly: yes-yes, yes-yes. It was 4:45.

As soon as I crossed the threshold to the doctor's office I was overcome with memories of rainy afternoons, the twilit hours of my childhood. A barrage of familiar smells brought back my father's office, all the marvelous things I was forbidden to touch: test tubes, brown bottles with gold labels, the black bag my father carried when he left home suddenly, blue pharmaceutical syringes, a small alcohol burner, the microscope with which you could see tiny sea creatures sporting in the water. In the corner was the phantom chair my father used to tell me to sit in, instructing me to breathe deeply and not to stir until he finished fishing with his microscope and filling his thick diary with row after row of tiny, antlike script.

Dr. Mayer sat behind a heavy desk, leading a line of ants across the white card in front of him. When my father used to bend over his desk in this fashion his bald spot would gleam, his small mustache would twitch as he wrote. Dr. Mayer's hair was gray, but his cheeks were pink and as smooth as a baby's. His warm, soft hands inspired trust. Peering over his glasses at Barbara, then studying me with a stern expression, he waved us toward the upholstered chairs.

"Now then, children," he said quietly, as though someone might overhear us.

I didn't know how to begin. Finally, after a few faltering words, I summoned all my courage and as casually as I could described the signs of doom. He nodded with understanding. When I finished my tormenting account, he asked if we were married. We shook our heads.

"I see," he said. "And when was the last time?"

"Yesterday," I said.

"And the first?" he asked.

"Two days ago."

"I understand. And before that, when were you in contact?"

"About a week ago," I said.

"And you?" he asked Barbara.

Staring through the window at the gray sky she was silent for a minute. "About a month ago," she finally replied.

"Very well, then," he said. "We'll have a look. You can undress."

"Here?" I asked uneasily.

"There if you prefer," he said, pointing toward a flowered curtain.

As he examined me I mentioned that Max Herman had referred me to him and added, in Hebrew, that I was also from Israel. He stopped what he was doing, clasped my hand, and exclaimed, "Hello there!" as if he had found me at last after a long search. His sudden delight was disconcerting. It seemed inappropriate, not to say downright ridiculous. I stood before him half naked, my pants dangling to the ground, my hand clasped in his. In this posture we discussed the state of my country. He had left Haifa ten years before and his curiosity was insatiable. He wanted to know if the city had grown, how was the famous Professor Feingold with whom he had worked, now minister of health. How did I know Max? Where had I learned German? What was the situation at the border?

He had forgotten for the moment why I had dropped my pants, and I glanced helplessly toward Barbara, who was watching this comic scene. I tried to provide brief answers to his questions. He asked softly (my hand still in his) if she (pointing to Barbara) was Jewish. This question, which had not occurred to me, hovered in midair. How did I know, actually, that she wasn't Jewish? Barbara Stahl. The name itself, of course, proved nothing. Neither Lampel nor Herman are Jewish names. Her father was a manufacturer of optical equipment— that didn't exclude the possibility that he was Jewish. The photograph over her desk? I had assumed it was the picture of a German officer, but I had no proof. The telephone conversation, "You don't have to love Jews nor do you have to hate them," could be interpreted either way. I told him I didn't know, I wasn't sure.

"Barbara, are you Jewish?" I asked.

"Does it matter?" she asked in dismay.

"Of course not," I said. If she is Jewish, it will be vaguely disappointing, I thought. "The doctor asked," I said, "and I didn't know what to say."

"Is the information medically significant?" she asked innocently.

"Don't be silly. It's not important," I said.

"Sorry to disappoint you," she responded. "I'm not Jewish, to my regret."

"Why to your regret?" the doctor asked, releasing my hand.

"It's a long story," she said without further comment.

"*Nu, ja,*" the doctor said as if he understood the implication of her words. "Now, let's see what we have here," he added in Hebrew, returning to his work. With one assured notion he squeezed out the poison and placed it on a narrow strip of glass which he held in his hand. "That's that!" he pronounced in the tone doctors use to announce the end of a painful procedure. He shuffled back to his desk, moved the microscope into the light, and placed the glass strip on its metal tray.

I went back to my chair, and saw my father stooped in that precise manner beside the big window that faced our garden. Once, in a moment of grace—I cannot recall how I earned it—he had lifted me up and let me look into the microscope. He had said the tiny spot I saw was a vast sea, the minute creatures swarming in it were great leviathans. I could imagine myself amid the leviathans with God peering at us through a great magnifying glass, wide as the skies.

We received the results of the examination much more quickly than I had expected. For some reason I had assumed we'd have to wait a day or two to receive a verdict, two miserable days filled with long silences, loneliness, estrangement—a period of unmitigated horror. But looking up from the microscope, the doctor pushed away his glasses and reported simply that all was well; there was nothing to worry about. Just a cold, a variety of catarrh—urethritis to be precise. Barbara, sighing in deep relief, looked at me with new eyes— eyes I had seen in the stuck elevator.

"It's definitely not what you thought," the doctor said and proceeded to lecture us, in laymen's terms, on venereal disease. There was no doubt about it—one glance through the microscope was enough to convince him that this was a case of simple urethritis. He would still send the specimen to the laboratory, a routine procedure, though there was nothing to worry about. Three pills a day, and in two or three days the ugly, alarming symptoms would be gone. He noted some personal data on a smooth white card. When I told him I was born in Frankfurt, he asked my father's occupation.

"Dr. Lampel!" he cried, shocked, pushing his glasses up to his forehead. "You are Dr. Lampel's son?"

"Did you know my father?" I asked. We reverted to German.

"Did I know your father?" he exclaimed, his voice cracking with emotion, "of course I knew your father. I knew your mother too. Dr. Erich Lampel. I knew him well. He had two children, if I'm not mistaken."

"Three," I said.

"Three, three," he corrected himself. "You are undoubtedly the youngest."

"Yes," I said, glancing at Barbara. She was watching the doctor in amazement.

"I must tell my wife," he said. "Excuse me for a minute, I'll be right back. She will be so pleased. Dr. Erich Lampel . . ." He left the room, closing the door behind him quietly, then opened it again to look at me in wonder before he disappeared, shaking his head.

I got up and began to stomp around Barbara's chair like a caveman, pounding my chest with a clenched fist, and wailing in rhythm, "I'm healthy! I'm healthy!" She pulled me toward her. I ruffled her hair and planted a long kiss on her mouth. She struggled to break away.

"Madman," she said. "The doctor will be back in a minute."

"After what he saw in the microscope, nothing will surprise him," I said.

"You've convinced me," she said. "Shall we take our clothes off?" And she stuck her tongue out at me.

"Poor Barbara, you were worried, weren't you?" I asked earnestly.

"Right," she said.

"And you were beginning to regret the whole affair," I said.

"Almost," she said.

"And there was a moment when you didn't want to see me again?"

"No," she said.

"Why not?" I asked.

"Because, it wasn't your fault even if you thought it was, and because you felt so miserable, and because of all sorts of other things," she replied.

"And because of all those things . . . ," I said, coming close to her. But she moved away.

"Just the place to be on the make," she laughed. "A sex clinic."

"OK, let's run away!" I suggested.

"Don't you want to hear about your parents?" She asked.

I wasn't sure. More questions, and again those issues I didn't want to discuss. They will want to know what, how, where, and when. Their eyes will fill with tears, they'll shake their heads in pity. Poor thing, alone in the world. To hell with it, I thought. I came to Frankfurt to close the matter once and for all, to seal the stone on all that had happened. And here they are, about to force me to dig up the corpses. I don't want to talk about it anymore, and that's that. In addition . . . in addition, I was curious to learn what sort of people my parents were. They were dim images to me, odd, assorted phrases: "Time to eat, wash your hands, don't disturb your father." And that's all. I wanted to know who my parents actually were. What did they think about? What things troubled them? What interested them? Which of their characteristics did I inherit? What sort of impression did my father make on others? The fact is, I thought, I have no notion of what I am burying, who is entombed in the cave I want to seal.

"Let's wait," Barbara urged.

"All right, we'll wait," I said. Linking her arm in mine, she moved closer and whispered something. "What?" I asked.

"I would like to know your parents too," she said quietly.

The door opened and Dr. Mayer came back. At first we didn't recognize him. He had taken off his white jacket, and in his dark suit he resembled a retired official. Something in his face was altered. The gray hair was gone. He was bald.

He must have noticed the question in our eyes, for he pointed to his head and said, "Oh, that? Only when I work. Gray hair suits a doctor. As soon as I finish, I change my clothes, take off the wig, and I'm a free man. Come now, children, let's have coffee. Come with me." He motioned us closer and added in a low voice, "I would like you to meet my wife. She is not so . . . ," he said, pointing to his temple. "But she is all right. Poor thing. She went through a lot."

"We don't want to trouble you," I said. "Maybe another time."

"I hope there won't be another time," he laughed, shaking an admonishing finger. "It's no trouble. I told my wife I would invite you. She remembers your parents very well, and it's not every day that we have company. My wife meets people so seldom—it's not good. Come, come. She's waiting."

He led us into a parlor lined with shelves and chests cluttered with small china objects. The large upholstered pieces in the center of the room were covered with spectral white throw cloths. The air was stale and musty. Heavy velvet curtains were drawn over the windows. In the dingy yellow light the room had the look of an abandoned furniture warehouse. A thin woman in a stiff white dress sat at a table set for eight, peering out at us with large, wide eyes. She seemed to be about sixty, and despite her graying hair, sagging neck, and pale lips pressed tightly together it was obvious that she had been handsome in her youth.

"This is Miss Stahl and this is Dr. Lampel's son, my dear," Dr. Mayer said gently when we were at the table. She stared at us and smiled nervously as she offered her left hand. Her other hand dangled in front of her, stiff and bony. "Sit down, do sit down. Please," he said. "I'll bring the coffee." He left the room. As I sat down my chair made a grating sound.

"Do you live in Haifa, sir?" she asked in German.

"No, Jerusalem," I said.

"Ah," she echoed in a thin voice, turning to Barbara, "then the lady lives in Haifa."

"No, I live in Frankfurt," Barbara said politely.

"Oh, I see," she said. "We lived in Haifa. We had a little house with red tiles. In the garden we had a lemon tree."

"How long did you live there?" I asked.

"Oh, it was a long time ago," she said, using her left hand to lift her right hand from the table as she gazed over my head into the distance.

"Do you speak Hebrew?" I asked in German.

"Hebrew?" she said. "No. No. I didn't have a chance to learn the language. It was so hot outside and we spoke German at home. My husband speaks Hebrew."

"Here comes the coffee," Dr. Mayer announced festively, setting the flowered china pot down on a straw mat. He went back to the kitchen and returned with cream and a dish of cakes.

"Did you close the windows, Franz?" Mrs. Mayer asked.

"Yes, dear, the windows are closed," he said and began to pour. "She suffered a great deal during the war," he added in Hebrew.

"Can I wash my hands?" I asked in German.

"Of course," he said, leading me to the bathroom. Turning on the light, he took a towel from a high shelf and hung it near the sink.

"Soap?" I asked. Placing an anxious finger on his lips, he whispered, "Shhhh!" and tiptoed to the door, peeking out to make sure that we weren't observed. He reached up to the very top of the closet and took down a dried-out bar of soap.

"Here," he said. "When you are finished . . . ," he whispered to me, pointing to the closet. I nodded. Dr. Mayer got down and left the room, closing the door behind him.

When I returned to the table, Mrs. Mayer stared at the palms of my hands. I hid them quickly.

"You remember Dr. Lampel, my dear." Dr. Mayer spoke in the gentle tone reserved for invalids. "Erich Lampel. This is his son."

She lifted the cup to her lips, stopped a moment to study me, and without sipping the coffee, put the cup down with a bang that made the saucer rattle. "No one would know," she finally said, "no one would know he is Jewish. Too bad you weren't here during the war. With such a face you could have been saved." A faint smile was fixed on her face.

"Drink some coffee, Marta. Take a sip," said Dr. Mayer, patiently.

Barbara and I exchanged glances. Her eyes were wide with wonder. "He was a marvelous person," we heard Dr. Mayer say. "Isn't it true, Marta, that he was a marvelous person? Dr. Lampel. You remember Dr. Erich Lampel?"

"Yes," she said warmly. "He once came . . ." She let the rest of the sentence drop, as if she had forgotten what she meant to say.

"He once came and what happened?" the doctor said, placing his hand on hers.

"He said . . . ," Mrs. Mayer hesitated for a moment, "he said 'I am not very well today. You may return to your quarters, ladies.' He always spoke nicely to us. He didn't like his job."

Silence. Barbara tightened her grip on my hand, which rested on my leg. I was afraid to look at her.

"She sometimes forgets," Dr. Mayer explained in Hebrew. "Her memory is not very good."

"Franz, your wig is showing," she said.

The doctor checked his bald spot, then turned around and stared at the heavy chest of drawers behind him. The wig was poking out of one of the drawers. He got up to close it.

"Where do you live, sir?" Mrs. Mayer inquired politely.

"In Jerusalem," I replied.

"And the lady lives in Jerusalem too?" she asked.

"No," I said, "the lady lives in Frankfurt.

"So," she said. "And your parents?"

"Your father was an unusual person," Dr. Mayer cut in. "Ah, such a man, such a fine man!"

"Did you know him well?" I asked.

"Oh, yes. I knew him well," he said. "We used to meet often. And your mother—what a woman! What a woman!"

"Where were they?" Mrs. Mayer asked. I didn't understand the question.

"Marta means which camp were they sent to?" Dr. Mayer explained.

"In the beginning?" I asked.

"No," he said. "In the end."

"Teresienstadt," I said. "And then Auschwitz."

"Yes," she said. "I was there. Then they sent me to Dachau. No comparison. Right, Franz?"

"Drink your coffee, dear," he said. "It will get cold."

Mrs. Mayer lifted the cup to her mouth carefully and drank the coffee. Barbara was pale. Reaching under the table I shielded her cold palm with my hand. In the silence we heard the faint ticking of the wall clock. It was 6:30. I looked into Dr. Mayer's eyes. He shrugged sadly.

"You have lovely furniture, Mrs. Mayer," I said after a prolonged silence.

"We like old things," she said. "Before the war we had many beautiful things in our home. We had a table that was very similar to this one, made of red walnut." Again oppressive silence.

"Were you ever in my parents' home?" I asked.

"Yes," she said and fell silent.

In the distance the clock continued to whisper: yes-yes, yes-yes. Would my mother have become such a woman? As I asked myself this question, I could see her staring at me with large, frightened eyes. Would they, too, have returned to Frankfurt? As I pondered these questions, I could hear Dr. Mayer describing the ride in the train, the camp where he and his wife were separated. I assumed the mournful expression that people adopt almost mechanically when one of these camps is mentioned. I wished he'd finish his story quickly so we could leave. I'll take Barbara out to dinner, an elegant dinner, I was thinking as I nodded gravely to the doctor, whose lips moved incessantly: heaps of eyeglasses, heaps of shoes, bare feet in black melting snow; *achtung!*

"But now all is well," Mrs. Mayer said. "People are good to us. They . . ." Her words faded out, her chin began to tremble, her eyes filled with tears. "They love us," she continued in a broken voice. "They visit us. They ask if they can be helpful in some way. . . . From time to time one of the neighbors brings a basket of oranges or lemons, or a watermelon. In the early days a child—I remember her name . . . Elana—Elana used to come regularly and translate for my husband. Hello, Marta. Hello, Elana. Isn't that right, Franz?"

"Yes, that's right, Marta," Dr. Mayer said lowering his eyes.

Finally, after a long silence, we rose to leave. Dr. Mayer followed us to the door. He refused to accept payment. I tried to protest, but he wouldn't listen. At the door he clasped our hands warmly for a long instant.

"Thank you, thank you both very much," he said over and over with moist eyes. "She needs to see people. She always sits alone at the table. Thank you. Really, thank you so much."

Barbara promised we would visit again. He shook his head without a word and stood at the door, waving until we were out of sight. We hailed a cab at the corner and rode home in silence.

19 | *moons of honey*

The next day I packed my things and moved into Barbara's apartment. It was her idea and I must admit it made good sense. "Why keep the hotel room if you don't sleep in it?" she reasoned.

"I get the message," I said in a chilly tone. "I'll sleep in the hotel tonight."

"Don't be ridiculous," she said. "I want you to sleep here, with me."

"What about your good name?" I asked ironically.

"My good name is lost anyway," she said.

"And if one of your lovers should turn up . . . ?"

"I'll put a sign on the bed: NO VACANCY," she countered. "You have permission to come home after midnight, and I promise not to ask questions," she added, beaming.

"Of course!" I teased, "you have your trusted watchdog to guard me, to report a new smell as soon as he detects it . . ."

"You could wash and sprinkle pepper on your clothes before you come home," she said.

"And what happens when you get tired of your new roomer?" I persisted.

"I'll ask him to clear out," she said.

"Promise?"

"Promise!" she said, raising her right hand in oath.

"And the rent?" I asked.

"Warm relations with the lady of the house," she retorted.

"Every day?" I protested.

"Three times a week will do," she said.

"Dishwashing too?" I asked cautiously.

"No," she said.

"And walking the dog?"

"That's my job," she promised.

"The terms are acceptable, madam. When can I move in?"

"Right away," she said.

"Have two kisses, on account," I said kissing each warm cheek.

The first three nights I slept on the living room couch. We played "landlady and roomer." ("Good morning, sir. Did you sleep well?" "Yes, madam. I slept very well, thank you.") When my symptoms finally disappeared we shared the big bed again. After a week we found ourselves playing "the happily married couple." ("Wake up, sleepyhead, coffee is ready. I have to run." "Barbara, have you seen my socks?" "If you don't finish making up we'll miss the first act." "Uri, I can't open this drawer. Could you fix it?")

One morning when I took my toothbrush from her cup, I caught a glimpse of myself in the mirror and couldn't believe that this husband-figure clad in pajamas and slippers was me. What's happened, I asked myself. What am I doing here? I never imagined this episode would last more than a week or so. It was two weeks old now, and this seemed to be just the beginning.

Before I met Barbara I'd never lived with a woman, sharing the everyday business of life: three meals, waking up in the same bed, small compromises—the normal routines of marriage even an unmarried couple can experience. I hadn't savored this with any of the various women who had made nightly excursions into my life. In general those nights were snatches of time, nights that began with a chance meeting, one-night passions at any time of day, waking from dreams beside someone strange and superfluous, a monotonous round of hot advances followed by evasive gestures.

Now, after two weeks with Barbara, I began to regard these relations, which I had always considered a means of communication, a nonverbal dialogue of bodies, as a mess of blighted conversations and idle chatter. My love affairs were not devoid of exciting exploits, new and surprising insights. I recall moments of revelation, moments when it seemed to me that a wondrous new world was unfolding. But these were mere moments, glowing like fireflies in the night. Later, in the first sober instant,

I would realize, with considerable disappointment that the balloon I had inflated with hope was gradually shrinking.

I remember a number of occasions when I was compelled by circumstances to spend two or three days with a woman following a night of passion. Those days were maddening. Everything irritated me: the futile efforts to make conversation, the tableau of "understanding" staged on my behalf, the meaningful silence, the constancy and devotion, the strange toothbrush stuck in my glass, a book out of place, an endless telephone conversation, an open drawer, underwear in the sink just when I wanted to wash my hands—every trivial thing.

At such moments when I could not run away, I would withdraw, enclosing myself in walls of silence. ("I'm thinking about something. No, it has nothing to do with you.") I would hide behind a newspaper, lie on the bed with my eyes closed, pretending to be asleep, inventing excuses for leaving the room, evading stares, waiting for the moment when the door would finally close and I would once more be together with . . . myself. I would panic at the vaguest allusion to time ("How long . . . ? When . . . ? Don't you think it's time . . . ? When will we meet again . . . ? That's what you say now, but tomorrow . . . ?"). Any phrase of this sort would abruptly terminate my relationship with women whose beds I had shared. The vaguest suggestion of permanent ties would set off all my alarms and send me flying to the shelters I had provided for just such a crisis.

But now, with Barbara, none of my alarm signals seemed to function. After a month together it seemed as though we had just met. I marveled at my undiminished hunger for her company. How could it be, I asked myself. Why don't I run for shelter? It wasn't just that I made no attempt to escape. I actually feared that this idyll could not last much longer and I woke up every morning marveling at my good fortune. I was afraid she'd get tired of our setup and say we couldn't go on like this forever. The fact that I was the one who began to think of permanence was a novel twist—I couldn't believe all this was happening to me, I couldn't explain how such a fundamental change could occur so suddenly.

Even today, though I can be objective about those first weeks with Barbara, I still can't understand them. There were special aspects to my situation—no doubt about it. I was a stranger in Frankfurt. Except for Max I knew no one and no one knew me. I had come to Germany seeking myself among people whose conduct had affected the course of my life so decisively. Barbara was the key to this whole mystery. Through her I could see the world from which I had been expelled, I could penetrate the bewitched garden called Germany. She was my birthplace, claiming me, restoring me to her bosom, justifying my faith in that "other" Germany, a people one could love though they were German.

But objective factors don't explain everything (though naturally they did make me more dependent on Barbara). Barbara herself was reason enough for the revolution in my life. Apart from being attractive (at times she was actually beautiful), she was a remarkable person. I realize that I haven't mentioned this yet, but she was different from any woman I'd ever known. I don't mean to suggest that she was perfect. She had faults just like the women who preceded her, but—and here she was the exception—those faults didn't offend me. In fact, they added to her charm.

Her good and bad traits seemed somehow to complement my own qualities. But this involves a realm of mystery which to this day I cannot fathom. On the surface it seemed that we were of distinctly different worlds, separated by language, education, the chasm of a cemetery. Nonetheless, in no time we found ourselves suited to each other like two fragments of a single object. Our sense of identification and complement was embodied in a pet name: Yalie. Sitting in a chair and toying with the key Barbara had given me ("Here, sir, is the key we give to our roomers") I suddenly understood that the sum of virtues and faults isn't what determines two people's compatability. We are all composed of projections and ridges, like this Yale key, I thought, and only a singular alignment of notches and humps endows a key with power in terms of the lock it's made for. Add a single quality, displace a notch, and a particular key loses its value. This metaphor pleased her. I recall that we talked about compatibility at some length, borrowing as many terms as we could from our knowledge of carpentry.

What did we do in the first weeks of this honeymoon? What were the elements of our life during this segment of time? Many hours, entire days, are forgotten. I remember only the sweet feeling that enveloped me, the sense of belonging, of mutual concern, of intimate partnership, stability I had never known—all of which can be summarized simply: the feeling of home. Yes, a cozy spot from which you have no wish to venture into the cold rainy street; an orderly home, fragrant and clean, with shirts arranged on the shelf and mended socks, three meals a day at regular intervals, afternoon coffee, a fire on the hearth, books, newspapers, records, and endless conversation—a house you can really live in.

All of this was new to me and imbued me with a sense of tranquillity and rest that gradually began to manifest itself. I almost took to smoking a pipe, but the smug image of myself seated in an easy chair, soft slippers on my feet, a pipe in my mouth, put me off at the last moment.

I don't remember exactly what we used to discuss in those days, but I do remember the settings. We would talk in the morning or into the night at the wooden table in the kitchen, over coffee; on rainy nights we would sit on the wide couch, with a fire on the hearth or in "my" easy chair, the newspaper basket at my feet. I remember the big pillow, the red one, she loved to sit on cross-legged; or her head resting on my shoulder on the wide, dimly lit bed, her eyes studying the ceiling. We talked about everything and about nothing: the lead article in the newspaper, a book she was reading, a trip to the mountains, people she met, buildings I saw in the city, a film, an unwritten poem, a recurring dream, childhood fears, trivial things—everything and nothing.

Once when I had a headache she told me that as a child of seven or eight (she had two thin braids—I could see her standing with her parents near a sleek black car, a small puppy in her arms) she used to think every person had a private pain that followed him everywhere, a pain that hovered near the ceiling like a mute, white bird, like a stain of light. When a person is hurt this pain dives down from its perch to the injured spot, and burrows and rages there until it is spent; then, slowly releasing its grip, it soars upward to wait for the next fall. She told many such stories, especially when she was tired or almost asleep; I've forgotten most of them.

Our days were short and our long nights passed quickly. A week or two after I moved into her apartment she went back to her classes. One morning I opened my eyes to see her dressed in a bright raincoat, drinking coffee on the run. Our honeymoon was over, she informed me with a mischievous smile. Time to resume the routines of life and work, to deal with responsibilities, commitments, and so on. She would be at the university until two, she said. I could go right on sleeping or get up. There was hot coffee, breakfast was on the table. Before I could question her, she blew me two kisses and fled. Later, when she got home, I learned she was studying German literature and history, and was in her final year. She had to devote a few nights to lectures she had missed, or the vacation she had taken on my behalf would backfire.

The next four or five nights I felt superfluous, but then we resumed our normal routine. At first I would sleep late when she left the house, but I began to be disturbed by my idleness. I asked her to wake me in the morning so I could have breakfast with her. When she left I would read or translate news articles from English to German. She would check my work rigorously, marking errors with a red pencil. Sometimes in the afternoon I'd read aloud to her and she would correct my accent.

I would list new words on a slip of paper beside their English counterpart and, like Jack London, study the new words, then shift my lists from one pocket to another. More than once I sparked our conversation with an unusual word. Barbara would clap her hands in astonishment and give me a good mark in her imaginary book. Sometimes the teacher would even bestow a kiss on the diligent student.

After a while we began to go out in the evening, usually to the theater or a concert and at least once a week to the movies. After the show we'd stop at the Voltaire or at a dark jazz cellar, crowded with long-haired beatniks, black American soldiers, wild young artists. One of the first films we saw together was an anti-Nazi documentary on concentration camps and Gestapo methods of interrogation. Afterward we went to the jazz cellar and sipped our beer in silence. At first I was grateful that she voiced no opinion, but then her silence began to baffle me. She sat with her eyes closed, swaying to the rhythm of the music. Finally, I could no longer bear it—I asked what she thought of the film. I had to repeat the question twice before she grasped it and replied (I remember this distinctly) that the leading actor, the one who played the humane Gestapo officer, was a superb actor. I was stunned by this response. For the first time I saw her as a German. There are two possibilities, I thought. Either they have been glutted with atrocity scenes presented by the Office of Education as lessons in history, or she means that only a superb actor could portray a humane Gestapo officer. That night when we went to bed I asked her to explain what she had said.

"What did you expect me to say?" she asked. 'How terrible!'? What can you say about a movie like that when the horror is beyond words? How can you say, 'It's awful' when something is *so* awful? I had to comment on the performance rather than grade the horror. Only someone who has lived through that hell can grade it and say that Dachau was better than Teresienstadt."

I kissed the palm of her hand and told her I was a fool.

"You're no fool," she said. "But don't try to trap me. I might fall in."

Small wonder, then, that I loved Barbara. She was smarter than I and despite her twenty-one years I felt more than once that her life experience was greater than mine was. Her perceptions were sharp and canny; she was sensitive as a seismograph to moods and states of mind. She was remarkably considerate, her tranquillity was infectious. She had an uncommon talent for saying the right thing at the right time, for silence that was appropriate. After just a few weeks she learned to recognize my weaknesses. She seemed to know better than I when I was serious and when I was pretending.

In the very first week, when I began to feel my liberty slipping away, to realize I was attached to her in a special way, I made a futile attempt to rebel by assuming a façade of indifference. When she spoke to me I answered with detachment. When she was silent I, too, was silent. After a few rounds of this she observed, "So, you've decided to be indifferent to me today," and despite my vigorous protestations I was disarmed by her mischievous smile. Finally, unable to suppress a smile, I yielded. "I am fighting my War of Independence," I said, "and you won't cooperate." She came and curled up in my arms. "First I began the war; then I surrendered," she said gently. "Why don't you surrender too, my love? It's a losing battle."

For some reason she seemed to avoid the subject of her family. From various references and comments she'd made now and then I pictured a large estate, a liveried chauffeur, cows grazing in a pasture, servants in white, a stone wall covered with moss. I saw Barbara's braids flapping as she sat on a swing suspended from a great oak tree. I saw the chauffeur take her schoolbag as he opened the door of the black limousine on the way from school. I saw her fall from a galloping horse (the thin scar above her right knee). I saw her mother's face, stiff, frozen, expressionless. ("I never saw her laughing or sad. I saw tears in her eyes only once," Barbara said. "I was passing her room, and the door was open. She was in her nightgown, sitting at the mirror and combing her hair, with tears streaming slowly down her cheeks.") Though her mother's hair was actually black, I pictured smooth flaxen hair drawn tightly back; I saw a flat-chested woman in a dark suit and high heels, every phrase that emerged from her small pinched mouth beginning with a prohibition ("Don't sing. . . . No talking while you eat. . . . How many times have I told you not to touch that? . . . Don't talk to me like that! . . ."). It was obvious that Barbara didn't love her.

She rarely mentioned her younger brother, but it was clear to me that she loved her father. I pictured him short and plump, with moist, round eyes. In family quarrels he took Barbara's side, though he never dared raise his voice to Mrs. Stahl. She needed only to dart him a withering glance, and he would avert his eyes and start to finger the tablecloth penitently. Barbara would plant a good night kiss on his forehead and his knees would rock with pleasure as he whispered, "Barbara, my girl." Later, when I met her parents, I was shocked to discover how wrong this image was.

I remember asking her a number of times that first week about the man whose picture was over her desk. Each time she managed to change the subject and avoid an answer. One day she told me it was Uncle Gustaf but added no further information, though I looked at her expectantly. The following day, or some days later, perhaps, she elaborated. Uncle Gustaf had been executed by the Germans on the Russian front after his first and only battle. A group of Russians stationed in the ruins of a building, having fought fiercely until their ammunition gave out, then threw their weapons out the window and emerged with their hands above their heads. As they stood shivering in the cold, waving white handkerchiefs, their eyes expressing terror, one of the German soldiers opened fire and continued to shoot until their shrieks faded in the blood-red snow. Uncle Gustaf shot the soldier. He was arrested, taken before a military court, and executed on the spot. I didn't question her further. Some months later, when we were visiting her parents, we spoke of him again.

Now and then Barbara would invite friends to dinner. I must admit that I felt uneasy on these occasions, for many reasons: I disliked the small talk, the proper manners, Barbara's efforts to play the good hostess partaking politely of her guest's empty patter. Sometimes I would look at her and ask myself, Who is this woman? How can all this gossip interest her? How can she tolerate their insipid jokes? Why doesn't she at least look at me and shrug in apology?

During these meals I would feel out of place, though she was always careful to introduce me as Mr. Lam, a good friend. The alienation usually began when my birthplace was discovered. The guests would grow silent and then bring up some topic remote from Germany or Judaism. Now and then someone would ask a polite question about my country and after receiving a polite answer would quickly change the subject. Once or twice there were dinner guests who eagerly declared their sympathy for the Jewish people and expressed perfunctory regret for the crimes of the German people. These declarations were worse than the evasions. At moments like these Barbara would close her eyes in despair and try to steer the conversation in some other direction, for which I was always grateful.

At one such dinner, Karl, a political science student and a charming fellow, initiated a frank discussion, touching on issues that troubled me. "I can't accept the concept of collective guilt," Karl said. "Collective responsibility, yes. I do consider myself responsible for my parents' actions, but I'm not guilty of their madness. I'm willing to rebuild the house they set on fire." Later in the discussion he said there was no reason to hide the Nazi corpse in a closet and pretend it never existed, as if the stench had a chemical source. "The rotting corpse must be dissected," he said. "We must learn what we can through an autopsy, arrive at some conclusions,

and bury the dead, once and for all. We must learn to
live with the Hitler period as we have learned to live
with the atom bomb, with Hiroshima, with Nagasaki."
Here, as I recall, Barbara interrupted and said that one
couldn't compare the two things. "The atom bomb," she
said, "is the terror of the future, whereas Hitler is a
terror of the past. For Jews the atom bomb has already
exploded."

After a while, noticing my distress during these
dinners, Barbara began to avoid them whenever possible. Once or twice, when she did have to fulfill previous
commitments she proposed that I go to a movie, take a
walk, hear some jazz. "Don't misunderstand," she said.
"You're very welcome here and I'd be happy if you'd
stay. But there's no need for you to suffer just because
I sometimes have to invite people over." Taking her up
on this, I spent one evening with Max and saw a movie
or two. Once she asked me to take Pluto for a walk but
I refused. I didn't like him.

About two weeks after I moved into her apartment
the dog bit my leg. I must admit that relations between
us were strained from the beginning. I didn't like him
because he was a German dog. (Sometimes at night I
would see him sinking his sharp teeth into my brother
Martin's empty sleeve; once, I woke up in a cold sweat
after picturing him burrowing in a mound of bodies.)
But there was no doubt that the dog's hostility stemmed
from jealousy. He was unwilling to share Barbara's love
and attention. When I embraced her he gnashed his
teeth and growled, a deep menacing growl. I didn't view
this rivalry with favor.

One day when Barbara and I were embracing on the
couch I became aware of laughter rattling in her throat.
When I looked down I saw the dog embracing her leg
with his front paws; his eyes were clenched in passion,
saliva streamed from his pink tongue, his back was
arched, his body swayed rhythmically. When I tried to
disengage her leg, he sank his teeth in the fringe of my
pants, refusing to let go, as if trying to push me away
from her. Barbara shouted at him and slapped his head

several times. From that day on we were careful of our behavior when he was around. This alone was enough to make me hate the dog. Wherever we sat he would settle down beside us, following me with his eyes. When I made a move Pluto would stare at me, irritated and ready to leap. When I got up he would follow. When I sat down he would crouch in his usual place. Wild as this may sound, I had to call Barbara into the kitchen or the bedroom if I wanted to kiss her. In time the dog began to understand our private language and as soon as I would say, "Barbara, let's go into the kitchen for a minute, I'm hungry," Pluto would run ahead and station himself there. Then we'd close the door behind him and stay in the living room or the bedroom. During our nights of love we could hear his melancholy wails beyond the door, his nails scratching at the threshold. He would keep it up until Barbara shouted, "Quiet, Pluto!" As soon as we were back together, as soon as she began to breathe heavily, Pluto would resume his lustful wails.

One night when Pluto's noisy outcry drove Barbara away from me, literally, I decided to get rid of him, come what may. I already saw him crushed by a huge truck, swallowing a slice of poisoned meat, sinking to the bottom of the river with a stone around his neck, devoured by a lion escaped from the zoo. Suddenly, as if aware of my dark schemes, he stopped wailing. When I began to pursue Barbara—in words—he remained silent. But as soon as my hands sought her body, his wails became murderous.

"This is impossible," I said to her once. "It's either me or Pluto. Choose."

"Cut the melodrama," she laughed. "I love you more than I love him."

"Thanks a lot," I grumbled and fell asleep nursing my schemes.

The next day after Barbara left I fed the dog (which I generally avoided doing) and even before he had finished eating I took his leash from its hook and rustled it in his ears. "Want to go out, Pluto?" I asked as fondly as I could. Swallowing the rest of his food he leaped to-

ward the outside door. I attached the leash to his collar
and we went out. "A German dog!" I muttered to myself with venom. He stopped and looked balefully at me.
"You are charming," I said. When we reached a busy
thoroughfare I removed the leash and let him go. He
sniffed the trees at the curb, then lifted his leg and left
his mark on each one. When the light changed from
green to yellow I crossed the wide street quickly. By the
time I got to the other side the light was red and heavy
traffic flowed across the road. I whistled for Pluto. Lifting his head he looked this way and that before he
sighted me and ran across the street between the cars—
without a mishap. I repeated this procedure a number
of times, with no results. Twice, cars came to a screeching halt and he retrieved me, wagging his tail happily.
He liked this game. Just when I was beginning to
despair of my plan, Pluto noticed a yellow dog across
the street and began running toward it wildly. In no
time the two were out of sight and I headed back home.

On the way it began to rain hard. Stopping at a café,
I took off my drenched coat and ordered a glass of warm
wine. Though I tried not to think about the dog, he
preyed on my conscience. What will I tell Barbara
when she comes home and misses him? I will tell her
the truth: I took him for a walk and he simply disappeared. But why did I take him for a walk all of a
sudden? I wouldn't be able to hide the truth from her
even if I tried. She might forget him in a week and at
long last I'd be free to kiss her whenever I wanted. One
less German shepherd in the world, I thought to myself.
No loss.

When I got home an hour later Pluto was stationed
at the door. He looked at me with narrow red eyes. The
moment I tried to open the door, he lunged at me and
bit my leg. The injury was not serious—he tore my
pants and left two deep scratches on my ankle. Still, I
was furious and kicked him hard in the balls. He hung
his tail between his legs and screamed frightfully. I saw
fear in his eyes for the first time. I opened the kitchen
door and shouted, "Inside. Quick!" He lowered his head

and went to the kitchen. I closed the door behind him and tended my wound. From that day on he no longer wailed at the bedroom door. When I took Barbara in my arms, he would turn away and pretend to be asleep.

"See," Barbara said, "he's used to you."

"And you, my love?" I asked.

"I still bite . . . sometimes," she said, nibbling my hand in a most charming fashion.

20 | *moment of decision*

I was stunned by the news; it woke me from a peaceful slumber. Barbara returned from a weekend with her parents in a dejected mood. I didn't ask what happened there, although I was waiting for her to bring it up. Two days passed and she said nothing. She'd get back from the university late in the afternoon and in the evening, when she thought I wasn't watching, she would sit with a book, preoccupied, her eyes drifting in the distance. When she noticed me watching her she would force a smile and return to her book with a frozen stare. After a period of oppressive silence she would yawn pointedly, announce she was tired, and go to bed.

"Did something happen at home?" I asked finally.

"No, no, nothing," she said.

"But something is the matter," I said.

"It's nothing," she insisted. "I was thinking about something that has nothing to do with us. Something that happened in class. Really, I'm very tired."

Again, the next evening, she went to bed shortly after dinner. I put aside the problems of urban construction which I had been considering, undressed, and lay down beside her. Her eyes were closed but her breathing was strained.

She's told them about me, I thought. I could see her father, his knees rocking with delight. "You're sure you love him?" he asks. Then, learning I am from Frankfurt and Jewish—he hesitates, not knowing how to say what must be said. "Try to understand, Barbara, my child . . . I have nothing against them. I know they suffered great hardships in the war, and I know some Jews who are very fine people. But your mother . . ." Then the exchange with the mother: pale-faced, her thin lips tight and obstinate, the biting remarks, the repressed shouts, the veins in her neck twined tensely together. "You must pack your things and come home immediately!" The father trying feebly to ease the strain. "Maybe we should invite him here so we can get to know him. Henrietta, my dear, you know you mustn't get upset. It's bad for your blood pressure, my dear." She decrees, "I won't have a Jew in this house." Poor tormented Barbara, how can she communicate these difficult things to me? She is lying there, her eyes focused on the ceiling. She doesn't dare tell me the truth.

"What is it, my love? What's the matter, Yalie?" I said softly. She turned her head and stared at me for a long minute.

"I . . . ," she stammered. Then, turning away from me she whispered, "I missed my period."

At first, I didn't understand. Then the shock registered.

"I should have gotten it four days ago," she said. "This has never happened to me. I am always very regular."

"Are you sure?" I asked, knowing she was sure. She nodded.

"I checked the date on my calendar," she said. "It should have come the day I went to my parents'. Saturday, Sunday, Monday, Tuesday. Four days. Exactly four days late."

"It happens," I tried to comfort her.

"But not to me," she said decisively.

Not knowing what to say, I was silent. My mind was blank. I was stunned by this possibility. Once when I whispered to her, wanting to be sure, she had assured me it was all right, I needn't worry. Now suddenly this! From the frying pan into the fire. First my sickness, now nine endless months of pregnancy, a young vibrant woman growing heavy with motherhood. Nausea, blotches, a bloated face, blue veins on her thighs, elastic stockings, a large, tight stomach, swollen breasts, paperback books on infant care, painless childbirth exercises; every five minutes she would ask me to feel the kicks of the raving monster. No doubt about it, a monster would emerge. High-powered nurses would pull her legs apart and with iron forceps drag out a creature, deaf, dumb, blind, with short, distorted hands, and three fully developed legs—a model in great demand for horror illustrations. A featured attraction of the German circus: Adolfus Lam, three-legged monster, marries a bearded woman forty-five inches tall.

"You could be mistaken," I said in alarm.

"I'm sure I'm not mistaken," she said.

Assuming she bears a normal infant, assuming all goes well—come and see our child, he's so cute. Only two months old and he's already smiling. Kutzi, mutzie, putzie. See him laugh. Screaming all day and all night, a refrigerator full of sterilized bottles, diapers drying in the living room, a foul smell in the bathroom. That's it —the end of our youth and liberty. Prisoners to the end of our days, captives of this egotistical creature. Who needs it?

"Still, four days doesn't mean a thing," I said. "Some women are as much as a week late. Don't worry, Barbara."

"I'm not worried," she said. "It doesn't bother me at all."

"What do you mean?" I asked switching on the bedside light.

"A baby is a nice thing. It could be very nice . . . ," she said, her eyes flashing.

I said nothing. The sparks in her eyes were genuine. Cold terror began to spread across my back. She means it, I thought. She's out of her mind. She wants a child. That's all I need! ("What do you think of Uri? He went to Frankfurt, caught a rich German girl, and made her a baby.") I pictured her in Jerusalem, with a prissy child in a little suit, whispering something in his ear after supper, to which he nods in a docile manner and recites: "On a high hilly pass/all covered with grass/a gentle brown cow/empties its ass." Bravo, Adolfus! Very good. Now say good night nicely and off to bed. I heard the stubborn refrain on the other side of the door: "No, I won't, no, I won't!" I saw my married friends, the Saturday visits with them in two-and-a-half-room apartments, good neighborhoods, every convenience. I saw myself growing old, graying, pot-bellied, my pants held up with suspenders.

"It's not possible," I said. "I know I was careful. You said it wasn't necessary, remember? I asked you, and still I was careful."

"Yes," she said with cloudy eyes.

"Barbara, my love. Yalie, my dearest. Are you certain . . . that you want it?"

"I think so," she said. "How about you?"

"I'm not so sure," I said, busying myself with a cigarette and avoiding her eyes. "I . . . I'm not sure I am ready emotionally," I said, searching for a more effective way to put it. "It's so sudden," I said. "You understand . . . I'd rather it wasn't an accident." I looked at her but she averted her eyes. "I think that . . . that you should want a child before . . . before bringing it into the world . . . you should be ready for it. Emotionally ready. Frankly, I don't know. I'm not sure, Yalie. And . . . and besides, we're not married."

She shook her head a couple of times, saying nothing as she struggled to overcome her emotions.

I wanted to comfort her but I didn't know how. I turned away and saw the large clear eyes of a child. A boy of six or seven stood before me, listening in fascination to a tale of pain that hovered like a white bird. "Where is Mommy?" "Mommy went to pick flowers." "And your sister, Miri?" "She's with her friend." "Good. Go and do your homework." I saw a drowsy boy huddled over his desk late at night, addressing an envelope painstakingly: De Amicis—Italy. "Father?"

"What is it, son?"

"I love you, father." I held my breath.

"Don't worry, Uri," I heard her say, "I'll take care of everything."

"What do you mean?" I asked.

"Simple," she said. "I'll get rid of it."

In a small, filthy room, as in all the books, I thought. An ancient midwife, her hands trembling and soiled with blood; an alcoholic doctor whose license was revoked twenty years ago; a bed covered with a smelly brown blanket. Bony fingers poking, scraping with an infected knife. Fever, a torrent of blood, and my Barbara is no more. It happens. It happens often. Miss B. Stahl, a senior at the University of Frankfurt, died today of mysterious causes. The police are investigating. A tiny embryo floating in water. The idea of a human being, the bud of a fertilized egg (you, your father, your grandfather, all the members of her family), a tiny creature, one week old, executed for a hundred dollars.

"You mustn't even think like that," I said. "Do you hear me, Barbara? It's out of the question." She looked at me and was about to speak. I placed my fingers over her mouth and whispered, "Shh . . . don't say a word."

You are inhuman, I told myself, thinking only of yourself. Not for a moment did you think of her. Only of yourself and your own comfort! It upsets you to think she will have blotches on her face, nurse the baby, change its diapers. You're worried about the loss of your youth and freedom. What about her? Did you ever think what it means to her? The daughter of a proper German family takes up with a Jew and gets pregnant. She doesn't panic. She is willing to bear your child, yet you would close your eyes and allow someone to kill the you inside her. Rat!

"It will be all right. Don't worry," I heard her saying halfheartedly. "I know a very good doctor. It's foolish to have an unwanted child. You're right."

"I didn't say I don't want it," I said.

"Yes, you did. You said you're not sure. You said you don't want it to be an accident, and that's the same thing. Somehow, for a minute . . . I toyed with the idea that we could have a child. I was imagining him. Little Uri . . . OK, that's enough. We won't talk about it anymore. I'll wait another day or two and then I'll go to the doctor."

"Get that out of your head," I said. "I won't allow it. It's dangerous. You could die. There's no telling what they could do to you . . ."

"Don't be stupid," she said.

"I don't want you to," I said firmly. "And besides . . . it's a child! A small human being. I won't let it be murdered even by silence. Let's wait a few more days and see. We won't do anything to make a child. Not yet. And we won't do anything to unmake a child. If he comes he is welcome. Let him come. We'll take it as a sign, and we won't intervene. Absolutely not."

"Are you sure?" she asked, her eyes beginning to sparkle.

"Yes, I'm sure," I said, wrapping her in my arms. She lit a cigarette and gradually a smile began to light her eyes.

"Can we call him Jonathan?" she asked suddenly.

"Why Jonathan?" I asked.

"I don't know. I've always liked the name," she said. "Jonathan . . . That's nice. And it's a Hebrew name, right?"

"Yes," I said. "But it might be a girl."

"A girl? she gasped.

"A fat girl with thick glasses and braces on her teeth," I teased.

"No, no, it will be a boy, I'm sure of it. And he'll look like you. He will have blue eyes like yours."

"Yes, and his questions will drive you crazy," I said. "He'll tear books, scribble on my sketches, break dishes, and I'll have to tell him stories to make him open his mouth and swallow a spoonful of cereal."

"You won't have to do anything," she said fervently. "I'll take care of him. He won't bother you. I'll bring him up in the attic and when he is eighteen I'll introduce him to you. You won't have to take care of him. We'll buy him a huge cage and I'll throw him crumbs of bread every morning, we'll build him a little bed in the shape of a coffin." She laughed.

"Madwoman," I said, joining in her laughter. "He'll burn the house down and spill ink on your rugs."

"That's all right, I'll clean it up," she said. "You'll see how nice it will be."

"Jonathan," I called out, "stop making so much noise. It's time for bed."

"Did you hear what Daddy said?" Barbara shouted, her eyes glowing. "Come, give Mommy a kiss and go right to sleep."

I kissed Barbara's cheek and showed her my shiny, scrubbed hands. She nodded her approval and wrote down a good grade for me. "I want to sleep in your bed tonight, Mommy," I whined in a spoiled child's voice. She pulled me close and turned out the light.

The following day she came back from the university in high spirits, hugged me, and announced festively from the doorway, "I made the decision!"

"What decision?" I asked.

"I decided to stop smoking," she declared.

"All of a sudden?"

"For his sake," she said, placing a gentle hand on her belly.

"You're not normal," I whispered, biting her ear passionately until she began to shriek. "You are already reading the literature?" I asked.

"Yes," she said, flinging her books on the sofa. "That's how I spent the morning. I sat in the library reading books about pregnancy and birth in animals and humans. No more pills for me, either. Not a sleeping pill, not a headache pill. No more. Do you have a cigarette?"

"Sure," I said, reaching for the pack.

"Then smoke it," she said. "I'm not smoking anymore."

After lunch—which we ate in the kitchen with Jonathan beside us in a high chair, stuffing his mouth with food—she went to the bathroom and began discarding all the pills, singing cheerfully to herself.

Late that afternoon when I returned from the lawyer's

office (the day I moved to Barbara's, I began, under her influence, to deal with the business of reparations) I found her sitting in the chair opposite the window, a book on her knees. At first I thought she was asleep, but when I put the light on I saw dark depression in her face. The ashtray beside her was full of cigarette butts. I sat down, waiting for her to say something.

"It's impossible," she said finally.

"To stop smoking?" I asked.

"No," she said. "Everything. The child. I can't. It's too complicated. I'd better go to the doctor and get it over with."

"What's the matter? What happened?" I asked.

"I can't go through with it," she said, shaking her head in despair. "It's not so simple. What about my parents? It's out of the question. My mother will have a heart attack and poor father won't know what to do. A bastard child in the family! They'll die. It would be the most awful thing I could do to them."

"Is that all?" I cried, dismissing her concern. "If that's what's worrying you, let's get married."

She stared at me, her eyes heavy and preoccupied, saying nothing.

"One wedding more or less—what's the difference?" I chirped.

"You've been married?" she faltered.

"Wake up, darling. You've been living with a man more than a month and you don't even know if he's married," I replied, a mischievous smile on my face.

"You didn't tell me," she said.

"You didn't ask," I reminded her.

"Well, I'm asking now," she said.

"Actually . . ." I hesitated, "I should have told you right away. But as the saying goes, better late than never. Let it be known that I am not now married, nor have I ever been married though I have received many attractive propositions. But you're the first woman . . . it's true . . . that I really like."

"Be serious for a minute, Uri," she begged.

"I am serious," I said. "I'm willing to marry you this

very instant. For your money, of course. We will go to Switzerland, where I'll push you off a cliff and inherit your fortune." She smiled.

"You don't know how rich I am," she said.

"Are you rich?" I cried in alarm. "Then it's out of the question. I would never marry a rich woman. It's against my principles."

"I am not so-ooo very rich," she retorted.

"That's different," I was quick to retrieve my position. "When would you like to get married?"

"That's enough," she implored. "Be serious."

"All right. I am serious," I said raising one eyebrow.

"You are impossible," she sighed.

"OK, OK, let's be serious," I said. "True, I don't have much faith in this institution called marriage. In fact, I find it revolting and . . ."

"Same here," she cut in.

"Don't interrupt. I have the floor," I said, "and I still haven't concluded my treatise on marriage. Where was I?"

"You find it revolting," she obliged.

"Exactly. You were paying attention," I said. "Now then: true, the institution of marriage is revolting to me and in most cases the marriage ceremony signifies the end of love; true, the legal and religious sanctions strike me as an outrageous vulgarization of the finest of human emotions, the epitome of submission to the conventions of organized society, a means of aligning oneself publicly with the norms—and get this: (all in one sentence) these things inspire deep revulsion, the shame of a man betraying his ideals, for I would prefer to be the father of your child and live a life of true love with you without contracts requiring that the marriage be consummated, without the signatures of witnesses—my German is improving isn't it? But in your case, with the sanity of your poor parents in the balance, and since I don't especially value the formal marriage contract, I am willing to pledge you my troth, definitely, as the law prescribes, whenever you see fit."

She shook her head for a moment in deep wonder and then asked, "Why?"

"Very simple," I said. "Because I, excuse the expression, love you; and because it's suddenly not so important to me that I am violating all my principles. It's more important that this is what you want. Incidentally, I forgot to ask you—is it, in fact, what you want?"

"Just what do you mean, sir? Is this a marriage proposal?" she asked archly.

"Forgive me," I said, kneeling at her feet. "My dear lady, will you marry me?"

"I will," she said, from her regal throne. "What is your name, sir?"

"Uri. Uri Lam," I said. "And your name, exalted lady?"

"Barbara Von Stahl," she said hiding her face behind an imaginary fan.

"My pleasure," I said.

"And mine too," she said. With a sweeping gesture I lifted her dress and buried my face in her hot, perfumed thighs.

"How dare you, sir!" she exclaimed, tapping my head lightly with her fingers.

"My dear wife, let's have a drink in honor of the event," I proposed.

"Yes. I'd like that," she said. "I think we have some champagne in the refrigerator."

"Jonathan," I called, "bring the champagne, quickly. Mother and I have decided to get married." Pluto, bounding out of the kitchen, looked at us and wagged his tail in delight when we began to laugh. "No smoking!" I added sternly. "See how much you smoked."

"I was in a terrible mood," she said. "I never thought you'd agree and I thought I'd have to get rid of our Jonathan, so I decided to drown my misery in tobacco. It's good I threw out the pills or I would have taken tranquilizers."

"If it would help you, my love," I said, "I'll stop smoking too."

"That's not necessary," she said. "It's not your problem."

"So that's how it is," I said. "Already I'm dismissed. I've done my share, now I might as well be on my way."

"No sweetheart," she said, kissing my forehead. "I won't let you go. I need you. But I don't want this to change your life. You're still free as a bird. You can do whatever you like—on one condition: you must be in bed by 10:30 and follow orders, do you hear?"

"Yes, ma'am," I complied.

"Very well." Then, suddenly coming to her senses, "Are we really getting married?"

"Really-really," I said. "With a ring and . . . how is it done? Are you Catholic? Protestant?"

"I'm not anything," she said. "My parents are Protestants. When I was sixteen I stopped going to church."

"Naughty girl," I said, waggling a finger at her.

"That's exactly what my father said. Naughty girl. Mother wouldn't see me for two months. I was sent off to boarding school. How about you? Don't tell me you're Jewish."

"I'm a poor Jew," I said. "When I was in Aunt Anna's house they taught me to cross myself before bed. I've been in a synagogue two or three times in my life."

"Naughty boy," she said, shaking her finger at me. "Why don't you go to synagogue?"

"Because it's not air conditioned and the people are too noisy when they talk to God; He can't hear what I tell Him."

"We're both headed for hell," she said. "I'll end up in the Christian hell, you in the Jewish hell."

"Ours is nicer," I said.

"How do you know?" she asked.

"I saw the coming attractions when I was a kid," I said.

"You're hopeless," she said in mock exasperation.

"And what will Jonathan be?" I asked.

"A flyer," she said.

"Yes, but what sort of flyer—Jewish or Christian?" I asked.

"When he's eighteen he can choose for himself. As far as I am concerned he can be a Buddhist flyer."

"That's a deal," I said, shaking her hand. "A civil ceremony, right?"

"Yes, a civil ceremony," she agreed.

"Another small thing, Barbara. An important one, though," I said.

"I know," she said. "The answer is yes. Wherever you go, husband—I go."

"Even to Jerusalem?" I asked.

"Especially to Jerusalem." We shook hands again and I kissed her, a long kiss. "Now, dear husband," she said, "I will bring on the champagne."

The following morning when I opened my eyes I found Barbara lying beside me, leaning on her elbow and staring at me with fresh eyes.

"What is it?" I asked. "Aren't you going to class?"

"No," she said. "Our honeymoon begins today." She drew me close and kissed me on the lips.

"Before brushing our teeth?" I asked as soon as I regained my breath.

"Wretch," she said running off to the bathroom.

I stretched my legs and folded my hands under my head, enjoying the gesture. OK, I'm married, I thought. Married to Barbara, a German girl. Did you hear the news? Uri married a German girl and is living in Frankfurt. Impossible. It's true. He lost his whole family in Germany, went there to collect reparations, and married a German girl. How's that for an outrage! He marries the daughter of his family's murderers, is awarded reparations, and uses this money to raise a family. Actually, he doesn't need this money. I hear she's rich. Or he wouldn't have married her, that's obvious.

Let them talk! Let them say what they want to. Let them point me out on the street, erase my name from the list of holy martyrs. I am tired of my crown of thorns. Let them stop sending me material on "preserving the memory of the holocaust"; let them stop inviting me to memorials. I don't care. I want to marry Barbara. Why not? To hell with the rest. Really, why not? Forget, for the moment, that she is Barbara. Very well! The dog is buried here. (Murik, Murik.) How can you forget she's

German? It's horrible. When you love someone anything is possible. And I love her. She's a human being, not just a body; she is a soul and a mind. I never knew a woman I could be so close to. Her passport doesn't interest me. She's living proof there's another sort of German in the world. The king gives his only daughter's hand to the vanquished general or the defeated king. There is no better road to permanent peace. If only Ben-Gurion's son would marry Nasser's daughter. . . . The new generation will bridge our two peoples, overcome hate and anger. Jonathan will be the mediator, our one remaining hope. All the better: let a rational solution be the outcome of love. I want her as a woman. I want, if possible, to live with her in my country, in Jerusalem, city of peace—there in particular. I want to forget what happened—she can help me forget. We'll convince the world that it's possible to forget, to start a new chapter —a chapter called "Jonathan."

The bathroom door was ajar; Barbara poked her head out. She was wearing a yellow robe, her eyes were downcast. I thought she was playing the shy bride on the wedding night.

"I won't look," I said. "You can get back in bed, Margot."

"Our problems are solved," she said softly. "It was a short pregnancy, only five days."

"What?" I cried, sitting up in bed with a jolt.

"Just what I said," she explained. "I got it . . . my period. I'm not pregnant. There is no Jonathan and you don't have to marry me."

I leaped out of bed and took her in my arms. She turned away.

"My sweet Barbara, how awful," I said.

"It's not awful," she said. "Now you're free."

"Don't be silly!" I cried angrily. "I want to marry you. And yes, I want us to have a child. I love you, Barbara. It's awful."

Suddenly there was mischief in her eyes and peals of laughter.

"I was lying," she said, clapping her hands jubilantly.

"Nothing happened. He's here inside me. Jonathan is here. I . . ."

Without waiting to hear anything further, I kissed her passionately on the neck, face, hands, belly, and smacked her behind a few times for good measure.

"You are a witch," I said. "I almost had a heart attack."

"You did look pale," she said, studying me with amazement. "Don't be mad, Uri. I had to know if you really want him and if you would marry me even if you didn't have to. I feel better now."

"Madwoman," I said pulling her toward the bed.

"Careful!" she cried, shielding her belly with her hands.

"You nut! Of course I want him," I said kissing her whole body under the robe. "And I want you too. All of you. Now. Always. I assembled a model plane for him already and helped him with his math. I let him use my rulers. And then all at once, you appear with bad jokes. Don't ever do that again, do you hear?"

"Yes, sir," she said submissively. "I promise, sir."

"And now, off with your clothes!" I ordered, tugging at her robe.

21 | *assault in the street*

Saturday night, when Barbara went to Düsseldorf to impart the big news to her parents and ask their permission to marry, I went for a walk to relieve the tension.

I walked the streets of the bustling city, feeling odd and not at all the way I expected to feel. After seeing Barbara to the train I came home and sank into the armchair, telling myself with a sigh of relief, That's it. I'll go out, be young and carefree, open to adventure. I'll have a beer in some dim bar, engage strangers in conversation, sit in a café waching passersby, clear my mind of everything. I wouldn't concern myself with the crucial decision I had arrived at so lightly, with Barbara's parents, her father's wartime activities, Jonathan, that poor son of mine, the future which suddenly assumed such urgency. I sat in the chair a long time, walking the streets of the city in my mind until I fell asleep. When I awoke in darkness I was hungry. I washed and ate standing up. Phoning Max I learned with considerable relief that he would be out of town for a week. So I fed the dog and left the house, heading for the center of the city.

I found myself on a bustling, brightly lit street, thinking of Barbara against my will. I strained to picture her seated at a long table with her parents, saying, "I have something important to tell you. I'm going to get married." Instead, I saw her naked beside me in the wide bed, whispering, "Yes yes yes." I wanted more of the bedroom scene; I wanted to see her writhing under me, galloping over me. Instead, I saw her mother's waxen face and heard her decree: "It's out of the question. I won't hear another word." Afterward, when Barbara's head was beside me on the pillow, insensible, I saw her father, his knees rocking in pleasure, his eyes covered with a moist film. Barbara whispered breathlessly, "Uri . . . dear Uri," as Mrs. Stahl in a nightgown combed her hair before the mirror, tears streaming down her cheeks.

I wanted to clear my head of such thoughts, but I heard Barbara saying, after an oppressive silence, "I have no choice, Mother. I'm in my first month." Then, "For God's sake. Run upstairs my child, quickly, and bring your mother her pills." But maybe not, I thought. The mother takes Barbara in her frail arms but when she learns that I'm Jewish and a native of Frankfurt she faints. My own dear Barbara may be enduring great pain at this very moment while I stroll along the streets. She turns pale in the middle of the meal, she feels sick. If she were here beside me now, I'd slip my arm about her waist and inhale the fragrance of her hair as we sit on the broad couch in front of the fire and . . . scram, Pluto, scram!

In the jazz cellar we would sit close together, drinking beer and listening to my brother, Martin, play Ravel's "Concerto for the Left Hand." What will come of it? ("He married a German girl and works for I. G. Farben.") What will I do with the reparations money? What will she do in Jerusalem? Will she be willing to live in an Arab house on the border? (Last night Arab Legion soldiers fired at one of the houses on the border. A complaint was filed with the Mixed Armistice Commission. The shell tore through a window and struck the wall above Jonathan's bed. "Let it go, Jonathan, we mustn't cross the fence. That's no-man's-land out there. I'll buy you a new ball. Come on in.")

A light rain began to fall. I turned up my collar and walked close to the buildings. The gutters began to sing. Someone passed me mumbling. A small, well-dressed man walked ahead of me, his lips moving. I remembered seeing lots of people in Frankfurt—on the street, in cafés, in buses—talking to themselves. I tried to hear what this man was saying, but couldn't catch a single word. His lips moved incessantly, his gaze was remote. What sort of interrogations do these Germans conduct in the middle of the street, I thought. To whom do they address themselves? "No, your honor, I had no idea of our product's function. I was in charge of sales. I was instructed to send a certain number of tanks of gas B to that address, and I did as I was told. I didn't know, I never dreamed . . ." To whom is he speaking, this little man? Is he confessing the truth to his son?

As I passed him I noticed three figures, their faces expressionless, standing in the rain and staring into an alley. Even before I reached them I could hear groans and the sound of a fight. My first instinct, I must admit, was to turn around and go the other way, to lose myself in the crowd darting quick glances at the scene as they passed. But curiosity got the better of me.

Coming closer I saw two figures wrestling in the alley. At least, that's what I thought when I first saw them.

Then I noticed, over the bystanders' shoulders, that the man in the bright raincoat was standing there passively, his hands dangling at his side, a bitter smile on his lips. The other one, a man in black leather, clutched the lapels of his victim's coat and shouted violent imprecations which I couldn't catch. He suddenly let go and pushed the other fellow away, lashing out at him with swift blows from the shoulder and leaping about in a comically professional manner. The man in the bright coat made no attempt to evade the blows to his stomach, chest, and face. His legs suddenly buckled and his head struck the brick wall. He slipped and almost fell, but the man in the leather coat caught him as his knees began to fold, propped him up against the wall, and continued to pound him. Still the victim made no attempt to resist. From time to time he emitted a hollow groan but the bitter smile was fixed on his face, wielding some hidden power that seemed to frighten his assailant, despite his force.

My first impulse was to intervene and separate the two, but I dismissed this thought at once and found myself joining the observers who looked on coolly as the scene unfolded. What do I care, I thought. Let them kill each other. It's nothing to me. If these Germans pass right by without intervening, if those three at my side, their hands in their pockets, can accept violence with such detachment, as if it was a movie, why should I meddle? Aren't these the very people who beat my father and brother? Let them beat each other to death. I'll stay out of it. What's more, I'll stay and enjoy the performance.

I told myself this but my conscience wouldn't rest. I was tormented by a humiliating sense of guilt. This is undoubtedly how it began after his rise to power in '33, I thought. Two hoodlums attack an old man and smash factory windows, some kids paint JUDE on doors as a crowd looks on, and others pass in the street without slackening their pace. Not a voice is raised. No one protests. It's no concern of theirs, just as what I see is of no concern to me. The spark smolders, the blaze spreads through the land, leaving ruins, destruction, death in its wake. It's more than a matter of one man beating another before your eyes. Your brother is being beaten. You are being beaten.

The victim turned his face to me and in the light of the street lamp I noticed soft lips and blue eyes that I had seen somewhere before. Though the man in the bright coat looked familiar, I probably wouldn't have been able to place him in my memory if it hadn't been for a distant train whistle that blew at just that moment. Of course, the train from Milan to Frankfurt. Martin. Martin Schiller, the well-dressed, effeminate designer, suddenly silent when he learned I was from Jerusalem. Why the silence? An unsolved riddle.

I elbowed my way past the three observers toward Martin, who lay on the sidewalk. His attacker was kneeling over him. He slipped his hands under Martin's shoulders and propped him against the wall. Gesturing with his chin, he spat and said, "Tomorow at ten at my place! Do you hear!" Then with a decadent laugh he turned away and disappeared into the crowd. Martin tried to sit up. When I helped him to his feet, he fixed his bright eyes on me and looked puzzled. He didn't remember me.

"We met on the train from Milan," I said in English.

"Yes," he said and the last vestiges of the smile disappeared. "Lan?"

"Lam," I said. "Uri Lam."

"Yes," he said, "I remember."

Only then, standing near to support him, did I notice something odd—his face was made up, like an actor in a cheap melodrama. His brows were black and overstated, his lashes painted, his cheeks ashen; rosy lipstick extended beyond the lines of his mouth. He was drunk and the ridiculous makeup dripped down his collar in the rain. His lids were heavy and red.

"Shall I call the police?" I asked.

"There's no need to," he said.

"Are you all right?" I asked.

"Fine," he said, smiling bitterly. He slipped out of my

supporting grip and touched the corner of his mouth and his cheekbone gingerly.

"Does it hurt?" I asked.

"It will be all right," he said, trying futilely to clean his coat.

"Let's get out of here," I said. "Have some coffee and you'll feel better."

The three bystanders followed us with their cold gaze. Finally they concluded that the show was over and moved on. We turned down a side alley and entered a dim room, a restaurant or a cheap bar. We found a table far from the entrance and ordered coffee. When I asked Martin if he wanted something to eat he shook his head. "Have something if you're hungry," he said. I ordered two sausages. Martin brushed his cheek with his hand and stared at his stained fingers. "A sad evening," he said. "My evenings are all sad. Excuse me for a minute." He disappeared behind a door at the other end of the room. A moment later, just as the waiter was bringing the coffee, he returned; his face was washed and there was hardly a trace of the makeup.

We sat in silence. It didn't seem right to question him. At one point he pushed away the coffee with revulsion and said, "Besides, I don't love him. He has cold, clammy hands." Then he lit a gold-tipped cigarette and offered me one.

"I forgot," he said, closing the silver case. "You stick to your own brand."

I nodded and lit my own cigarette with his lighter. He looked at me with a disconcerting smile. The poor faggot, I thought. The waiter brought me a platter of steaming sausages, two small rolls, and a jar of mustard. Putting out the cigarette I began to eat.

"Did you find that 'other Germany'?" he asked sarcastically.

"I saw signs of it," I said, my mouth full.

"They should be castrated, all of them," he said, clenching his teeth, "without exception. Where did you find that other Germany? Who did you meet? Who did you speak to?"

I told him I had met all sorts of good people—poets, students. I lied brazenly—I was really thinking of Barbara.

"Normals?" he asked.

"Decidedly normal," I said, hearing Barbara say, For Jews the atom exploded long ago. And on the phone, You don't have to love them or hate them. I worry when I discover symptoms of the disease in my friends.

"Impossible," Martin said, shaking his head for emphasis. "They couldn't be normal. My father was normal. I know his sort. They make me vomit! I had a lot to drink tonight. The idiot. He thinks I'll come tomorrow, but I'm through with him. The little man, the average German, the ordinary citizen, the man in the street— monsters who fulfill their civic duty—that's who the normal ones are, Lam. I very much doubt if you met them or spoke to them. They fill the streets, the movie houses, the stadiums, the trains. Millions of normal people. Talk to them and you won't believe there's another Germany. The merchants, officials, the lower middle class. Good citizens who did as they were told, who neither knew nor wanted to know what was happening behind the fences, right under their noses—they are the normal ones. The scar-faced students, the new rich gaping at Germany's industrial wonders, the Nazis in government offices who speak of democracy as if they invented it, the aristocracy, sated with culture, switching from the production of arms, soap, and poison gases to the production of washing machines, cosmetics, optical equipment, and insecticides. Did you see them, Lam? Did you hear them sing Germany's praises, lament the evil perpetrated against us, agitate for the return of occupied lands, for a strong united Germany armed with nuclear warheads, claiming it was Germany that saved Western culture from the Communist scourge? Have you heard them praise the healthy instincts of the people, the common man, Germany's disciplined citizenry?"

I told him I had heard, had spoken with people, read newspapers. He nodded with finality and gulped down his coffee. I said not all Germans are like that, there's another sort, thinking again of Barbara.

"Of course there are others," he said heatedly. "Of course there are. I'll order more coffee. The crazy, the eccentric, the ostracized, living on the fringe of society. Those who refuse to forget and forgive, those who refuse to conform. Disturbed, scorned, detached from reality, beatniks, pot smokers, priests of opium and hashish, homosexuals, deviates—there's no limit to society's wish to degrade anyone who pisses on its sanctified institutions: purity of family, race, nationality. Of course there's another sort who insist on asking questions, who want to know why. There are those who refuse to play the games of society and government, who question the need for a strong united Germany, for any nation to exist—and not Germany alone, but any nation that toys with anthems, boundaries, and flags. Why salute? Why die for one's homeland? Why not violate the family nest? Another Germany does exist for sure—the Germany of the un-normal."

As he drank hot coffee the alcohol fog seemed to lift. He lit another cigarette and looked into my eyes, about to speak; then he changed his mind.

"Why are you telling me all this, Schiller?" I asked. At first he seemed bewildered; then, gazing off into space he began to laugh.

"That's a good question. On the train, when I learned you were from Jerusalem, I didn't want to talk to you. Or rather I didn't dare—I wasn't sure you would listen. Our sense of guilt is so oppressive—this is true only of 'us,' not of the 'normal' segment of German society—that we don't allow ourselves to dislike particular Jews even if they are uncongenial. Understand? I feel compelled to vindicate myself with Jews, always, everywhere.

"I don't mean to defend all Germans—I just want you to know there's another sort of German. But you've got to look for him elsewhere. He is rejected, imprisoned, isolated. And this is natural, for the un-normal society which Germany defends itself against with every means is a public menace, refusing to forget. More than once I've considered joining the Aktion Sühnen-Sachen, and undertaking a special task to atone for Germany's crimes, but I was afraid my personal life would discredit the cause. My father was an army officer—in the occupying forces, not on the front. But why am I telling you all this? If you'd rather not listen, Lam, I'll stop."

"I'm listening," I told him. "And I want to listen."

"I wanted to go to Israel," he went on, "and do something there. Anything. But I didn't want to suggest that all the good Germans, the un-normals, are homosexuals. That's how *I* am. And believe me, if I hadn't been born this way, I would choose it. This is my private revenge against my father. He was a stiff Prussian officer, displaying his sexual organ proudly in the form of an iron cross, which he wore around his neck. He regarded homosexuality as un-German, an English invention. Germany's defeat in '45, which wrecked his military career, was a meaningless episode compared with the tragic fact that his only son is a homosexual. My conspicuous life-style is a humiliating slap in the face to the family, its tradition of manliness, and the German people. I remember the lectures to which he subjected me, endless, exhausting sessions in which he ordered me to be normal, like him, like everyone else. When this failed, the stern commands became pleas. He begged me to try to appear normal. He said he'd forgive everything if I would hide my depravity. Wouldn't I at least take another name? I refused, delighting in his torment. I'll never forget the beatings that preceded these enlightening sessions and the blows he bestowed on me regularly until I was sixteen. I enjoyed the sweet revenge I inflicted on this little man, this monster who happened to be my father."

The hate in Martin's eyes was transformed into a wicked smile; the smile in turn became laughter, repressed laughter culminating in a cough that wouldn't go away.

"I can't stop laughing when I remember our festive farewell," he said, still coughing. "Whenever I think of my father, I always remember that scene. I'm overcome with hysterical laughter, like this, at least once a day. Sometimes I wake up in the middle of the night and find myself laughing aloud."

I didn't ask him to go on. Interpreting my silence as an invitation Martin began to recount his tale. He hadn't been invited to the surprise party arranged by friends for his father's sixtieth birthday. His mother, a delicate, aristocratic woman with a perennial tear in her right eye, suggested that he go to a concert that night and come in late, through the back door. She wished to spare his father's feelings on this occasion. Martin, pale with rage, said nothing. He left home early and at the height of the festivities, when the house was swarming with guests—old friends, soldiers and officers who had served with his father, all looking ridiculous in civilian clothes —Martin appeared, wearing a tight, low-cut gown, a blond wig, earrings, a pearl necklace, his lips and fingernails painted red. The servant who took his fur coat didn't recognize him. His father, assuming that he was the daughter of one of the guests, extended a carefully groomed hand, clicked his heels, and bestowed a polite kiss. Martin lifted a glass of champagne to offer a toast. His mother, in black lace, stared at him intently; then she suddenly clasped her brow and ran out of the room. The guests were silent. In a feminine voice Martin invited them to drink to the eternal German male. Against a sea of raucous cheers he pulled off the wig abruptly and placed it on his father's head. The guests responded as if this was an amusing prank. But they fell silent when the father staggered backward and collapsed, the wig still perched lopsided on his head. In the awful stillness that followed, Martin made his speech, interrupted by derisive calls. Finally he was dragged to the door and thrown out into the rain by several of the men.

"That party came to mind tonight," he said. "I even remember my speech. I remember wishing everyone a long life. 'I hope you will remember your heroic deeds,' I told them. The torture cellars, the dull daily interrogations. (In an old suitcase, I once found letters my father had sent to my mother from Amsterdam and Paris and Copenhagen, and a snapshot of my father in a black uniform, at the entrance to an ancient castle with a high barbed wire fence and a military guard in the background.) It was utter madness—though I didn't get to my theory about suitable penalties for war criminals —they threw me out as soon as I mentioned the cellars.

I was only fourteen in '45. Too bad—someone might have listened to me at Nuremberg. When I try to discuss my theory now no one listens. It includes everyone who was implicated in Germany's crimes: those who executed orders without protesting, who refrained from shooting themselves, from setting their clothes on fire in front of the Reich Chancellery. These criminals must not be executed, for that's too mild a penalty. And they shouldn't be imprisoned—that would allow them to escape from the past. They should be dressed in uniforms with yellow patches inscribed WAR PRISONER and compelled to circulate through the streets—to be seen and noted everywhere. I would rank them by levels of shame. Those who programed the 'final solution,' the architects of death, would be generals. Camp commandants would be colonels. Transport chiefs, like my father, would be majors. Those who turned in Jews, who plundered and raped, would be captains. Those who knew but were silent would be lieutenants. And so on, down to the most humble private. None of them would be executed. To fight murder with murder is contrary to logic and morality. Anybody who has been judged guilty should be castrated, their memory and genes erased forever."

"Schiller!" I interrupted.

"I'm quite serious," he said. "Don't you understand? A monster was born, through some spiritual mutation, a mystical configuration, a unique convergence of events . . . not unlike the seething gases which formed the mass called earth or the phenomena that created the first living cell. Without getting involved in the details of how and why this monster has developed, measures must be taken to arrest its growth, to protect the world from another generation of monsters. Castrate them so they can't reproduce. Castrate them all, every last one. Castrate them, castrate them!"

Martin's voice, charged with emotion, rose to a shriek. His finely chiseled face assumed a hard and cruel expression. As on the train, he became the soft-spoken interrogating officer. People at nearby tables turned to stare at Martin curiously. A long-haired old drunk at the bar, who had fallen asleep over his beer, looked up at us drowsily and repeated, "Castrate them." His head drooped and once more he was asleep. Martin lowered his voice and went on speaking feverishly, ignoring my attempts to slip in a word.

"But Martin," I began, "Martin, listen. Let me say something. Sons of Nazis don't usually become Nazis. In general they rebel against their parents. I know lots of cases like that. You, for one."

"I'm hardly a normal case," he said, laughing bitterly. "The normal ultimately follow in their parents' footsteps. At sixteen, eighteen, twenty they play revolution, proclaiming disillusionment. But in the end they begin to 'understand' their fathers. The poison absorbed in small doses three times a day begins to show its effect, destroying that youthful passion, the fiery faith with which they intended to burn the older generation's refuse— and believe me, even in their period of faith these youngsters regard their parents' past as a humiliating disease, a hereditary syphilis never to be mentioned in conversation with a stranger. Even the most fervent passions dwindle with each addition to the family, with the first car, mounting expenses, accumulated debts. The fire is diminished, and by degrees at age thirty, what remains of it couldn't even serve as . . . what do you call it? I've heard that Jews light candles in memory of the dead." He frowned, straining to recall.

"Memorial candles," I obliged, seeing myself lighting three candles for the first time in my life, and saying the prayer for the dead in a Sephardic synagogue where on Yom Kippur (or was it on the eve of Passover?) I had once seen men sitting barefoot on rugs, their eyes closed, their white beards swaying.

"That's it. A memorial candle. The dwindling fire is not quite adequate for a memorial candle. They become realists—normal, level-headed; they too begin to say, 'It's not simple. You have to consider the special context of these events. It's time to bury the Nazi corpse, to turn over a new leaf. What was, was; it will never recur. One must forget.' They simply deny what happened. Life, after all, must go on."

I listened to his words though I didn't want to. I was totally bewildered. My head began to droop. I remember cracking my knuckles continually, a detail I recall because he became aware of it. I quickly hid my hands under the table. I wanted him to stop talking, to stop sounding so right, I wanted to get up and go. Yet I did not stir.

He is wreaking havoc in my ordered room, I thought bitterly, and breeding unrest. A madman. Suspicions relegated to the past, doubts I had diligently dealt with, apprehensions I had sorted out and enclosed in chests of steel were floating about before my eyes, blown by the wild wind he stirred up. In my imagination the first proper German I met would sit before me, stuttering defensively while I responded with the cold, obstinate silence of the righteous. Now the roles were reversed. I was bewildered, stuttering, defensive; he was obstinate in the pursuit of irrefutable logic, unfurling banners of justice I had long since cast aside. . . . He was demanding that I remember what I wished to forget. Forgetfulness—the one remedy with the power to soothe my throbbing head, to put the maddening shrieks, the long fall from the roof at a distance—he regards as deadly poison providing a slow, continuous death, so that those who forget, those who try to forget, will never distinguish death-life from living death. My emergency exit leads to a blank wall—so he says. What, then, should one do? Should you *not* forget, and commit your mind to madness? Should you live (for life must go on) by the premise that this is not so simple, that special circumstances must be considered?

I tried to change the subject, but he refused to turn away from the ravine which the flow of his words transformed into an awesome abyss. I asked him about the outcome of his father's party. Refusing to be distracted by this bait, he dismissed the question briefly and then proceeded to deepen the abyss at my feet.

After the party he moved from Berlin to Frankfurt. Some months later his mother died. His father "liberated the world from his presence" at the age of sixty-six, leaving all his money to an organization for disabled veterans. "Thank God," Martin said, "he didn't leave me anything. I'm not sure I would have had the strength to reject his money." Then he lapsed into dejected silence. When I thought he had dozed off he opened his eyes abruptly, grabbed my hand, and confronted me with the awful question from which I seek refuge to this day: What would I have done in 1933 if I had been eighteen and German? Am I certain I would have protested?

There was a prolonged silence. I knew he was watching me, expecting quite a different answer from the one I offered. I had asked myself this very question, remembering that I had joined a youth movement in Israel because of a pretty face, that I had prayed the war would not end before I had a turn to look like a fighter, to join the Underground. In an awesome moment of truth I gave myself this answer: I can't be sure. I really don't know. Nonetheless, I said to Martin, "Yes, I am certain. I know I would have protested. I would have stood on the sidelines and resisted the current."

He looked straight into my eyes. I recall the effort I invested in the steady gaze with which I confronted him. Still, I didn't bat an eyelash. "I envy you," he said finally. "I, myself, for instance, am not certain. I'm really not certain." He shook his head and fell silent. I scanned the faces at neighboring tables, the posters on the walls, the bare flourescent lights, the damp sawdust on the floor. I didn't want to meet his eyes. I was afraid he would discover my lie. Why not tell him the truth, I asked myself. Why am I afraid to admit it? Yes, it's quite possible that at eighteen, in Germany, in 1933, I would have been swept along by the current for the sake of a dazzling uniform or a girl's pretty smile. I am sure that now, at twenty-eight, knowing what I know, I would escape, hide, perhaps take my life. But at eighteen? I'm not certain. I really don't know.

"I used to have a recurring nightmare," I heard him say as if to himself. "When my father died I was finally free of it. Always that same dream. I enter an ancient castle in a black uniform, go down a spiral staircase leading to a dank cellar lit with a blinding beam. Dark dry skin stretched over living skeletons, moaning skeletons in striped pajamas hung on barbed-wire fences, like the photographs I had seen. And I . . . I am beating them with my father's belt. Sometimes the belt is transformed into a machine gun. I shoot them and watch as the life ebbs out of the holes I have bored in their bellies. My poor mother raises her hand feebly and says 'Heil!,' tears streaming from her eyes into a puddle of blood on the stone floor. In this puddle of repose I see a reflection of myself saluting, my lips emitting a hearty 'Heil!' "

The drunk at the bar mumbled "Heil" without so much as raising his head. Martin laughed raucously and again a host of eyes turned on us.

"And do you know what was so awful about those dreams? It wasn't the fact that I was in uniform tormenting all those victims that disturbed me. This seemed natural after all the testimony I've read, after the photographs and documentaries I've seen. No, the worst thing was my sadistic pleasure, my own laughter. I would wake up screaming, bathed in sweat. The very things that terrified me when I was awake were sources of pleasure in my dreams. Do you understand? It's not so much the thought that I could have been like the others that's so distressing, but the suspicion that I could *enjoy* it.

"Thoughts like these have led me more than once to consider turning on the gas, succumbing to a razor in a

warm tub, a handful of sleeping pills. Try and understand—in that spartan atmosphere I would have been
required to prove my manhood, to deny my fears, to accept these supposedly normal events. I don't have to
describe the means by which I would have been expected
to demonstrate I was a man any pure German could be
proud of. In my adolescent years, thank God, we had a
democratic regime, in a, quote, prosperous decaying Germany, unquote. No one demanded that I prove my
manhood—except for my father, of course. I could see
myself as I am and accept the facts—over which I had
no control anyway. Today's 'decadent' society allows me
to be a normal person by being un-normal. It sounds
absurd but actually it's very simple. Do you understand
me, Lam?"

I understood him. Of course I did. The very thought
that this distorted creature with soft feminine features,
this pathetic queer, is actually far more manly than I—
this thought infuriated me. I, who experience puritan
revulsion at every homosexual mannerism, am the queer
and abnormal one, I thought. Whereas Martin is truly
normal, a candid human being and a man. For I would
never be capable of the manliness he displayed at his
father's sixtieth birthday. What bitter irony, I thought.
How absurd! Posing as a woman he had been more
manly than I could ever be. If I were a man, the wild
thought flashed through my mind, I would kiss him now
on both cheeks in front of everyone. I would kiss the
wounds of this poor Christ, his revolting lips. But instead I glanced at my watch and, remarking on the
lateness of the hour, paid the waiter. I left Martin in
the rain and shouted, "Be seeing you" from the taxi that
took me home. I remember tossing restlessly in Barbara's
wide bed before I finally fell asleep just as the day began
to dawn.

22 | *abandoned property*

The phone roused me out of dank cellars, their walls covered with white mushrooms. Figures in nightshirts and pajamas stood in a long row, passing bricks from hand to hand, mumbling *danke-schön-bitte-schön-danke-schön-bitte-schön* in the rhythm of train wheels. I took a long trip in a ringing elevator before opening my eyes to the light of day. I picked up the phone and closed my eyes again.

"Where were you last night? I called three times and there was no answer. At one you were still out." It was Barbara. Where was I? Where was I, I thought. Martin. What time is it? It's 9:15. I'd been asleep three hours.

"Please call back between ten and one," I said in an old man's voice.

"Who is this?" Barbara asked, puzzled.

"This is the city nut house," I answered in the same voice.

"Cut it out, Uri."

"Good morning, my love," I said in my own voice. "Don't people say good morning anymore? And 'How are you?' You begin with a cross-examination?"

"Good morning, darling," she said gently. "I was really worried."

"And rightfully so," I said.

"What happened? What's the matter?" she asked anxiously.

"Nothing much," I said. "I was run over by a bus. I lost a leg but I still have both arms, and my left eye was hardly injured. I had two stitches . . ."

"I was really worried. It's not funny," she said in a sullen voice.

"I was drinking coffee until dawn with a homosexual designer," I said.

"That's enough. I'm not in the mood for jokes."

"I'm not kidding," I said, finally coming wide awake. "I met him on the train to Frankfurt. An interesting fellow. Odd. A bit crazy, in fact. I'll tell you about him when you get back. He thinks all war criminals should be castrated. Did you talk to your parents?"

"Nice of you to ask, Uri," she teased. "Are you really interested?"

"Cut the crap and answer me," I said. "They say it's out of the question, I suppose."

"Sorry to disappoint you," she said. "True, they almost had apoplexy. But in the end they more or less agreed— at least they didn't say no. They want to meet you, of course."

"Did you tell them about . . . ?" I asked cautiously.

"No, I'm saving that surprise for after the wedding."

"You didn't tell them I'm Jewish?" I asked.

"Idiot. Of course I did," she said. "I didn't tell them everything, but I think they understood."

"Understood what?" I asked coldly.

"That . . . you know. Your family. I had to tell them something. Don't be angry, Uri."

"What did they say?" I asked.

"They didn't dare say anything," she said. "They were silent."

"Blackmail," I said.

"Maybe," she admitted. "But what's the difference? The point is they want to see you. That's why I called. They want you to come today."

I said nothing. I didn't know what to say.

"I told them you could come next week maybe," she said. "Is that all right?"

"Definitely," I said with relief. "And how are you? How do you feel?"

"Great," she said.

"Nauseous? Vomiting?" I asked.

"You've been reading the literature," she laughed.

"Is everything really all right?" I asked.

"Perfect," she said.

"When will you be back?"

"On the 9:44. Will you be home?" she asked.

"No."

"Where will you be?"

"At the station—with flowers, a black raincoat, and a plumed hat. You'll surely know me."

"Go back to sleep, my dearest nut," she said.

"Speak softly. I'm asleep," I said, pretending to snore. "Are you in bed?"

"Yes," she said.

"Move a little closer," I whispered.

"OK," she whispered in my ear. "Keep your hands to yourself."

"That's not *my* hand," I said. "Alphonse, take your hand away."

"You nut," she laughed, adding furtively, "Just a minute, Alphonse. Stop it! I'm talking to my husband!"

"Good night, wife. A kiss for Jonathan," I said.

"I can't reach," she said.

"Put him on," I said, blowing three kisses into the phone. "I love you," I shouted.

"I love her too," she said, affecting a male voice, and hung up.

I couldn't fall asleep. Alphonse, in a long shirt and nightcap, was standing over Barbara's bed, twirling his mustache as he blew the candle out, rubbed his hands in wicked delight, and slid under the covers. I buried my head in Barbara's fragrant pillow and kissed her soft belly. She's turned it all around, I thought. They didn't say no. They agreed. They want to meet me. I'll put on a bedouin abaya and a white keffiyeh. "*Ahlan-wasahllan hawaja* Stahl, *kif schtek wakif martek: Ahlan, ahlan!*" How exotic. They'll surely be impressed. But why not a black *streimel*, earlocks, a long kapote, and white socks? I'll invite Frau Stahl to dance a *scherele*. She'll hold the end of my handkerchief. "Reb Ludwig," I'll exclaim, "your wife, may she live long, is a wonder. Such splendid dancing! Splendid beyond words. A woman of valor. May my sons and my sons' sons be deemed worthy of such fortune." Reb Ludwig Stahl will close his eyes, stroke his beard, and retort, "Ay-yay-yay-yay-yay."

Nonsense. A dark suit, white shirt, knitted tie. Not the red one, the black one. Conservative. Serious. Yes, sir. Remain standing until the ladies are seated. Get up when they get up. Ask permission before lighting a cigarette. Remember not to pick my nose at dinner and absolutely not to stick snot under the table. Flush the toilet after pissing. Be civilized, well-mannered, restrained. European. (Charming. Hard to believe he's an Israelite.) Yes, Herr Stahl. Of course, Herr Stahl. A schmuck, Herr Stahl. From your point of view, Herr Stahl, it's quite logical; but there are two sides to every coin, don't you agree? Or, Thank you very much, Herr Stahl. Believe me, I'm flattered by your offer, but unfortunately I cannot agree to manage your business. After all, you did produce periscopes for German submarines which sank Allied ships every day in the North Sea; you sold telescopes to the Wehrmacht through which they watched the Warsaw Ghetto go up in flames and Lidice vanish from the face of the earth. You supplied the fine microscopes with which camp doctors studied my brother's tubercular lung after removing it from their experimental freezing units. I hope you understand, Herr Stahl, that under these circumstances I cannot manage your business, though the salary you offer is very seductive. I am a citizen of Israel, don't forget. And I am a Jew. I want your daughter to live in Jerusalem with me. We mean to live there—right, Barbara? I couldn't remain in a country whose citizens . . . Barbara, did you tell your father what the Germans did to my father? You told him about my sister and my brother, Martin, the musician? See? It's impossible. And please, sir, stop crowing over the German industrial miracle. I would just as soon piss on it and if you don't move a bit I'll be glad to piss on you as well. If I marry your daughter it doesn't mean I'm marrying you or that scarecrow you call your wife. Don't bother. We don't want any favors. We can do very well without your money. Come on, Barbara, let's go. All right, all right. I'm very sorry, but he got me so mad. He thinks he can buy the whole world with his lousy money. Let's go. Don't worry, we won't starve. No one can take away our dreams, our hopes. Don't exaggerate. Thank you very much, Herr Stahl. I'll think it over. I'll consult Barbara. I value your daughter's good sense. Skoal, sir. *L'chayim.* Frau Stahl, my compliments on the dinner, it was superb. A lost cause—I'll never get back to sleep.

Getting out of bed I danced into the shower. I was in high spirits and stood in front of the mirror making faces. When I got out of the shower I began whistling to myself. The dog, sitting in the doorway, his head cocked to one side, wagged his tail contentedly.

"Don't flatter yourself, you German dog," I told him. "I'm not your friend."

The dog stopped wagging his tail and lowered his eyes. "Want to go out, Pluto?" I asked, and he leaped toward the door, barking excitedly. I let him out and waited for him to find a suitable tree, then the spot in the garden which he favored for his needs, circling it again and again before performing. When he was finished I whistled to him from the hall but he still got to the kitchen before me. Rolling up my sleeves I began to prepare our breakfast. I took a small package of chopped meat from the refrigerator, cracked an egg, and kneaded it into the meat. I divided this into five equal patties, which I placed on a bed of lettuce leaves, adorning each patty with a black olive. I set this festive dish before the dog. "Eat," I said to him. "Enjoy, while you can, *capo.*" He surveyed the dish suspiciously, approached it with caution, and sniffed it before beginning to devour the food with great appetite. He didn't touch the olives, the wretch. I made myself a royal breakfast. The omelet was excellent, the salad splendid. The herring was out of this world. The bread tasted like cotton but the coffee was very fine, and the first cigarette—paradise. "Life can be beautiful, right, Pluto?" I said and he wagged his tail twice. After I washed and dried the dishes and put everything in its place I didn't know what to do next. A nice day, I thought. A glorious day. A fine day for a walk. To my parents' house, why not?

From the day I arrived in Frankfurt I had been thinking of this visit. One morning shortly after I moved to Barbara's I found myself alone, and it was then that I was possessed by a crazy notion. I searched through my papers and found my parents' old phone number. I'll call home, I thought, and ask to speak with Dr. Erich Lampel. Maybe Martin will answer. Maybe Miri will say, "Dr. Lampel is out on a call. He will be back in the afternoon. Is there a message?" With pounding heart, I dialed 62582 and held my breath. I heard the phone ring. It didn't seem possible that this number was still in use after its owners had been expelled, imprisoned, murdered, cast out. Where is this phone I hear ringing now? Is it still there in my parents' home, on the white table in the hall? Someone picked up the receiver.

"Hello," I cried out in a broken voice.

Deadly silence. Irregular breathing on the other end.

"Hello!" I repeated, trembling.

"Hello," a child's voice answered.

"Is your mother there?" I asked in the sweet voice strangers reserve for children.

"No," the child said. "Mommy isn't home. Just the cat and me are home."

"Where is your father?" I persisted fondly.

"He went on a trip."

"Where did he go?"

"I don't know," the child said. "Once he was sleeping and some people came and took him away in a big box. My mother said he went away."

"Aren't you afraid to stay home alone?" I asked.

"Yes," he said quietly, "I am afraid."

"Where do you live, son?" I asked. The child was silent. "I'll come and play with you. Where do you live?"

"I know the number, but I don't know the street," he said.

"What's the number?" I asked, my heart pounding fiercely. Nine, if only he would say nine, I prayed.

"I forget," the boy said.

"Nine?" I asked. "Wagner-Gasse 9? The child remained silent. "What's your mother's name? Is it Miri?" I could hear his breathing on the other end.

"My mother doesn't let me talk on the phone," he said and hung up.

That evening I called my parents' home again but got no answer. I counted ten rings but no one picked up the phone. The next morning the boy answered again. Once more I failed to extract any information from him. He told me a long story about an aunt who bought him a tank, about the neighbor's dog who had puppies, about another aunt who was sick, and finally he told be about his mother who instructed him not to talk on the phone. In the evening there was no answer again. I dialed 62582 five times at fifteen-minute intervals. The phone rang but no one answered. Barbara, who was huddled over her notebooks, looked up finally and asked who I was calling. I told her the whole strange story. She rolled her eyes, twirled a finger at her temple and, instead of pronouncing me crazy, proceeded to open the phone book, which was arranged by street names. She found Wagner-Gasse 9 and showed me that the number listed for that address was not the one I had dialed.

"Is there any way to find out who has my parents' number?" I asked.

"That's fairly complicated," she said. "But if you want to you can write to the postmaster and explain the whole thing to him."

"It's really not important," I said.

"Then why did you call?" she asked.

"I don't know," I said. "Just one of my crazy ideas. Sometimes when I go out I call myself on the phone. I know no one will answer and yet I expect—or maybe I'm afraid—that one day someone will pick up the receiver. I'll ask, 'May I speak with Uri Lam?' and my own voice will answer, 'Speaking.' "

"So you thought you would call your parents and one of them would answer," she said.

"It's crazy, I know. But that's what I thought," I told her.

"Would you like me to come see the house with you?" she asked.

"No," I said. Puzzled, she turned back to her books.

I put off the visit from one day to the next, dreading an encounter with the occupants of the house. I don't know how to explain it. I didn't want to make them uncomfortable. Maybe it sounds odd, but I experience deep shame at another person's embarrassment. Once in school I caught someone stealing from my locker. I'll never forget his face when he saw me standing there staring at him. I didn't mention the incident to anyone nor did I say a word to the boy himself. I was ashamed to meet his eyes. His humiliation seemed to extend to me. To this day when I meet the fellow, who has become a government official, I turn away, pretending not to know him. It sometimes seems that this penalty of silence is too cruel, that I ought to tell him that I bear no grudge, that I forgive him, that I'm not scheming to blackmail him. It appears to me, absurd as this may sound, that there is an element of injustice in the silence of the righteous. This is probably why I kept postponing the visit to my parents' home. I was convinced that my very presence in the house would shame its occupants and place them in the position of oppressors, as if they had stolen my parents' property, even thought it was legally acquired. Whenever I saw myself revisiting my parents' home, I was haunted by a scene I had witnessed some years back.

I was visiting a painter in Safed whose house belonged to a government agency that took over the property of absentee owners—Arabs who fled to Nazareth during the battle to liberate Safed and were not occupying their homes at the time of the census. Their property, confiscated by the government, was leased for a symbolic period of ninety-nine years to Jewish artists "who succeeded, through diligence and love, in converting the old Muslim quarter into a charming colony of artists, a spot which to this day attracts large numbers of visitors and tourists." At the home of this painter some two or three years after the war I met the landlady, who had received permission from the military governor to visit her home in Safed. Relations between the artist and the lady were quite cordial, as I quickly discovered. The painter, who spoke elegant Arabic, treated her with great respect, addressed her as "mother," and served her coffee, cold water, and grapes from the yard. He was altogether gracious. He told me she visited every six months to check the house, pointing out peeling plaster, cracks in the roof, and so on. Though he was not required by law to listen or even to let her in the door, he respected her wishes and promised to make the repairs. He would lead her to his most comfortable chair, listen politely to her complaints, and assure her that Arab leaders would one day open their eyes and recognize the State of Israel; they would make peace, and arrive at a logical agreement about Jewish property in Arab countries and the property of Arabs in Israel. In short, everything would turn out all right. When I was visiting we sat in the formal room. The woman's eyes sparkled as the painter spoke, and when he concluded this charming fantasy her breathing was heavy with emotion. She smiled as if waking from a sweet dream and said, "*Ya-rt, ya-rt,*" which the painter translated as, "So be it." I remember that the air in the room seemed suddenly stifling and I asked my friend to open a window, but the shutter refused to yield. The woman, noticing his struggle, climbed up on a stool and with a skilled tap of her finger opened the shutter. "It's a special sort of hook," she said, stepping down. For an instant I recognized the same expression in the painter's eyes as I had seen when I caught that boy stealing.

I was afraid I might see that very look in the eyes of those who now occupied our house. Despite this (or perhaps because of it), I decided that fine Sunday morning to visit the house the German authorities had seized from my parents and passed on or sold to a German family.

I must admit when I got out of the taxi I didn't recognize the house I'd spent my first ten years in, even though the street was Wagner-Gasse and there was a white number 9 set over the doorway. The enormous house I remembered from childhood seemed small. The stone wall that separated the snip of land in front of our house from the sidewalk, the wall I used to walk on, eyes closed, hands stretched out for balance (to this day I have a scar on my chin), had been replaced by an iron fence and a gate that screeched. The windows, once a series of small squares, had large panes now, and the front door had been painted black. I'm almost sure that in my childhood this door was white or some other bright color. I couldn't have scribbled with pencil on a black door and I distinctly remember being slapped by my father for doing this. The five stone steps at the entrance were the steps where Miri and I used to play "Mommy and Daddy," where I used to count my supply of chestnuts; here, on Saturday mornings in the sunshine, I would sit waiting for the household to wake up, for my mother to call me for coffee in a thin china cup and a piece of coffeecake.

Walking up the steps I noticed our bell in the center of the door, a simple gadget that sounded like a bicycle bell. The top of it was attached to the inside of the door and only its handle, which consisted of two wings, was on the outside. This handle had to be turned back and forth. I used to have to stand on tiptoes to reach it but now it was only as high as my shoulders. As soon as I touched it the door opened slightly and a woman of about fifty peered out anxiously, waiting for me to declare myself. I didn't know what to say.

"Are you looking for someone, sir?" she finally asked.

"No," I said bewildered. "I'm not looking for anyone. I was noticing the handle of this old bell."

"Yes?" she said without opening the door any wider.

"Madam," I finally ventured, "I was born in this house and I'd like your permission to see it again."

Her face darkened. "Just a minute," she said. "I'll ask my husband." The door closed and I heard footsteps fading in the distance, then silence. I lit a cigarette and went down the steps. There were once rosebushes in front of the house, red roses that spilled their sweet petals on the table. In a far window a white curtain stirred. I was being scrutinized. I turned my back on the house and a minute later I heard a door open behind me.

"Please, sir," the woman said, "won't you come in."

The anticipated encounter with the house in which I spent the golden years of my childhood was less moving than I expected. Truthfully, I was a bit disappointed. The house was like an old trunk, violated and empty. This trunk, in which I had hoped to find the lost treasures of my soul, the aroma of childhood, faded pictures, forgotten melodies, myriad scenes holding the true reflection of my life—this wondrous trunk, the very thought of which so stirred my soul, was desolate. The grave robbers had beaten me to it and emptied the family treasury of all its choice objects. The purple flowers that used to climb the walls of my room were gone, replaced by wood paneling. The sky-blue ceiling in our game room was covered with a revolting cloud pattern and not a trace remained of the blinding whiteness in my father's examining rooms. The hall, with gleaming parquet floors that always smelled of wax, now reeked of wurst and sauerkraut. The wooden steps to the second floor no longer squeaked like new shoes. I couldn't believe that I once lay in ambush for Miri behind my parents' door, that once when she passed me in the dark, clutching three dolls to her bosom, I grabbed her ankle shrieking like a wild animal in my picture books. Now, when I peered behind the door (to the dismay of its present occupants), I couldn't picture the terror in Miri's eyes as she fell and her favorite doll, Suzy, with its china head, slipped from her hand and rolled down the steps, smashed to bits. This tableau, which had recurred many times with such brutal clarity that I felt my heart pounding with terror, refused to be revived now that I was back at the scene of the crime. Those childhood memories which for so many years had animated my dreams, my yearning fantasies, expired right there in my parents' home. I felt remote and alien. No one in my family accompanied me on this melancholy walk to the brink of the past. I was alone in the house. My mind was empty. The house, may its memory be blessed, was dead.

I don't want to remember the dialogue with my host at the end of the tour, yet I can't seem to forget it. The silver-haired German, sitting motionless in an easy chair, had irritated me from the outset with his possessive manner and his way of resting his hands on the table, as if to say, "This is all mine and you have no claim to it." There was no shame on this man's face, though he was living in a house stolen from my parents. He didn't even lower his eyes when I told him that the house he now occupied was loved by my parents, that my father had worked many years to pay off the mortgage. (Even this lie, invented on the spot, didn't move him.) He dared to nod impatiently when he heard we were expelled from Frankfurt, and that I was the sole survivor of the family that had once lived in this fine, comfortable house. His "yes, yes," as if to say "I know all those sad stories," infuriated me so much that I riffled through the Bible I had noticed in the living room and poked it under his nose, pointing to the verse: "Hast thou killed and also taken possession?" He stared at me as if I was deranged before slamming the book shut.

"Sir!" he said turning pale, "I owe you nothing. I live in this house by right, not kindness. I stole it from no one. We had a house too, a two-story house in a suburb of Leipzig. It was taken over by the East German authorities. We left our belongings there and escaped to the West. We are refugees too, sir! The beautiful house you refer to was in ruins when we found it. We rented this ruin in 1948 from the town, which by law—yes, by law—appropriated the property of absent owners. The roof was crumbling, the plaster was falling, not a single window was intact. We worked hard, saved every penny, and renovated it. We installed electricity, replaced all the plumbing, put on a new roof, laid new floors in four of the rooms, repaired windows and doors. We invested a phenomenal amount of money. And you dare say to me, 'Hast thou killed and also taken possession?'

"I have killed no one, nor have I taken anything. You wished to see the house in which you were born. We showed it to you, though we are not required to. And you accuse me! Your parents loved this house? Well, I loved my home too. I inherited it from my father, who built it with his own hands. I'm very sorry about your family's fate but it wasn't I who took this house away from you, sir. I acquired it legally. I can prove it. I owe you nothing!"

I wanted to go, but the man wouldn't let me. He ignored his wife's attempts to calm him. (She brought a tray of cookies and coffee. Though I refused emphatically, she poured me some coffee and passed the sugar and cream.) Little by little I found myself apologizing. I asked him to try to understand the extent of the evil which had been perpetrated—not by him of course. This I was willing to admit. But you must understand, I said, that though you're not the oppressor, I am nonetheless oppressed. He shrugged and said, "Yes, but what can a person do? That's how it is, that's life."

When I left my parents' house, closing the door behind me for the last time, I was agitated and confused, more distressed than I had been at any time since arriving in Frankfurt. When I got home I fell on the bed in my clothes, and buried my head in the pillow, tossing about for a long time, unable to put my visit out of mind. I finally got up and went out. I spent the afternoon walking the streets in a daze. In the evening, at about nine, almost an hour before Barbara's train was due, I went to the station and fell asleep on one of the hard wooden benches in the waiting room.

Sleeping soundly I saw my mother and father pushed through the corridor of a train with thousands of others. Soot streamed down their grimy faces and a soldier I knew (a paratrooper who was killed in a retaliatory attack) was eating a sausage sandwich pressed against Miri's behind—her hairdo was bouffant like Edna's. I heard a train whistle. People coughed and laughed. "Open the windows. Turn off the heat, we're choking!"

The persistent whirr of train wheels droned, *"Danke-schön bitte-schön, danke-schön bitte-schön,* smoke-stacks-shine! Smoke-stacks! Smoke-stacks! Stacks!"

The shrill wail of a siren woke me up. It was ten o'clock. The train from Düsseldorf had arrived and by now the platform was deserted. I called home but there was no answer.

Taking a taxi home, I leaped up the steps and stood in the doorway huffing and puffing, as the damned dog circled around me, jubilant. Barbara was calmly setting the table. She tried to pretend nothing was wrong, though I had promised to meet her at the train with flowers—still, I detected a cold, steel gleam in her eyes. When I tried to kiss her she gave me a peck and moved away before my lips could even brush her cheek.

I started my tale from the end, from the startling bit of information I had acquired during this unnerving visit to my parents' home. She was as shocked as I had been; she too was agape with wonder—my brother, Martin, was apparently still alive! When I repeated the sentence that had driven me to walk the streets in a daze all afternoon, she wrapped her arms around my neck and covered my averted eyes with kisses. I was overcome with emotion. "Wait, wait. Don't say a word," she said, her eyes flashing with excitement. Pulling me toward the couch, she settled in the opposite corner and curled her legs under her. "Now, tell me."

At the end of the visit, I reported, my host suddenly turned to me. "You say you're the only survivor?" he questioned. I nodded. It never occurred to me that his next sentence would be a haunting one. "If that's so, who is the other man who came here claiming he grew up in this house?"

"An hour must have passed before I recovered my voice," I told Barbara. "I don't know how long it was before I could ask when this occurred, what the man looked like, what he had said. There can be no doubt about it—it was Martin. He had visited the house ten years earlier, in 1949. November or December, sometime in the winter. His right sleeve was empty, his hair was gray. He hardly said anything. He asked to see the house because he had grown up in it. He walked through the rooms with a lost expression and left without even saying thank you. I asked my host if the man resembled me. He stared several minutes before replying, 'I'm not sure, it was a long time ago. Maybe something . . . Around the eyes, perhaps. . . . No, I'm not sure there is a resemblance.' I asked if he ever came back or called. The man shook his head firmly. 'He didn't say anything except that he grew up in this house. Oh, and one other thing,' he suddenly recalled. 'He looked into the garden and remarked, "We used to have an apple tree here." ' Those were Martin's only words."

23 | *the search*

My first attempts to locate Martin were almost involuntary. At first I didn't even stop to consider why I was searching for him or what I would do when I found him. The urge to find him seemed obvious, a reflexive act which I began to examine only a few days later.

Barbara suggested that first we look for his name in the Frankfurt directory. Shocked by this simple approach, I could hear the dialogue: "May I speak with Martin Lampel?" Someone on the other end would answer, "Speaking." Why not, come to think of it. He's in Frankfurt too, I thought. He survived the camp and was liberated by the Americans, after which he returned to Frankfurt not knowing I exist. Suddenly the phone rings in his apartment and his kid brother is speaking.

In the phone book we found eight listings for Lampel. One of them (my heart stood still) had the initial M. My hand trembled as I dialed. A man named Manfred Lampel answered. No, he knew of no Martin Lampel. Very sorry. And that was that. When Barbara called

information to see if my brother's name was listed somewhere else in Germany, she was referred to another
number and told to wait. During the infinite moment it
took to look this up, I saw Martin teaching music in
Munich, a bank clerk in Hamburg, an insurance officer
in Cologne. The answer, however, was negative.

When she hung up I was overwhelmed with fatigue
that had been mounting throughout the long day and
night. But when I lay down I couldn't sleep. My eyes,
focusing on the darkness, watched Martin feeding a
cloud of pigeons at the Milan train station. After a while
Barbara whispered, "Uri? What is it, Uri?" I didn't know
what to say. "I can't fall asleep," I said. I pictured him
at the window that faced the garden, saying, "We used
to have an apple tree here." I closed my eyes and saw
him at the black grand piano in the living room playing
"Moonlight Sonata." I remember my emotions when I
heard this sonata on the lawn of the Youth Center. It
was then that I discovered the name of the piece my
brother used to play almost every evening that last summer in Frankfurt. Sometimes I would wake up in the
middle of the night and see the moon reflected in our
river, the Main, tossed on the peaceful waves of the
sonata's opening phrases.

I wanted to tell Barbara about my brother, Martin,
to share my misty fantasies with her. But it became
clear that I actually knew nothing about him. I know
much more about Barbara, I thought, than I know about
Martin. "I was ten," I told her, "and he was nineteen
when I last saw him. I'm not sure I'd recognize him now.
I don't know if I loved him or if he loved me. He used to
read a lot. More than once I heard my mother calling,
'It's late, Martin. Turn off the light.' Once I pryed open
his secret drawer with my penknife and found a thick
notebook filled with mysterious writing and a funny picture of a naked lady in a garden smelling an enormous
flower."

Barbara giggled in the dark. Closing my eyes I could
see her naked in our garden, standing beside the apple
tree and smelling a rose. I tore myself away from this

scene and pursued the quest for Martin. Shreds of paper were blowing in the wind. I chased them through the garden, through every room of the house. When I spread them on the table, I saw something of Martin's everywhere. Though I struggled to fit the pieces together, the snatches of memory, the elusive scenes refused to form a single clear picture. I called his name in the depth of my self and strained to raise him from the profound silence of memory. But my net yielded only fragments of a picture: the stench of his white sneakers at the bathroom door; a plump girl standing shyly at our steps, asking, "Is Martin home?"; the slap he gave me when he found me rifling his drawer; his feet on the brass piano pedals; his long face and gray eyes. "Once," I told Barbara, "my sister asked me at supper, if one of us had to die whom would I choose? I remember answering, without much thought, 'Martin.' A day or two later he got sick. I was sure it was my fault and resolved not to eat until he was better. Luckily his fever was gone the next day and he was out of bed. I had visions of myself dying of hunger at his bedside."

"You loved him," Barbara decreed, placing my hand on her belly.

"Maybe," I said. "What's the matter? Does it hurt?"

"No, no," she said. "I just wanted your hand. Weren't you glad to have a big brother to protect you?"

"Yes," I said. "A boy threw a stone at me once. His name was Horace but we called him Horseface—he really did have a face like a horse. We saw him throwing stones at our big window; then he turned his behind toward us and bent over, making an obscene gesture. I remember how proud I was of Martin for slapping his face. That winter Horseface fell into a puddle and I laughed until Martin slapped my face and sent me into the house."

"You were no angel," she said.

"That figures," I admitted. "I probably would have been just as mad if I'd been called Horseface."

She kissed my neck and we lay there motionless and silent.

"Do you think we'll find him?" I said.

"Tomorrow," she said drowsily. "We'll see tomorrow. But just a minute . . . ," she suddenly remembered. "You mentioned a homosexual fashion designer. What's that all about?"

I told her about my first encounter with Martin Schiller and our conversation in the train corridor as the Germans demolished their chicken in the compartment. I had begun to describe the street brawl, when I realized she was asleep.

The next morning, right after breakfast, we went to search for my brother. First we checked the list of city residents and the municipal archives in the mayor's office. The clerks were gracious and tried to help, but we found nothing. Then we turned to the Jewish communal organization. While we waited our turn I called Barbara's attention to the door: unlike the others in the building it was made of heavy metal meant to be locked from the inside with a double lock and a heavy steel bolt. "Jews have come back to the other Germany," I whispered, "but safety is safety." Dismayed by the door, she said nothing.

The secretary of the organization, his face veiled in chronic sadness, asked in a whisper how he could help me. As soon as he heard my business he began to nod, as if to say, "Yes, yes; that's how it is." This sort of problem was apparently not new to him and even before I finished, he asked his secretary, an elderly woman, to bring the register of the city's Jewish residents. "Go on, sir, I'm listening," he whispered, closing his eyes. I couldn't decide if this was an effort to concentrate or if he was simply dozing.

The secretary shuffled off to the bookshelf, bringing back a thick ledger from a row of crumpled files and placing it on the desk. The man leafed through the book. Running a clean finger down each row, he found the name Lampel and confirmed the fact that my family had been expelled from the city in 1941. He knew nothing further. He didn't know of my existence and had no record of my brother's being saved, but hastened to note my name and address in the margins of the ledger. "Your brother may turn up some day and ask if we know anything about you," he said, closing the book. He jotted down the names of institutions that might be useful to us in our search. As I took the slip of paper he extended his hand, lowered his head mournfully, and concluded the interview.

We didn't get any further that day. By the time we arrived at the Joint Distribution Committee, office hours were over, and the same was true at the police department. We were told to come back the next morning, that the clerk in charge of citizens' registry was gone for the day.

After two days of dashing from office to office we drew a blank at the Joint, IRSO, the police. We still had hopes of getting some information from the Jewish Agency in Jerusalem, the Missing Persons Bureau of the Department of the Interior, or the International-Zuchdinst in Arolson, a small German town near the Swiss border where Nazi archives were kept; these contained the names of victims, refugees, and persons liberated from concentration camps.

I remember the particular street corner where I was struck by the crucial question—I was coming home from the post office, the letters were on their way. Suddenly, at the corner, the red light flashed STOP! Halt. Perhaps you should stop for a minute and consider. Why are you searching for your brother?

A foolish question, it would seem. Still, it troubled me. Why? Why *was* I searching for my brother? The answer seemed obvious: because he was my brother. Simple, yet not quite. Why my brother in particular, even though others were saved and need help? What is it that makes X, Martin Lampel, my brother? How are we connected? I hardly know him at all. Our common blood means nothing to me; every one of my friends is closer to me than my brother. Any random passerby is potentially closer to me than my brother. If I were to discover he's a thief, a criminal, a man without conscience, what then? In that final second beyond all hope when the ovens were extinguished, he was granted life as a gift to use as he sees fit, without any accounting. He has a right to steal, deceive, exploit, oppress, destroy—and it's not for me to judge his actions. But even though he is my brother, I maintain the right to respond to him as I would to anyone else. In other words, I seek Martin conditionally, only if he merits being my brother. I seek myself in him, just as I shall continue to seek myself in everyone I meet to the end of my days.

When I got home I found Barbara at her typewriter.

"Working?" I asked.

"No," she said, "I had an idea. Why not put notices in the newspapers? Most of them have a missing persons column. Something short and simple: 'Anyone with information pertaining to the whereabouts of Martin Lampel, thirty-five, native of Frankfurt, etc., is requested to contact . . . ,' and then give this address and phone number. What do you think?"

"I don't believe anything will come out of it," I said, sprawling on the sofa.

"You never can tell," she said. "Maybe someone knows Martin. Do you have a picture of him?"

"No," I said, and told her about the two snapshots, the diary, and the letters I had burned in the empty lot behind the Youth Center.

"Why did you burn them?" she asked.

"Don't you understand? I wanted to forget, not to remember—to be reborn far from here and what happened here. I even changed my name. It used to be Hirsch."

"Hirsch?" she asked with surprise.

"Yes, Hirsch Lampel. I changed Hirsch to Zvi and Lampel became Lam. In Hebrew, Zvi is Hirsch. To get a little more distance I changed Zvi to Uri. Martin may have also changed his name. He may not even know his real name."

"What makes you think so?" she asked.

"Did I tell you about the man at the Technion library

in Haifa who asked me if my name was Lampel?" I asked. She shook her head. "He was a childhood friend of Martin's. They were in the same class. When he saw Martin at Teresienstadt during the war Martin stared at him vacantly without recognizing him. And the man who lives in my parents' home gave a similar description. He may have amnesia; he may have forgotten what happened to my parents, my sister, even himself. The nightmare he lived for four years may have been erased from his memory. That often happens."

"Still, I'd put an ad in the paper," she said.

"Yes, let's," I said, seeing Martin in the camp, liberated, standing before the Classifying Committee in striped pajamas, a nervous smile drifting across his fragile face. "What is your name?" they ask him and he blinks silently. The question is repeated gently—in Russian, Polish, English, French. No response. The committee members sigh, the secretary shrugs and makes a note on the white card alongside a number, like the one on Martin's arm. Later he moves through the garden, which is enclosed by a high wall. He rakes the gravel path, collects the falling yellow leaves in a heap—a quiet gracious man, eternally sad. Perfectly normal—only he doesn't know his name, where he comes from, how old he is, what happened before the American army flung open the gates of the camp. Day after day he sits in the doctor's office straining to remember. What is your name? He is finally released and granted a certificate with a name on it, any name: Willy, Maurice, Manfred. When he meets someone he extends his hand and says, "My name is Manfred Sacks. Do you know me?"

What if I should meet him on the street, on the bus, in the park? What if he should approach me and offer his hand? "Yes," I would say, "I do know you." I would lead him to Wagner-Gasse 9, show him his room and the steps where I saw him kiss the plump girl who had asked, "Is Martin home?" I would tell him I'm his brother, remind him of the time he slapped me for rummaging in his drawers, of the picture of a nude woman in a garden, smelling an enormous flower, of Horseface, the kid who threw a stone at me and broke one of our windows. I would whistle sections of "Moonlight Sonata." Suddenly his eyes would light up; he would frown and stutter, Ma-Ma-Martin, and all the rest would begin to unfold. He would remember the piano, the sneakers, my father's black bag, the apple tree in the garden, Miri's dolls, the scarecrow chair in my father's office. Every day he'd remember more and more.

Then what, I asked myself in alarm. What will happen when he remembers the day we were expelled from Frankfurt, when he remembers Miri's cropped hair, my mother's cough, my father, barefoot in the black snow, the white ashes on the lakes? What then? Would he not run to the window with a searing shriek? Why recall the horror, when forgetting is our only salvation, our only escape from madness? Why tamper with the refuge nature offers? Let him forget what happened before 1945. Let him forget me as well. Should I meet him on the street one of these days, should he offer me his hand and say, "I am Martin, Martin Lampel. Do you know me?" . . . I would shake my head vigorously. I would answer in English. I would say I don't speak German, I don't know him. Then I would follow him—at a distance—to his home. I would ask the neighbors about him: who is the charming gentleman on the third floor? What does he do? How does he live? I would send him money every month, anonymously—all my reparations money. Maybe I could visit him, just once, casually, as a stranger. We might become friends and I would play Ravel's "Concerto for the Left Hand" for him. He would sit on the couch listening to Telemann and Buxtehude.

"We'll invite him to dinner some night, OK, Barbara?" I asked.

"Who?" she said, not looking up.

"My brother," I said. "Martin."

"Of course," she said, studying my face.

"And if he really has forgotten, and I hope he has," I said, "if he really doesn't remember what happened to them and to him—we won't remind him. Even if he doesn't know I'm his brother, if he doesn't know who he himself is. Better not to know. What's the difference, really? I'll be *more* than a brother to him. I'll give him all the reparations money. Gladly. It'll be a relief. I have my doubts about that money anyway, I've already told that."

"Yes, you told me," she said. "And I told you I don't understand. That money is yours. It was taken . . ."

"Yes," I said bitterly, "five marks per diem for labor in the quarry. How many marks for the final solution?"

"Nothing will make good those murders!" she cried heatedly, "but that's not the point of the *wider-gut-machung* law. That's not why you collect reparations. I don't understand you. How could you—"

"I know, I know," I said. "Still, I can't forget that this money is for *something* even though I don't want to remember for what. I want to forget. I hope my brother has forgotten. I won't be able to bear it if he remembers and tries to remind me every day of what I'd rather forget."

"But why forget?" she said angrily. "Why must you forget? It's impossible to forget—don't you understand?"

I told her yes I understood, but it was many months before I really did understand. At that moment I didn't want to listen. I pursued my own thoughts. You must forget, I told her, because you cannot forgive. And without forgiveness there is hate, and everything, no matter how trivial, becomes a reminder of those horrors. Her dog isn't just a dog, he's a Gestapo hound hunting skeletons in the forests. The smoke that trails picturesquely from chimneys beyond our window merges with that other sweet smoke. A bar of soap—has she forgotten Dr. Mayer's wife?—is no longer a simple object, and the gas oven in the kitchen is not just an appliance for baking. There is no refuge from these horrors except forgetting. I told her about an article I had read in an English newspaper on the sleep cure. After a patient is put to sleep for a week or two, he calms down and recovers. We all need this treatment,

I told her. If Martin has forgotten, I envy him. I really do.

"Once, in Jerusalem, I heard an odd Yiddish song," I told her, "from a construction worker. He was sitting in a small restaurant in his work clothes, drinking vodka and eating herring. He sang on and on. He was drunk but his faced glowed. When I began the search for Martin the song suddenly came back to me with haunting persistence. I'm just beginning to understand it. Listen:

> *"Hast fargessen tatte mamme*
> *Zayer gut, wider-gut!*
> *Iyz dein bruder dir a soneh*
> *Zeyer gut, wider-gut*
> *Zeyer gut, wider-gut!"**

I explained the unfamiliar words (without completing the phrase that popped into my mind at the end of the song: *"wider-gut-machung"*—as if anything could be "made good" again). She stared at me in deep dismay, not saying a word, until I got up and pulled her toward me onto the couch. When I tried to catch her eye she looked away. She didn't want me to see how worried she was.

"You haven't forgotten anything," she finally said, cracking her knuckles, "with one exception. You forget this is 1959, twenty-six years later. The nightmare is over; it will never recur—not here, not anywhere. The world has learned a lesson. So have we."

"Yes," I said, nodding.

"Isn't that true?" she persisted.

I remained silent, not wanting to offend her. But it was plain she expected an answer. "I have my doubts," I finally said.

"Just what sort of doubts?" she countered.

"Doubts," I replied, with no further comment.

"Such as . . . ?"

---

* "Mother and father both forgotten,
  Very good, good again!
  Your own brother? You say he's rotten?
  Very good, good again!"

"I read the papers," I said. "Not just the ones you read. Sometimes I buy a paper on the street. The *Deutsche Nazional und Soldaten Zeitung*, for example."

"A lunatic fringe," she said.

"Free to walk the street and incite others," I said.

"You think they should be locked up?" she asked bitterly.

"No," I sighed, "that wouldn't help, it wouldn't help at all. The winds of madness are blowing. Take the NPD program: the return of occupied territories, a united Germany, strong and proud. . . . We have paid enough to the Jews. . . . We saved the West from the Communist menace. . . . We demand respect . . . power . . ."

"Shit!" she interrupted, "not everyone talks like that. Listen to the radio, watch TV. Read *Die Zeit* and forget about those yellow journals. There are others—"

I didn't let her finish. Of course there are others, I said impatiently, but you can count them on the fingers of one hand. They make a good show—their stage sets impress the world. An elegant backdrop despite the foul stench from backstage, a stench that prevails to this day, fifteen years after the close of the Nazi tragicomedy. I asked her not to be angry, to listen without interrupting, to hear me out. I could be exaggerating, I told her, but I don't know how to emphasize the truth without overstating it.

Germans, I said, love the theater, especially a hit. Two productions are making it big these days: the East Germans are staging an educational show they call communism; in the West, night after night Germans fill the halls of the great hit, democracy, otherwise known as "how to succeed in business without even trying." Simultaneous productions, in two "other Germanies," not one. The "free world," I told her, its heart filled with suspicion, follows the West German production—democracy—while "tomorrow's world" keeps a watchful eye on communism, the performance in East Germany. No one knows what surprises are in store for us in the third act, whether the performance will assume the character of sweet melodrama or grand tragedy. The citizens, the yawning masses at these government-sponsored events, wait restively for the final curtain, for the moment when the happy circus, the NPD, presents its nationalistic pyrotechnics. They want to see Germany in the popular tightrope act, spitting fire, swallowing swords, galloping over the death wall, executing breakneck historic feats.

I detected a faint smile on Barbara's face. She was, apparently, enjoying the picture. In any case she had to admit that my German had improved considerably. ("The credit is yours, dear teacher, all yours," I said.)

"The metaphors are elegant." she commented, "but the facts are flimsy: they are not all performing." ("I didn't say all," I interrupted.) "There are plenty of people in West Germany who sincerely believe in democracy, the great majority, if you can trust the election returns. And their ranks are growing every day. They fill the universities and—"

"My own darling sweetheart," I said gently. "You are clinging to illusions. You and all the good liberals are listening to yourselves. You gaze into your little mirrors every morning and are pleased with what you see. You read the good newspapers that express your opinions, you listen to commentators who share your views, you mingle with people you like. It's natural—that's how everybody is. It seems to me, and I hope this is a mistake, that you're completely out of touch with the man on the street. The *Deutsche Nazional und Soldaten Zeitung*—'shit.' The NPD—'a lunatic fringe.' When was the last time you talked with the guy at the bar, the average citizen? You have nothing in common with them, you say. But one day, when the volcano erupts, when the murmur becomes deafening, when the earth begins to blaze underfoot, when the results of your democratic elections begin to come in, you'll be shocked and shout 'Help!' "

"You exaggerate, yes, you do, you do, you do," she exclaimed.

"I know," I said. "But let me ask one simple question. What would you do, Barbara, if one of these days—and

I hope this will never come to pass—if the democratic fiasco of 1933 should recur?"

"It won't happen again," she said confidently. "But if it happens I'll get out of here. I'll go to England, America, Israel—it doesn't matter where. I'm not required to cast my lot with the democratic majority."

24 | *the test*

That night I fell asleep at Barbara's side in Edna's bed in Jerusalem. I sat with her in some café, surrounded by strangers who pressed my hand incessantly and ignored her. I saw her napping with Jonathan in the shade of a fig tree beside my house on the border. When I woke up beside her I enjoyed the sweet shade of the yard, though all the rest was washed away with the water dripping in the sink.

The search for my brother, the tense wait for answers from the institutions we'd contacted, the visit to her parents' home, preparations for the wedding—all these concerns pushed aside our decision to go to Israel. As soon as I stopped assuming she would be reluctant, on principle, to live in Jerusalem, I felt free to prolong my stay in Germany. There were other reasons for postponing the voyage. I had to be in Frankfurt to press my reparations claim, and Barbara wanted to finish her courses at the university.

About ten days after I learned of Jonathan's existence (a visit to Dr. Mayer confirmed it) I went with Barbara to Düsseldorf to ask her parents for the hand of their only daughter. I was nervous about this meeting and in the train, Barbara's hand clasped in mine, I prepared several monologues.

"You look good in that suit," Barbara said, scrutinizing me with her father's sharp eyes. "The tie is nice too. You'll make a good impression."

"That's the point, darling. Solid, serious, self-sufficient —a man to whom one can confidently entrust a treasure like you."

"Not so fast. They're not entrusting you with the treasure just yet," she said, sticking her tongue out at me. "You have to convince my father you're the man for the part."

"My bank account won't impress him," I said.

"He won't care about that," she said.

"What *will* he care about?" I asked.

"All sorts of trivial things," she said.

"Like?" I asked.

"He'll want to be sure you love me."

"Very bad," I said. "I'm not prepared for that question. What should I tell him? Help, what should I say?"

"Tell him yes. What do you care?" she smiled.

"And what will you say if he springs that question on you?" I asked.

"I already told him I love you," she said.

"Oh, fine," I said in an offended tone. "Why do you tell other people things you don't tell me?"

"It's embarrassing, I'm shy," she said, fluttering her lashes coyly like a movie starlet.

"I understand," I said. "But tell me anyway. I'll look the other way. Say it. Imagine for a minute that I don't understand German."

"You're cuckoo, and I love you very much," she whispered, though we were alone in the compartment. Pluto leaned his front paws on the windowsill and surveyed the passing scene, his pink tongue trembling like a leaf in the wind.

"I love you, Uri," she repeated, in a whisper.

"Why?" I shouted. Pluto's ears perked up and he glared at me suspiciously.

"I want to know why," I repeated in the tone of an orator. "I want some reasons. Logical, compelling reasons."

"Idiot," she said. "If it were logical I wouldn't trust the feeling. I have no reasons. That's how it is, and that's that."

"There must be some reason," I said. "I want to hear at least one good reason. Not just 'That's how it is, and that's that'."

"I don't know why," she said. "You passed all my tests. I have no idea how my computer makes its calculations or just what data it uses. Smells, colors, chemical reactions. . . . Perhaps. The intensity of your whispers in the dark, the consistency between what you say and your gestures. The fact that you're not stupid has something to do with it, no doubt, though that's not the only reason. It's just one of many factors that my calculator examines automatically and irrationally when it's asked, 'Do you love this man?' I don't even know the coding system of this mysterious computer. Anyway—and this should be clear to you—I don't try to understand why I love you, but I'm sure I do. Yes, yes, I definitely do love you very much. Is that clear?"

"Too bad I didn't take down your speech," I said.

"I'll give it to you in writing sometime," she promised and I kissed her hand.

"Not sometime," I said. "Before the wedding, in triplicate, with two notarized signatures."

"Yes, sir," she replied dutifully.

"OK," I said. "I'm convinced. "Now, the problem is to convince your father."

"Very simple," she said. "Be straight and open like you are with me. Don't be intimidated. Flash your charming smile from time to time—yes, like that. And remember to close your mouth; your teeth are frightening."

"Don't be such a smart-alec," I barked. "Our future is at stake. What if his computer works on an entirely different scheme?"

"There's no doubt," she said, "that he functions not only on emotion; he has a useful, and effective rational computer too. Still, his instincts are decisive. Don't for-

get: the transistors in my computer are inherited from
him. The apple falls close to the tree, as the saying goes.
The odds are pretty good in your favor."

"Still and all, what if he says no?"

"Don't worry. If worse comes to worse we can use our
secret weapon," she said, placing her hand on her belly.
"Jonathan is a most compelling force. And you, my love,
are a considerable force too."

"I'll use every weapon," I promised. " 'Mr. Stahl, I
tried to resist your daughter's charms. I struggled
fiercely to preserve my freedom, but in the end I had to
surrender. Having failed to withstand her power, I
hereby request that you approve the surrender terms.' "

" 'Mr. Lam,' " she said in a deep voice, swinging her
shiny knees, " 'before taking any stand in this struggle
between you and my daughter, permit me to ask a leading question: do you love her?' "

" 'Yes, Mr. Stahl,' " I declared confidently. " 'Yes, yes,
yes, I love her.' "

" 'I shall consider your request,' " she said, nodding
pompously.

The meeting with her father was not as I had
imagined it. I expected the fateful interview to be conducted in a dim room lined with books; I imagined that
after a formal introduction, a drink in the living room,
an exchange of appropriate comments about the weather,
the Common Market, modern architecture, Mrs. Stahl
would say, "Now Barbara, dear, let us leave the gentlemen alone so they can talk."

Mr. Stahl would get up, link his arm in mine with
a show of warm affection that I would disapprove of
and lead me to the library, where we would face each
other in silence, each waiting for the other to begin. But
that's not how it was.

When we got off the train at Düsseldorf, Barbara
dropped my arm suddenly and exclaimed, "Father,"
offering her cheek to a man about my height, neither
short nor stout, with short gray hair that made him
appear younger than he was. His face was tan and he

looked about fifty. A thin wire trailed from his right ear to a hearing aid in the breast pocket of his dark suit. After kissing Barbara on both cheeks he extended his hand to me. "And this is Mr. Lam, I assume," he said. As we headed toward the exit he proposed that Barbara go on home while he and I stop in for a drink. Barbara looked into my eyes and considered this.

"You're not afraid to leave us alone are you, my dear?" he said.

"Actually," she said, "I *am* a bit afraid."

"Don't worry," he said. "It'll be all right. Mr. Lam looks as if he can take care of himself."

"That's just what I'm afraid of," she said. "I don't want him to be put in that position."

"Go on home, my dear," he replied, smiling, "and don't worry. We'll be back for lunch." They exchanged kisses.

We waited until the taxi was out of sight and then went to a nearby hotel. Since it was so early in the day the bar was empty. The waiter appeared with a bowl of salted almonds and tilted his head expectantly.

"Whiskey?" Mr. Stahl asked.

"And soda," I requested.

We scanned each other's faces.

I remained silent.

He loosened his tie. "These places are always overheated," he remarked.

I nodded and loosened my tie too. We smiled in confusion.

He cleared his throat to say something but just then the drinks were served. He lifted his glass and said, "*Prost.*"

"Skoal," I toasted, clinking my glass against his. The ice cubes jingled as we took long sips and exchanged glances, silent again.

"Mr. Lam," he said finally, so quietly that my heart began to pound. "This situation, though I have brought it on myself, is bewildering." He took another sip and cleared his throat uneasily before going on. "On the way to the station I prepared a long lecture. I intended to point out the rashness of your decision. I planned to question you thoroughly, to point out that you and my daughter are incompatible. You're from Israel, she is German; that's quite a gulf to bridge. I intended to intimidate you with a hard line, one that was uncompromising and obstinate. But I see—and I saw it right away—that this tactic will fail. I'm afraid reason isn't much of a weapon when it comes to affairs of the heart and I assume that you do love my daughter . . ."

I nodded, straining to visualize him in a black Gestapo uniform, which was totally inconsistent with his soft eyes and restless hands. The Gestapo man I conjured up was actually more like Martin Schiller.

"If I had only you to fight," he continued, "I might have managed to sustain the role. But war with you involves war with Barbara, and here I throw up my hands." For a moment I saw him marching through the snow, wrapped in a blanket, hands raised in surrender. "Barbara is a powerful woman. You're in for a lot of surprises in this respect. I, at least, as well as my wife and son, are no match for her. She generally knows what she wants, and once she decides, no earthly force can sway her. I respect her good sense, so I tend to give in to her. When she stopped going to church, she almost convinced me to drop it too—she was about sixteen or seventeen then. This time, too, I feel it would be futile to oppose her. All I ask is that you make my retreat easier by convincing me of your personal integrity and declaring your intentions toward my daughter. Skoal."

We clinked glasses and drank up. He looked at me expectantly. I lit a cigarette to occupy my hands and finally, after a long silence, I told him I loved his daughter. I pictured Pluto swinging his flank over her leg, which was stretched before the fire, and told her father in utter candidness that my feelings as well as their intensity were a new and surprising experience. I spoke of other women who had made excursions into my life but swore that his daughter was the first woman whose appeal never dwindled though I had assumed that this chapter would end like the others. I found myself in love with her and overwhelmed as if this was a first romance.

"I asked myself the same questions, Mr. Stahl," I said, and he moved closer so the hearing aid in his pocket would pick up every word. "During those first weeks I challenged myself constantly, seeking reasons to flee and escape what appeared to be a frightening trap. I argued endlessly and finally yielded, finding no further reason to resist. Please, Mr. Stahl, don't underestimate my own preying doubts. After all, as you say, I'm from Israel. I'm a Jew, Barbara is German. There's no need to dwell on the problems *that* presents. No doubt Barbara has told you things I'd rather relegate to silence, at least for the moment. But understand this: having come to terms with myself and decided that our love is greater than all the horror—and the prosecution fills my dreams with evidence of that horror every night—you have no reason to distrust my intentions. And now, to dispose of the formal aspect of our conversation, let me ask *you* a question. Will you, Mr. Stahl, grant me your daughter's hand in marriage?"

He pondered this a moment, then lifted his glass, and said softly, "Skoal. To you, young man. I wish you much happiness." We clinked glasses once more and shook hands heartily. The steel gaze I had noted in Barbara's eyes, on occasion, and in his as well was replaced by a soft, youthful smile.

When we left the bar two drinks later, Barbara's father knew things I myself didn't know. He saw me in several roles: a young architect supporting himself handsomely, hopeful that one day his daring dreams would be realized in concrete; a young man who left school to fight in the war and was wounded in one of the Jerusalem battles (I didn't mention that it was a stray shell that struck my right arm); a dedicated worker in the orchards and fields of the kibbutz—he was reassured when I explained the difference between kibbutz and kolkhoz. I told him about the Sinai campaign and how I had sketched its every turn with a ruler and colored pencils.

Though I tried to avoid the subject of my family, I couldn't bypass the matter of reparations or the astonishing news about my brother. He was moved, and before he could turn away I noticed that his eyes were distinctly moist. I told him I intended to go back to Israel after settling my reparations claim, that Barbara had agreed to join me, that if she found Jerusalem agreeable we would settle there. He would visit us and I was sure, I told him, the country would delight him. "We'll come back to that," he said, glancing at his watch. "Right now it's time to go. Our women are probably worrying."

When we left the hotel and headed for the parking lot, I felt as if I had just passed an exam in school. I wasn't drunk, but if Barbara's father hadn't been there I would have leaped in the air. When the chauffeur in a black uniform opened the rear door of a large Mercedes Mr. Stahl made a point of letting me, his guest and future son-in-law, climb in first. He, too, seemed high. I noticed a tiny smile lurking in the corner of his eyes. As the car picked up speed we caught each other's eye and began to laugh.

Barbara's house wasn't what I expected. True, it was a large two-story structure surrounded by wooded grounds, with a private driveway leading to broad steps at the entrance. But it wasn't very different from other houses we had passed. Barbara was standing in the doorway looking concerned. Pluto leaped toward us barking a joyous welcome. At the top of the steps her father linked his arm in mine. Barbara's eyes lit up. She ran to greet us, planting one kiss on her father's cheek, one kiss on mine.

"As you see, everything is all right," Mr. Stahl said to Barbara, adding, "It didn't hurt, did it, Mr. Lam?"

"The shot of whiskey was a great help," I said.

"I can tell," Barbara laughed.

The house was filled with the fragrance of wax and lilac soap. The elderly maid who awaited us at the door took our coats and hung them on gleaming brass pegs.

When Mr. Stahl introduced me as Barbara's fiancé she bowed stiffly.

"Else," Mr. Stahl explained, "brought Barbara up. She carried her in her arms when she was a baby. What do you think of our Barbara's fiancé, Else? Will he do?"

"Yes, sir," she said curtly. Without a further glance in my direction she retreated. Barbara and her father exchanged meaningful looks.

"Never mind," he said. "She's jealous. Someone is running off with her baby. It's natural—I'm a little jealous myself. Where's your mother?"

"She's waiting in the living room," Barbara said.

"What kind of a mood is she in?" he asked.

"A little better," she said. "How about you, Uri?"

"Splendid," I said. "But don't let me have another drink, or I'll ask your mother to do the cha-cha-cha."

"She can only waltz," Mr. Stahl laughed.

"That's a possibility too," I said.

We walked through a long hall flanked with dark portraits—Barbara's ancestors in nineteenth-century dress escorted us to the living room. At the far end of the room one such portrait, a woman with gray eyes like Barbara's, sat on an antique sofa staring at us, her face an enigma: Mrs. Stahl, just as I had pictured her from Barbara's few references. A tall, slim woman, with black hair pinned away from her face, thin legs, flat shoes, a narrow upper lip which barely moved even when she spoke. As we entered the room all traces of laughter shriveled under Mrs. Stahl's severe gaze. Thick Chinese rugs absorbed our footsteps and in the unbroken silence I thought I could hear Barbara's heartbeat. An antique clock pounded rhythmically as its pendulum swung from side to side.

"Mother, this is Uri," Barbara said.

She extended a frail, bony hand, saying, "Sir," and nodding in a brusque, highly formal manner as she stared at me with eyes full of rebuke.

"Now I know where Barbara's enchanting gray eyes

come from," I said with exaggerated calm to conceal the flattering intent of my remark.

"And I know how you won my daughter's heart," she said, looking toward her husband, who stood to one side enjoying the opening moves of the game.

"I hope it doesn't displease you," I said.

"My opinion carries very little weight in this house, but thank you for your interest," she retorted bitterly.

"Mother," Barbara said in a disapproving voice, and her father quickly intervened to suggest a drink in honor of the occasion. "Vermouth, Henriette?" he asked, and poured it without waiting for an answer.

The vermouth didn't have much effect on her mood, but the additional alcohol made it difficult for me and for Mr. Stahl to control our irrepressible smiles. Barbara linked her arm in mine as if to say, "Look, this is my man," and once when her mother turned her back for a moment she quickly kissed me on the lips. At the sight of such abandon her father, in a broad theatrical gesture, hid his head in his hands.

We managed to eat lunch in peace. Between courses, served by Else, the elderly servant who didn't stop muttering to herself, we discussed the weather along with a variety of trivial matters from the newspaper. Barbara's father caught on to the game rather quickly, but her mother listened gravely to the tales we invented, one of which became part of our repertoire. For years afterward whenever a friend would introduce a topic at dinner and begin with, "Did you see the item about . . ." Barbara or I would volunteer, "You mean the one about the driver in Michigan who collided with a truck, was thrown out of his car, and flung through an open window—only to find his wife in bed with the man who sold him the car?" Mrs. Stahl listened to stories like these without a smile. Barbara sat beside me at lunch, her fingers whispering utterly different stories under the tablecloth.

"What are you two up to under the table?" her father asked.

"Counting fingers," was Barbara's response.

"Are they all there?" he asked.

"We're missing one," she said.

"Take it out of your nose," her father retorted, and we all laughed. Even Mrs. Stahl hid a grudging smile.

I can't remember what we did after lunch. That day, or perhaps the one that followed, when her parents went to church we toured the house. Opening an old bureau drawer and taking out a pile of photographs, Barbara asked me to find her in a class picture of forty children. Naturally I pointed to a girl in glasses—the ugliest kid in the class. Then she took a suitcase down from a chest and showed me her dolls; one of them was like Miri's china doll. The autograph album in which her classmates had written bits of rhymed philosophy ("Know people well/ for it's a human trait/ that today's love/ may turn to hate") also contained some prophetic material: "First comes love/ then comes marriage/ next comes Barbara with a baby carriage."

The walls of her brother's room were covered with photographs from magazines: war scenes, pictures of Khrushchev, Kennedy, de Gaulle, Adenauer, a starving Indian child, an atomic mushroom over the ocean, racing cars, the sad eyes of Anne Frank, Wehrmacht soldiers in a victory march, palm trees, sand, a green sea. "You wouldn't like Gunther," she observed. "I'm glad he's not home." But when I asked her why she only shrugged.

We went out to walk through the gardens. In the greenhouse as my hand dove under her dress, we breathed in the sweet scent of flaming flowers tended by her mother. On the way back to the house she showed me the oak tree that used to hold a swing she had fallen from when she hurt her knee. (So she didn't fall off a horse after all, I noted.) Later, when we were in bed in her room in the attic, I brushed my finger over the thin scar and then kissed it. We heard Pluto barking under the window as we dozed off in the narrow bed in which my future wife had spent her nights when she was a girl.

Barbara's father won my heart on that first visit. In

those two days I had several opportunities for conversation with him—not all real conversations: sometimes a few sentences, sometimes a single remark made me see him in a surprisingly positive light. His frankness, already apparent in the bar, was thoroughly appealing. Once I remember finding him in front of the TV, biting his lips as a cowboy and an Indian battled near the edge of a cliff. He pointed to a chair and placed a finger on his lips; only after the Indian plummeted into the abyss, leaving the cowboy to mount his horse and ride into the setting sun, did he turn off the set and talk to me. After we had exchanged a few idle comments he interrupted me abruptly (I no longer recall the train of thought— I may have said something about Martin or mentioned the visit to my parents' house) and said he would like to tell me a dream.

"I dreamed this before," he said, "many years ago. I saw myself leaving the house, standing in front of a train jammed with people. They held small parcels in their hands and the guards were closing the doors. It was right after the war. I mean, it was right after the war when I first had the dream. I remember walking alongside the cars, here, in front of this house, and asking myself in the dream, 'Why not get on the train and go with those people?' I knew where they were going. The Jewish clockmaker who used to check our house clocks regularly stood in the door of one of those cars. He took off his hat and said, '*Auf wiedersehen*, Herr Stahl,' as he always did when he finished his work. I remember saying to myself, 'I can't go with them. I told Henriette I would be home for dinner. The children will ask for me, and she won't know what to say. Besides, I have to attend to some important matters in the office, the sort that can't be postponed. I have commitments to others.' But when I woke up I knew I hadn't boarded that train simply because I lacked the courage to commit an act of madness, which in this case was just and decent. All my reasoning about responsibility and commitment were excuses. Now, about a week ago, after

Barbara told us about you, I had this dream again. The very same dream. But this time as I walked alongside the train, I knew I had no commitments: my son is in Berlin studying; Barbara is on her own; my wife is provided for. Still, I didn't have the guts. Do you understand? Even in my dream I didn't have the guts to board the train and be led with my watchmaker to a destination from which he never returned."

The room was dark. We remained silent for a long time. I couldn't see his face, but I knew he was looking at me. I wanted to tell him he was a fine and decent human being even if he didn't board that train in his dream. I wanted to tell him that the very fact that he was disturbed by such a thought proved his integrity. But I was silent. Maybe I did say, "Yes, I understand." I remember putting myself in his position for a moment and knowing that I would not have boarded that train either. Good God, I thought, I wouldn't have boarded it even if I had seen my brother Martin's face beside the old clockmaker's.

Our other conversations during that visit were more prosaic. Once, after we had set the date of the wedding and convinced him to settle for as modest and intimate a reception as possible, he asked me with a grave expression how I intended to support his daughter. Though the question was not meant to be a serious one, I told him the reparations money would last us at least a year. When he heard this he turned pale and decreed with unexpected finality, "I can't possibly agree to that." In all innocence I asked him why not. He insisted it was out of the question to entertain such a diabolical idea; he would never agree to have me support his daughter with money paid by Germany for what was perpetrated against my family. "Such a thing is inconceivable," he said, "it's absurd, macabre. I'll take care of you until you get back to work." I tried to argue, but he refused to listen. "I don't want to hear another word on the subject," he declared and left the room.

When I reported this conversation to Barbara on the train back to Frankfurt, she shrugged and said, "My father is crazy, like you." There were, in fact, many more fights in store for us on this issue.

25 | *the wedding*

The wedding ceremony took place at the beginning of November. Jonathan was "five weeks old" when our marriage was registered in the appropriate office in Düsseldorf. I read somewhere that our Jonathan already had fingers, ears, a small nose, lips and eyelids that were just beginning "to float, like petals, around the fringes of his eyes." I remember, as I slipped the ring on Barbara's finger, peering through a microscope at a child aflutter in a sea full of fish.

Besides Barbara's parents there were two other persons present on the bride's side: her brother, Gunther, and a small, thin, frightened woman who reminded me of Dr. Mayer's wife. (Later, when we were alone for a moment, Barbara whispered that this was Aunt Clara, the wife of Uncle Gustaf who was executed by the Germans on the Russian front.) On the groom's side the sole witness was Max, who to my great relief arrived alone.

"I'm glad you came," Barbara said, shaking his hand warmly. "Someone should testify for the defendant before the awful verdict is pronounced."

"I'll even provide bail," laughed Max. Barbara referred the matter to me with a magnanimous gesture.

"I don't want to be released," I said. "I insist on serving my term."

"The defendant's plea will be considered," Barbara said gravely. Only her father smiled.

Later, when I asked about Edna, Max shrugged.

"What happened?" I whispered.

"It doesn't matter," he said.

"Come on, what's up?"

Max said, with an exasperated sigh, "She was offended because we didn't get a formal invitation. A phone call wasn't good enough for her, I guess."

"So that's it," I said.

"I didn't think you would mind," he said with a smile.

Truthfully, I was glad Edna didn't come. Since that first evening, when I appeared in their apartment drunk and battered, we had met several times for coffee or dinner. After each encounter I vowed I'd never see her again. I couldn't bear her pasted-on face, but rather than offend Max I tried to be polite and behaved with a reserve that bristled with hostility. To this day I don't understand how I could have been fond of her once, how I could have . . . but the very thought was revolting to me. I never dreamed she could become such a monster. There was no trace of the old Edna, with a short boyish haircut and jeans, listening to Segovia on her bed in the room on the roof. All I could see now was a little housewife with a bouffant hairdo, a chronic talker with no mind of her own, a gossip whose culture was derived solely from women's magazines and conversations in the beauty parlor, an empty-headed coquette taking great pains to express thirdhand opinions on a standard range of topics. I couldn't understand how anyone could live with such a creature.

Still and all—and I can't quite digest this—Max loved her. Or so he claimed. And since I was fond of Max and delighted to rediscover the Maxie who had marched hand in hand with me onto the boat, Max the clown, who used to share cookies with me, left for him by his "mother" in other children's drawers, I swallowed the rage and revulsion inspired by Edna and treated her with grudging courtesy.

About a week before the wedding, yielding to Edna's persistent demands that I introduce her to my future wife, I had invited them to dinner. The tension between Barbara and the wife of my childhood friend was overwhelming. ("It's so cosy here," Edna exclaimed when she walked in. "And so artistic, just the kind of disorder that's the in thing now." Barbara, staring at her in disbelief, flung a pillow down in the middle of the sofa, studied it with a critical eye, and retorted, "Yes, I copied it from a French magazine.") We both treated Edna with bristling politeness which poor Max endured in silence. All in all we certainly were relieved to learn Edna wasn't coming to the wedding.

At one point in the ceremony, when I glanced toward Barbara's parents and brother, when I saw Aunt Clara's trembling chin, the tears glistening in Mrs. Stahl's eyes, I was overcome by an embarrassing sense of relief. I said to myself, Thank goodness I have no "loving" parents and that I'm free to do as I please. Then, having involved my parents in my festive wedding ceremony, I panicked and the palms of my hand were bathed in sweat. My father placed a cold hand on me and whispered in a broken voice, "How could you do such a thing to us, my son?" A procession of yellow insects marched across my back. Max's touch. I looked at him and he gestured toward the justice of the peace.

"Uri Lam," he repeated, in a remote and empty voice, "do you take Barbara Stahl to be your lawfully wedded wife?" As I turned I saw my mother in Aunt Clara, who stood beside Barbara, dressed in black, muffling a bitter sob in a moist handkerchief, her dim eyes repeating, "How could you?"

"I do," I said, brushing my parents out of the picture. I glanced at the crowd of strangers and was relieved.

"I do," Barbara responded, and suddenly there was silence. Someone whispered, "Ring." I searched my pocket and when I slipped the ring on Barbara's firm finger I saw Jonathan aflutter in a sea of fish. Max's eyes twinkled mischievously and Reb Ludwig Stahl beamed with delight. Barbara's brother peered at his watch with a sigh, a nervous tremor passed across Mrs. Stahl's lips, and Aunt Clara turned away. The justice of the peace was muttering something about the graveness of the moment, the responsibilities of each partner in marriage. He repeated the word "love" again and again so that it suddenly seemed meaningless to me.

Again I saw my parents in Barbara's parents' faces and I held my breath. If they were alive, I thought, would they be standing here with us? Would they accept the verdict with such equanimity. (Don't cry, mother. I can't bear it.) And my father . . . would he tear his jacket in mourning to signify the loss of a son from the family of Israel? "Cursed is he and cursed be his name unto eternity"—I could hear his hollow voice, then a chorus of men in striped pajamas mumbling the age-old, "Amen, amen."

Thank God, I reiterated to myself, that they aren't here and I'm free to take Barbara as my wife.

". . . for better or for worse, in sorrow and in joy, until death do you part." The man's voice soared with pathos and echoed through the room; the ensuing silence was pierced by good wishes and hearty hand-shakes. As Barbara's father embraced me, the scent of cologne rose from my own father's face; then, as I pressed my clenched lips on Mrs. Stahl's drawn cheek, the sour smell of sweat and unfamiliar soap flooded my nostrils. My wife's tightly buttoned brother waited for me to offer my hand and Aunt Clara stood aside timidly, not daring to look up. Max flung his arm about my neck, crying, *"Mazel tov,"* as we ran down the steps, Barbara's hand in mine, and out to a wet gloomy street where the new Mercedes, her father's wedding present, was waiting for us. There was a shower of confetti and rice, and the crowd cheered as we pulled away, dragging a cluster of rattling tin cans behind—and then I knew we were married!

"Chicago!" I shouted, making a sharp turn so the wheels screeched and I was thrown against the horn.

"Nut," she said. "Are you ready for death to do us part?"

I slowed down. Barbara took off her shoes, flung her head back, and sighed. "Well, what do you think of Mrs. Lam?" she said, affecting a reckless manner. She began to blink nervously. I put my arm around her and held her close. The cars behind us honked impatiently.

"Come on, let's run away!" I proposed and we were off.

"Let's go," she cried wildly. "Where to?"

"It doesn't matter," I said. "Let's go somewhere quiet, where there's not a soul. Let's go to Dachau."

She stared at me in utter bewilderment. "You know," she said, "you have a strange sense of humor."

"That's how it looks from the outside," I said. "You should see the mess inside—it's terrifying! You think I didn't see my parents at the ceremony? My brother was there and my sister was right next to you."

Her clever, earnest face froze like a candid snapshot. She was looking straight ahead, but her eyes were lost in the remote regions of our first conversation in bed. I was convinced she could see my brother and sister, and I wished I could see them with her eyes. They looked different. Her brother, Gunther, stood beside her father, one-armed, and poor Ophelia was walking through the garden, naked, a flower in her hand.

"Don't be so grim, my own sweet Yalie," I said. "I didn't invite them, they simply appeared. It's natural. But then we parted. They went their way and we go ours. . . . Where to, my love?"

"Home, of course," she said.

"Do we have to?" I asked.

"No choice," she said. "They're waiting for us. I invited people. Don't make faces. It's not so bad. You can talk to Max. I like him."

"He's a nice guy," I said. "I'm glad she didn't come."

"That's just what I was thinking," she said with a smile.

"I know. But she used to be different—very different." I could see Edna washing her hair in the sink, reaching for the towel in my hand. I turned to the right and the car coasted down Ben-Yehuda Street in Jerusalem. Safi, the painter, waved to me and called out, Look at Uri in his Mercedes; he's caught a real German bombshell.

"You are very beautiful, dearest Barbara. Especially today," I said, stroking her thigh.

"You too. Thanks for the compliment . . . ," she said.

At a red light I turned on the radio: schmaltzy music. I turned it off and lit a cigarette. The light turned green.

"When will you tell them about Johanna?" I asked.

"Johanna?" she echoed in dismay.

I kissed my fingers and then patted her belly. Laughing, she took my hand from the steering wheel and put three kisses in it. "You're cute," she said. I crossed my eyes. She shrieked and wiped away my weird expression with her hand. I slowed down and kissed her on the lips, a kiss that lasted a full mile.

"Our prospects seem fairly good," I said.

"That's what you think," she countered. "You'll ruin this day yet."

"It's the seventh of November," I said. "A day I'll never forget. Do you know why?" She shook her head "I got the Soviet Union to celebrate the October Revolution on our wedding day. They will always remind me it's our anniversary."

"Genius," she said. "I never thought of that."

"Of course," I exclaimed in my most pompous manner, "for you, this wedding is a simple event. For me it's a revolution, an October revolution. I speak for myself and for my country."

"Stop the car," she proposed. "Let's get out and sing the anthems of Israel and Germany."

By the time we reached her parents' home I had taught her the melody of "Hatikvah," but the words were a problem. Instead of "a Jewish soul murmurs" I came up with something like "a Jewish soul aflutter."

When we arrived the house was full. We were greeted with cheers and serenaded by a small jazz combo (they had promised a modest reception!) that began with variations on Mendelssohn's "Wedding March." Then chaos set in. We were engulfed by hordes of people who hugged and kissed Barbara, strangers who shook my hand and slapped my back. Someone handed me champagne. Waiters in uniform floated around the room carrying trays of sandwiches—black caviar and smoked salmon. Sounds merged in my mind: popping corks, shrieking women, the men's ripe laughter, and "Uri, I would like you to meet Herr So-and-so and Frau Such-and-such; I told you about her, remember?" The band began to play "Tzena tzena" in my honor and I pictured a column of German soldiers marching down the main street of Hadera singing in unison, "Tzena tzena—come all you pretty maids and cheer/soldier boys from far and near." Mr. Stahl peered out from the throng and grabbed a glass of champagne from the tray for me. Just as I lifted it to my lips—darkness: Edna swooped toward us, exclaiming, "So here is the happy couple!"

She changed her mind, swallowed her pride, decided to overlook the issue of the formal invitation. Now here she was in Barbara's parents' home, introducing herself as an old friend and telling everyone about my exploits in the war. My husband and Uri, she told everyone (as I learned later), were awarded medals for bravery. They risked their own lives to save the Palmach officer who captured Kastel and killed Abdul-Kadar, commander of the Legion army in Jerusalem. She met us both, so she said, in the hospital, where we lay wounded; she herself escorted a convoy, Sten gun in hand. We both loved her and she loved us both, but in the end Max won because all the girls in Jerusalem were after me and I always knew how to elude their traps. So she was glad some woman finally trapped and tamed the great Don Juan—and other nonsense and lies in a similar vein.

Now, as she approached us, she flung her plump arms around Barbara, kissing her as if they were best friends and offering her cheek to me, but I turned away in time to see Max watching us with a wretched look on his face. When I finally forced myself to shake her hand and thanked her politely for coming she turned to Barbara and said in a loud voice, "No one in Jerusalem will believe Uri Lam is finally hooked. My dear, you should have heard his views on marriage: who needs to marry, to settle down and be buried alive with a wife, and children . . . remember, Uri'le? See, it's not so terrible after all. Right sweetie? I'm so glad you're happy."

I didn't know where to hide. All around us the guests were laughing in amusement. I took Barbara's hand and pulled her after me, getting as far away from Edna as possible. By now she was announcing to the crowd clustered about her (and these were the last words I heard) that Max and I were born in Frankfurt and that our parents . . . Grabbing Max by the arm I dug my nails in his flesh and hissed, "Get her out of here before I lose my cool! You've got to shut her up!"

I knew she would embarrass me. I was humiliated by her ghastly behavior, but, as I later learned, she struck them as the typical Israeli: energetic, plucky, vibrant. They listened eagerly to her repertoire of war stories. Naturally, their curiosity about me was insatiable. To my chagrin after her revolting chatter and vulgar lies they began to picture me as a brilliant architect, a modest hero who, having lost his entire family in Germany, succeeded in overcoming the past, choosing Barbara over all the rich and beautiful women that were pursuing him—a sign of real guts, for "after all, she *is* German."

In short, Edna's efforts sent my stock rising, not only in the eyes of the guests, but even Barbara's mother began to see me in an exotic light. After listening to Edna with rapt attention she actually smiled in my direction. As I say, all this was reported to me later. My impulse was to flee when I heard Edna advertising me and Max as survivors of the holocaust, but Barbara clung to my arm and insisted that we have another drink and still another, which was, of course, a grave mistake. The results of my excessive drinking were soon apparent. I don't recall exactly what happened, but detailed accounts of my conduct were rendered by Max and Barbara the following day, and somewhat later by Erna, a close friend of Barbara's. If I add their descriptions to the foggy fragments retained by my own memory, the following scene emerges.

After six or seven rounds of champagne and two or three whiskeys, I wandered away from Barbara and began to circulate among the guests with Max, my trusty guard. At first I was simply high and engaged in light banter with anyone who crossed my path. I lavished compliments on the ladies, expressed my views on Germany's economic situation, offered schemes for global peace, and in one conversation—or rather in one of the conversations Max overheard—I told the production manager of Opticum, who had been trying to reduce for years, about a new diet which allows an unlimited intake of food. Naturally, the man was eager to hear more, so after elaborate questions about his eating habits I finally suggested that he abandon any dietary regimen, eat what he pleases without counting calories, and simply end every meal by tickling his palate with a goose feather to induce vomiting, in noble Roman fashion. Moving from him to Mrs. Stahl, I coaxed her to drink to brotherhood with me, then whirled her around the dance floor in a fiery Viennese waltz (I remember this only dimly) which brought color to her drawn cheeks.

From this high I escalated to the level of tipsy charm, following my feet wherever they carried me, ready to share my feelings and my wealth with the entire world. I sang a children's jingle: "Turn to the left/turn to the right/then circle round with all your might," and explained (incredible as it may seem) that this sad song was the anthem of the center parties in Israel, constantly battered by leftists and rightists. Anyway, that's what Max reported—he *must* have been lying. He claims I gave my car keys to a student who had to get back to town, saying it was my gift to him, but Max retrieved them in the nick of time. I dragged timid Aunt Clara into a corner and whispered with her for a long while. I argued with Gunther about Germany's position in Europe. Actually, it was no argument; he would voice his opinions and then I would grade them—Gunther, you're even more of a fool than I imagined—so the exchange with him was brief. He left me in the midst of these evaluations, but I had my say to a waiter who happened by.

After several encounters with Barbara, each of which

evoked the same phrase: "Madam, haven't we met some-where?" I flopped into a soft sofa between Erna and a young man whose name I didn't catch, both of them close friends of Barbara's, both active members of the Catholic organization "Aktion Sühnen-Sachen" dedicated to atoning for Germany's war crimes. The man had spent three months in a kibbutz founded by survivors of the resistance movement in Europe's ghettos. He had harvested potatoes and weeded carrot beds. Erna was planning to spend the summer rehabilitating amputees in Jerusalem. I don't remember what I told them, but Barbara, observing me from a distance, said I never stopped laughing and stroking Erna's leg, though the two of them remained silent. When I met Erna a few months later she reminded me of the lewd jokes I had told her at my wedding. She said that the young man she was with had moved away in disgust. I had no recollection of this, though I vaguely remember stroking Erna's full, flaming thighs and once, when I whispered something in her ear, she sighed voluptuously and pressed her leg against mine. At this point we were joined by Barbara. Again I said she looked familiar and told her I'd invited Erna to live with us in Jerusalem and to share our bed, an act which would deepen her understanding of the cooperative movement. Barbara, who was also drunk, was enthusiastic about the whole idea, but Erna blushed and said nothing.

Later the champagne went to my head and my drunken chatter gave way to clumsiness and incoherence. Max claims that I approached one of the older men from be-hind and whispered "Nazi!" in his ear. The man paled and stared at me in shock; then without a word he snatched up his coat and left. Max tried to restrain me but I refused to cooperate. People began to notice my wild behavior. Once Max almost managed to herd me into the library but I jerked away violently and pulled Barbara's father into a corner and, according to Max, demanded to know what he did during the war. Looking at me coldly he said, "Am I expected to account to you?" to which I answered, "Yes, Herr Stahl, you owe me an accounting. I, Uri Lam, alias Hirsch Lampel, a citizen of Frankfurt until 1941, have taken your daughter as my wife and you owe me an accounting."

Max tried to intervene, but Barbara's father, his face white, countered, "What if I tell you I cooperated with the Nazi regime, would it change anything with respect to my daughter?"

"It would, it certainly would," I muttered to myself.

"If so, why didn't you ask yesterday, before marrying my daughter?" I didn't know how to answer this challenge. "I don't owe you an accounting," Barbara's father continued in a whispered shout. "And I can't tolerate vulgarity. You are drunk, Mr. Lam, and under the circumstances my words would be wasted. I suggest you sleep it off and when you're sober, if you have the courage to repeat your question, I'll be happy to answer it." At this point, according to Max, I grabbed Mr. Stahl's lapels. Max succeeded in disengaging me, but I continued to shout obscenities (in Hebrew, luckily) until Max slapped my face (a quick slap which no one noticed) and I lost consciousness. The two of them dragged me to an adjoining room, took off my shoes, and put me to bed.

After an hour—it seemed like an eternity—I got up, my head heavy; groping in the dark I found the bathroom and vomited my soul on the floor. Then I washed my face with cold water, took off my jacket, and flopped back on the bed. Far away I heard a familiar tune. The whole house lay profoundly silent and someone a long way off was playing the last part of a sonata in which there was a full moon and rippling river waters. Halfway to dreams I heard applause and then succumbed to a deep sleep from which I wished I'd never waken.

26 | *the wedding trip*

The next day I couldn't remember a thing that happened at the wedding reception. A mixture of champagne and dust weighted down my head when I pried my eyes open. Barbara was sleeping at my side, fully clothed. "What happened?" I cried in a sour, scratchy voice. I couldn't understand why we were there, nor would I believe her drowsy words. Seeing the alarm in my face, she broke into mounting laughter.

"What's so funny?" I asked.

"You—you make me laugh. You look like a little boy who's just been scolded."

I would have stuck my tongue out if I hadn't been too upset. "You're not telling the truth. Stop keeping me in suspense," I said.

Convinced that the things she was telling me had no basis in reality, I was sure she was just embellishing the little I remembered with made-up details. I remembered Edna's chatter. I vaguely recalled waltzing with Barbara's mother, sitting with Erna, speaking with Gunther. I was willing to believe that I sang an Israeli song with Max in two-part harmony, that I goosed a woman balancing champagne in one hand and a dish of sandwiches in the other. That much seemed plausible. But I would absolutely not concede that I shoved Aunt Clara (literally) into a corner and gave her a detailed account of our first days in bed when we had no common language. I didn't believe that Herman the translator was at the party and that I tried to explain in German just why I had refused to speak German. I didn't remember proposing that Erna share our bed in Jerusalem, though the idea was exciting. And of course I didn't recall the conversation with Barbara's father—Max had recounted the details of this little episode. But she swore repeatedly that it all really happened, that she had witnessed some of it personally and had reliable eyewitness accounts about the rest. If I didn't believe her, why didn't I ask Max, who never stirred from my side the whole evening? When she saw the confusion in my face she drew me close and said it was no tragedy. After all, I was drunk, and there's nothing wrong with being drunk at your own wedding.

"Are you sure I asked your father what he did during the war?" I asked, incredulous.

"That's what Max told me," she said.

"Why all of a sudden? How could I do such a thing? What a remarkable lack of tact!" I said.

"It's not so terrible, Uri," she said. "You were drunk."

"I hate people who get drunk and can't remember what they did the next day," I said. "It's a good thing I didn't break anything."

"As a matter of fact, you did," she retorted. "But it doesn't matter."

"What? What did I break?" I asked in alarm.

"Nothing much. Three or four champagne glasses. You drank the champagne in one gulp, like vodka, and flung the glasses away with a regal gesture. It was pretty funny."

"Who, me?" I asked in astonishment.

"Yes, you," she said. "I saw it myself, it so happens."

"Why didn't you stop me?"

"I tried, but you said you couldn't remember where you knew me from, or some such line."

"That's not true," I insisted passionately. "I never said any such thing."

"You certainly did, but it doesn't matter. No one cared how many glasses you broke either. It's better to break a glass with a flourish than to drop it by accident and make an awkward apology. Don't worry. Plenty of glasses were broken yesterday."

I heard a door open in the distance. Someone said good morning. I looked at Barbara. Her eyes were glowing. I kissed her on the mouth, a perfunctory morning kiss. "Good morning, husband," she said.

"It's not morning and it's not good," I grumbled, a sour taste in my throat.

"But you *are* my husband."

"That's right," I agreed, cradling her face in the palm of my hand.

"They'll be here soon to check the sheet," she said. "You know, the wedding night. It's a tradition."

"What can we do?" I said. "We violated the tradition. Shall we get up?"

"Let's," she said. "I'm going to take a bath."

"Is it all right?" I asked placing my hand on her belly.

"Idiot, of course it's all right," she laughed. "Do you want to take one too?"

"No," I said. "I've got to commune with my soul in the john."

When I got out of bed the floor was whirling and my feet were like lead. I closed the bathroom door with a sense of relief.

Now what, I asked myself. I have to leave this room and face her parents' chilly stare. How could I have asked such a question? They'll overlook the incident with brutal tact. Breaking glasses, goosing ladies, shouting obscenities—what did I whisper in Erna's ear?—poor Aunt Clara in a corner with me. And the climax: Where were you during the war, Mr. Stahl? What nerve! What vulgarity! I know them, that well-bred bunch. They'll smile at me politely and pretend nothing happened—and add my humiliating behavior to their list of forbidden topics. Another subject to be avoided, like syphilis, like those camps, like the years 1933 to 1945 which vanished so miraculously from German history. (In the Baedeker guide to Frankfurt, the list of important dates jumps from 1934, the year the airport was opened, to 1943–1945, with this entry: "Heavy air bombardment; the center of Frankfurt was utterly demolished and transformed into a heap of rubble." And that's all.) They'll deny my embarrassing performance, just the way they deny so many other compromising events, and torment me with cruel silence. I know.

"I'm almost finished, Uri," I heard Barbara call from the other side of the door.

So I asked him what he did during the war, so what,

I reasoned to myself. Is it wrong to ask a murderer how he slept the night he killed your father? In the victim's home it may be gross to refer to a noose, but in the hangman's home, why not? Why should I feel guilty? What did he do during the war years—a legitimate question! Let him give me a simple yes or no answer. If he had nothing to do with it there's no problem. And if he did—even if it was only the slightest involvement, say, adding a signature to many others on the list of those to be deported or weighing gold fillings—what then? How would I respond? Barbara, explain to your father that I can't accept the car, that I can't eat at the table with him. He's part of the nightmare I am trying to forget. How can I forget those horrors when I see him strolling in the garden, brushing his teeth, washing his hands, saying *gut Nacht*? He says *gut Nacht* and I hear *gut Nacht und Nebel*; I see the night and fog that swallowed up my parents, my brother, my sister.

"Are you asleep, darling?" said Barbara's voice through a fog.

When I came out she was dressed. Her hair was shampooed and fell smoothly over her face. As I shaved I saw her face peering at me in the mirror and for a moment I didn't believe this handsome young woman could be my wife as well as a daughter of one of *them*.

"Still," I said, "what did he do in the war?"

"Who?" she asked.

"Your father?"

'You really want to know?" she asked.

"I'm not sure," I said, hesitating.

"Why didn't you ask sooner, before we were married?" she asked.

"I was afraid of the answer," I replied weakly.

"And now?"

"Now you're my wife, and I want you to be my wife. Your father's past has no bearing on it."

"Even if . . . ?" she asked.

"Even if," I asserted to bolster my own confidence.

"What do you think he did?" she asked, studying my reflection in the mirror with large, grave eyes.

"I don't know," I said. "I'm afraid to guess. Besides, it seems impossible. Horns and tails went out of style with Goethe. In our day the devil's disciples wear Orlon suits, drink whiskey, smoke cigars. They're married, raise children, have heartburn, spend the evening watching TV. I really don't know. At first, right after the war, they were considered monsters, wild animals, madmen; now it seems they were just average—honest merchants, white-collar workers, ordinary middle-class families, like your own neighbors, like the charming people one sees at concerts and—who knows—maybe like your parents."

"Relax," she said. "It's not what you suspect. But talk to him. Ask him. I'm sure he'll tell you the truth."

A few weeks later, when Barbara informed her parents she was pregnant and her father came to visit us in Frankfurt, I got to discuss the war years with him again. That morning, however, when we found him sitting near the fire reading, I didn't dare raise the subject. I said good morning and he put down his book, returning my greeting with his usual warmth. As I predicted, no one referred to the events of the previous night. Even Barbara's mother claimed she had too much to drink and to prove it placed her shriveled hand on her forehead and closed her eyes.

Only Gunther's manner was chilly—he left the table as soon as we sat down. But Barbara assured me this was his usual way. "He ignores me too," she said. Barbara's parents joined us for coffee, and after clearing my throat once or twice I apologized for my behavior. "Nonsense, we all had a lot to drink," her father said, dismissing my words with a casual gesture, and though I searched his eyes I didn't detect any further meaning.

"Have you opened your gifts?" her mother asked. They were piled up in Barbara's room: a colorful array of bags and boxes wrapped in bright paper and tied with gay ribbon. The excitement with which I opened the first box took me back to the sweet birthday parties of my childhood. I could taste the chocolate cake and count seven, eight, nine candles. These were my last birthdays, with my parents watching in the doorway as

I unwrapped each package, enjoying the gleeful squeals evoked by such things as a red tin flashlight, a book of jungle animals, a real football, a watch, a grown-up watch.

We spent a long time opening the presents and reading the messages. There was silver, kitchen utensils, a carpet sweeper, Rosenthal china for twelve, a TV set, books, ashtrays, two drawings we didn't like, a Persian rug, linens, and assorted household goods without which, in the opinion of the senders, married life was unlivable. One of Barbara's close friends sent us a package of diapers and a set of pink and blue baby clothes with a note: "I hope you soon have use for the enclosed," which amused us no end. Max sent a giant package of candy, chocolate, cookies, and other goodies. "A gift from other children's mothers and from Maxie," the note said. There was also a check.

The most valuable presents were in envelopes: money and stock in various Düsseldorf industries. While I busied myself with the boxes, Barbara read out the sums in a festive voice. I saw a mark slip from one envelope and noted an odd expression in her eyes as she scanned the letter. She read it, glancing quickly in my direction, and with a slow gesture that contradicted the pallor of her face, returned the letter to its envelope, stuck it under the pillow, and opened another.

"What was in there?" I asked.

"Where?" she asked innocently.

"In the last envelope," I said. "The one with the mark that you slipped under the pillow."

"Nothing special," she said, straining to be casual. "Someone's idea of a practical joke."

"Show me the envelope," I demanded.

"Nonsense," she said. "It's nothing."

"Barbara," I said, looking her squarely in the eye, "you're not much of an actress. It's lucky you don't play poker. Anyone could see through your bluff. Show me the envelope, please."

"It will make you mad," she argued, "and I don't want you to get upset. It's just some fool's idea of a joke."

I persisted. All her pleas were to no avail; it was no longer a matter of idle curiosity. I insisted on my right to see the letter, which was addressed to both of us. The issue almost led to a fight. She tried to destroy the envelope and I tried to force her to hand it to me. "That hurts!" she cried, but I didn't relent until she handed me the crumpled letter.

"It's nonsense. I can't imagine who could have done such a thing," she said when I finally had the letter in my hand. It contained a five-mark bill wrapped in a sheet of paper with the following typewritten message: "Mr. Lam, accept six marks, a last and final payment of the reparations you claim as your due. As for you, Barbara, we extend our sincere sympathy to your parents and friends in their untimely bereavement." The letter was unsigned. I studied it for a while in disbelief. Barbara reached for the letter—I don't remember if I put it on the bed or if it slipped out of my hand—and tore both the letter and the money to shreds.

"A terrific sense of humor," I said bitterly, trying to force a smile. "Who could it be?"

"I have no idea," Barbara said quietly. She turned to me with moist eyes. I got up and went to the window. I couldn't stand to look at any more presents.

"Barbara," I said, finally.

"What is it, Uri?" She was standing beside me.

"Let's go home," I said.

"Now?"

"Yes, now. We've had enough wedding. Let's go home."

"You're so stubborn," she said. "I knew it would upset you."

"I'm not upset," I said. "I'm just tired of the whole production. We didn't need it—we went along with it for your parents' sake. But now the show is over. The audience has gone home."

As we stood near the window in a long embrace I remembered our first morning, together at her window, naked. She rubbed her cheek against my shoulder gently and rested her head on my chest, saying, "Yes, let's go."

To this day, whenever I think of winter I'm reminded of the drive from Düsseldorf to Frankfurt over the rain-swept *autostrasse*. A violent downpour lashed the fogged-up windshield, the wipers squeaked mournfully from side to side. Pluto stood in the back seat watching the infinite road being swallowed up behind us. Barbara was beside me, silent. I don't think we exchanged a word throughout the trip. I remember wanting to talk to her, but not knowing what to say. Every sentence I composed seemed inane and meaningless.

We left the presents on the bed. Barbara announced to her mother that we'd be back for them in a week or two. Though her father was surprised by our sudden departure (the wedding took place on Friday and they'd expected us to stay at least until Monday), he made no attempt to dissuade us. As we drove along I thought of Stahl's periscopes and the letter. Who had sent it? Her brother? Herman? I remember being depressed and not knowing exactly why—the letter alone couldn't have affected my mood to such an extent. More likely it was the gloomy day, the dark skies, the jazz from the radio. Or maybe it was Edna, Herr Stahl, a headache, the sourness in my mouth, the broken champagne glasses. Any of these trivial things could account for my depression. Even the new car irritated me. Look at him! Driving around in the Mercedes he got as a gift! Six marks as final payment . . . I was about to swerve off the road and plunge into a dark valley when I suddenly met Barbara's eyes, which were soft and doleful. I slowed down.

At home two letters pertaining to my brother, Martin, awaited us. The Jewish Agency had no record of him but promised to contact me the minute there was any news. The Department of the Interior had sent a form for me to fill out and send back, along with a small fee; in return I'd be informed if the party in question was listed in the census. All at once, for the first time since I arrived in Frankfurt, I was overwhelmed with longing for my own country. I yearned to be in Jerusalem, in my house near the border, among friends. I wished I was at work at my drawing board, even if this meant working on those awful Brumberg developments. I was tired of speaking German.

We had a bite in the kitchen, standing up, and went to bed. As soon as the light was out I closed my eyes and fell asleep without even saying good night.

I don't remember what we did the next day, but the day after that in the morning mail there was another letter about Martin. The Nazi archives in Arolsen informed us that a man named Martin Lampel, born in Frankfurt in 1924, was released from Dachau in 1945 and sent to a mental hospital in Goeting, near Munich. (Dachau? How did he get there?) Without taking in all the implications of this letter I decided to set out for Goeting that very morning. I wanted to go alone, but Barbara was determined to come too. Though I tried to dissuade her, explaining that it was a long trip and that in her condition it wasn't wise to travel unnecessarily— I even suggested that it might be better for me to be alone if and when I found my brother—it was no use. "I'm going with you," she decreed.

"What about the dog?" I argued. "Who'll look after him?"

"We can take him along," she said.

"I can't take a dog on this kind of trip," I said, disgruntled. I almost slipped and said "a German dog."

"He won't bother you," she promised. "He'll stay in the car with me."

Another long exhausting drive in heavy rain. We traveled four hours in silence, driving at high speed. I saw myself entering the hospital, a gloomy walled structure, and finding my one-armed brother, Martin, staring at the rain that was falling in the garden, a lost expression in his eyes. I would speak to him, but he wouldn't hear. I would question him; he wouldn't respond. In one of many hospital scenes, this one framed by bare chestnut trees, he would approach me and say, "My name is Martin. Martin Lampel. Do you know me?" I would turn away in silence. In another hospital—this one an ancient moss-covered castle—I would find Dr. Mayer, who would remove his wig and say, "I'm very sorry." I wouldn't know just what he was sorry about. Was Martin dead? Gone? Released leaving no traces? Then the doctor would say, "I remember your brother well. He was an exceptional person. Quiet and modest. He used to play Bach for us—on a comb.

But when we finally arrived at Goeting and, after many inquiries, found the hospital, I didn't notice if it was walled or if there were trees around it, and if so what sort of trees they were. Leaving Barbara in the car I bounded up the broad steps. Inside the white door I was received by a man in a white jacket with black sleeves, who searched at considerable length through a large book. Lampel, Lampel—yes. Here we have a Lampel, Martin. He was released in 1949 and went to Frankfurt. No, he didn't leave an address. You could try the Frankfurt police. The mayor's office might have some information or the Jewish communal agencies. I'm very sorry—really.

I was already in the hall on my way out, but I turned back and asked to see the director of the institution. Yes, of course, sir. Follow me. A hard bench in the hall and a long nerve-wracking wait. When he was ready for me, the man behind the desk, the director, looked up with a mechanical show of understanding. Lampel, Lampel. We'll check his personal file. Then, to the intercom, "I would like the folder of Lampel, Martin Lampel: 1949. Do you smoke, sir? They'll bring the folder and we can check. Many patients have been accommodated in our institution and of course I don't remember them all." His narrow, precise lips moved tirelessly. I forget what he asked and what I answered in that nightmarish interval. Finally the black-sleeved man appeared, holding a tattered green folder. "Yes, yes," the director said. "A common enough pattern. Dachau. Then four years in our care. Schizophrenia and paranoia. Very natural in his situation. What? No, he didn't speak of you. He was sure he was the only member of the family to survive. And I see two attempts at suicide. Yes, yes. Just a minute. There is an address here, Wagner-Gasse 9.

Frankfurt. He kept a bill for piano tuning which had been sent to that address."

I walked down the steps slowly, despite the heavy rain. I got into the car and asked Barbara to drive. She drove in silence, waiting for me to speak. "Apparently he *is* alive," I said as the car began to move, "but no one knows where." I was tired and closed my eyes. When we got home Martin was on the sofa covered with a white sheet. His face was yellow and transparent, like wax. When I pulled his hair to wake him up, the skin began to peel away, hair and all. I heard the jingle of coins in tin cans, and under the window someone crooned, "Charity saveth from death."

Barbara brought coffee and cake from the kitchen and set the cups on Martin's back. As we sat beside the fire the dog settled at our feet, staring at the cake and wailing plaintively. I awoke and found myself in the car beside Barbara. "Quiet, Pluto," Barbara was saying. We had stopped in a large empty parking lot. It was no longer raining, and through the foggy windshield I saw a large building with a black-tiled roof, bathed in mist.

"Where are we?"

"Dachau," she said. "Do you want to go in?"

27 | *on the threshold*

I was half asleep and at first I wasn't sure if the situation was real or part dream: Martin on the couch, the dog wailing at the gates of Dachau. What happened? How did we get here? What did she say? Do I want to go in? Why did she bring me here, anyway?

I now know her intentions were good. We were on the highway from Munich to Frankfurt and she lost her way. But at that moment, for a fraction of a second, I felt trapped; as if Barbara had plotted the confrontation I was hoping to avoid, as if she was deliberately pushing me toward this terrible place so I would make peace with it at long last. The wicked image of a boy named Dave, Davey-Knavey we called him behind his back, was conjured up in my mind. He was the strongest kid in our class, and from the very first day I hated him bitterly. Not long after school started Max summoned the courage to wear shorts like the other boys and expose his bony white legs. When he appeared in class Davey-Knavey's cruel taunts resounded throughout the room. "Get a load of that skinny refugee. They took him out of the oven before it was time." Silence. No one dared speak up. He would single out one of the weak children to be his slave: make his bed, shine his shoes, stand up when he passed. Once when I was walking through the pine grove I saw Max tied to a tree, his hands bound behind his back, as Davey-Knavey beat him up. I threw a stone and hit the bully's ear. He ran to the infirmary, screaming; his shirt was soaked with blood. He never touched Max again. Whenever he came near me I would pick up a heavy stone and toss it from hand to hand. We didn't speak to each other for a whole year, although he tried to make peace with me more than once. His mother used to bring him special treats, and once he sent one of his little slaves to me with a slice of cake and two yellow candies. I saw him hiding behind the dining hall, watching, so I promptly threw the cake down and crushed it with my shoe. One day some of the boys pushed me into a room and closed the door. Inside Davey-Knavey was smiling ingratiatingly. The kids thought this would force us to come to terms with each other, but I opened the window, tore off the screen, and jumped out. He's now a senior officer in the Israeli army, with a distinguished record in the Sinai campaign, so I hear. Not too long ago we passed each other in the street and nodded politely.

Sitting in the car (do you want to go in, she asked) I felt for a moment that Barbara would have liked to push me into the camp and close the door. She thinks, so I speculated, that if I find myself face to face with this terrifying place, I'll have to come to terms with it.

But my first impulse was escape, self-preservation. I heard the shrill sound of the shell that fell beside me in Jerusalem without exploding. Then too, when I saw the shell in the ground six feet away from me, I wanted to run. And then, as now, I couldn't stir. The time that elapsed before I could mobilize myself was the longest interval in my life. I recalled taking a few steps, retracing them almost against my will, kneeling over the shell, and finally picking it up. I studied this instrument of destruction which had appeared from heaven for a crucial rendezvous. Why did it fail to fulfill its destiny? Why am I alive and someone else dead? I wanted to take it apart and analyze it, to learn the components of terror. I wanted to tempt fate, though I knew that if I insisted on handling the damn thing it was likely to shatter in my hands and split my gut open. I finally hurled it down the hill and cleared out.

I experienced something similar, terror mixed with fierce curiosity, when I found myself at the gates of Dachau. To take apart the terror, stare it in the eye without turning aside, that's the only way. Time for the inevitable encounter, I told myself, and nodded to Barbara.

"Yes," I said. "Let's go in."

We got out in the damp mist. The dog barked happily and raced toward the gate.

28 | *stigmata*

When we got home that night I didn't feel anything unusual. Fatigue seemed natural after such a long trip and I thought a warm bath and supper would refresh me. I sat on the bed and took off my shoes. Barbara undressed lazily. As soon as the bathroom door closed behind her I flopped on the bed and fell asleep in my clothes. A minute later, I stepped out of the car into the fog. I opened my eyes and saw Barbara naked. I asked why she wasn't taking her bath and was astonished to learn she had been in the tub more than half an hour.

I flung my clothes on the floor and a chill passed through my body. Closing the bathroom door I stood beside the sink for a moment and wiped the fogged-up mirror. The face that confronted me was my everyday face. The same mustache, the same high forehead unburdened by worry. Even the eyes were unchanged. If I were to see myself on the street, I thought, it would never occur to me that this is me. Something has, after all, happened. Why is there no trace of it in my face? You have married a German girl, I told the face that peered at me. You have received a slap and six marks in the mail. Your brother, Martin, was not destroyed with the others; you saw that awful place—and it's impossible to discern any of this in your face. You don't even need a shave. Try for a second to relax your face muscles, to discard the mask. Make an effort. Your face might reveal something, a fleeting tremor in the corner of your mouth, a tear in your dry eyes. . . .

The floor was cold and I began to shiver. I stood on the mat at the foot of the tub but my teeth continued to chatter. I turned the hot water on, then off. Want a warm bath? I slapped myself. The little brat wants a warm bath. I yearned to feel the crown of thorns, to reach my hand into the fog and touch their frozen fingers. I searched for a sign, the faintest sign of stigmata. Turn on the cold water and test your endurance. See if you can take it.

I turned the faucet and saw the canal in the clover field, the pond in the abandoned orange grove, the people lined up for water on Mamilla Road, the damned ashes floating on bewitched waters. I put my foot in the tub—torture. The cold water burned my feet. I counted to three. I started over and counted six marks, seven fires of hell, age ten in a train to the border. I turned off the faucet and, all at once, closing my eyes and holding my breath, I dove into the icy bath.

Twice I've swum in the sea in winter—once of my own free will when I read in the sports section about a Swedish club whose aged members take a morning dip regardless of the weather, and another time because of a bet with friends. So I expected the sensation to be familiar: a moment of shock, but after a few vigorous strokes your body adjusts. At least that's what happens in the sea, where you can thrash around. But to this day I shudder when I think of that cold bath in Barbara's apartment. As soon as my body was immersed in water I had an impulse to leap out of the tub screaming. I thought I was losing consciousness. I tried to inhale but my lungs were enclosed in cold steel. When I managed to snatch a few rapid breaths I felt as though the flesh was being plucked from my body, as if I was being skinned and dipped in a tub of vinegar. The soles of my feet were suddenly numb. I felt dizzy and my head began to sink. With the last shreds of consciousness I surfaced, climbed out of the tub, and began to jump in place, to swing my arms, to stretch, to knead every muscle. I regained some sensation in my legs but my teeth kept on chattering. I went back to the bedroom; tore the covers off the bed and curled up under the blanket, folding my knees under my chin and hugging myself tight. "Barbara!" I shouted, "come here!" She was surprised to find me in bed.

"Supper's ready," she said. "Don't you want to eat?"

"Later," I said, my teeth rattling. "Lie down with me for a minute. I'm freezing."

She laughed and turned to go back to the kitchen, but I leaped at her and threw her on the bed. I covered us both with blankets and began to writhe convulsively. With trembling, impatient hands I opened her robe and pressed my body against hers for warmth. She screamed.

"You're cold as ice!" she cried in alarm.

"I know," I said. "I took a cold shower. Warm me up, my love. I'm cold, I'm cold."

"Cold water!" She was shocked. "Are you out of your mind?"

"I was trying to wake up," I lied, and pressed her to

me until the warmth of her body began to flow gradually into mine.

"You certainly *are* awake," she laughed, and I realized
that my efforts to warm up had indeed assumed another
character. Before I knew what was what we were locked
together, panting, my mouth was buried in her neck and
in her warm breasts; her eyelashes fluttered, her nostrils
were tremulous, she bit her lip until it turned white
between her teeth, and on and on—until my breath
expired with hers and all at once we found ourselves on
the mattress beneath a heap of blankets and sheets.

I took the elevator down from the roof and at every
flight I sank into deeper slumber. The elevator lurched
and stopped. "Sweetheart," I heard, then Barbara's laugh.
"Don't go to sleep. Supper's ready." Her eyes were
radiant, her cheeks ablaze, like the night when I first
feasted my eyes on her naked body. "Food, din-din," she
said, opening and closing her mouth in pantomime. I
pictured an omelet floating in grease and was nauseous.
My mouth was dry and scaly. I was thirsty, I wanted
tea with lemon.

"Get up, darling, I'm starved."

When I got out of bed I felt dizzy and the room
seemed to whirl. I lit a cigarette, then snuffed it out in
the ashtray. It tasted like tar. The kitchen table, set
with leftovers, was enough to induce vomiting: cheeses,
salad, a chunk of smoked eel, jelly, black blood sausage,
cold chicken. I asked for tea, tea with lemon. Barbara
filled the kettle and set it on the stove. I had no desire
to eat, but she buttered a slice of bread and placed a
piece of chicken on my dish. I ate unenthusiastically,
my eyes were riveted on Barbara. She apparently was
very hungry. She usually peeled everything, even a pear,
cutting it into sections to eat with a fork, but all at once
she seized the chicken in her hands and was devouring
it. I couldn't believe my eyes. When she finished tearing
off the meat, she began to pull apart the joints with her
teeth and to suck the marrow. There was a peculiar
smell in the air. "Gas!" I said. "You turned on the gas

and forgot to light it." She got up (a cup fell and shattered; Pluto started) and turned off the gas. When she opened the window to air the place out a strong wind whirled through the kitchen scattering the paper napkins, which flew about the room like giant snowflakes.

Later, when we were back in bed, I took two small sips of tea and wrapped myself in her arms. As I closed my eyes to shut out the light I heard Barbara whisper, "Good night, my love." I opened my eyes in ruddy darkness and would have asked why she took me there except that it required too great an effort. I saw myself at the camp, marching through the fog. I saw Pluto burrowing in the earth near one of the cabins and I dozed off. When I awoke a few seconds later I was bathed in sweat. My face was flaming and the damp sheet clung to my body. The room was dipped in red light. All the electric heaters were on. Electric coils, red and blinding, glowed along the walls. My nose was dry and my saliva sticky. I tore off the blankets, uncovering Barbara's naked body. I had a choking sensation. For a minute I wasn't sure if the heaters were coming at me or if I was drifting toward them. I closed my eyes and the red coils continued to float toward me in the darkness. When I put my foot on the cold floor the bed creaked but Barbara slept on with long relaxed breaths. I got up cautiously and groped my way to the bathroom. I drank cold water from the faucet and washed my face before I went back to bed.

I closed my eyes. Again the room was filled with blazing ovens. I must turn them off, I thought to myself. First a cold shower, now these ovens. I'm sick. When did she turn them on? It's impossible to breathe. Tea. Tea and lemon. This heat is intolerable. And the sight of it is even more awful. The red light will drive me out of my mind. What was the dog looking for? A bone? Whose bone? I should have simply said no, I don't want to see the place. It's stifling. Have to open a window. Train wheels pounding in my head. Chimney-smoke, chimneys, chimneys!

I got out of bed, fumbled with the cords, found the plugs, and disconnected them one by one. The red light died slowly, then the room was dark. I went back to bed but I couldn't sleep. Tomorrow, I said to myself, tomorrow I'll get up and it will all be over. The white gravel in the yard, the road, the ruins of the cabins and these ovens, extinguished at last. Like those ovens. (Which?) There. (Where?) In that automated bakery. (Whose?) I. Kopf and Sons, Inc.: a technological wonder, a *Wirtschaftswunder*. Those Germans have good business heads. Kopf and Sons. Fifteen hundred loaves an hour. Maybe more. An oven a hundred yards long. Maybe less. You put the molded dough in one end and loaves of bread come out. All so well calculated. So precise. *Wirtschaftswunder*. The machine is oiled and running. Like a watch. German or Swiss. Once the oven stopped working and half an hour later, when it was repaired, ashen molds emerged at the rate of fifteen hundred an hour. Where was it? Where exactly? What was the name of the place? Man and oven! Man in oven. Ova-in-oven; blood-in-oven. Something to that effect. Ashen molds. Ovens blazing in my head. I feel sick. Tomorrow I will wake up dead with my parents and my sister at my bedside. My mother will be smiling in her black dress. My sister, Miri, will mend my brother's torn lapel and my father, Dr. Erich Lampel, will hold out his cold hands to me and say, "Come, Hirschen, let's row across the lake of ashes." It's my own fault, I know. No one made me go in. She thought I'd want to see the place. I could have stayed in the car and said no. *You* go and see. I've seen everything. It was crazy. To take off my shoes and stand barefoot on the cold floor under the shower—utter insanity. Five long terrible minutes. And the cold bath? To test my endurance. Now, here are the consequences. I'm sick. The flu and a fever. But I had no choice—I *had* to do it. I couldn't stand there like an outsider and photograph that monstrous *"Suendrencropolis"* in Kodachrome. I couldn't stand there any longer, detached, dry-eyed, contemplating the remnants of terror. I had to take off my shoes. For five minutes, at least. Five minutes to signify so many days barefoot in snow and ice. Otherwise I could not have seen them. There, of all places, I would never have found them. Everywhere else, yes. But there, no. Tens of thousands of people passed before my eyes on their way to the final lineup. Anonymous persons with no identity. A great sea of strange eyes. Names inscribed on cold, damp walls, names from every corner of the world, and dates before and after the cataclysm. Still, I did not find Martin. I should have made room for my name alongside the names of the survivors. I should have engraved it with my fingernails: Hirsch Lampel—Uri Lam. Jerusalem—Frankfurt. I had to take off my shoes. Five minutes barefoot in an icy inferno. Five minutes during which I saw them at last (for the first time since I passed through the gates of the camp). I saw Martin's long, tormented face, Miri's tearful eyes, my mother's finger, menacing, from the kitchen window, my father's bald head bent over the microsKopf (and Sons). Rising up from the floor, their voices penetrated my frozen feet. There were no more barriers. As in the bath. They seemed to come closer to me, or was it I who came closer to them? I am cold. Cold. The ovens . . .

I don't know how long I tossed at Barbara's side, clinging to her and trembling. She woke up. Turning on a blinding light to investigate, she declared me sick. I spoke in broken fragments. She gave me a blank stare and said she didn't understand a word, that I was talking Hebrew. When she turned on the heater I said I was hot, and made some reference to ovens. She stuck the thermometer in my mouth and studied me with concern. Swallowing two pills with my tea I fell asleep.

In the morning I had a coughing fit. My head was blazing. Barbara said something about 104 degrees. She was standing at the window, which was gray with rain. My tongue was dry, my lips parched. When I said, "Water," she lifted my head and put a cup of tea to my lips. My body was wracked by another round of coughing. She said something about a doctor. She was going out to get a doctor. Would I like to listen to the radio while she was gone? I opened my eyes and stared at her. I heard music, familiar strains. Then the room was empty; a door closed. I shut my eyes.

When the music ended two candied voices came on, extolling a new petrochemical insecticide by Shell: "Destroys flies, roaches, moths, bedbugs, spiders, lice, and other household pests in seconds. Press the button and they're dead."

"So economical," said the woman.

"So effective," the man added.

"Easy to use," said the woman.

"Shell-toxica," they sang in chorus.

The final solution for the problem of pests and parasites. "Try it and see for yourself," the woman said.

Your house will be fly-free (*Fliegenrein*), free of roaches and bedbugs. Everything-*rein*. *Ho, du wunderschoener deutscher judenrein.* Then the two of them sang a jingle, each line ending in "Shell-toxica," and then in the very same voice the woman announced some music by Mozart for the glory of home and hearth (the gas oven).

I woke up. A man in a black suit was holding my hand. He had a head but no neck and a double chin which spilled onto his tie. His lips were soft and decadent. His black bag lay beside me on the bed. Barbara smiled reassuringly.

"This is Dr. Hess," she said. I pulled my hand away with a sudden jerk and began to cough.

"I don't want him!" I finally managed to shout.

Barbara took my hand and tried to soothe me. "He'll give you a shot and you'll feel much better." I watched him take a syringe from his bag and attach the needle, I watched him come toward me.

"I won't have him!" I said, in a faint voice, seized by another round of coughing that tore at my lungs. "Get him out!" I screamed in Hebrew. "Get rid of him. He'll press the button that brings death. Shell-toxica." They looked at me in dismay. When the doctor approached me cautiously I threw an ashtray at him. "Get out!" I screamed in a hoarse voice, like an actor in a war movie.

"I want a young doctor, Barbara. It doesn't matter who, as long as he's young. Get out of here, Dr. Davey-Knavey. *Raus*, you Nazi pig!" His bloated face turned white. He flung the syringe into the bag and grabbed his coat. I heard receding footsteps and the sound of a door closing. I gaped at Barbara and began to cough so I wouldn't hear what she was saying.

"He's a good doctor," she maintained calmly, but I wouldn't let her go on. "I want a young doctor," I repeated obstinately. "Or Dr. Mayer. I want Dr. Mayer, Barbara."

She left the room and I could hear her dialing. I had another attack of coughing and spit a mouthful of phlegm into the glass of tea. For the moment I felt better and fell asleep.

Once I opened my eyes to an empty room. I called, "Barbara," and went back to sleep. When I opened my eyes again I saw her in a chair near the bed watching me. Then I heard her talking to someone in the other room. I called to her but she kept talking. I heard a man's laugh. I got out of bed and peered through the doorway. She was sitting on the couch talking to my brother, Martin. When he noticed me he winked in my direction. Hearing rapid footsteps I got back into bed.

Barbara shook my shoulder and said, "Dr. Mayer is here." I woke up and saw my father sitting on the edge of the bed, smiling at me. His bald head gleamed in the light. The curtains were drawn. Dr. Mayer's hands groped in my father's black bag. He put the stethoscope around his neck and held my hand. "How do you feel, Uri?" he asked in Hebrew. I nodded and ran my tongue over my dry lips. Pulse, thermometer, and now sit up, please. That's right. Breathe in, then hold. Breathe in again. He tapped my back with his soft, cold hand. He wrapped a cold strip around my arm and pressed the red rubber bulb. Like the photographers on Rothschild Boulevard. Smile, please. An old-fashioned rubber car horn. Open your mouth. Say ah. A cold spoon on the tongue and a fit of coughing. You can lie down now, Uri.

I heard him say pneumonia. Antibiotics to bring the fever down. Lots of liquids. A vaporizer. Inhalator. Annihilator. I opened my eyes. His pink cheeks were smiling at me. I asked him to come closer. When he leaned over me with his medicinal smells I told him in a whisper that there was another doctor who wanted to give me a shot of benzene. His syringe was filled with air; he wanted to shoot it into my veins. A typical doctor. A fool, I said, and Dr. Mayer laughed, dismissing my complaints with a sympathetic shrug. Lie on your stomach; I'll give you a shot and you'll be better. I heard a bag open, metal rattling, the delicate jingle of glass. One prick and, "That's it!" the doctor said. My arm sank into the blazing pillow. I heard a pen scratching on paper. Two pills three times a day and please call me in the morning. Footsteps. A door slammed.

They've gone? Left me alone? No, Barbara is here. Footsteps on the parquet floor. "Uri, I'm going to the drugstore. I'll be right back." I nodded and reached for her hand. She pressed her lips to my hand and was off. I heard the clang of metal and Pluto's excited bark. "Quiet, Pluto, quiet," Barbara called out. The door closed, then silence. Hush. Shhhh. Hushhh. Like the showers. Barefoot on an ice floor. The silence of death.

Don't fall asleep now, I said aloud into the pillow. If I fall asleep—I will never wake up. Wait for her. (Who?) Barbara. (Which Barbara?) My wife, Barbara Stahl, Barbara Lam, Yalie, Yaeli, Yael Lam (I think she is German), is coming back with the medicine. I don't want to die of pneumonia. I wanted to take a step in their direction but I took too big a step. Laryngitis, an advanced case of stigmata. Barefoot. Both hands on the dank wall. I wanted to be eleven again, to be there with my father and mother, with all the other naked bodies (I once saw my mother in the bath, but how did father look naked?), to be pushed with the others (move in, please, there are more outside), to hear the steel door sealed hermetically with a final bang. Dr. Hess, in a white robe, pours the proper amount of potassium cyanide into the funnel. How much? A hundred grams per two hundred souls? A hundred and twenty grams? Crystals of KCN. Bluish gems from the death laboratories singing in the pipes like raindrops in a gutter. KCN sinks softly into a tank of H_2SO_4; the deadly gas rises magically. HCN filters into the room, stealthily. It oozes from the showers ever so quietly. A death rattle of letters: HHH . . . CCC . . . NNN . . . H . . . C . . . N . . . Like the song. What song? A folk song, with a woman's melancholy voice. Quiet, hush . . . hush little baby. "Hush little baby, don't you cry/you know your mother was born to die/all my trials, Lord, soon be over."

Lord, God, don't let me go to sleep now. Sit up. Stand. Do something until she gets back. Piss, little baby, don't you cry.

I got out of bed. Instant darkness. Sharp needles pierced my chest. I sat back on the bed and gradually the forms in the room became distinct. Hammers were pounding in my head. My cough was harsh, like a dog's. I got up carefully and groped my way along until I found the cold threshold of the bathroom. As I looked in the mirror an involuntary shudder flickered over my dry lips. I tried to comb my hair but the comb fell from my hand. I didn't dare bend down. Instead, I picked up one of Barbara's lipsticks. Then I found myself back in bed, shivering under a heap of covers. I heard my teeth chattering an SOS. S-O-S. Help! I'm drowning in a sea of ice. Frankfurt. Wagner-Gasse 9. Six-two-five-eight-two. Dr. Lampel, please, He's not there. Is Mrs. Lampel asleep? She's not there. Could I speak to some other member of the family? They're not there. No. The tremors began to pass. My hand was still. I saw the red coils of an oven.

I lay in a white bed. The window opened onto a small garden flooded with sunlight, and apricot trees in full bloom. In the distance I heard the sad wail of jackals. Maminka, her plump arms draped in silk, popped a pill into my mouth and gave me a drink of water. I opened my eyes to say, *"Non mi sento bene, Zia Anna,"* and there was Barbara in a wet raincoat. The dog was wailing by the window. "This will bring the fever down and you'll feel better, darling," I heard her say. I took her hand and pressed her fingers to my lips. "An unavoidable meeting," I whispered. She looked at me with an expression I had never seen in her eyes. Fear. Worry. She covered me and tucked the edges of the blanket under my feet. The door was opened, Pluto barked, then more footsteps and a door closing.

I was dozing under the fig tree on a straw mat—a lazy summer day. Flies buzzed quietly in the shade over my head. Someone was dialing and after a moment I heard Barbara's voice. She said good evening to someone and then how are you and I would like to ask you something. What is KCN H_2SO_4 arrow HCN? (Where did she get the formula?) Oh, I see, she said. No, she said, I was just curious. I saw it in a book. Thanks very much, she said. Yes, absolutely. Fine, she said. A little sick. He caught a cold. What? Yes, maybe in a week. I'll call you. Definitely. And then the slam of the receiver. What does that mean? Where did she see the formula? Maybe there, in the central building of the concentration camp, among the photographs I chose not to look at. She stayed inside while I went for a walk. "Those who cannot remember the past are condemned to repeat it." Santayana. Santa Rosa. Santa Croce. Santa Maria. Maybe he was right. The more I try to forget, the more I remember. Did she hear me talking in my sleep? Did I mouth the secret formula for the final solution, the key to the sheltering gates of hell, of Gehenna, Gehinnom? My house at the edge of the Valley of Hinnom. The house on the border. The border of sleep. Sleep.

I opened my eyes. Morning, alien and gray beyond the window. I wanted to wake Barbara but I fell asleep again. Lost in dreams I returned to a room where once I saw Barbara and another time Miri. Someone rolled up my pajamas and I felt a gentle sting. Cold hands on my body. Dr. Mayer spoke to me and my mouth was stuck together. I emerged from a dream to an empty room and was sucked into the spongy depths of uneasy sleep. Once I opened my eyes to scarlet darkness. I was thirsty but couldn't reach the glass.

Barbara's voice in the next room reported, "Yes, doctor, a hundred and four point two," and then the bedside light was on and she was there. Distant and very small. She handed me some water. My throat was sore, the pills were large. I mumbled something and she said, "Still talking? You've been talking all day." She took off my striped pajamas (where did I get them from?) and rubbed my body with alcohol; it smelled like vodka. I remember seeing myself: a yellow corpse on a white table. Purity, I thought, an act of final charity. The mountains of fever were beginning to shrink. I shuddered. Then I heard myself speak, a cascade of random words that failed to form a picture.

Burn these pajamas, I told her, I want another pair. With flowers like the ones in front of the house, and red leaves that fall on the tablecloth, like the garden in autumn. Ask him why he's digging there. He's digging a grave. For himself. For me. He said, "I am digging pits for trees." Very simple. Pits for weeping willows, dark-row-trees, Dachau-trees, wail-low willows, grieving beside those empty cabins, amid gravel, crushed monuments, and teeth. *Ho, du heiliger* Max! I told him, *"Arbeit Macht frei."* He stopped digging and looked up at me without a word, his square hands gripping the handle of the spade, his fingers pale. They picked some prime potatoes/in Dachau's pretty patch./Prime potatoes/proudly picked/in Dachau's pretty patch./Rich black earth. Minerals and nitrates. All the rest is gone with the soul. Dust and ashes. For out of dust hast thou come and unto ashes thou shalt return, courtesy of Kopf and Sons. Calculated to the end, to the last fraction of an inch. Ten point seven inches. Paint the cabin with antique brown and the smell of carbolic acid. Reconstruct every detail. One model cabin and a warm welcome to tourists. Preserve the scenes of horror. Like the medieval torture cellars. Oil the torture devices regularly or they will rust. Catacombs of wood. An auto-da-fé, made in Germany. Photograph the extermination camps in Kodachrome. Follow the trail of terror. We recommend an unforgettable weekend, authentic extermination camp atmosphere. Round-trip air flights, superb restaurants, first-class hotels, a tour of the gas chambers at unprecedented low prices. Photograph your wife beside the death ovens. Perpetuate Auschwitz in 8mm. Don't smile, I'm taking a picture. It's cold here. Put your hand on the oven. Now you can see the film we just made. There's coffee and cake in the lounge. Tea. I would like tea and lemon. I'm burning up inside. The ovens are burning inside me. Speak to me, Barbara. Don't say a word. I know. What do I know? I don't know anything. That hovering pain is embedded now, it won't go back to its place near the ceiling, to flutter there like a white bird.

I don't know how long I ranted. Much of the time it seemed to me I was silent, watching the pictures flash through my head. I would suddenly hear, "Yes?" or, "What did you say, Uri?" and see Barbara struggling to fathom my monologue. Once I saw fear in her eyes. The damp towel she pressed to my forehead was soaked with tears. I sank into a deep sleep and emerged knowing the crisis was over. The sky was bright through the window. As I was taking my temperature Barbara appeared in the doorway.

"Good morning," she said, a smile crinkling her weary eyes. "How are you?"

I took the thermometer from my mouth.

"Ninety-eight point two," I replied.

"At last," she said. "Take your pills. I'll bring some tea."

She was back in a minute, setting the tea down near the bed and propping up the pillows. I was hungry so she went to get me toast. I had lost all sense of time and was astounded to learn I had been almost unconscious for two days and totally incoherent, that my fever had climbed to 105.8. "Does your hand hurt?" she asked. My right hand was bandaged. It seems I tried to get out of bed and fainted at the bathroom door, bruising my hand.

"All because of a cold shower in November," she reflected.

"What shower?" I asked.

"The shower you took when we got home. How do you think you got pneumonia?"

"Oh, yes," I recalled.

"It wasn't very smart," she said, shaking her head.

"I admit it," I said, coughing. "Was Dr. Mayer here again or was that a dream?"

"He was here twice," she said.

"And you talked to someone on the phone yesterday?"

"Why do you ask?"

"I heard you talking about some formula," I said. "Where did you get it from, Barbara? Was I talking in my sleep?"

"No. I found it two days ago, when I got back from the drugstore."

"Found what?" I asked suspiciously.

"Look up there," she said, pointing to the wall behind me.

The formula was inscribed on the white wall in bold lipstick-red letters and underneath it, "Hirsch Lampel– Uri Lam. Frankfurt–Jerusalem. 1941–1959."

"I wrote that?" I asked in disbelief.

"Well, it wasn't me," she said. "I didn't even recognize it. I asked a friend, a physicist. He knew immediately: hydrogen cyanide."

"That's right," I concurred.

"Feeling better?"

"Much better," I said. "I have no fever and the pain in my chest is almost gone. I want to get up and wash. Besides, I'm hungry—I want a soft-boiled egg and some cocoa. And I want to tell you something."

"What?" she asked.

"I love you, Barbara," I said. "Really."

"You're sick," she said. "You'll get over it."

29 | *days of sickness*

I was exhausted. I didn't want to talk anymore or even to listen. I slid under the covers and closed my eyes. Barbara's chair squeaked. The clatter of a cup and saucer, the tinkle of a teaspoon, soft footsteps in slippers, a faucet in the kitchen . . . I opened my eyes. But for these sounds the room was empty.

Sweet fatigue in every muscle, the limpness that follows a siege of illness. Like my first trip outside when I was in the hospital; wearing a blue robe and slippers, I sat on a green bench in the blinding garden sunlight, enjoying a delicious sensation of vulnerability. Sit still as a lizard. Don't stir. Open your eyes; drink in the grass, green leaves floating in a sea of sky, birds flitting about, chirping their message of peace, the sprinkler whistling among the flowers. The big beautiful world one needs time to retrieve. Rest, dream, think nothing. Don't touch me. I'll make my own way, I'll revive slowly, step by step.

Sunlight shimmered on the wall, like that distant, hovering pain. A car horn sounded. A puppy barked, a white puppy. A trip to the sea on the Sabbath. "Jonathan, help your mother; take the mat to the car. Daddy will carry the basket, it's too heavy." Roaring waves in the kitchen sink. "Don't go too deep. Yes, I see. That's very good, Jonathan. You're a good little swimmer." Transistors on the beach. Palestrina in Palestina. "It's nice here, Barbara, isn't it? It's probably raining in Frankfurt. What does your father write?" Then, in the shade of the blanket: cool grapes, peeled cucumbers, firm red tomatoes, sardine and cheese sandwiches, cold cuts wrapped in brown paper, a thermos of coffee. Eilat in winter; eternal sunlight. "Give me the paper for a minute, Barbara." She reads Hebrew already and speaks it fluently, my dear greenhorn. This light dancing on the wall, the tiny shadows darting about like a silent film . . . "City Lights." Turn on the radio? It's not worth the effort. He's asleep. Let him sleep. If it hadn't been for her blazing body I would surely have frozen, right here, after nearly doing myself in in the tub. Am I asleep? No. I hear someone leafing through a book. She is at her desk, writing, under Uncle Gustaf's watchful eye.

"Barbara," I called.

"Yes, Uri?"

"What are you doing?"

"I'm reviewing a boring lecture. Do you want something?"

"No," I said. "Why aren't you going to class?"

"And who will nurse my sick husband?"

"You could call a baby-sitter," I offered.

"I'd have to find one over eighty," she said.

"But I'm healthy," I objected. She sat down beside me and touched her cool hand to my forehead.

"You still have a fever," she said.

"Ninety-eight point two isn't a fever," I argued.

"But ninety-nine is," she countered.

"Nonsense. You can go to class. I don't want you to have to repeat the year. When your exams are over we go home to Jerusalem."

"Is that final?" she asked, smiling.

"That's it," I answered.

"Without consulting your partner?"

"No backtalk," I pronounced. "It's the male prerogative to decide; you accept with love and submission. Thus Spake Zarathustra. And if he didn't say it, I say it. Besides, you promised. You said we'd go right after your exams."

"We'll talk about it when you're better," she said.

"Do you have some doubts?" I asked.

"Not in principle," she said. "It's just a matter of timing. But we'll talk about it. Are you sure it's all right for me to go to school?"

"Positive," I said.

"And you'll be good?" she asked. "You won't get out of bed? And no more cold showers?"

"It's a promise: no more cold showers," I said, my hand on my heart.

"Good boy," she said patting my head. I pictured a velvet skullcap on my head, with the words "good boy—Jerusalem" embroidered in gold.

"What if I have to make peepee? Can I get out of bed?" I asked, pointing primly to my organ.

"You may," she said. "But be sure to wear your slippers. I'll be back at two. If you're good I'll make chicken soup."

"I'll be good, I'll be very good." I said. "Are you taking Jonathan along?"

"Yes," she nodded solemnly.

"I want to give him a kiss," I said.

"Please do," and she opened her robe. Her skin was scented with eau de cologne. She kneeled over the bed, motionless, her fingers playing with my hair, a gentle silence taut between us. Then her breath seemed to fly away and she clutched my head. "That's enough, that's enough . . ." she implored softly, without letting go of me. I heard the faucet dripping in the kitchen.

Afterward, she lifted my head and looked at me, her eyes brimming with light and wonder. As she closed the bathroom door she exclaimed, "You're crazy." My heart pounded wildly.

I didn't hear her leave the house. When I woke up I found a cup of tea, a red rose in a glass of water, and a note: "I almost fell asleep at your side. Jonathan says thanks a lot. We love you. I called Max and asked him to come over. I told him you caught a cold, but I didn't say how. He said he would come tomorrow or the next day. Without his tutti-frutti. Remember: two pills at noon. Barbara (née Stahl), who is Mrs. Lam, your loving wife."

I took my temperature: ninety-nine. Still sick, after all, I thought. Have something to drink. The tea's cold, so she must have been gone awhile. What time is it? Time for my pills. Max will come. Good. What will we do? Talk. Talk about what? I'll ask if he was there, if he went there on the number 11. Maybe we'll play our game again, "Concentration Camp," in the old packing crate near the barn. We had our own versions: number 4: you are evicted from your home, your property is confiscated; number 11: take the first transport to a concentration camp; 19: hard labor; 28: last stop . . . the infirmary; 45: death by firing squad; 52: last-minute reprieve in exchange for your fortune; 61: seven days on an illegal boat to Palestine; 99: deported to Cyprus, begin again. He will pretend not to remember. Good Edna isn't coming. She would probably say, "It's awful what they did to us." Tutti-frutti, the name suits her. A real fruitcake. "Such a talented architect, a valiant fighter, a man who lost his entire family in Germany. And all the rich and beautiful women . . ." She's not normal. Rich? How did she hear about Carmela, any-way? Airmail gossip. "We heard you have a girl. Her father is a big-time builder or something . . ." Right, Buckman the Builder. He made his first million on cement he managed to store up while building defense systems for the British. "Uri'le, Daddy wants you to spend the weekend with us." A huge villa in Herzliya filled with shit. Shit on the walls, framed in gold. "My father is mad about Israeli painting, but personally I prefer the Europeans." Brains in his ass and a head full of shit. "Uri, stop it, darling, get your hand out of there. You drive me crazy." She wanted to marry an architect. Her father a builder, her husband an architect. How neat! Carmela, honey, you're wasting your time. I'll marry when I'm forty. She'll get the news by airmail. Edna will write everyone: Uri Lam married a German girl. I don't believe it. I got a letter from Edna—she was there. What do I care? Let them talk, let them choke, let them point their fingers at me. Here he is, the guy who married a German girl. I'll ask Max what they're all say-ing. We'll sit close, the way we did in that hut, the way we did in the old packing crate near the barn, with its smell of pepsin and chocolate cake. Maxie, how did you get the cake? My mother left it in the girls' cabin by mistake.

The hut, the only remnant. All the rest were razed. One hut was left as a model, restored to illustrate the past. Built of new pine with whitewashed walls, planks on three tiers, floor and benches as they were—and eyes, hosts of eyes. The horror reconstructed in its every detail. Precisely, scientifically, on the basis of testimony from witnesses, no doubt. "Excuse me, Mr. Isak, as one of the occupants, perhaps you recall the exact distance between planks? Was it sixteen inches or eighteen? And do you by any chance remember the color of the wood?"

I had sat in that hut on a narrow bench near a window inhaling the fragrance of pine, and now, in my bed, I heard echoes of the voices that were there. An agitated voice. "Can't you read the plans, Mr. Kramer? It says right here specifically: nine and a half inches, not ten and a half. And what about the color?" A penitent response. "Antique brown number 202. Here is one of the original planks and a sample of number 202. The color is identical. A coat of oil will preserve the wood." I did not quite catch the response to this.

Sane people, I thought, met one day to consider ways of improving the tourist attraction known as Dachau. One of the speakers contended that the display of photographs in the central building was inadequate. An impressive exhibit, he said, with great educational impact, arranged tastefully from the graphic point of view (clear enlargements, fine mat paper, appropriately subdued layout), but all in all a dead exhibit. A growing number of tourists visit the camp each year but there is nothing for them to photograph. It was admittedly essential to destroy the old structures—for reasons of security and sanitation. By demolishing these structures, covering their foundations with fresh gravel, and numbering the blocks clearly, our first goal—order and cleanliness— has been achieved. But, at the same time, gentlemen. some of the authentic atmosphere of this place has, alas, been forfeited. I propose, at least as a first step, that one of the huts be restored in a move to break the monotony of the landscape and liven up the scene. This reconstructed hut would, obviously, make the entire experience more real, especially for the younger generation. Bravo, Herr Doktor, Bravo! A superb idea. The wall of conservativism begins to crumble. New horizons.

Commission Madame Tussaud to fill the huts with wax figures. In fact, why not fill the shower rooms with figures of naked, screaming women? The sound could be taped. What a dramatic effect! There could be light shows like the ones at the Acropolis, the Roman Forum, Versailles . . .

I saw myself sitting there in the hut on a narrow bench and again I heard, "This place is closed to the public." The man in the long leather coat eyed me sternly. He carried architectural plans in his hand (a colleague) and was followed by a silver-haired gentleman who brandished a yellow yardstick.

"The door was open," I said.

"We're not ready for visitors," the fellow snarled.

"I only wanted to see how—" I tried to explain, but he wouldn't let me finish.

"There's nothing to see now," he said decisively, showing me to the door. Outside in the wet fog I could still hear his voice: "Herr Kramer, please lock the door. Your floor is already dirty."

The phone rang a half ring.

Pluto burrowed in the ground under the gravel. A young man was digging a deep pit in the dirt at the side of the road. I asked what he was digging. He was about to say he was digging pits for trees when the phone rang. Someone with an odd, hollow voice asked if Mr. Lam was home. I answered yes. A nasal voice snapped, "Dirty Jew. We'll settle with you yet."

"Who is this?" I asked, though the question sounded foolish even to me—obviously the caller wanted to remain anonymous—but it was instinctive. "You will hear from me again," the caller went on, and hung up.

I held the receiver, not knowing what to do. For a moment I wasn't even sure the phone had really rung. It was conceivable that I had misunderstand—dirty Jew. Who? (Me!) We will settle our account with you. Why? (Barbara.) What should I do? Call the police? And say what? I have a complaint. Someone called me on the phone and said thus-and-so. They're probably used to these complaints; they receive dozens every day. Maybe no one has the nerve to complain—besides it's agony to repeat the words. The policeman will ask over and over again for the precise message, mouthing the words with a trace of pleasure. Which was it—"dirty Jew" or "filthy Jew"? Are you actually of Jewish extraction? The letter. Six marks. For your untimely demise. No doubt about it—the letter and the call come from one and the same person. Herman? Gunther? One of Barbara's rejected suitors? What do they want? They're after me and they won't relent. Day and night: Hello. May I speak with the *Untermensch*? You who dare to violate the purity of our Aryan race . . . Jewish scum! *He* didn't finish the job, but we will. A ring in the middle of the night: heavy breathing, but not a word. Modern torture devices . . . Inquisition by mail. Should we change our number? Move? Go home—to Jerusalem. And there? Will the phone ring with a menacing message: "Dirty Jew. We'll settle with you. You dare to violate the Jewish race, in this holy land? . . . Get rid of her!"

I set the clicking receiver in its place and went back to bed. As soon as I lay down the phone rang again. Five, six, seven rings, then I answered. This time a woman asked for Mr. Lam.

"Speaking," I said.

"Just a minute please."

"Who is it?" I asked, but there was no one on the line.

It's a whole network, I thought. A Nazi underground with offices, phones, secretaries. "Eva, would you please get me that little Jew who married the Stahl girl." Eva leafs through the notebook of intermarriages—she has a notebook of death camp survivors, a notebook of reparation claims, a notebook of merchants. All meticulously organized. A personal folder for every victim. Letters. Telegrams. Phone calls.

"Hello," I heard a muffled voice on the other end.

"Hello," I responded.

Silence.

"Hello, who is it?" I asked.

"It's me again," in the same voice.

"What do you want?" I asked.

"I want to make you miserable, you stinking Jew," said the muffled voice.

"Who is it? Who is it?" I shrieked on the verge of hysteria. Again silence. "Yellow-bellied coward!" I screamed. "Vile Nazi. Identify yourself and we'll see who settles what score!"

"Ha, ha, such an excitable fellow," a shrill voice chirped in perfectly articulated Hebrew. It wasn't Max. My rage was mounting.

"Who is this?" I demanded in Hebrew.

"Guess," the voice taunted.

The blood rose to my head—I could never stand that kind of an answer. You pick up the phone and instead of simply announcing who it is they torment you with playful small talk: "Guess who. Don't you know my voice? It's a good friend." It seemed clear to me that only an Israeli would be capable of such infantile behavior.

"I don't have time for jokes," I said. "Tell me who it is or I'll hang up . . ."

"What's the matter with you, Uri?" the voice asked in dismay. "Where's your sense of humor?"

"Who is it?" I hissed through clenched teeth.

"Can't you guess?"

"No," I cried. "And I don't want to try."

"It's Danni," the voice replied, expecting to evoke gleeful peals of welcome and surprise.

"Danni who?" I didn't remember anyone called Danni.

"Ha, ha! You have no memory. Danni-boy! We came to Genoa together and later we met at the train station, remember?"

"Did you call before?" I asked.

"Yes," he said, relishing his success. "That was great, wasn't it? You thought the Nazis were after you. You fell for it, come on, confess! I've driven quite a few Israelis mad, here in Germany, with the same line."

"And did you write the letter too?" I asked.

"What letter?" He was surprised.

"Never mind," I said. "Who gave you the number?"

"Leave it to Danni-boy," was his retort. "I have agents throughout Europe."

"Tell me how you got the number!" I persisted.

"What's the difference?" as asked.

"There's a difference," I said. "I have no time for your foul jokes and I don't want any more calls from scum like you. Understand?"

"Get a load of this," he sulked, offended, "he marries a German girl and it's beneath his dignity to talk to Israelis. Just you wait . . ."

"Listen here," I enunciated slowly, "if you dare to call once more I'll beat the shit out of you!"

"You and who else?" he challenged. "I wouldn't wash my ass with soap like you. Go ahead! Kiss their asses, you and yours. A mess of *dreck!* I'll show you . . ."

I hung up in a fury and was on my way to bed when everything blacked out. I sat down again. If I could only get my hands on him now, I thought, I'd break a chair over his head. I'd give him two black eyes. I'd kick him in the balls, trample his corrupt face. He calls it suspense, the idiot; that's his idea of humor. To finger me as a jewel smuggler—that's hilarious. Then this phone call. "Dirty Jew, we'll settle with you"—what a weird sense of humor. I would have him shot, empty the barrel into him, do him in in cold blood. Relax: easy does it. . . . Take a deep breath. Count to ten and it'll go away. Your heart is playing games with you. Breathe in. One, two; one, two. No use getting upset over every lunatic. Impossible—Max wouldn't give him my number.

I called Max. He wasn't at the office. I called home. Edna didn't know where he was. He'll be home late, she said. She heard I was sick and wanted to know how I was. I said I had a cold. She wanted all the details. How much fever? How was I now? Who was my doctor? Did I need anything? I told her I was all right, I was being looked after, they were taking good care of me. "You were very naughty at the wedding," she said abruptly.

She's going to tell me everything I did, I thought; she'll quote me word for word. She'll say who I sat with. (Erna.) Who I drank with, what I said. I don't have the strength.

"Do you know a guy from Israel named Danni . . . 'Danni-boy'?" I ventured.

"Sure," she said. 'He's dark and terribly funny. We met him yesterday at a party. Lots of Israelis were there. They wanted you to come so we called, but Barbara said you were sick. You were asleep at the time. When Danni asked about you, I described your gorgeous wedding. What do you mean? He said you were best friends, that you came to Genoa together on the same boat."

"And you gave him my number?" I asked.

"Naturally," she replied. "He said he'd surprise you, so I gave him the number. Did I do the wrong thing?"

"It doesn't matter," I said, eager to hang up. But she asked again if I was sure I didn't need anything. "I've got last week's newspapers and a pile of recent magazines," she offered.

"I have enough to read," I said.

"Aren't you interested in what's going on at home?" she countered disapprovingly.

"Did something happen? What happened?" I asked anxiously, picturing Davey-Knavey leading an armored division across the Sinai border. War. They're bombing Tel Aviv. The executive branch of the government is in the direct line of fire. A child clutches a doll amid a heap of rubble. Yad Mordecai is cut off and enclosed in barbed wire. Don't sit under the apple tree/with anyone else but me. You and your apple trees!

"Nothing special," I heard her say. "Not very much news. Zippi, you know her, the one who married the orange grove magnate, gave a party at Savion. Everyone was there. Pictures in all the magazines . . ."

I stopped listening. Yes, I said impatiently, I know. I heard. I didn't stop saying yes until she lost interest and concluded the conversation. I fell on the bed, exhausted, and sank into a deep sleep.

When Barbara got back I didn't tell her about the calls. I was afraid to. I didn't want to expose her to the ugliness of my compatriots—it was enough for her to know Edna. If she heard about Danni she'd conclude that two out of every three Israelis (Max, Edna, Danni) were vulgar, aggressive, arrogant, and endowed with a gross sense of humor. I didn't want to confirm any doubts she might be harboring about our trip to Israel.

After lunch (chicken soup with soft white rice) the conversation turned in that direction. Though she listened with interest I sensed she was concealing something. I described our house at the border (but didn't mention that the neighboring building was an Arab Legion military post). I described our yard, enclosed by a wall, and the fig tree where I planned to hang a hammock. I saw her lying in it at sunset, gazing beyond the Valley of Hinnom to the wall of the Old City, bathed in glowing purple. I saw Jonathan in the swing I would suspend from the tree. As for me, I would watch from the window, delighting in this scene.

"What are you doing there at the window?" Barbara asked.

"Planning a city, a city in the desert," I said.

"Have a rest, Uri. Come on, lie down beside me," she called, waving as though she was far away.

"The hammock will break," I called in a whisper, cupping my hands around my mouth.

"Then I'll join you," she said. "Move over."

She lay down beside me, her shoes falling to the floor. I put one arm under her head, the other on her belly. Her eyes were smiling.

"Jonathan!" she called. "Come and do your homework. Now then, Uri, what kind of a house do you have? Tell me."

I took her hand and led her from room to room. She was delighted with the thick walls covered with blue plaster. I opened empty closets for her, took two or three Hebrew books she knew in German from the shelf, made Turkish coffee which we drank on the broad windowsill that overlooked Mount Zion. The bells of the Dormition Church were ringing, the wall of the Old City blazed in the sunlight. We moved from the windowsill to the wide sofa and fell asleep in each other's arms on the Moroccan rug I once bought at the market in Machane Yehudah. As we walked through the darkness hand in hand, over the narrow road that winds its rocky course to my house, Legion soldiers sniped at us. I saw their fire soar over our heads. We lay among the rocks in a bed of rosemary and thyme. When we got home I discovered that someone had scrawled in tar on the door: DEFILER OF ISRAEL. Barbara lowered her eyes, pretending not to understand. Jonathan lay in his blue crib, not breathing. I opened my eyes to darkness. Barbara was asleep in her clothes, breathing evenly. Jonathan slept soundly inside her.

30 | *convalescence*

I spent almost the entire first month of my marriage in bed. The cold I had contracted in such a rash moment developed into pneumonia—I owe my recovery to Dr. Mayer's devoted care.

"Did you imagine we'd spend our honeymoon this way?" I asked Barbara once as she came out of the bathroom carrying a bedpan. It was the second week of my illness. The fever had dropped suddenly, and I had a great thirst for conversation. I reached out my hand, and when she took it with a smile I drew her toward me. Kicking off her shoes, she settled herself at the foot of the bed.

" 'What did you do after the wedding?' " she asked in the affected tones of a well-bred snob. " 'Oh, nothing special—on the first day we visited a mental hospital in Goeting, a charming little village; then we toured Dachau for a bit.' " She shook her head. "Who would believe it," she reflected. "What a morbid sense of humor. I don't understand how I could have taken you there."

"Nonsense," I said. "I had to see the place. It was, as you might say, an inevitable encounter."

"That could be," she said, sliding her legs under the covers. "But why right after our wedding, and why did I have to be the one to take the initiative? I could have waited for that wretched idea to cross your mind. I don't know why I did it. I saw a sign at a fork in the road and without giving it much thought I just turned in that direction. I may have intended to surprise you. I really don't know what I was thinking. How incredibly stupid!"

"Stop accusing yourself," I said, placing a gentle kiss in the palm of her hand. "How could you have foreseen the effect it would have on me? Even I didn't know. I was convinced I had seen everything, that I couldn't be shocked. In effect I had seen the place even before visiting it. I had read every eyewitness account, every book— and there was a documentary film. Night after night I saw myself there. It never occurred to me that a real encounter with the place, or what remains of it, the hut restored with such diabolical precision, that room which resembles an empty warehouse now—I never imagined that could revive anything for me. I assumed that I understood what happened there. I *seemed* to understand. But how can you understand? How can such things be comprehended without experiencing them? Is it possible to understand hunger without fasting? I wanted to feel something. A little bit—something."

"So *that's* why you took a cold shower," she said, her eyes scanning the formula on the wall, then looking off into the distance.

"Not a shower. A bath. A cold bath. Yes." I said, and she nodded.

"Dr. Mayer understood immediately," she said. "I told him about the visit and he understood why you threw out the other doctor. I, fool that I am, didn't understand. He's quite a person, that Dr. Mayer. I really like him.

He has a baby face and the eyes of a devil. A somewhat sad devil, but a devil nonetheless."

During that conversation or one like it she told me that in the first days, when my fever verged on delirium and I barely knew what was going on, Dr. Mayer would come every day, sometimes twice a day, to give me a shot and would often stay for coffee. They would sit in the kitchen talking in whispers.

I have a hazy memory of these conversations. Through heavy curtains, damp and seething, I would sometimes hear her whispering with my father, whose black bag lay on the chair near my bed. I thought I heard him tell her everything that had happened since we parted at the border. Once I was certain I heard him say something about hunting dogs and I knew he was referring to the man in a hunting cap who took me to San Castello in his car. Once I heard her whispering with my brother, Martin, while he played Mozart and I recall that there was something very odd about the scene— I couldn't understand why she was talking to him as he played. I saw myself get out of bed and stand in the doorway, signaling for her to be quiet. Later, when I fell asleep, I saw Martin drinking coffee with his one hand. Barbara stood over him feeding him cookies.

From what Barbara told me later it appears that something similar did actually occur. Dr. Mayer loved music and she would sometimes play Mozart on the record player while they drank coffee. He mentioned that his wife, Marta, used to play flute in a chamber ensemble ("Many years back, before you were born"). One winter in a camp where scientific experiments were being conducted ("mild ones, thank God"), her hands were frozen and only the fingers of her left hand revived. He wasn't with her there and she didn't remember just exactly what happened—her memory was somewhat affected (again he said "thank God"). He had a fine record player at home, but listened to records only when alone in his office, while Marta was resting.

Dr. Mayer also told Barbara that my father spent a few years treating animals. When she mentioned this

I recalled the dogs and cats that suddenly began to appear in my father's office. Well-groomed puppies dozed under the furs of sad, nervous ladies, and cats wailed, frisky cats that broke test tubes and bottles. I saw a green parrot whose eyes were tearing, and one day I discovered three yellow canaries in the trash, a procession of ants marching across their open beaks. I didn't know then why my father was treating animals and why people no longer sat in his waiting room leafing through magazines. In 1938, so Dr. Mayer told Barbara, Germans were forbidden by law to consult Jewish doctors. Since my father was very popular with his patients, they began to bring their dogs, cats, and birds to him—the ban didn't extend to pets. In some cases he would treat the dog and in other cases he would, secretly, treat its master. Apparently some patients brought their animals as an alibi.

Telling her about the dogs in our house reminded him of a good story about Dachau or some other camp. One man had his dog with him in the camp. The dog's name was Murik and the man loved him dearly. He used to share his bread and his meager dish of soup with the dog. He stole bones from the kitchen for him, though he himself was very hungry. One day when he could no longer bear the hunger, he killed the dog and ate him. When he finished eating the meat and only the bones remained, the man sighed and said sadly, "Hey, Murik, Murik, if only you were alive—how you would enjoy these bones."

I nodded in wonder and laughed.

"Why are you laughing?" she asked.

"Because," I said.

"Is it funny?" she asked.

"I don't know," I said. "The incident is sad, but the story is funny."

"Gallows humor," she said. "I never heard such insane logic. Do you remember what Dr. Mayer's wife said when she first saw you?" I strained to remember. "Too bad you weren't here during the war. With your face you would have been saved. Understand? She wasn't content with the fact that you're alive. She was sorry you missed such a great opportunity to be saved."

"There's a certain logic in that," I said. "Especially for her."

"Yes," Barbara agreed. "Nonlogical logic. The logical absurd. Do you know Buber?"

"I saw him once," I said.

"You saw Buber?" She was astonished.

"Yes," I said. "Why? What's the matter?"

"I admire that man," she said. "Did you read—"

"I haven't read anything of his," I confessed.

"That's impossible," she said, deeply disappointed, almost offended.

"It's true," I said.

"You must!" she cried enthusiastically. "You must read him."

"I heard him lecture on Hassidism once," I offered. "He was invited to our class. I was sixteen, maybe. We sat on the grass in front of the dining room—it was a hot summer day—he talked for two hours about Hassidism and I didn't understand a word. I wasn't even paying attention. I was sprawled on the grass and right next to me I saw the legs of a certain girl with braids and I wanted to have my dialogue with her rather than with God. She didn't usually notice me but that day on the grass, as the sun set and twilight was suddenly upon us, I rested my cheek on her brown leg as though by accident, and she didn't move away. I wanted—"

"What does he look like—Buber I mean?" she interrupted.

"Just the way he does in his pictures," I said. "A high forehead, fine white beard. He was wearing a suit, even though it was very hot that day, and he spoke with great fervor, as I recall. From time to time he would close his eyes. But I don't remember what he said. He spoke with a German accent, and in those days I was completely unsympathetic to German accents."

"Did you know his wife was German?" she asked.

"No, I didn't. Do you mean Christian?"

"Yes, a German Christian. She converted, of course, and went to Jerusalem with him in '26, as I remember."

"Very interesting," I said. "But you don't have to worry. You can come to Jerusalem with me without converting."

"It doesn't frighten me," she retorted.

"That's all I need!" I cried with panic and she laughed.

She had read Buber before we met, but after I moved into her apartment and especially during my sickness, she read any book about Judaism and Israel that she could get her hands on. She even made room for the new subject on the shelf over the picture of Uncle Gustaf. Among the books aligned there in their sparkling new jackets I found a history of Jewish settlement, something on the Hassidic movement, two volumes dealing with the Israel-Arab conflict, Palmer's book on Jerusalem, a history of Judaism, Edmund Wilson's *Dead Sea Scrolls, Hebrew Sources,* and a book called *Prolegomena to the History of the Jewish People.* She bought the *Encyclopaedia Judaica* at a bargain price after seeing an ad for it in the paper. When I asked why she hadn't bought the whole set she stared at me in disbelief. "Didn't you know they stopped working on it in the thirties?" she informed me. "They only got as far as the letter J and then they had to stop."

"What a coincidence," I retorted.

My own knowledge in these areas was very superficial, and I must admit that sometimes when she looked up from one of these volumes I felt like an object of scrutiny. It was as if she was observing me from a hidden vantage point and noting my every gesture with a knowing nod. At such moments her earnest gaze seemed to say, I know who you are, what you are, where you come from, and why you are as you are—I understand you. I've found the key to you in these books.

I don't mean to suggest that it gave me a sense of inferiority, but I did, gradually, begin to envy her knowledge. One morning, after she set out for the university I made a bold resolve and took *The Science of Judaism,* by someone called Rosenzweig, to bed with me. On page 3 I fell asleep and never picked that book up again. Incidentally, I have not read Buber to this day. I've heard so much about him from Barbara that without batting an eyelash I can discuss him at the dinner table, from the main course all the way through dessert. I've done it more than once—but not in Barbara's presence.

In time I got used to the idea that in our family the specialist on Jewish matters was Barbara, not I, consoling myself with the fact that at least in the area of architecture my knowledge surpassed hers. But one day she read some Lewis Mumford and began to express some highly interesting opinions in this field as well. One of the things that always irritated me about Barbara was her phenomenal memory. She doesn't forget a thing. She remembers names, numbers, facts, and she can quote whole passages from a book she read years ago. Moreover, she remembers the very things I want to forget. (She claims, for instance, to have read this very phrase in Oscar Wilde.) This talent is enough to drive a person mad.

While I was ill I seem to have had an argument with Dr. Mayer. A few days after I had tried, fruitlessly, to find out more about my father's veterinary talents he burst into my room like a tornado, flung his coat on the chair, and before I had a chance to scold him for bringing Barbara flowers he ordered, "Don't talk. Open your mouth. Say ah. Sit down. Hold your breath. Breathe deeply. Cough." After concluding the ritual by taking my temperature and checking my blood pressure, he finally said, "Now you can talk." Barbara, who stood in the doorway holding the flowers, surveyed the scene with a smile.

"What am I supposed to make of this flirtation with my wife?" I asked him gravely.

"You may conclude that something is not right. I'm angry with your wife," he said, and I couldn't detect even the ghost of a smile in his tiny eyes. "I'll continue to bring presents as long as she persists in sending checks in the mail. You two are offending me."

"Dr. Mayer, really!" I scolded. "You do your work and you should be paid for it."

"Nonsense," he said, dismissing my argument. "There's such a thing as professional courtesy among doctors. No doctor would accept money from me and I wouldn't accept money from another doctor, certainly not from the son of a doctor who was my good friend."

"Good friend?"

"Let us say acquaintance," he admitted.

"But he's been dead a long time," I said.

"So what? If the situation were reversed, if I had a son your age and I wasn't here, do you think your father would accept money from my son? You talk nonsense and I have no time for nonsense."

"Dr. Mayer," I sighed in despair, "you are impossible."

"It's not so terrible. And I warn you both: if you persist in sending money I'll . . . I don't know what I'll do. I'll buy furniture for your nursery."

"You'll do nothing of the sort," I said menacingly, and Barbara laughed.

"Yes I will. You'll see," he said. "I'm going now."

We, of course, didn't let him go. We urged him to stay for coffee and he refused, shaking his head stubbornly like a little boy. Only after I threatened to get out of bed and run to the door barefoot to block his way did he relent. We waited for the coffee in silence, but as we drank it his face became grim and he began muttering to himself. When we asked what was the matter he shrugged his shoulders without answering. After coffee we succeeded, through determined cross-examination, in discovering what had suddenly depressed him.

The previous night (we reconstructed this from his evasive answers) after leaving a patient's house he stepped into a bar for a beer. ("You don't drink it at home? I'll send you a case.") As soon as he opened the door a drunk who was draped over the bar shouted, "*Juden raus!*" The fact that the proprietor bounced the fellow immediately was no comfort. Dr. Mayer was stunned. "And there weren't even any Jews there," he said. "I didn't see a single one."

We began to argue, trying to allay his anxieties with insipid rationalizations: he may have misheard; the remark very likely was not directed at him, etc. Finding him inconsolable, I finally asked why he had come back to Germany.

"What do you mean?" he asked, astonished.

Why did he leave Haifa, I asked, where no one would say, "*Juden raus!*" I told him I couldn't understand Jews who came back and settled in Germany after all that happened there. Dr. Mayer stared at me without a word. Assuming he had no doubt addressed similar arguments to himself, I went on with my arrogant indictment, barraging him with words I hadn't dared to utter to Max the day before. (Max had come for a brief visit, bringing newspapers from home. We played chess and he never stopped grumbling about "the situation." I asked when he planned to come home to Israel and he shrugged.) I was attacking Dr. Mayer as I hadn't dared to attack Max. At first he seemed unperturbed. But then, suddenly aroused, he began to flap his hands as if to say, that's enough—I've heard enough. Barbara, who was sitting on the bed, placed a restraining hand on my arm and I finally shut up. The silence was oppressive. Dr. Mayer sighed deeply, and then in a calm, measured tone he said things I didn't expect to hear from him.

Even if his wife's health had been more stable, he explained slowly and with emphasis, even if she hadn't suffered from the climate in Israel, he would have returned to Germany. Germany was his native land (he said this explicitly!). And Frankfurt was the scene of his youth. German was the language he thought and lived in. I noticed Barbara nodding in agreement, which enraged me further. What the devil is this, I asked myself, why is she agreeing with him? How can he still regard Germany as his homeland? After the "mild" experiments conducted on his wife . . . ("Mrs. Mayer, would you

kindly place both your hands in this ice water and leave
them there for an hour and forty-five minutes, until the
timer rings. *Danke schön genaedige,* Frau Mayer.")
After the humiliation, degradation, torment that he himself endured . . . ("Dig, you damned Jew. Stick your
head in the trash. Run faster, pig. Dance, you Jewish
monkey, laugh.") Still, he was willing to live with these
murderers, these dispensers of death transformed into
amiable pharmacists, storekeepers, industrialists who
suffer indigestion and come to him for relief. Unbeliev-
able! Even Germans, Barbara among them, say they'll
emigrate the moment the Nazis regain power. Why
must he be superfaithful to this bewitched land? She
nodded, meaning, I suppose, I too, having been born
here, should consider Germany my native land. They're
insane, out of their minds.

That's what I told Dr. Mayer. I said he was crazy.
I offered all my proofs and arguments. I reasoned that
only in a Jewish state could every Jew . . . and so on;
that history repeats itself, that those who forget the
past are condemned to repeat it, that no self-respecting
person could live where he was unwanted, was even de-
graded, where his own patients—yes, yes!—murdered
his kin. I went so far as to say that I regarded his conduct as grossly disrespectful of the dead. But he denied
this, arguing that Germany was his home despite what
had happened, that an ill wind had swept through the
land, a fearful plague had wrought havoc all around, but
now that plague was reversed. And furthermore he
believed that those who were born and grew up here,
victims who survived through some miracle, ought—yes
ought—to return and concentrate their efforts on pre-
venting the recurrence of such a catastrophe.

"I came back to do what I can," he said, "to cure
people. There is no logic or justification for allowing the
culprits, the murderers, the madmen to inherit the land
and enjoy its fruits. Let Germany be the heritage of the
victims, the oppressed. Those who suffered ought to be
present as an eternal reminder, at the very least."

Much later, when I heard the evasive answers of Jews

returning to Germany to make their fortunes, or, as they themselves put it, to snatch what was available and enjoy some revenge for what was perpetrated; when I heard the feigned innocence, the hypocritical responses of Jews and Israelis who came to wash the soiled linens of the murderers, to fit them with new shoes, to forget the past in nightclubs housed in converted torture cellars —only then did I begin to value Dr. Mayer's integrity and courage. But in the course of that stormy argument I considered him pathetic, unworthy even of pity. I was quite merciless and went on berating him, even when his face went white, even after Barbara interceded, rising to his defense with a passion and fury she seldom displayed.

When he left that day I thought I would never see him again. In the evening, after hours of grim silence between Barbara and me, I phoned to ask him to forgive me if I had offended him, to forget what I had said and not be angry. He was glad to hear my voice and said he was not angry; my arguments were not new to him, he had been confronted with them many times, but he maintained the same position nonetheless. Yes, of course, of course he would visit us soon. How was I feeling, was my fever down? "Please, give my regards to your charming wife." And that was that.

Now is the time, it seems to me, to deal with various other unsettled matters. When did Barbara's parents learn of the pregnancy and what was their reaction? When did I meet her father again? And what about my brother, Martin? Did I give up the search? How was the reparations claim progressing?

The matter of reparations is complex and I'll get to it later. For the moment let me say that substantial sums were arriving in the mail by the first week of my illness, checks I put off cashing from day to day on various pretexts. I gave up the search for Martin after I received a letter from the Department of the Interior in Jerusalem informing me that there was no such person listed in the register of residents. There was nothing further to be done—all that remained was the hope, or rather the apprehension, that we would find each other through those mysterious turns of fate (often recounted in the newspapers) which reunite brothers after many years.

As for those other questions . . . Two weeks after I took sick Barbara called her parents to tell them the news about her condition. Naturally, they were surprised and her mother persisted in asking questions that amused Barbara. "Of course I'm certain, mother," I heard her say. "Do you think I'm a child? Yes, I did go to the doctor. What kind of a question is that? Of course I'm very happy." Her father interrupted, declaring that two weeks, or more precisely sixteen days, sets a new European record, and is "bound to make quite a stir in gynecological circles." At this point Barbara informed them that she was in her second month. "That's right, mother, it happened before the wedding. Don't be ridiculous, that's not why we got married. I wanted to get married." This reminded them of my existence and they asked how I was. Barbara said I felt much better; my fever was down and the doctor might allow me to get out of bed in a week. (They knew about my illness from earlier conversations, and at the beginning there were daily calls to check on my progress. Her father wanted to send his doctor from Düsseldorf, but Barbara assured him I was in good hands and there was no cause for worry.)

The afternoon after this conversation, while Barbara was in class, the doorbell rang. Pluto barked and began sniffing the threshold. I grabbed my robe and slippers as I ran to open the door. To my surprise it was Barbara's father, carrying flowers and wine. I was surprised and pleased, very pleased. We shook hands heartily, with the vigor of men who know how to make children. When he looked over my shoulder expectantly I said Barbara would be home soon. After setting the French champagne in the refrigerator and sticking the roses in a pitcher of water, he reached down to pat Pluto, who was jumping all over him. He shooed me back to bed

and sat beside me for a long moment without a word;
then he began to laugh. He got up and embraced me,
but suddenly embarrassed, he dropped his arms and
sat down uneasily. He asked if it was all right to smoke,
and quickly lit a cigarette. He seemed about to say something, then thought better of it. I waited for him to reconsider but he remained silent. When I asked what
brought him to Frankfurt he said he had come to offer
his good wishes, to see me and to chat a bit. I nodded
and asked no more questions. Did I really try to strangle
him at the wedding I mused, riveting my eyes on his
collarbone. His face was tan and youthful. It was hard
to believe this was Barbara's father—almost a grandfather. He could easily be one of her admirers—an
elegant one at that. The morning after our wedding, it
was possible to avoid referring to my shameful behavior,
but now, alone and face to face, how could we pretend
nothing had happened? Why was he silent?

"How's the weather?" I asked. He made some vague
response. A long pause. He asked how I was feeling. I
replied with a perfunctory "Fine thanks," or something
of that sort. After awhile I asked what time it was.
"Barbara won't be home until two," I volunteered.

"Very good," he said. "That gives us a chance to talk."

"That's right," I said. I didn't know where to look.

A fly fluttered on the curtain, or was it a black stain?

A dirty towel hung on the doorknob and a drawer was
open; Barbara's shoes were under the chair. Pluto,
sprawled at the foot of the bed, wondered why I hadn't
exiled him to the kitchen; he watched Mr. Stahl, wagging his tail in pleasure.

"That's how it is," said Mr. Stahl.

"Yes," I concurred.

A long silence.

"I see it's hard for you to restate the question," he
remarked.

"What question?" I said, playing dumb.

"You wanted to know what I did during the war," he
said.

"Yes, I did want to know. But I'm not sure I do now.

I was drunk. Forgive me. Later I didn't even remember what I said—Barbara told me. She heard all about it from Max."

He ignored my little speech. "Are you afraid of the answer?" he asked.

"Not anymore," I said. "I . . . I'm not sure I have the right to ask. Not now, that is. You were right, Mr. Stahl, I should have asked before marrying your daughter. Even then I doubt if your answer would have changed anything. Anyway, I already know the answer. Barbara told me. You manufactured optical equipment."

He verified this, adding quickly that his defective hearing kept him out of the army. "It was before this marvelous gadget was invented," he said, tugging at the thin string that led from his ear to his jacket pocket. "I was totally deaf. Or so I claimed. Luckily the doctors confirmed this." Smiling mischievously, he went to the kitchen and returned a minute later (I heard him opening cupboards) with a glass of whiskey. He assured me he did not mean to pretend he was a saint. It was sheer luck, he emphasized, that kept him out of the army and out of the Nazi party. In the middle of the war, in '42, he began manufacturing optical equipment. The first orders were from the War Department: binoculars, telescopes, cameras, lenses . . .

"Periscopes, microscopes," I added with the trace of a smile.

"Yes," he said, "that too. And I don't feel guilty about it. I knew very well what the periscopes were for, and I did what I could to guarantee that they would be precise and effective. I didn't declare the war. I wanted to live. As for the microscopes, I know. The formula you scrawled on the wall is familiar, the German *"Mene, mene, tekel, upharsin."* I produced microscopes for laboratories and hospitals. I could not—and it didn't occur to me to do this—sell them only for constructive purposes. I doubt if you would condemn a barbed wire manufacturer for his role in setting up concentration camps . . ."

"Or an oven manufacturer—" I started to say.

"No," he disputed, "that's entirely different. Kopf and Sons produced ovens for a very specific purpose. Their ovens were not meant for bread. They are definitely guilty. But I don't see how you can condemn an industrialist for producing sulfuric acid, even though H_2SO_4 does appear in the death formulas. It serves many functions in industry—it's used in metalwork and in my industry too."

"Mr. Stahl," I said, "I wasn't accusing you."

"Right. It's odd that I'm so defensive. I guess I'm really not so free of guilt." Smiling bitterly he took his empty glass to the kitchen. When he returned I tried to change the subject: I asked about his wife, the state of business, his views on Franco-German relations. His brusque responses made it obvious that he was preoccupied with other things. I began to tell him about a competition in which my design for a hospital had almost won third prize, when the phone rang; it was Barbara.

"How are you, darling?" she asked.

"Come right home and bring a special cake. We have important company," I reported gaily.

"Max?" she guessed.

"Even more important," I said. "Your father is here."

"And what are you two doing without me?" she asked sternly.

"We're doing the tango. Your father begs you to come and replace one of us. We are getting tired of each other."

"I'll be right there," she said, blowing a kiss into the phone before she hung up.

31 | *nocturne*

A week or two after I was out of bed, the first signs of crisis began to appear. I knew that this was inevitable. Our honeymoon would have to end and we'd wake up from our dream to discover reality, unlike what we imagined. Our blissful state could not endure. Its sheer bounty would surely drive us out of our minds. Somewhere along the line, I mused, there lies a snare. Unsuspecting, we will pull the thread and set off an explosion. We'll become remote and lie in bed with our eyes open, refusing to speak; we'll heap our silences on one another, working with obstinate diligence to erect a wall of alienation. It happens to everyone, I thought. I may as well be prepared for the shock.

Many times, before and after the wedding, I tried to foresee the crisis. Especially in placid moments. When I watched Barbara bent over her books, when I sat by the fire listening to music, I tried to picture the situation that would bring things to a head. The beautiful moments didn't mislead me or dispel my suspicions. The quiet before the storm, I reflected. Something isn't right here—too orderly, too neat. At any moment it will erupt.

I considered various potential trouble spots—specific pressures, complexities, frailties—and tried to anticipate their resolution. If she does this, I do that. I schemed to myself like the old men one sees hunched over a chessboard in a café. If she makes this move, I make that one. I pictured her in countless absurd situations: having an affair in the stacks with the medieval poetry instructor, with a gentleman-in-mourning at the Necropolis Hotel. I found myself responding to these scenes with a warm, tolerant smile. So what? Such trivial matters don't wreck a marriage. A woman needs to know she's desirable even when she's pregnant. She should hold the key to the prison of matrimony. I could see her peeling an apple with a knife and fork at a students' party in Jerusalem, and I shrugged. I imagined her gossiping about me on the phone. (She thought I was out, but I was hiding in the closet, meaning to surprise her with a kiss when she hung up her coat.) I overheard her from the closet dialing and saying I had come to Germany to demand five marks for every day my parents spent in the camps. Impossible, I thought; she wouldn't say such a thing about me. She couldn't form the words "damn Jew." And yet what will happen, I asked myself, if the word "kike" escapes her lips in a moment of rage? What will I do? Be silent, I decided. Two days of silence, three. A week. Until she gets down on her knees and pleads. I saw her in situations I prefer not to recount, situations that incensed me so that I saw myself slapping her face or, on second thought, saying something sharp and then proceeding coldly with everyday routines. Once when she came close to me while I was engaged in one of these mental battles, I pushed her away with repressed anger. It was a long time before I could joke about the incident.

A crisis seemed so inevitable that I actually found myself looking forward to it. I was impatient, a warrior tensed for battle, on the alert for signs of an offensive. I began to wish the crisis would come so I could overcome it and emerge from the experience, relaxed, fortified, and enriched. After many hours of mental calisthenics I was, so I thought, ready for anything. But when the moment came I was taken by surprise and utterly unprepared.

I was sitting in my usual spot, in "my" chair near the fire, reading one of Edna's new magazines from Israel. The story I was reading, translated from English, was one of those "great" love stories—a stormy night, an isolated castle, candlelight, a fire crackling in the ancient hearth. ("Oh, Skiff, I love you," said Karen closing her eyes and holding her breath. "Do what you will with me." Skiff McCann held her blazing body in his steady hands and carried her toward the canopied bed in which his father had breathed his last a few days before.) Barbara was at her desk, which was heaped with books and papers, studying as usual. Once I turned and found her watching me with a new sort of tenderness. I smiled an exaggerated smile to acknowledge her look but she continued to gaze at me with an earnestness that verged on tears. I went back to the story but couldn't find my place. Rain was pounding on the window and the record that fell onto the automatic turntable happened to be Chopin. I glanced at Barbara a few minutes later—expecting to find her studying—and was astonished to discover she was still staring at me. No longer able to elude her with a smile, I felt I had to say something. "What is it, Barbara?" And as if anticipating this, she said in a faint voice, "Uri . . . I love you very much . . ."

This sentence was like a cold torrent. I don't remember if I said, with disdain, "I love you too," which is what I wanted to say at that moment, or if I merely muttered something vague. Turning away from her I let the magazine fall to the floor and fixed my eyes on the wall. "She loves me," I repeated to myself in a scornful voice.

A chair stirred behind me. Footsteps. My neck muscles were taut. A hand, ever so light, touched my shoulder. I felt her breath, then her warm lips on my neck. "Uri, darling . . . ," she murmured. I bent down to pick up the magazine, hoping to slip away from her, but as soon as I straightened up I felt her hand again. I tapped it lightly, three gentle taps, and held my breath. The hand was gone. The footsteps receded. She's back at her desk, thank heavens. For God's sake, what is she up to, I asked myself. Why all of a sudden the need to declare her love in such a maudlin way? Great God, is she suddenly "in love" with me? A stormy night, Chopin at the piano, a fire in the hearth—and she loves me! What kitsch. George Sand kicks off her boots, slips out of her riding habit, slinks into a fine cotton nightshirt, and, "Chopin, my darling, I love you."

This is it, I thought. The crisis I've been waiting for. She will be soft, yielding, and in love to the point of revolting sentimentality, staring at me for hours on end with a soft, sad look, eyebrows compressed in self-pity. Tireless displays of love and attention. I reach for a cigarette, she rushes for a match. I head for the bathroom, she races to hang a fresh towel and pass a warm one over the toilet seat. I look up from my plate and with utter devotion she passes me the salt or the bread. Before I have a chance to swing my legs off the bed she hands me my slippers. She follows me with tiny steps wherever I go. I glance toward the dog, she banishes him sternly to the kitchen. And declarations of love: morning, noon, and night. Along with this—tender glances, tormenting expressions of surrender and self-sacrifice. It's enough to drive you mad.

Cautiously, without a sound, I half turned toward her. She was perched on the chair, ready to leap when I beckoned, filling page after page of a letter pad. Her brows were knit. She's writing me love letters, I thought.

"Barbara," I ventured tentatively.

"What?" She quickly put down the pen and turned to look at me.

So I was right, I thought. "Nothing, really nothing."

"What is it, darling? What?" she asked ardently, awaiting my command. "Would you like something?" Her yearning tone matched the schmaltz of Chopin's "Nocturne." (A storm in Majorca. Candles flickering on the black piano.) "Should I make some coffee, darling?"

"No, no," I said. "It's nothing. I only wanted to say 'Barbara.'"

She smiled knowingly and was about to throw me a kiss, but I turned away in time.

Well, it was clear something was wrong. Something must be up. An emotional crisis following the honeymoon—that happens. It could be the pregnancy. She no longer regards me merely as a friend, a lover, a splendid bedfellow. I have become a husband and father. Her maternal impulses are at work. My past, perhaps, the search for Martin, the visit to that camp, my illness—all this may have brought her to the absurd conclusion that I . . . (phooey) that I need warmth, sympathy, an outpouring of love. Hell, she's out of her mind.

Such a sudden transformation! She who was a mystery, opaque, perplexing—a sealed and enigmatic book. In all her actions and decisions she was completely independent and included me without in any way depending on me. "I'm going to the theater tomorrow," she would say. "Want to come along?" How I loved her in those moments. At last, I thought, I've found a woman who makes no attempt to hold me responsible for her existence. Every day I had to pursue her anew, as if

nothing had passed between us the night before. There
was an enchanting lack of certainty in our relations, an
element of suspense that made her all the more attractive to me. Now, suddenly, what a transformation! "Uri,
darling . . . I love you so." No more and no less. "I love
you so much, my darling." This in a candid yet tiresome
tone. She really means it. What a pain.

No, it's not the words that bother me, I thought—I've
used them too. From the very start we were free with
words, even extravagant ("Please pass the salt. Thanks
very much, I love you"). It's possible to look into someone's eyes, and whisper in a faint yet lyric voice, "I . . .
love . . . you . . ." but this is banal, downright vulgar.
Why not make do with a gentle caress, a pillow fight,
sweet curses and imprecations? These are clear enough.

"Barbara," I said, to prove my theory, "I can't bear
your ugly face."

"I know," she said after a brief silence.

See, I proclaimed to my audience. She has mis-
understood! I could say, "I love you" in the very same
tone. In school when a boy liked a girl he would pull
her pigtails, scatter her books, push her into the bram-
bles. All the kids would crowd around and sing, "Here
comes the bride." It wouldn't do to give her a flower and
admit that you had a crush on her. It was out of the
question to cling and coo like . . . like Toomi for example.

We had a teacher in our school named Ruth. Everyone loved her. She was plump and soft, with a lovely
smile and a dimple in her right cheek. To this day the
thought of her firm bare legs poking out from under her
white apron affects me. And I remember her bosom
(now I can say breasts) soaring gently over the lunch-
room table and the heavy braid flung over her shoulder
in such delightful disorder. Whenever she crossed the
cypress-lined path a noisy gang of children, led by
Toomi, would swarm around her. Toomi was twelve or
thirteen, and he, more than anyone else, was stuck on
Ruth. Every chance he got he would hug her, rest his
head on her bosom, and sometimes even kiss her neck

in front of everyone—displays of love that revolted me. Especially when he called her "Mommy." After all, he wasn't the only motherless kid in the country. Ruth never scolded him nor did she make an attempt to check his advances. At most she would say gently, "That's enough, honey. Ruth has to go now. Walk with me. Come on, Toomi." Maxie and I . . . Maxie was my good friend. The two of us were born in Frankfurt and went to Palestine together. Incidentally, he went back to Germany—but that's another story. Anyway, Maxie and I used to give Toomi a pinch whenever we had the chance, when Ruth wasn't looking.

One afternoon as we left the dining hall and were going to our rooms beyond the pine grove, I saw Ruth sitting on a bench with Toomi in her lap. At first, I didn't notice them—I was probably busy searching for a firefly or a scorpion. (I had an insect collection in my room in cardboard boxes with holes. I raised silkworms too.) Anyway, I was only two or three steps away when I noticed them. Instead of walking on or looking away, as I would usually do, I stood rooted to the spot, too bewildered and upset to avert my eyes. Toomi's head was buried in her bosom—really, right in her bosom! His frail arms were clasped around her hips. She murmured something to him and smiled her dimpled smile, her fingers caressing his head gently. Her apron was askew so that I caught a blinding glimpse of her thighs. I was fourteen. Imagine that. She suddenly became aware of me and said, "Come on, Uri, come and join us." At this Toomi opened his eyes and glared at me. When Ruth saw that I wasn't responding she came over to me and tried to be playful. Then—and this was the awful part—she drew me to her bosom. To her breast, that is. I was too terrified to move. My hands dangled tensely at my side, and I thought I would die of humiliation. Just then I turned around and saw a row of kids watching us solemnly. It was awful. I pushed her away, screaming, "Let go of me, you whore!" and ran to my room.

Years later we lay naked in her room in Bet-Kerem,

my hand on her flowing hips, my head in her sweet breasts. (I was nineteen, she twenty-five.) I had loved her then, at fourteen, she explained, even though I had been so nasty. "Remember?" I sensed a note of rebuke in her voice and buried my head in her breasts again to hide my shame.

That's it, folks. Why did I tell you this tale? Yes, please. Louder. Speak up so everyone can hear. . . . You're absolutely right, sir. I will elaborate on that point in my next lecture.

"Barbara," I said, "don't you think it's time for bed?"

"I'm not tired," she answered.

I was relieved. I can go to sleep unburdened by her love. Just as I drop my pants, looking ridiculous in crumpled underwear and drooping socks, she would croon in her most languid voice, "Uri, dear, how I love you." Now for a swift exit, before she changes her mind. Say a quick good night, get into bed, and turn off the light. When she comes in I'll be asleep, even if I'm not. But wait a minute! What's the meaning of this? She is *not* tired? She didn't even look in my direction. What am I supposed to make of this sudden defiance? Have I offended her? Is she waiting for me to go to bed so she can be alone?

I pushed my chair back noisily and stared at her. She didn't make a move. Her back was toward me, her feet curled under the table. She looked very striking, with the light over Uncle Gustaf casting a golden halo on her hair. She was writing furiously, never stopping to read what she had written or to consider what would follow. The words seemed to gush forth in an unending stream. To whom was she addressing those passionate phrases? I got up abruptly and stood waiting for her to acknowledge me. She wrote on, unrelenting. I went to the phonograph, leafed through the record pile and finally chose Telemann, the record we played that first day. I sat down again and cleared my throat. No response.

"Barbara," I began, aware of the tender note in my own voice.

"What?" she said without looking up. I stared at her in silence. Lady Von Stahl is writing, I thought; she is far away. Then without putting down the pen she looked at me and smiled patronizingly, to convey the fact that she "understood." I said nothing. She continued writing, but a moment later she turned to see if I was still watching her and asked, with a trace of impatience, "What is it? Do you want something?" in a tone that meant, "Why are you staring at me like that?"

"Would you like some coffee?" she asked a few minutes later, overemphasizing the "would you." It was clear that she didn't want to stir, that she only wanted me to stop distracting her. (Why? What happened?) She's writing a love letter, I speculated bitterly, a passionate letter to her medieval poetry professor or to that gentleman-in-mourning or the one with graying sideburns and an elegant scar across his cheek.

"It's late," I said. "Let's go to bed."

"You go if you like," she said, "I'm not tired."

She's not tired, I thought, derisively. Why doesn't she tell me to get out, to stop bothering her? Why doesn't she speak up?

"What are you doing?" I asked trying to be casual.

"Oh, nothing," she answered evasively.

"What?" I persisted.

"You insist on knowing?" she asked in a threatening tone.

"Yes," I said firmly. I might as well know the truth.

"Some thoughts on von Kleist," she said.

"Some thoughts on von Kleist," I repeated slowly, sardonically.

"Don't you believe me?" she asked, irritated.

"Of course I believe you."

"Then why did you say 'Some thoughts on von Kleist' in that tone?"

"I was just repeating your words," I said with a show of indifference.

"Yes, but you sound as if you don't believe me," she charged.

"What's on your mind?" I asked defensively.

"Nothing," she said. "It's empty."

"Who says so?" I asked, offended.

"You did," she answered.

"Me? What do you mean? When?"

"A few minutes ago. You said you love my empty head." She uttered the word "love" with revulsion.

"I didn't say a word about an empty head," I countered. "I said I love your ugly face."

"Thanks a lot," she said.

"What's the matter with you?" I shouted. "You know what I mean."

"First of all, stop yelling," she said. "I know what you mean. You may have said ugly face but you meant empty head."

"Are you crazy?"

"Listen here," she said, "you don't have to pretend. I can tell."

"Nonsense!" I said impatiently. "I never thought you were dumb. I said ugly because—"

"I know I'm ugly now," she said.

"You're not ugly," I said sincerely.

"Pretty soon you'll deny you said it," she taunted.

"That's what I *said*, but I meant to say . . ." I tried to explain, but she interrupted me. "Yes, I know. You're tired of this. You think it's my fault. These blotches on my face? They're natural when you're pregnant. All you do is sit in your chair all day, and you have the nerve to complain!"

"Complain? You're the one with complaints," I cried, becoming more and more agitated. "What do you expect me to do? I should look after the house, I suppose." I got up in a rage. "What do you expect me to do?"

"I don't know," she said. "But I don't see how you can sit home all day without doing anything."

This was the beginning of our first full-scale fight. I remember my excitement, even my glee, as I plunged into it. Even before she finished her sentence I turned off the phonograph with an ostentatious gesture and said to myself, So, she wants a fight? OK, I'm certainly willing. It's time we had a good fight! I'm tired of this insipid peace, of the gracious manners, the silk gloves, the polite masks! If there's going to be a fight, let's fight! Strike the sensitive spots, step on toes, shoot poison arrows. OK, step aside, everyone, you're about to see the real thing. Just what does she have in mind? Does she think I'll take it from her, bow my head like . . . a poor submissive Jew? She doesn't know me very well. I don't take that sort of thing lying down. I'm an Israeli and nobody, especially not a Germ—nobody can tell me what to do. The nerve! I sit home doing nothing! Sponging, she means. Get a job—aren't you ashamed to let me support you? Let's put the cards on the table and find out where we stand.

I no longer remember just what I said to her or what she said to me. It isn't especially important now. Every married man knows how easily a casual exchange becomes a grim quarrel and how tenuous the line is between love and hate. I remember that in the course of our argument there were moments when I enjoyed the stormy verbal clash, though in the long run I regretted it. Our quarrel began like most family quarrels: a polite game that gradually escalated into a complex match with two or three balls flying simultaneously; then finally it became a critical bout accompanied by abuse and insults too ugly to repeat.

At the outset of the duel I left the choice of weapons to Barbara. As long as she attacked with gentle though bitter irony, I, too, was content with cold blades of lethal sarcasm. When she raised her voice I followed suit. ("Don't shout at me!" she shouted. "And don't you shout at me!" I shouted.) When she struck below the belt I cast aside my gentlemanly restraint and chose my own weapons. I met each of her stabs with a strike and every strike with a blow. Most of the verbal darts missed their target, for neither of us was listening.

It was to Barbara's credit, I must admit, that even in the thick of the fight, when she was under constant fire, she made no attempt to crash the door to my past or to attack my real weak spot—the fact that I was Jewish—

not even by implication, though more than once I tried to push her in that direction. "What do you take me for?" I screamed over and over. "Do you think I'm some humble Jew who swallows every insult in silence?" I had a devastating sentence in my arsenal about the true character of Germans, which even the camouflage of so-called liberalism could never mask. I intended to undo her with this sentence as soon as she dared utter the word "Jew," but the clever shrew managed to circumvent all my splendid traps.

Who knows where this ugly fight would have led if Pluto hadn't rushed in from the kitchen barking at us with such fury that we had to direct all our energies toward getting him back to the other room, which required our joint efforts. We closed the door on him, tired and depleted, but remained silent—remote from each other a long, seemingly eternal moment. She went back to her desk and sat pretending to read what she had written. I stood beside the dying fire, my back to her. The oppressive silence was broken by thunder. The rain had stopped pounding on the window. I was beginning to calm down. When I peeked over my shoulder at Barbara, I could see she was still upset. Her knee was propped on the chair, and her thigh, encased in nylon, gleamed in the light of the lamp. I watched her restless fingers turn page after page and knew she was staring into space.

A self-indulgent bitch, I thought to myself, a preening cat with claws of steel. The face of an angel, the heart of a devil. So swift and so sharp—what a surprise. Not once did she flounder. Even before I finished my sentence she had a retort, snatching the words from my mouth. Clever tactics, a well-conceived strategy. Before I could even place my runner in the breach, her horse would advance, threatening assault. She was certainly on the ball, the little witch. But I wasn't bad either. "Your clever maneuvers arouse my deep compassion, my dear," I said. It didn't matter how she responded, I charged ahead: "Don't trouble your empty little head with questions that are beyond your scope." What was the point of this? It doesn't matter—a satisfying sentence is an end in itself. Her eyes flashed. This wild seething animal was very beautiful.

"It doesn't take a giant brain to grasp your superficial view, which arouses *my* deepest compassion, darling."

I continued to rant, pretending not to hear her. I must admit it wasn't a bad fight. We emerged tired but gratified. I felt better.

Now, somehow we had to make up. She had to be the one to take the first step; after all, I was the offended party. "I am sorry for you, you poor victim," she had said. I wouldn't forget this. So, I am the victim, and she is sorry for me! Never mind. I am willing to forget even that. If she had any sense she would come to me now (I won't look), offer her hand, and admit her position was somewhat extreme.

"Let's make up, Uri," she could say simply. "I lost myself. Forgive me if I hurt you. Come on, let me give you a kiss and everything will be OK." If she had the strength to place her head on my shoulder, I would take her in my arms and kiss her salty eyes, cheeks, lips, neck. (She was crying, poor thing.) I would confess in a whisper that I too was out of line and ask her to forgive the nonsense I flung at her so thoughtlessly. We would have coffee in the kitchen, the way we did in the beginning, when we used to sit in eloquent silence that yielded to smiles, even laughter. Remember how it was when I said thus-and-so to you, and you said thus-and-so to me? You were very sharp, Barby dear, a real bitch. And you were pretty good yourself, you devil. Know something, darling? Your German has really improved. We should practice like this regularly. When we live in Jerusalem let's promise to quarrel in Hebrew, or I'll never learn the language.

It could have been so simple and sweet—but she didn't make a move. She didn't even look at me, although I cleared my throat and began to whistle a South American song we both liked. Finally I decided to swallow my pride. I started toward her bravely, but at the last minute I walked on to the kitchen. I stood there a few seconds trying to compose an opening sentence, to predict her reaction, to formulate an answer. The palms of my hands were sweaty by the time I had the nerve to approach her.

"Barbara," I began in an appeasing tone, standing close to her.

I noticed her tensing up and touched her gently (too gently perhaps) on her shoulder. I touched my lips to her taut back. She squirmed and slipped away, shouting, with a look of revulsion (real revulsion!), "Leave me alone! You make me sick!"

I, of course, was deeply wounded. I felt as though a terrible injustice had been perpetrated and went into the bedroom, slamming the door so hard that the Chagall lithograph I had bought Barbara after my illness fell off the wall and shattered.

An hour or so later, a long tormenting hour during which I lay in bed fully clothed, my eyes rending the darkness, Barbara came in and got a blanket from the closet. She left without closing the door, without even a glance at me. I heard her undress and sink into the soft cushions of the living room couch.

32 | *complications*

It sounds absurd I know, but the next morning matters were no better and they didn't improve in the days that followed. In fact, the situation became more and more grave. It may have been my fault. I could have gone to her in the middle of the night. (I didn't sleep a wink, anyway.) A situation that can't be redeemed by day can often be resolved by night. I should, perhaps, have been up early, fixed breakfast, and greeted her festively with, "Good morning, darling. Coffee is ready." It is very possible that such a trivial gesture would have broken the ice. Even if she withheld her smile as I poured her coffee, buttered her bread, passed the jam the instant she reached for the knife, I could have said, simply, without a trace of malice, "Come on, Barbara, that's enough. Don't make a problem out of every little thing. If I have offended you, I'm really sorry. I'll get down on my knees and beg your forgiveness. But there's no point in behaving like children. This is our first quarrel, not our last. There will be many more silly fights—believe me, I don't even remember how this one started. We'll have to learn how to cope with these dead ends. Come on, honey, let's bury the hatchet. Enough is enough."

Quite possibly this would have settled the matter—but I decided to stay mad, not to give in. When I heard her in the kitchen in the morning I assumed the role of the offended party, closing my eyes and pretending to be asleep. I've already demonstrated my good intentions, I reasoned, by taking the first step, which wasn't easy. I swallowed my pride and asked her to forgive me. (For what? What did I do? What did I say?) All she could offer was, "Leave me alone, you make me sick!" These were her very words. What does she think I am? First she insults me and then I'm expected to apologize. No thanks, honey, not a chance. It's your turn. Now, I thought, closing my eyes, she should come to me, lean close, stroke my head, and say, "Uri, I am sorry." I'd be willing to forget, I'm not petty. I might mutter to myself to let her know it's not easy, but in the end I'd forgive and forget. (What happened? How did it all start anyway? What did I say to her?)

Such was my inner monologue that morning in bed. But she, the witch, the wretch, the stubborn bitch, made no gesture of goodwill. She didn't even come into the bedroom. (Later it occurred to me that she may have peered in and thought I was asleep, since I was lying with my back to the open door. She may have even been waiting for me to get up and acknowledge her existence.) She went out without a word. I heard her footsteps in the living room, then a door opening and closing. She could have left a note: "Good morning, Uri dear." Or "Good morning, Uri. What happened yesterday?" That would be enough. "Why were you so hurt? Acting like a little boy. . . . That's not nice. I expect an explanation when I get home at two. Yours, with a kiss for your empty head." She could have written something in this vein but I searched the whole house without finding any message—she left the dirty dishes on the table and took off. I'll show her, I said to myself. She'll find the dishes right where she left them. And when I hear her footsteps in the hall I'll be asleep—conspicuously asleep. Until she asks me to forgive her. Until she gives in.

That day she didn't weaken; she spent another night on the couch. Nor did she show any signs of yielding the next day, though I got up first and began to move about noisily. I gargled as hard as I could, dropped a few things on the bathroom floor, filled the sink, then let the water out with a great clamor. When I went to the kitchen to fix a festive breakfast she was lying on the couch, with the blanket pulled over her head. Later, when I was slicing the bread, she went by on the way to the bathroom, still wrapped in the blanket. She dawdled interminably. Tired of waiting I sat down with my coffee—just as she emerged from the bathroom. Seeing that I'd started without her she grabbed her coat and was on her way.

"No coffee?" I called.

"No," she answered from the doorway. "I'll have some at school."

She got home late that day. When I heard her footsteps on the stairs, I leaped toward the big table and sat down to work on some sketches I had made earlier. Let her see I'm doing something, I thought. I'm not as idle as she thinks. She'll be surprised. When she asks what I'm doing, I'll tell her I'm working on a new project. A school, let's say, a government institution, a housing development. (The fact is you can barely tell them apart.) One thing will lead to another, and somehow the clouds will pass. But she hung up her coat, responded perfunctorily to my warm hello, glanced at my sketch with no interest, avoided my eyes though they sought hers, and retreated to the bathroom again. I heard the shower and tried to picture her there under the water, in her second month. Five, six, seven minutes passed. (I checked the clock.) Twenty-two minutes later she emerged and sat down at her desk, her back to me. With her damp hair and her white sweater she looked like a diligent schoolgirl.

"Aren't you hungry?" I asked without intending to make an issue of it.

"I've already eaten," she said. A few minutes went by. I cleared my throat. Five minutes later I said, "Don't you even want to know if I ate?"

She asked politely, "Well, *did* you eat?"

"Yes," I said.

"That's what I thought." She went back to her books.

An hour or two later (I stopped watching the clock) her chair squeaked. I buried myself in my work and didn't look at her. A new sketch, almost complete, was spread before me: the front view of a long building; beside it, to establish the scale, I drew an avenue of trees and a man digging a pit. She stopped to peer over my shoulder as I was writing the first word of the caption: ARBEIT, in clear bold letters.

"What's that?" she asked.

"A workers' cafeteria," I said with annoyance, muttering to myself, Can't she see what it is?

"A workers' cafeteria," she repeated and went back to her work.

Time passed slowly. Behind the first building I sketched refineries, factories, roads, train tracks, and a bridge crossing a river cut off by the edge of the page. After supper, which we ate silently in the kitchen, we went back to our places. When it was time for bed I got up noisily and threw my sketches in the trash. I opened and closed the refrigerator door, took a sip of cold coffee, then went back to the living room, addressing myself to the heart of the matter.

"Look," I said, "if one of us has to sleep here on the couch it will be me. You sleep in the bed."

"I'm very comfortable on the couch," she said.

"That's just it," I said. "I know the couch is comfortable, that's why I want to sleep there."

"But the bed is more comfortable." She fell into the trap.

"Then you sleep in it," I said.

"I don't want to," she insisted.

"I won't sleep there either," I said. She lowered her eyes.

"Where will you sleep?" she asked suspiciously.

"On the floor," I said. "I'm used to that."

"Are you crazy?" she asked, irritated.

"I'll sleep on the floor," I said, "or we'll both sleep in the bed."

She grumbled but finally yielded. I undressed without turning on the light and got into bed. She stood in the doorway for a moment deliberating, then got into bed without undressing. After a period of silence—I could hear her holding her breath—I tried to put my arm around her. She turned away. I moved to the other end of the bed, granting her the distance she seemed to want. If that's how it is, forget it, I thought. I'm asleep, and I don't care about anything. Let her cry. I held my breath and listened. She wasn't crying. That was just a sigh. The gulf between us was now an abyss. I sought refuge in other scenes, in other bedrooms. But Barbara was everywhere, lying with her back to me. An hour or two later, just as I was dozing off, the bed creaked and I awoke. She got out of bed and went to the bathroom. After a minute or so—I saw her taking a pill, a sleeping pill, twenty sleeping pills—she was back. She stood near the bed looking at me (my eyes were closed) before claiming her distant corner. There was a large iceberg between us that lasted through the night.

When I opened my eyes the room was flooded with light—it was ten o'clock. Barbara was gone. I made coffee and drank it standing up, sliced some bread, spread it with butter and jam, then threw it in the trash with the plans and sketches from the previous day.

I was sick of everything. I considered packing up and clearing out, now, immediately, without further thought. I'd fling my old clothes into the suitcase, just the old ones, the ones from home, drop the keys on the table, and take off without leaving a note. Grab the first train south, wake up in Italy. (Say hello to Aunt Anna? No. I've had enough of the goddamn past.) Go straight to Genoa. (Hey, Maria Cristina, give me back my money, you goddamn whore-in-mourning!) Get on the boat, close my eyes, and wake up in Haifa. From there, a train, a bus, a cab to Jerusalem—home. My work, my plans, my dreams in concrete. Simpler still, buy a plane ticket with the reparations money and in four hours I'm home. Run, clear out, disappear!

I remember how these thoughts excited me. All at once, as in those other flights of mine (when I ran away from school to the war, when I left the kibbutz for the Technion, when I abandoned a woman's room because she began to clear a shelf for me), I felt like a young man set for adventure, carefree, liberated—what a glorious feeling!

I'll go for a walk, I thought. To unwind, stop thinking so hard, see people, amble through the streets, get lost. Then I'll figure out what to do. I'll come back at two; if she's not home I'll pack my things and figure out what comes next. She's really nuts—making such a drama of a little thing like that! What happened? So what if I said I love your ugly face. Is that so terrible? She won't talk to me, won't look at me, sleeps on the couch, turns her back as if I were a stranger. A vacuum. Air. Nothing. The hell with it! It's not as if I didn't try. I spared no effort to appease her. Barbara, I said tenderly—and she said I make her sick. She finds me revolting. I tried to touch her gently in bed, in the dark. She turned away. Maybe that was the mistake. Should I have grabbed her firmly and screamed, "Cut the crap or you'll get it from me! A smack or two will show you what's what! Shit on your silent treatment. If you have something to say—speak up! I won't stand for these games, do you hear?" She might break down, she might give in if I treat her rough. She would cry a little (two ringing slaps), but in the end she would know who wears the pants in this family. That's it, that's the way to treat a woman.

Later, as I walked through one of Frankfurt's main streets in the rain, I saw my reflection in a large display window: a young man in a black raincoat with a turned-up collar—talking to himself. Midst the array of cameras, binoculars, and microscopes in the window I saw my lips distinctly and realized, to my horror, that they were moving. My face was grim. This is her last chance, I told myself. If she's not home I'll clear out, I'll leave. For a day, maybe two. I'll take a room in a hotel. A cute chick of a chambermaid will bring the breakfast tray, saying, "But make it a quickie. If they catch me, sir, I'll lose my job." I'll make room for her under the blanket and pull up Ruth's white apron. If I do find her home, if she turns her back on me again, I'll bring her around, with force if necessary. "Cut the crap before I slap your face," and so on. That's what I'll do.

A few steps farther I saw myself in another window, my moving lips reflected in the desert sands of a tourist ad. Inside my coat pocket I pinched myself so it hurt. Stop these ridiculous dialogues, I lectured myself, biting my lip. People will stare, they'll think you're crazy. But no one seemed to notice. They're used to people talking to themselves, I thought. Everyone talks to himself in Germany. They're busy defending themselves at imaginary trials, relating the gruesome truth to their sons, truths they dare utter only to themselves, here in the street. I turned back to the yellow desert of the tourist poster: "Follow the sun—fly to Israel" splashed across the color photograph. A suntanned girl on a jeep, an endless vista of blazing sand and clear blue sky, the marble capital of a Roman column rising out of the sand. Climate, history, the here and now—all in one package. Luckily, no one had tattooed a number on her arm—such restraint. Hello, Shosh! What are you doing in the desert? "I'm on my way to Wadi Majnun, to change and make up. They're doing some shots of me in a bikini at the Nabatean temple. See you in Frankfurt. I hear you married a German girl."

There was a sudden downpour in the Negev Desert from which I sought refuge in a huge department store. Eying a fine leather suitcase (I could see myself carrying it off the plane at Eilat), I heard someone call my name.

It was Erna, Barbara's friend. At first I didn't recognize her. In her red wool hat she had a dashing air, and it was hard to believe that this girl with the captivating smile was a concerned member of an organization to atone for German war crimes. Her arms were laden with small colorfully wrapped packages so that she could barely shake hands. She said she was so glad to see me and naturally I said the same. We exchanged a few more banal remarks, ranging from her health to my health to the weather to Barbara; what am I doing, what is she doing, and so on. Though she didn't allude to my conduct at the wedding, the memory of her warm thigh was suddenly vivid. We stared at the rain in silence, exchanged an intense gaze, then recoiled from it in bewilderment. More questions and answers: Who are all the gifts for, Erna? Parents and friends. Where are you planning to spend Christmas, Uri? I don't know. With Barbara's parents maybe. We might not even bother. What are you doing now, this very minute, I mean? Going home. What are you doing? Nothing special, just walking. Barbara's at school.

"Then walk me to the car," she said, avoiding my eyes.

"Delighted. Give me the packages, and you can hold the umbrella."

I forget the opening moves in this bizarre episode but I do remember, first in the car, then in the elevator (it didn't get stuck, thank God) feeling young again—a charming rake, an experienced lover, a scheming devil —and thoroughly emancipated from the morning's depression.

When we arrived at her one-room apartment, she proceeded, with profuse apologies, to quickly clear away the traces of sadness and loneliness: nylon stockings and a bra drying on the chair, a wrinkled sheet flung over the convertible couch, a coffee cup filled with cigarette butts, an empty sardine can. After the kettle finally whistled we sat on the couch and drank instant coffee from yellow plastic cups. She tried to relieve the perilous silence with conversation about Barbara, our one common interest, but this struck me as tactless and I avoided the subject. I stared impudently at her bosom, her full thighs, her firm legs; she clasped her legs in silence, pulled her dress down over her knees, flashed me a bewildered smile, and finally threw a pillow at me, laughing and tossing her head from side to side.

Later my hands took the place of my eyes and we were soon playing an amusing game. I tried to catch her; she laughed and slipped away. I drew her toward me. Pretending to resist she brushed her fingertips through my hair with a tantalizing laugh. When I flung her on the sofa she made no attempt to escape. She lay at my side panting, shielding her body from my advances with her free hand. I pinned down her legs; she thrashed about in an effort to slide to the floor. Then in a sudden thrust I caught her lips. These gestures of resistance, along with feeble protests—"Stop it . . . Please . . . really, that's enough . . ."—and grunts of excitement were an essential part of the game. But she carried it so far that it no longer amused me. I sought her lips. She turned away and bit my shoulder. Enraged and impatient, I began to tear off her clothes.

I am convinced that had she not cooperated, if she hadn't pulled her arms out of the sleeves in a feigned effort to elude me, if she hadn't struggled to pull away from her skirt, which I clutched in my hand, I wouldn't have finally held her naked in my arms. "Subduing" her with one hand and tearing off my own clothes with the other, I declared to myself with considerable satisfaction, This is it, this is how you treat a woman. A firm hand, a strong show of force and authority, a tone that says "Cut the crap or you'll be sorry!" That's the only way.

Provide an excuse so she can tell herself there was no choice.

But our game of hide and seek was not over. We lay naked under the blanket. I thought the preliminaries were at an end, but she began to struggle again, to writhe elusively. When I clung to her, she sank her teeth in my back and bit me hard. I pushed her away, barely conscious of my own actions, and slapped her—twice—on the cheek.

I assumed that this would be the end, that she would dissolve in tears and jump out of bed. To my astonishment she began to tremble with animal desire and scream through clenched teeth, "Yes, yes. More!" It took me a moment to absorb her words—I may have preferred not to understand. I was regretting my own sudden outburst, and this made it difficult to digest her message. I remember feeling compassion for her, placing my lips on her neck tenderly, smoothing her hair with my hand in an effort to atone for my behavior. I was in for another surprise. Pushing me away, she dug her nails in my back and bit my hand hard, exclaiming, "No! Not like that! Beat me!" Though the words were clear I couldn't believe that I must beat her to give her pleasure. The though was repugnant. I would have gotten out of bed and left if she had let go of my hand; I'm certain of this. But she sank her teeth deeper in my flesh, swinging her head wildly like a mad dog. The blood rushed to my head. I slapped her so she would relax her grip but when she let go of me I kept striking her on her face, her breasts, her hips, her tremulous buttocks for the sheer thrill of her wild, tormented passion.

Many times since I've thought of these moments in Erna's bed. When I look back on that scene from a distance of years, when I see myself beating her with mounting fury and hurling abuse at her, phrases I am incapable of repeating, when I hear her ardent groans, see her close her eyes and bite her lip, wrap her legs around me, and wail with tortured pleasure, I begin to defend myself and make excuses for the cascades of hate and ruthlessness I discovered in myself. (She started it. She bit me and scratched me. She hurt me.) While this is the truth, it isn't the whole truth. To be frank—and I intend to be frank even it isn't to my credit—every blow I bestowed on her white flesh gave me a deep, hidden pleasure (over and above my impulse to avenge the pain she had inflicted on me). The link of pain to pleasure was a new and shocking discovery. The fact that I enjoyed my sadistic behavior as much as she did troubled me then and troubles me now.

When I left her a few hours later, hours which were so many black pearls on my string of pleasure-fantasies, I couldn't look her in the eye. I remember my relief when at last I was free of Erna's soft lips and delicate embrace. In the cab on the way home (it was already 3:15) my mind was blank. The decision I'd arrived at that morning seemed quite remote. Settling back in the cab I closed my eyes and was filled with a sense of deep peace. In the flood of family scenes I was straining to repress, I no longer saw myself slapping Barbara's face.

As soon as I opened the door Barbara's voice called from the kitchen, "Is that you, Uri?" My heart pounded with excitement and guilt. She's home. She got back on time, promptly at two. She's been waiting, she missed me, she may have even worried. There was no harshness in her voice; it had a placid note. As for me—Erna, the bite. Are there signs? She's sure to notice something. What if she asks?

"Yes," I said, turning up my collar. I went past the kitchen and saw her at the sink, a wooden spoon in her hand, a faint confused smile in her eyes. I slipped into the bedroom.

"I hope you haven't eaten," she called.

"Just a minute," I said, closing the bathroom door behind me. So, it's over at last, and that's that. Submission. She made lunch, she's ready to come to terms. And while she . . . there I was with Erna. The scent of her body was still on my hands. Taking off my jacket I rolled up my sleeve and checked my arms for teeth marks. I looked in the mirror. There was a purple mark on my shoulder, a spot that would soon turn blue, a

mark of Cain. I washed my hands, face, and neck with
warm water and soap. I changed my crumpled shirt,
put on a turtleneck, and checked the mirror again.
It's OK, I thought, no evidence. But she'll see it in my
eyes—the glow of contentment. She'll know. Cover it
with a frown. That's better. A stern face like yesterday
and the day before. Bury the shirt at the bottom of the
laundry hamper. Now, go ahead and make up with her.

Even before I sat down she asked penitently if I was
still mad. Without daring to look her in the eye I said
I wasn't. "I can't even remember how it started," she
said. I told her with a slightly bitter grimace that I no
longer remembered the start though I certainly remembered the end.

"What do you mean?" she asked.

"Don't you remember?" I said. "The very first night
I tried to make up. I said, 'Barbara,' and you said—"

"I remember," she interrupted, "and I'm sorry. It was
silly and childish. It's awful that a trivial fight can
assume such absurd proportions. By the second day I
couldn't believe we were married. You were a stranger
to me."

"You too," I said.

"Then have we made up?" she asked, offering her
hand. The curiosity and confusion of our first encounter
in the elevator were reflected in her eyes. We exchanged
a handshake and comradely smiles that melted into an
embrace. When she wrapped her arms about my neck,
I kissed her eyes and she found my burning lips.

"All is forgiven?" she asked in a whisper.

"And forgotten," I added.

"Then let's eat," she said.

We ate in silence. I was aware she was watching
me, studying my face. I pulled up my collar. She's suspicious, I thought. Why is she looking at me like that?
She sees something in my eyes, she sensed it when we
kissed.

"You're hungry," she said.

"Yes," I answered.

"Know something"—this after a pause—"when I came

home and didn't find you I began to worry. I saw you drunk, telling the bartender your troubles like a B movie, crossing the street with tipsy steps. You'll laugh, but I saw you run over, and then I realized how silly it all was. Where were you?"

"I took a walk," I said, "and stopped for coffee. I planned to take a room in a hotel if you weren't home."

"Thank God it's over," she said. "It *is* over, isn't it?"

"Yes." She was worried, I thought. She saw me run over as I stumbled through the streets. Just when she was deciding to forgive me I was in bed, an unconjugal bed at that, with Erna. Irony, what you might call "fate's trick," I reflected, laughing bitterly to myself. When I looked up I saw Barbara smiling at me.

33 | *armistice*

Waking late the next morning, we found ourselves locked in an embrace, as of old, clinging to the remnants of last night's pleasure. Broad smiles, very private smiles, flooded our faces. We knew that the storm was over, that there was nothing more to worry about, that life had resumed its idyllic course. We were newly in love, pursuing each other with the fervor of a young couple groping toward the bedroom.

I don't know what impelled Barbara to weave her spell with such maddening sweetness, but I was motivated, in part, by guilt over the bizarre episode with Erna. I loved Barbara fanatically, in the penitent way of a pilgrim atoning for his sins. We were fortified and enlightened by our crisis; it provided a new counterpoint for our relationship. We began to value every peaceful moment, to regard it as a peak of contentment.

But there were other factors too—objective factors. Barbara's nervousness, which may be characteristic of the second month of pregnancy, began to dwindle, and

I in turn relaxed considerably. Our nights became wilder and more primitive. We unlocked dim cellars of passion in ourselves, and in the mornings I noted a deep new glow in Barbara's eyes. Not only our nights, but our days as well were suddenly filled with interest, partly owing to Barbara's efforts, partly to mine, and mostly to a surprising letter from Amos.

A day or two after our end-of-the-crisis celebration I found an envelope in the mailbox, containing some blueprints and a marvelously exciting letter from Amos Avni.

"Uri," it said, "the city of Jerusalem is offering a prize for a school building design. I made so many sketches that I lost all perspective and was on the verge of giving up the project when I remembered your bitter complaints about the ways schools are built here, remember? Would you be interested in entering the competition with me? I am sending you the program, along with six different designs. Let me know what you think. If something suits you as a basic idea, work it up, take off from it, do as you see fit with it. I've had it. Feel free to reject everything and start from scratch. I won't be offended. Maybe we can solve the problem together. Want to try? Onward! Incidentally, I hear you're married, you devil you. Congratulations! When will you be home? If we win first prize (of course we will, no doubt about it), you'll have to come right back to supervise construction and sign checks. I'm tired of working at Brumberg-Avishai-Landau. Let's start our own firm. How does that strike you? Write soon. Amos (IIA)"

This letter arrived at precisely the right moment and set off a minor revolution in my life. After reading it with great enthusiasm three or four times, I realized it was just what I needed. Ever since I left home I had been without any real work, without any focus or purpose. My beautiful life seemed empty. What's the point of random sketches, of an architectural scheme that will rot in some drawer and never reach the hands of a foreman, a mason, or electrician? Blueprints are like unwritten poems, planes that never take off, a piano without strings. I needed something real, a dream that would become concrete. Amos's letter was just what I needed.

Many times I've had the experience of grappling with a problem on a sheet of empty white paper and I've accumulated scores of designs, few of which were actually realized in cement. But I don't remember ever approaching a project with as much enthusiasm as I brought to this one. The day I got the letter I cabled Amos agreeing to everything and went on a buying spree. In half an hour I had indulged myself to the extent of a drafting board, a superb T-square, an array of Rapidograph pens, colored pencils, erasers, India ink, rulers, letter and furniture stencils, a metal compass, triangular tacks, and sketching paper—the works.

When Barbara came back from the university at three I had already done the maintenance area of the school. Before she had a chance to ask what was up (I could see the question forming in her eyes), I read her the letter from Amos, spread out the sketches, pumped her with technical details, trotted out my precious acquisitions, covered her face with kisses, wrapped her in my arms, and danced her around the table gleefully, amid loud shrieks and giggles. Her books fell. When she bent down to pick them up I grabbed her from behind and led her to the sofa.

"You've gone completely beserk," she laughed with resignation. "Go look in the mirror."

"That's because I love you," I said.

"Liar. It's because you're working. You finally found something to do, something that interests you. I've been waiting for this moment—I'm glad it's finally come."

"You wait and see, we'll win first prize," I said, flinging myself on the couch. "You'll like Amos, I'm sure. He's a mixed-up guy with long fingers and glasses, a pleasure to talk to. You should hear him when he gets going on architecture and related topics. He's a raving poet—a dreamer, a madman with a head full of ideas mixed with bits of straw. What's that marvelous smell? You washed your hair? We'll open an office! AMOS AVNI AND URI LAM, ARCHITECTS. A discreet little sign. I didn't know anything was bothering me until I opened his letter, but suddenly there is logic and meaning everywhere. I'm starved. We'll build the most beautiful school in the world—our school will be the childhood vista of tomorrow's people: serious architects, engineers, electronic technicians, TV cameramen. I'm happy, dear Barbara, and I'm hungry. Come on, let's go to the kitchen or I'll eat you up."

"No," she ordered, "you sit down and work. I'll call you when it's ready. We haven't touched the champagne my father brought—want some?"

"Not now. Maybe tonight," I said. "Now I want food. And coffee! Lots of black coffee. This isn't simple—there are problems with this school."

From that day on a new routine was established. Activity and involvement replaced the boredom and idleness that had oppressed me since my illness, so much so that often when Barbara came home I couldn't believe it was already two and time to eat. These were the best of our days together in Frankfurt. We began to go out again, to movies, theater, concerts, sometimes dining with friends and at least twice a week inviting company to our house. After the movies we would drop in to the Café Voltaire or stop for a beer in our jazz cellar. We had time for everything.

We spent Christmas with Barbara's parents. Barbara's hesitation and tact when she began to consider going to Düsseldorf for Chrismas were amusing. "Are you crazy?" I said to her. "You know I'm not religious and I certainly don't have any bias against gift-giving holidays. Besides, when you ask so nicely, how could I possibly refuse?"

We spent a day and a night in her parents' home. While coffee was being served after the festive Christmas dinner under the tree, which was lit by scores of candles and decorated with gold and silver stars, cotton snow, and many colored glass ornaments, the scholarly discourse began.

"It's very nice of you to celebrate the birthday of a

fine upstanding Jew like Jesus," I said to Mr. Stahl. "He's not so popular with us."

"I can understand why," said Mr. Stahl, "he was your first nonconformist."

"That's not so," I said. "All our prophets were non-conformists, or at least they weren't normal. But their followers became such terrific conformists, and they're the ones who brought on all our troubles."

"But why did they crucify him?" asked Gunther, the innocent son.

"What would you have them do with a man that walked through the streets announcing he was the son of God and king of the Jews?" I asked. "Today he would be put in a mental institution and the problem would be solved."

"Still," Gunther persisted, "don't you think that cruci-fixion is a pretty harsh penalty for a man who, as you put it, isn't normal?" Barbara's mother cleared her throat and moved her chair. Barbara tapped the table with her fingers.

"Don't forget," I said, "that happened exactly 1959 years ago. We've always been considered a techno-logically backward people. Besides, we weren't the ones who crucified him; we left that to the Romans. It was the accepted method of execution in those days. Jesus wasn't the only one who was crucified. That was stand-ard treatment. I agree with you that the method is somewhat primitive. More primitive than the auto-da-fé or other advanced devices employed by the Inquisition. Technology marches on. Why, in the twentieth century, not many years back, in fact, human genius devised a final solution to the problem. . . ."

At this point Mr. Stahl changed the subject abruptly, proposing that we drink our brandy near the fire. The rest of the evening passed in silence broken only by remarks about the weather. "I hope," Mr. Stahl said as we began to turn in, "that there will be snow tonight."

At seven in the morning, when the household was still asleep, Barbara leaped out of bed and opened the blinds. There was no snow. Black tree skeletons floated in the gray fog. "Come on," she cried with excitement, "let's go down and open our presents!" She told me how she used to lie awake all night waiting for the moment when she could open the presents, only to fall asleep right before morning. Once her father woke her up dressed as Saint Nicholas and she believed that's who he was.

We went down in pajamas, sat on the rug at the foot of the tree and began opening our presents. Remembering Erna's woolen hat and the parcels in her hand, I gave Barbara a holiday kiss. She had many presents: maternity clothes, a big warm sweater, baby clothes, a complicated gadget for sterilizing bottles, pacifiers, a leather purse from Italy. The last present she opened was from me: an electric hair dryer she had admired in a store window. She welcomed each gift with childlike delight, which I shared with her. I got four presents: a Parker pen from Barbara, a splendid camera from her parents, a telescope (I could picture myself on the roof of our house in Jerusalem looking out on the Old City and surveying the Arab Legion positions), and an electric eraser ("it erases everything")—Germany's latest contribution to architecture.

That evening when we got home I lit Hanukkah candles, though the holiday was long past, and told Barbara about the great miracle that took place, about Judah the Maccabee, Antiochus, the evil king, may his name be erased, Hannah and her seven sons. She was very attentive so I gave her Hanukkah *gelt* and told her to go to bed like a good girl, since "Daddy has work to do." At 2 A.M. I cleared away the rejected sketches and lay down to sleep beside my good little girl.

It was four solid weeks before I produced a design that seemed complete to me. I tried several approaches and in the end I went back to one of Amos's sketches— a central space surrounded by various autonomous units. The plan I sent off to Amos was especially satisfying because it was the result of our common efforts. He provided the underlying concept and I developed it, revising it in ways that seemed significant to me. In the cover letter that I sent with my design I explained in elaborate detail why in the end I came back to his idea ("Your solution is ingenious—that can't be denied") and explained each of my revisions as well. I asked him to write his reactions to my work and let me know when the results of the competition would be announced. "Until then," I said, "send me more assignments. It doesn't matter what. We'll be back in May or June, and I'll lose my mind if I don't have some interesting work to do here."

There was nothing more for me to do but await an answer. Ten long, nerve-wracking days; then there finally was a letter from Amos. It turned out that he had been in Eilat for three days on business and it was two more days before his dizzy secretary found my envelope under a pile of magazines from abroad. The plan, Amos wrote, was very good and apart from one minor change (facilities for students' bikes) he had hardly touched it before submitting it in both our names. The results of the competition would not be announced until March 1. "Until then, my friend, you'll have to be patient." At the moment he had no further assignments to offer. As for our joint office, he suggested we wait until I get back. It's complicated, he wrote, and requires careful thought. And finally, "What else is new with you? Yours . . . etc."

A disappointing letter despite the compliment—I expected more. What did he mean, "The plan is very good?" Just very good? And "I hardly touched it." What about that "hardly"? Just what did he change? All in all, a cold letter. No further work for me at the moment. The new office requires careful thought? What is he saying? Has he changed his mind? Why? Was he offered a raise? Maybe because . . . Why didn't he send regards to Barbara? That's impossible. Something must have happened there. Why didn't he say what he is doing now? Why didn't he ask for advice, an opinion—on anything, it doesn't matter what, just to include me in his work, to give me a sense of partnership? What will I do until the first of March? Hell! What's the good of all my gorgeous equipment? I don't have the strength or the patience for doodles of buildings that will never be built. I want to work on an actual project—something that will stand many years after no trace is left of me. I'll be out of my mind by March 1. Now that I know the taste of work I can't bear being idle.

The long wait for Amos's letter and its disappointing contents had a perceptible effect on my mood. I don't know how else to account for the renewed tension between me and Barbara. This time it was not a childish falling out, but a long series of misunderstandings, squabbles, sharp remarks, heated arguments that mounted into quarrels. I now know that in most cases the fault was mine. I was the one who brought these squabbles to a head—but at the time I refused to admit this even to myself. I was convinced that it was all Barbara's fault. The first fight had to do with reparations, and, in this connection, let me fill in a few gaps.

Even before the outbreak of hostilities the issue of reparations hovered over us like a heavy cloud. We both tried to deny this, though we knew the storm would strike and there would be no shelter. In one of our early conversations, when we were marveling over the lucky coincidence that brought us together in a broken elevator, Barbara asked me what I was doing in that particular building on that particular day. (She was on her way to see the editor of some literary journal.) I told her briefly about my reparations claim. This was the first and last time we discussed the subject, though she took quite an interest in it, and more than once when I got back from the lawyer in a depressed state she would ask for details. But I firmly refused to include her in this chapter of my life, don't ask me why. I didn't care if she knew every detail of my past. On various occasions, in bits and fragments, I told her about my parents, my brother, my sister, about Aunt Anna, who hid me in her house for three years. I didn't care if she knew all this, but I was reluctant to speak about the reparations claim, just as I had refused to take her with me to my parents' house or to the mental institution in Goeting where I hoped and dreaded that I would find my brother, Martin.

In the camp, too, I had the same response. Leaving her
in the main building to study the horror photographs,
I ran off with Pluto to confront the remnants of terror,
the reconstructed showers, the oven. I did not want her
to witness my alliance with the past. It was a private
matter, between me and myself. I may have been afraid
to expose myself in a moment of weakness. I don't really
know why, but the fact is this is what I felt.

In any case, despite a succession of meetings with
Ernst, the young and dedicated lawyer who took my
case, despite the depression that followed these meetings, I never discussed the progress of my case with
Barbara. I never recounted the grisly sessions I had to
endure, the horrendous testimony Ernst uncovered (with
my help) to support my demands, and of course I never
told her about the experiments . . . pardon me, the
medical examinations I had to undergo at a government
hospital to establish whether or not I really deserved
reparations for physical injury. To this day, deep down I
try to deny the humiliating nightmare I endured before
meeting Barbara.

I know I lied. I wrote that two days after arriving in
Frankfurt I went to the lawyer's office but decided not
to see him, because of unresolved doubts and hesitation.
I wrote that I walked back and forth in front of the building, then returned to the hotel and secluded myself there
with my conscience. But this is not how it was. I lied.
I did go to Ernst's office and he repeated, word for word,
what my lawyer in Tel Aviv had said: it's complicated,
the papers at hand are inadequate. Evidence must be
presented, witnesses produced. We had to find my parents' names on the lists of those deported to Teresienstadt and later to Auschwitz—unless, of course, their
names were on the list of survivors. Also, if I intended to claim reparations as an orphan I had to present certified proof that I was a student until the age
of twenty-four. Property confiscated from my parents
was an intricate matter in itself. Ernst spoke to me in
a complacent voice that suggested that this case was
primarily a matter of conscience for him and only

secondarily a routine piece of business for which he would be paid at the accepted rate (15 percent, to be shared with the lawyer in Israel).

"First of all you need a medical checkup," he said. "I have connections, so it might be possible to arrange this immediately. We have to establish that your health was impaired, which shouldn't be difficult. I'm sure you suffered periods of sleeplessness and nightmares; you may have required sedation," he suggested. "Perhaps you have suffered some digestive disturbance. We can determine its extent in the course of the medical examination. Between us, this is the most serious of all your claims and promises the highest returns. When we conclude this section we can deal with some of the other counts: parents' loss of freedom, being orphaned, interrupted studies, compensation for property, etc."

I resented the physical checkup yet at the same time, in some mysterious sense, I welcomed it. There was a succession of tests, slides, analyses, electrocardiograms, encephalograms. When I stood in the X-ray room, when I lay on the examining table, I saw myself in other laboratories with other doctors. I subjected myself to these procedures with a tinge of excitement. I didn't want to talk about myself, about actual events, how I felt when, when . . . Still, I told the droopy-eyed psychiatrist about nightmares, terror-filled dreams, recurring fears, sedation prescribed for me in school and later in the kibbutz and at the Technion. I had an attitude of bizarre curiosity toward myself. I wanted them, the Germans, to know with scientific objectivity what they, the Germans, had done to me. I think I would have been pleased if they had discovered I was tubercular. Only after the examinations were over did I begin to react. I holed up in the hotel for two days, as I've already related, to struggle with myself and be plagued by doubts.

I'll never forget the smug note in Ernst's voice when he presented the results: "Excellent. Distinct disturbance in the neurovegetative area, disturbances in the digestive tract. Just as I thought. The implication of this

diagnosis, my dear friend, is as follows: a single outright payment of twenty-five thousand marks and a
further grant of two hundred marks a month. Very
good."

Later, when I phoned to tell him the whole futile saga
of my search for my brother (I was sick in bed and
Barbara was in class), he listened anxiously and said he
was glad my brother was alive (he couldn't explain how
Martin got from Teresienstadt to Dachau either), but
that this fact weakened my case. (As sole inheritor I was
claiming total damages.) "Unless," he added in a considered tone, "unless we can convince the court to regard your brother as a missing person, which certainly
seems reasonable."

When I recovered I went to Ernst's office and he informed me that I would be granted five thousand marks
for interrupted studies and that upon receipt of my
papers from the Technion I would be eligible for an additional payment of fifteen thousand marks. "It's not un-
likely," he added, "that we will succeed in establishing
your status as sole inheritor. I'm working on that now.
In that case you could receive ten thousand nine hundred and fifty marks for your parents' loss of freedom—
five marks a day doubled for your mother and father,
then multiplied by three years—and fifteen thousand
marks for your father's loss of livelihood." He went on
talking but I was no longer listening. The figures were
staggering. I'm rich, I told myself. Rich and worthy of
pity, deprived of self-righteousness, the sole wealth of
the oppressed. All my rage, every last drop, will be
traded for marks. They will send me away with full
pockets and an empty heart.

I tuned in to Ernst again. "As for your father's house,
which he was compelled to leave behind—there are no
prospects." He spoke softly, as if to emphasize that these
matters were confidential, the hard-core truth. "I've in-
vestigated the matter thoroughly and have consulted
colleagues who have dealt with similar cases. I searched
for some loophole through which I might be able to press
your case—which is, perhaps, justified—but believe me,

there is no chance. It would be a waste of time and money to pursue this matter. Your father refused to sell the property at a symbolic price, which is what many others did. He simply abandoned it. Since the present occupants acquired your parents' home by legal means from the city of Frankfurt, which by law was declared Custodian of Absentee Property, we have no grounds for prosecuting them. We can't sue the government—it already paid reparations to Jewish organizations, to IRSO, against Jewish property unclaimed as of 1948, assuming, of course, that IRSO demanded compensation for specific property. At IRSO I did establish that no claim was made for your parents' house, nor was compensation received for it. The circle is closed. That much is lost."

Now, having explained as well as I can the intricacies involved in my claim, let me go back to the dispute that arose between me and Barbara in this connection. One day when she was hunting for something in the drawer, she was appalled to find three checks totaling 30,200 marks (impaired health, interrupted studies and my first monthly allotment). With obvious displeasure she asked why I hadn't deposited the money in the bank. I turned away muttering a vague response. I thought she would realize I didn't want to pursue the subject. But she repeated the question over and over until I told her in a loud, angry voice that I hadn't cashed the checks because I preferred not to touch the money, that I still did not know what I would do with it, that I wasn't sure if I wanted or even had a right to it.

"What do you mean by that?" she asked in dismay. And I told her what I meant. I said that earlier I had questioned my moral right to accept reparations for each day during which my parents expired slowly in that hell (I had not yet received that particular sum but I spoke as though it was in my hands); that these doubts had become even more intense after my visit to the hell pavilion of Dachau. The very existence of that money in the drawer preys on my conscience, I told her. "I still don't know what to do with it. Do you want to deposit it in the bank? Please, put it in your account."

This infuriated her, of course, and led to the outbreak of hostilities. For several days the battle raged in fairly civilized terms, but by degrees it became violent. (It was I who screamed. Barbara spoke with contained anger that provoked me more than shouts.) Before long we were engaged in an ugly quarrel, with bitter remarks we both regretted later on. I have already outlined my position, and Barbara's arguments in favor of reparations are familiar too. The West German government had agreed willingly to pay reparations to victims of the Nazi regime, she said. Nothing could atone for the crimes; that wasn't the proclaimed goal of the reparations law. It was supposed to compensate victims to some extent and to help survivors recover. Etc.

When the battle deteriorated to personal attack, Barbara asked derisively why I hadn't used my own money to pay for my drafting equipment. At this point I lost my head and said I would never invest that money in anything permanent; I wouldn't build a house or build our future on those funds. Do you imagine, I asked her, that I could draw a straight line with a ruler that cost my father four days of slave labor?

Even this argument, which seemed decisive to me, didn't sway her. She continued to barrage me with straightforward, logical points and I kept on attacking with twisted, emotionally charged rationales. My position grew weaker as my tone became more vehement. There was no end in sight. I am convinced now that if she had been silent, if she hadn't made it an ideological battle, I would have yielded and finally found some justification for using the reparations money. But after she backed me into a corner the issue became one of dignity and self-respect. I saw no possibility of conceding any ground to her, though she was right on many accounts—a fact I was unwilling to forgive.

I remember, for example, recounting the status of the claim to my parents' house in the dramatic manner of a man who has been grievously abused. Rather than agree or sympathize with me, rather than decry the injustice, she began to compare my situation with that of the Arab refugee. From her reading on this question she maintained that our treatment of the Arab refugees was in no way superior to West Germany's treatment of Jewish refugees. The very comparison drove me wild. How can anyone compare the crimes of the Nazis to our War of Independence, I shrieked. The Arabs tried to destroy us and we fought in self-defense; we wanted peace while they threatened to drive us into the sea, and so on and so forth. But I made no impression; she stuck to her guns. No one would compare the Nazi crimes to the policies of the government of Israel. ("Thanks a lot," I retorted.) But still, to the Arab refugee his situation is very similar. Let's assume the Arabs were not expelled, that they were misled by their leaders, that they fled out of fear. I am willing to grant for the sake of argument that all this was so. How is their situation different from yours, she asked. "You live in an Arab house," she said coldly. "The man you bought it from acquired it legally from the Custodian of Absentee Property, just as your father's house was acquired legally by its present occupants. You can't expect them to be evicted, just as no Arab refugee could demand that you be evicted from his house." Not letting it go at that, she raised the issue of abandoned property in Israel. She was well informed. First, she said sarcastically, a man is chased out of his home or flees of his own free will, and later he is prevented from returning for security reasons; then it is legislated that anyone not occupying his home by a given date is considered absent and his abandoned property is confiscated by the government.

The actual argument, of course, was rather different from this account—I didn't sit back and listen as she lectured. I seethed, interrupted, shouted, and wouldn't give her a chance to finish a sentence. I insisted that she had been reading the wrong books and misunderstanding them, that she was unfamiliar with the reality of Israel, that she had to live there before forming opinions, that the government of Israel had offered reparations to the refugees, but the Arab governments were using them as political pawns, that when a peace treaty was signed every refugee would receive full reparations ("I hope so," she said) for property abandoned as a consequence of government policy. "If the situation were reversed," I continued, "not only would the Arabs take our property, they would slaughter us all. You should see the condition of Arabs in Israel and compare it with their condition in neighboring lands. We have built schools and hospitals for them, introduced electricity to their villages, paved roads, raised the standard of living." I bombarded her with these and similar points, absurd points I'm ashamed of now. But in the heat of argument, when I was compelled to fight for my life, I fervently believed my arguments.

I recount these incidents not because they are so significant, but as a backdrop for what happened later. I am trying to understand the elements of my depression and to single out the factors that motivated my bizarre behavior at the carnival late in February.

First, I was upset by the idleness that followed the disappointing letter from Amos. Then there was a long series of bitter disputes, which ended when I deposited my reparations money in the bank in a surge of goodwill. Just when I thought the situation was improving, a casual comment of Barbara's brought on another crisis more severe than any of the previous ones.

One evening when we were dining with friends the conversation turned to the subject of Israel. One of the guests began to praise Israelis lavishly. "It's sometimes hard to believe," he said, "that Jews and Israelis are one people. They're so different, in behavior, in personality, in outward appearance. Take Lam, for example, who'd guess he's a Jew? He looks like any one of us." Barbara cut in, "To me he is Jewish. I don't see what difference—" and she in turn was interrupted. "That's clear, my dear, you know him from close up." All except Barbara laughed wickedly. I smiled at this remark, missing the point for the moment.

Today, thanks to Barbara, I know better. But that
evening I was offended by her comment. Whenever
Israelis were singled out for valor, pride, integrity, psy-
chological soundness, etc., I would glance at Barbara
with a trace of pride, as if I was being praised, and
wonder at the revulsion, almost hostility, I would
glimpse in her eyes. I actually felt flattered by these
compliments (how incredibly stupid!), for as a matter
of fact (why pretend?) I found the Jews I met in Germany to be an unappealing lot devoid of self-respect,
selling their souls for money. Of course I was pleased to
hear how different we Israelis are. I considered Barbara's
comment a personal insult and confronted her angrily
when we got home. "What did you mean," I asked with
annoyance. "Do I seem so Jewish to you? I'm no Jew,
I'm an Israeli—and the two are not synonymous." She
waited for me to finish before she began to sound off.

"You enjoy their hypocritical compliments," she
charged. "Rather than admit they hate Jews and consider all Jews ugly cheats, money-mad monsters devoid
of self-respect, they say you Israelis are different. And
you support their ugly racism with your silence. Do I
have to explain that there are all kinds of Jews, just as
there are all kinds of Germans? Are you ashamed to be
Jewish? What's happened to you?"

I must admit that I didn't have the courage to bow my
head and accept this torrent of criticism—justified
though it was—but embarked on a childish counter-
offensive. "Of course I'm not ashamed of being Jewish,"
I retorted. "How could you suggest such a thing?" I recall changing the subject as swiftly as I could and attacking her on irrelevant grounds. I saw myself in a
state of war with Barbara. Victory was more important
than justice.

After our long argument, which ended in alienated,
back-to-back sleep, I began to emphasize my origins at
every opportunity, especially in the presence of strangers,
just to irritate her. "We Jews . . ." I would say in a loud
voice in a café, at a party, or on the street. Sometimes,
and it didn't matter what the subject was, I would begin

with, "As a Jew, I naturally see things differently." Or, "We Jews have a proverb which says . . ." and so on. One evening after I had gone overboard with remarks of this sort Barbara suddenly lashed out at me. "Listen, you don't have to announce you're Jewish at every turn."

"Aha!" I leaped at this, "so, you're the one who's ashamed. The truth will out!"

"Don't be ridiculous," she said. "It sounds silly when you inject it at every turn, whether it's relevant or not. Imagine if I were to say, 'We Germans . . .' or, 'As a German I think . . .' I'm sure you'd be annoyed. No one is attacking you so why don't you stop defending yourself."

"Let me tell you," I said, "Somewhere deep inside it makes you uneasy. I know you've made peace with the fact that I'm Jewish, but it's obviously not a source of pride. You'd prefer it to remain confidential, and you're uncomfortable to hear it declared publicly."

This quarrel, which could only have erupted in Germany, reached a peak of absurdity at the costume ball to which we were invited at the end of February.

34 | *masked ball*

When we first received the invitation to the carnival I didn't want to go. Barbara pleaded so eloquently that finally, to make up for various bitter outbursts of mine, I agreed to go. Her tender "thank you" was utterly captivating. "It's the most elegant, gay, and celebrated evening in all of Frankfurt," she chattered, "you'll love it. It's a fabulous event—we were only invited because of my father's connections. You have to buy the tickets, of course, and they're expensive—a hundred marks— but it's only once a year . . . and not everyone has the chance. You'll see, it's really the end." I kissed her and pulled her down on the couch. I hadn't seen her so exuberant in a long time.

"What will you wear?" she asked.

"Striped pajamas and a crown of barbed wire. Something simple like that."

"You're kidding," she said.

"Of course I'm kidding. I have no idea what I'll wear. A black mask over my eyes. Will that do?"

"They won't let you in," she said. "You have to come in a real costume. Let's think up something special, something shocking. How about a can-can dancer in her fifth month?"

"Being pregnant *is* a problem," I said.

"It could be an advantage. Once I dressed up as a fat opera singer and I had to stuff my dress with pillows. Look at me now!"

"I suppose we'll have to buy half a ticket for Jonathan," I joked, patting her taut belly.

We tried to recall costumes from books, films. I conjured up a procession of policemen, pirates, Arabs, soldiers, cowboys—the standbys at Purim carnivals at home. But these characters seemed banal to her, and she was right. I never had the patience for elaborate dressing up; my standard get-up on Purim was a nylon stocking pulled over my head, and that was all.

"I have an idea," she cried excitedly, "a great idea! It'll be so much fun."

"Romeo and Juliet after ten years of marriage?" I exclaimed. "You knit while I read the evening paper."

"No, no," she said. "We won't tell each other what we're going to be. We'll go separately and see if we can find each other: mystery, tension, a glorious adventure. OK? Will you do it?"

"And what if I don't recognize you?" I asked. "What if we don't meet at all?"

"Of course we'll meet," she said. "I'd know you in any crowd. Besides, if we don't find each other we can take off our masks at midnight and meet at the door. OK?"

"I'll dress up as a gynecologist; see if I don't find you then," I suggested and she laughed.

All that day I tried to come up with an original idea. I saw myself in leopard skin, wailing like Tarzan as I made my way through the hall. I danced a *kazatska* in leather boots and red silk pants. I was a Frenchman in black beret and striped undershirt, a Scotsman in kilts ("Please, madam, feel free to check for yourself"), a singing gondolier, an Arab sheik in a gold embroidered abaya. I'd been through the entire atlas when a diabolical scheme popped into mind. A Jew! Why not dress as a Jew? With a beard and earlocks, white stockings, a kapote and a *streimel*. Why not, really? Why a Russian or a Scot but not a Jew? That's brilliant: to appear here in Germany as a Jew. A ringing slap in the face for everyone. A test: for myself, for Barbara, and for all the rest. How will they feel when they see me? How will I feel when they stare at me and avert their eyes? I, Uri Lam, would be a Jew for one night. I will finally know what it means to be a Jew. What will Barbara say? Will she be ashamed? Will she be angry?

It's easy to decide to be a Jew, but how do you go about it? Where in Frankfurt do you find a kapote and a *streimel*? I scoured the thrift shops. I found an SS uniform, but no one had heard of a Jew's uniform. The storekeepers were polite but cautious, treating me as if I were demented. In an antique store that specialized in insignias, emblems, distinguished service awards and decorations, I found a yellow star of David inscribed with four block letters: JUDE. The proprietor, a pleasant fellow with long delicate fingers, wanted forty marks for this prize patch. I tried to bargain. Forty marks for a yellow arm patch! This struck me as an inflated price.

"What's the matter with you?" he protested. "See the quality of the work, feel the silk. You won't find anything like this anywhere today. This must have belonged to a rich man of fine sensibilities. It's a rare piece, of museum caliber. I have others at a lower price, but the work is quite ordinary, of course."

He opened a drawer and with a broad demeaning gesture fingered a pile of worn, faded stars of David. I bought one for fifteen marks and paid him out of my second reparations check. (I'm ashamed to admit that I spent the first check on a luxury item—a fine leather suitcase.)

I didn't see a *streimel* anywhere, but with the help of one of the synagogue functionaries I finally obtained a kapote and a black broad-brimmed hat. Incidentally, the Saturday morning I spent in the synagogue was an experience in itself. (I'd been told the sexton could see me after the Sabbath service.) I sat in back like an actor studying a role and watched the swaying heads, the closed eyes, the lips mumbling incomprehensible prayers in a Hebrew that sounded foreign to me. Suddenly, a voice soared over the mumbo jumbo; the fragments were becoming meaningful and rich with impact. "Pray, O Lord, secure my soul . . . ," an intense voice beseeched. After a while another verse rose to the surface: "For Thou hast delivered my soul from death, mine eyes from tears, my feet from stumbling. . . ." I became aware of my neighbor's searching eyes and began to move my lips as if there was prayer in my heart.

What am I doing here and who are these people, I asked myself. I pretend to be one of them, but who are they? These robust, well-fed figures—were they once skeletons impaled on barbed wire? Are these the white bodies that lay naked on the damp ground? The murmur I hear—is that the murmur emitted as smoke from swollen lips and swallowed up by the murky fog rising from the lake? "Pray, O Lord, secure my soul." All these prosperous people wrapped in prayer shawls of blue on deathly white—are they really fugitives from hell? "I had not thought death had undone so many." *Non avrei mai creduto.* ("That corpse you planted last year in your garden, Herr Kaltenbruner, has it begun to sprout? Who would believe it could bloom? *Jawohl, mein Herr.* The sudden frost has not disturbed its bed. You do a good job, Herr Kaltenbruner.") Here are the winners, returning from a long journey (*non avrei mai creduto*) upon which I have not yet embarked. To whom do they address their prayers now? By the banks of the Main, here they sit and here they weep . . . ? What for? Is it all waste? Is it my haste that sees man as waste? Let's try a simple exercise.

Study number one: with a pair of scissors, cut out from the general scene the prosperous face of the man to my left. Consider him close up, without the silk skullcap and the blue prayer shawl. Consider his facial expression, his gray eyes, his broad neck. Let's put another name on his picture: Sturmbannführer Bernadet. See the cruelty in his decadent lips, his cold ruthless gaze? (What's he doing here? He escaped with the others, burned his uniform in the forest, took striped pajamas from a corpse at the wayside. He fasted, tormented his soul, grew a beard. The dread of death peering out from his eyes completes the role: a Jew, his back bent, his head dropping—a driven scapegoat like the others. He's been hiding here these twenty years, among his one-time victims. Here, in this sanctuary, no one will find him.)

Study number two: take a photograph of SS officers and cut out the face of the real Sturmbannführer Bernadet, without his insignia. Write the name Josef-Chaim Brand under his face. Now look at his large steel-gray eyes (like Uncle Gustaf's eyes)—they assume a melancholy cast; that tormented face could belong to a persecuted Jew. Incredible, isn't it?

An end to the exercise in metamorphoses. What can you conclude? Conclusion A: We see what we want to see. (Take the woman in black in the Eisenstein film. If the preceding scene shows a funeral procession, the woman in the window is in mourning. If it shows a shot of children playing in the street she is simply looking out the window. Like those Germans on the train from Milan to Frankfurt.) Conclusion B: If I wear a kapote with a yellow patch, not only will they consider me a Jew—I will consider myself a Jew. If I consider myself a Jew I may even *be* a Jew. Even if for one night.

The prayers, strange and incomprehensible to me, seemed interminable. My eyes began to close. When I opened them again, the men were folding their prayer shawls, putting hats over their skullcaps, shaking each others' hands. All at once the synagogue was empty. The head of the congregation, a short man with a little white beard and suspicious eyes, received me in his over-heated office. After I declared my business he wanted to know why I needed a kapote and *streimel*. I told him a long story about my uncle, an Orthodox Jew from Bnei Brak, whose entire family had been lost in the holocaust. As this uncle was about to marry a woman of good family, I would like to please him by coming to the wedding in the attire of a proper Orthodox Jew.

"And you are not such a Jew?" the man asked, mildly scornful.

"Observant—yes," I lied, "Orthodox—no."

He wanted to know my uncle's name, the name of his bride, the date of the wedding. I muttered that his name was Lampel and the wedding would take place at her parents' home in Düsseldorf.

"Are you, perhaps, related to Dr. Lampel, of blessed memory, from Frankfurt?" he asked.

"No, no," I quickly responded, feeling the blood rush out of my face. "Our family was Lampelman, but in Palestine it's the custom to shorten names. As far as I know, we had no relations in Frankfurt."

He nodded as though praying. "And you, what are you doing here?"

"I am studying architecture," I said.

He wasn't satisfied. He wanted to know how long I had been studying, where I lived, why he hadn't seen me before. I scarcely managed to evade his questions. Finally he gave me the address of a Jewish tailor who would make me a kapote. (I was about to take out my pen and jot down the address when I remembered it was the Sabbath.)

"Glad to know you, Mr. . . . ?" he said, extending three soft warm fingers.

"Lam," I mumbled. "Lampelman."

Many years have passed since that awful day, but my heart still pounds wildly when I see myself (me!) in a black silk kapote, a broad-brimmed hat, a four-cornered garment, with fringes flying, black pants folded over white stockings—in this attire I climbed the steps of the

elegant Hofgarten Hotel, holding a small tattered suitcase tied with coarse rope. If it weren't for the photograph, which I have before me now, I'd dismiss the
whole episode as a nightmare, a hallucination. But it all
did really happen.

I doubt if I could have traversed the endless distance
from the main entrance of the hotel to the ballroom, the
first station of my "Via Dolorosa," had I not started out
drunk.

I had my first drink with the tailor, an old Jew from
Vilna with tearful eyes and a tobacco-stained beard.
When I put on my new clothes (and the white socks I
had bought that morning at the Kaufhaus), he rubbed
his hands together gleefully and giggled as he pushed me
toward a cracked mirror. There I saw a young Hassid
with a chalk-white face. After I paid him generously out
of my third reparations check he spread an old sheet of
Heint on the worktable, produced half a loaf of black
bread, some herring in a spicy onion sauce, and some
vodka, which he served in a tea glass. I drank to him,
he drank to me, we both drank to my uncle from Jerusalem and his bride from Munich. After the third round
he began to recount his woes in broken German, his
doleful voice reminiscent of our veteran actors in *The
Dybbuk.* Even the most pious, he groaned, no longer
wear kapotes. Soon, when it is his time to appear before
the Creator, there will be no one in all of Frankfurt to
sew such handsome garments nor will there be a pious
man like me to wear them. I glanced at my watch and
got up to take leave of him. He shook my hand warmly
and wished me much pleasure from his handiwork. When
I asked him to wrap my old clothes he brought me a
tattered suitcase, saying, "Take it. I've wanted to get rid
of it for a long time; it's the one I arrived in Frankfurt
with after the war. You can discard it when you get
home." I stuffed my things into it and tied it with a
coarse rope—which added to my bizarre appearance.
The doorman at the hotel eyed me suspiciously. Though
I presented my ticket, he asked my name uneasily and
checked it against the list. After adding a check to the

names Mr. and Mrs. Lam (Barbara was already there, I noted) he let me in. As I went by he asked, "Incidentally, sir, what is that costume?" "The dybbuk," I said, and moved on, followed by derisive laughter.

In the men's room I put down the suitcase and stood in front of the mirror like an actor making up. I worked diligently, pasting on a beard and earlocks which had been made for me in a wig salon. A red-faced Bavarian hunter turned away from the urinal and stared at me in perplexity as he buttoned his short leather pants. I smiled sourly and he left. Pinning the yellow patch to the lapel of my kapote I stepped back to survey the total effect in the mirror. Suitcase in hand, I looked very much like a Jew from Meah Shearim in Jerusalem dashing to catch a bus. I covered my eyes with the black mask and dropped a coin in the startled attendant's bowl. His eyes followed me as I left. I had intended to leave the suitcase in a locker but since they weren't conveniently located I had to drag it around all evening, the coarse rope trailing behind me on the floor.

I will never forget my dramatic entrance. The hall was crowded with kings, princes, all manner of royalty, several of whom took notice of me. Whispers, at first a few nearby, then swelling, rippled in all directions like a pebble flung into the quiet waters of a lake. Finally there was a hush; even the orchestra was silent. In the profound stillness I could hear only the pounding of my heart. At this orgy of revelers, who thought themselves safe from the plague, I was like Black Death penetrating the gates of a barricaded palace. My nightmare recurring, I saw myself naked in the street in the midst of a gaping crowd. I wanted to run away, but my legs were fixed to the spot. I found myself in the center of a throng that kept a cautiously calculated distance (so it seemed to me) as if I had cholera. The silence, though it probably lasted no more than a second, seemed endless, like a fall from a high roof. I knew that unless I woke up immediately, unless I broke out of this bewitched circle, I would fall and be trampled. With a superhuman effort (my hands were moist and cold sweat bathed my face), I made my way through the crowd to a round of polite applause. The band began to play, a waltz, and all at once the scene was lively again. More whispers— one woman laughed, a thin, hysterical laugh. Three musketeers bowed solemnly, their lips twisted in mockery. A Roman nobleman made a remark I didn't hear. His flattering coterie laughed raucously. A one-eyed sailor pointed at me and a thick-fleshed *belladonna* hid behind her fan. My head began to droop under the weight of scornful glances and contemptuous whispers. For the moment I forgot where I was. All I could see now was feet. I saw men's feet, women's feet, tens, hundreds of pairs of feet. Far above my drooping head and my bent back, I heard rustling wings of shame. I could pick out snatches of conversation: "What's that supposed to be?" A breathless response: "For God's sake, a Jew! What a dreadful lapse of taste!" The whispers resounded in every direction. "Look, look. Did you see that? What nerve! Imagine coming to a party in that attire. What a pig." Someone stopped me. "Where are you running to?" This was followed by decadent laughter. "What's in that suitcase?" someone asked. The response from the crowd—"Dollars, no doubt"—evoked peals of laughter. "I think he's cute," a coquettish voice declared. "He looks just like a Jew. What a perfect costume, and watch him walk. He doesn't crack a smile. He's really a great actor." "Sheer vulgarity, that's all," someone countered, "a caricature from *Der Sturmer*. The contemptible Nazi. I'm surprised they let him in. They should have been more selective at the door."

Walking through the crowd, my back bent, my head bowed, I asked myself, What's happened to me? Why am I dragging myself around like a crucified Christ? You'd think I was really Jewish. I came to remind the amnesia victims of their past, in case they've forgotten the scarecrow image of the *Untermensch*, in case they've dismissed that subhuman specter. One slap on their smug faces will remind them who I am. What do I care what they think of me? No one here knows me. Let them be embarrassed and confused. I should walk among them erect, a Jew proud to bear the banner of righteousness. Ha ha! Let them bow *their* heads, the monsters!

As soon as I lifted my eyes, straightened my shoulders, and shifted my physical bearing the whispers seemed to stop. The masked celebrants continued to laugh and talk in loud voices, but this was no longer related to me. One fellow, spared from the gallows (the noose still dangled from his neck), accidentally caught my eye and smiled at me; he even greeted me with a polite nod. A fat opera singer winked at me in her most sultry manner and for a moment I thought she was Barbara. Coming closer I saw the lines of sixty years in her sagging neck. Where is Barbara, I asked myself, searching everywhere. Surely she knows it's me. Who else could have come as a Jew? More likely she is embarrassed to be seen in my company. She's probably keeping her distance.

At last my dolorous route, the heart of which I'd just traversed, was at an end. I was being swept along by the general movement of the crowd toward the buffet, which was laden with delicacies. I reached for some smoked pork and my fringed garment trailed in the mayonnaise. A sea of black masks was focused on me. I took a hard-boiled egg, a slice of bread, and a tomato instead, and muttered something that passed for a blessing, I suppose. The hell with this disguise I thought. Now I have to pretend I eat only kosher food. I grabbed a whiskey from the waiter's tray, muttered another blessing, and downed it in one gulp. A duke in a plumed helmet fished two fat frankfurters from a steaming pot and waved them at me tantalizingly. "Frankfurters?" he offered. His eyes were swollen and he had a Bismarck voice. I took some cheese and a glass of apple wine. A rotund man in a smoking jacket and a top hat grabbed my sleeve and said, smiling sourly, "Forgive me, sir. I'm from the organizing committee, and I don't think your costume is suitable. I'm very sorry, but you will have to leave." I disengaged myself from him and disappeared in the crowd.

The apple wine, along with the other two drinks, lifted my spirits considerably. I began to circulate among the guests, smiling vacuously at anyone whose eyes met mine, chattering foolishly with anyone willing to lend an ear, intruding on other people's conversations. I even found a woman, no longer young (two flaxen braids rested on her cascading bosom), who was willing to dance cheek to cheek with me, a sight which inspired widespread smiles. As we danced in one of the adjoining rooms where a forest of paper streamers dripped from the ceiling, she called me "my Tristan" and rubbed her warm thighs against me. "My nerves are bad tonight," she whispered into my neck in English. "Stay with me. Speak to me. Why do you never speak? Speak. What are you thinking of? What thinking? What?"

I told her I didn't know what to think.

She raised her moist eyes and said, "Do you know nothing? Do you see nothing? Do you remember nothing?" (Actually, I remembered another *Festnacht* at Wagner-Gasse 9. My sister, Miri, was Queen Esther and I was Mordecai the Jew with a white cotton beard. My brother, Martin, shouted from his room, "Quiet! There's too much noise down there!") She rested her head on my chest and sang a song which was meaningless to me.

> *Frisch weht der Wind*
> *Der Heimat zu*
> *Mein Jüdisch Kind*
> *Wo wohnest Du?* *

This poor lady was completely drunk, and before the end of the dance she was asleep in my arms. I sat her down on the couch next to Chamberlain, who was catching a few winks with his head propped on the handle of his umbrella. I slipped away from this colorful forest and went to claim the suitcase I had left under the buffet table. As I wandered from room to room without finding it I drank beer from a huge wooden barrel and

* [A paraphrase of Eliot's *The Waste Land*, which quotes *Tristan und Isolde*, I, verses 5–8.—trans.]

snatched some whiskey from a tray that seemed to float over the dancers' heads. One fat fellow, either Churchill or Erhard, belched at me drunkenly, "Take my advice, my friend. Remove that patch. There are Jews here and they might be offended. It's an unpleasant business, decidedly unpleasant."

"But I *am* a Jew," I told him.

The confusion in his eyes melted into pleasure and he shook my hand warmly, handing me a cigar and proclaiming that he was especially fond of Jews. "Such clever people," he said, "the spiritual elite of Germany. The pepper in the soup. The bitters in the cocktail. I have many Jewish friends, and I am very pleased to know you, sir."

Many things happened that evening; some were forgotten by the next morning, some are vague in my memory—I was, after all, very drunk that night.

I well remember the fortune-teller who spread her diabolical cards before me in the game room and said, "I see barbed-wire fences." (She saw the patch on my clothes, the witch!) "And ashes floating on water." (She is literate, this daughter of the devil!) "I see a woman searching for you." (Very clever! A logical guess.) Later she said something about a letter from a distant land, shots in the darkness, a one-eyed man who would determine my fate, unrequitted love, and a large sum of money that would cause me distress. "You want to forget," she concluded her speculations, "but you can't. Only if you remember will you forget; and what you refuse to remember you can never forget."

I remember the tattoo artist. I found him in a maze of lottery stands, archery games, confessional booths (for five marks you could lie down on a couch and bare your soul to an old charlatan playing the part of a psychiatrist), portrait painters and silhouette artists. He worked with a cobalt pen (by-product of the atomic era) and guaranteed that his product would withstand a week of soap and water. In a moment of sheer insanity I asked him to put a phone number (my parents') on my arm. He refused, offended by the idea. I persuaded him to let me do it myself with his magic pencil, explaining that the number was given to me that evening by a mysterious woman. I remember that it hurt as I scratched the number, 62582, on my arm. When I asked what he thought of my handiwork, he dismissed it with contempt: "Dilettante."

I bought a little bottle from him that contained a blue transparent liquid. "The latest German invention," he said. "A secret chemical that erases everything. Two drops on cotton and the number will vanish." I put the bottle in my pocket, I'm sure of it, but it wasn't there the next day. After about a week the number disappeared, or rather almost disappeared, from my arm. Actually, on cold days even now it seems to me that I see the pale bluish lines under my skin.

At the caricature artist's booth I ran into the fellow who had given me the cigar earlier. He fell on my neck, belching profusely. "Where did you disappear to, my friend?" he said. "I must have a picture of you, so everyone can see." I tried to shake him off but he dragged me to the photographer, who took a picture of us in a congenial embrace against a backdrop of the Eiffel Tower. He wanted me to come with him and find his wife. "She'll be so glad to meet you," he mumbled. With great difficulty I finally succeeded in getting rid of him.

I searched all over for Barbara and did actually see her once. I recognized the feet and the bright hair falling down her back. I came up from behind and embraced her, but she turned on me and said in a rasping voice that was nothing like Barbara's, "Get away from me, you pig!" It wasn't Barbara, after all. Her partner, whose back was covered with medals, seized me by the fringes of my garment and snarled, "Keep your distance or I'll call the police."

I don't know exactly when I began to be revolted by this scene, but I remember searching for the exit and finding myself in dim rooms with swaying walls, rooms filled with signs, arrows, pointing hands that swung in every direction, oversized posters proclaiming NO EXIT,

NO WAY OUT, DO NOT ENTER, NO TRESPASSING, NO OUT-
LET. I remember running away from the man in the
smoking jacket and top hat who took me by surprise
again and again, always coming up to me with the
same words: "I'm from the organizing committee and
I don't think the costume you have chosen is suitable."
In the course of many escapes from this polite pest I fell
into the hands of my philo-Semite, who refused to let
me go. I ended up giving him a hard push and hugging
an old woman who lost her false teeth in the excitement.
I remember a hall of distorting mirrors that made me
dizzy; Jewish faces, ridiculous ones, pathetic ones,
grotesque ones, peered out at me from every side.

From the hall of mirrors I wandered into a dim room
filled with dancers. The band was playing a slow, quiet
tango. Then I noticed that the dancers were asleep; their
hands hung limp, their feet were nearly immobile. "How
do you get out of here?" I bellowed into the ear of a
Supreme Court justice. He opened his eyes for a second,
then fell back asleep on the neck of a nun who snored
placidly. When I asked the pianist the same question, he
was startled out of his lethargy and pointed toward a
low door at the opposite end of the room.

Beyond this door I discovered an enormous beer hall
I hadn't seen before. Those very people who were paying
me reparations sat at long tables in tight rows, swaying
from side to side, tapping their mighty beer mugs, and
singing, "Wer soll das bezahlen? Wer hat so viel Gelt?"
No one seemed to notice me as I passed through, though
I stuck my chest out so the yellow patch on my lapel
would be conspicuous. Then I remember losing control.
I stood on a chair and began to orate.

"What are you thinking?" I cried. "Are you trying to
ignore me? You drink your foul-smelling beer and forget. See this yellow patch! Does it remind you of anything, you swine? I am a Jew! Have you forgotten what
that is? Did you think you could liquidate us all with
your ingenious devices? You thought you had a final
solution? You were mistaken, gentlemen. Here I am,
alive and thriving. And you will not ignore me though

you ignore the haunting horror when you light the gas oven in your kitchen, when you wash your hands with soap, when you lie down on a hair mattress. I will not let you forget. See this number on my arm!"

When I rolled up my seleve and displayed the number on my arm the singing stopped, and the room fell silent. Someone shook my chair and I found myself on the floor, my face splattered with sawdust. "What did he say? What did he say?" someone asked anxiously.

"He didn't say anything. He wasn't speaking German."

Someone else asked, "What language was he speaking?"

The same voice answered, "No language. He was just pretending to say something. Must be an actor."

Two masked figures helped me to my feet. "He's Jewish," someone said, "he stinks of onion." One of the men who was helping me whispered, with great authority, that I must follow him. Rather than waiting for me to oblige, they lifted me up and carried me out of the room.

From here on I remember the details very clearly, having recounted them so often. The men in black who dragged me out (they were merely ushers) led me to the director of the carnival, a slight man of about sixty who sat behind a desk wearing a red clown's nose and spectacles without lenses. The ushers hauled me right up to him before they let go of me.

"Sir," the director said in a haughty but polite tone, "I'm terribly sorry, but this is impossible. True, this is a costume party, but everything has its limits. Your costume as well as your behavior have offended many of the guests. You have exceeded the limits of good taste. We cannot allow any individual to interfere with the mood of the entire event. We've had enough of this nonsense."

At a signal the two ushers pounced on me. One of them ripped off my beard and threw it on the floor; the other tore at the yellow patch as well as the lapel and pushed my hat off my head. When I bent down for the hat one of them gave me a professional kick and they both laughed.

"And now," the director said, "be so kind as to rid us of your unpleasant company. You are not welcome here. Get out immediately and take your suitcase with you, if you don't mind!"

He threw the suitcase at my feet. As I picked it up the two guards grabbed me and began to drag me out of the room. Some of the guests stopped to see what was going on but turned away quickly and resumed their conversations as though they had seen nothing. "They're kicking me out!" I shouted, but no one even glanced my way. The guards pushed me so hard that I fell. I picked myself up and offered them my arms so they could lead me. And here, at the very last moment, as in all the fairy tales, a miracle occurred. Martin Schiller, the good German I had met on the train from Milan, the poor tormented pervert, this man of rare integrity, came toward us in the black uniform of an SS officer. Recognizing each other immediately we embraced. A familiar perfume filled my nostrils. "What do they want from you?" he asked. When I told him, he insisted that they leave me alone. "But—" one of the guards protested. "No buts!" Martin ordered curtly. "Mr. Lam is my friend and I'm responsible for him." The guards let go of me with an obedient "*Jawohl, mein Herr*" and vanished.

I was glad to see Martin and he was glad to see me; he beamed as he clasped my hand. I told him the uniform suited him well. He said with a bitter grimace that he was sorry he couldn't say the same for me. (We spoke German, and he nodded in total understanding when I explained why I had spoken English when we first met.) I asked why he had come as a Nazi. He said for the same reason I had come as a Jew—we both wanted to remind them of what happened here. "Come on," he said. "Let's go in and make them uncomfortable."

Arm in arm we entered the main hall. To my surprise our entrance didn't excite much interest. A few people noticed us and smiled, this time without a trace of scorn. The smiles were simple and warm. There were a few polite nods and even some gentle applause as we passed. The response was one of pleasure, even pride.

Someone said, "Look, what an excellent idea!" Martin's face was pale and his hand, locked in mine, was trembling. We headed for the bar, where two Venetian merchants gave us their places. Ordering two large beers we drank them down without a word. A morose clown who stood near us caught the bartender's eye, pointed to us, and two more beers appeared. No one paid any attention to us. The crowd continued to drink, chatter, laugh, as if we did not exist.

"Our performance is a flop," I said bitterly.

"Yes," Martin agreed. "Instead of shaking them up we're fulfilling their most cherished dream. For them we seem to symbolize an acceptance of the past, the wish to forget and turn over a new leaf. There's no choice, Lam, if we want them not to forget, if we want them to remember that it can all happen again—today, tomorrow, here or anywhere—we must play out our roles. There's no choice. I must be the Nazi and you must be the Jew."

"I understand," I said faintly.

"Forgive me," Martin whispered as he got up. He took the beer and threw it in my face. Those at the bar reacted with frozen terror. The clown's face was distorted by a weird smile.

"Get out, you damned Jew!" Martin screeched in a hysterical voice I recalled from war movies. "Scram, you pig!"

An awful silence reigned. The dancing stopped. A sea of unmasked faces, pale and expressionless, turned on us all at once. Suddenly, I thought, they see the Black Death seeping through the barriers of their palace. A sobering chill has possessed the revelers, those who thought to escape the plague. Beer streamed down my cheeks and dripped down my torn kapote. I picked up the shabby suitcase, which seemed heavier than I remembered, and turned to go. In the oppressive silence I heard only my pounding heart and the thump of Martin's boots on the marble floor. Head bowed, back bent, I traversed the "Via Dolorosa" cleared by the crowd. I did not see faces, only feet. Tens, hundreds, thousands of pairs of feet in endless procession.

"Beat it, you Yiddish shit!" Martin's voice lashed at my back.

When we were a safe distance from the hotel, after checking to be sure no one was watching we let go and laughed and laughed, our voices resounding in the rainy street. Martin put his arm across my shoulder and we walked and laughed until real tears appeared in my eyes. Later, in the taxi he grew quiet and shook his head sadly, saying, "Forgive me for my performance."

"You did very well," I said. "For a minute I thought you were a real Nazi."

"And I thought you were a real Jew," he said.

When Martin got out at the opera house we parted with a long, wordless handshake. I watched him take off the black SS hat and disappear in the rain. This is how I picture him to this day: walking hatless, in the rain, the ruins of the opera house in the background. I never saw him again.

When I got home at 3 A.M. Barbara was asleep. She had walked out of the party as soon as she saw me dressed as a Jew.

35 | *an end and a beginning*

That's that. Now, I have only to pack my things, tie up the loose ends, and conclude my account.

The day after the party I couldn't elicit a word from Barbara about my mad disguise, which was designed to test us both. She saw me at the party and went right home. She was determined to let the matter drop. "I don't want any more fights," she asserted with finality, realizing that the mildest disapproval would incite a new round. She sensed that I was girded for battle.

Some days later, when she began to press the matter of our trip to Israel in direct contradiction to her previous position and was even willing to forgo her final exams if we would leave Germany immediately and begin our new life, I began to understand how deeply distressed she must have been by my conduct that evening. If she's willing to miss her exams, I thought, and make such a great sacrifice for my sake, she must have considered the issue carefully and concluded that a longer stay in Germany involving further encounters with my past would strain our relationship and undermine it even more.

I could tell that this was her logic by her worried manner. I remembered the day two or three months earlier when her father had tried to convince me, using many of Dr. Mayer's arguments, that I belonged in Germany. Barbara didn't join in the conversation, but she stood beside him with her hand on his chair, as if to indicate that he spoke in her name and with her total support. Now she suddenly felt pressed, regarding each additional day in Frankfurt as a waste. She wanted to pack up and go immediately, having apparently decided that I was in danger, that the sooner we leave, the better.

I couldn't accept this, eager as I was to get back to Israel. To me the situation didn't seem so drastic that we couldn't hold out another two months. There was an element of insult in her excessive concern, concern that was akin to pity. I wasn't ready for a retreat, with its implicit panic. I was unwilling to receive her great sacrifice, to incur so heavy a debt. I knew very well that this noble gesture was essentially a generous one, intended to dramatize the extent of her concern. "I'm willing to drop everything and go immediately," she had said, yet I hesitated to put her to the test.

I pretended to consider her proposal seriously. "All right, Barbara . . . I hear you, and my answer is . . ." (brief pause to heighten the suspense) "no. Let's wait another month, as we planned originally. Don't worry, I can take it." I said this with mild scorn. "You take my performances to seriously—I like to fool around," I added, laughing nervously.

She stared into my eyes, trying to fathom my words and finally gave me her hand. I clutched it as if to conclude the bargain and threw in a kiss for emphasis. She sighed, much relieved and grateful that I hadn't betrayed her trust. I have behaved like a gentleman, I thought, and she will surely cherish my altruism.

My gravest problem now was idleness, how to occupy myself in the two months that remained before Barbara's exams. The reparations claim was proceeding well without me and no longer required my attention. The papers that arrived from the Technion won me fifteen thousand marks, and an oath sworn before a district judge established my position as sole inheritor, yielding an additional twenty-five thousand marks.

The high hopes I had invested in the competition in Israel were smashed abruptly by a cable from Amos with the news that we didn't even get honorable mention. I was about to pack away my drafting equipment (the sight of it reminded me of the idleness ahead), when Barbara's father called and solved the whole problem. He was planning to add a wing to his plant and wondered if I would be willing to take a look at the plans before he authorized construction. Of course I agreed, and that same day I went to Düsseldorf. I planned to stay a day or two and then come back to spend the weekend with Barbara, but as things developed I spent more than two months in Düsseldorf.

On the way to Düsseldorf I remember listening to the sleep-inducing drone of the windshield wipers and hoping that I would disapprove of the plan. I'll find errors and flaws, I thought. I'll prove to Barbara's father that one can build a bold, handsome, functional structure at a lower cost. Then he'll ask me to design a new plan and I'll begin work immediately. The long months will pass without my noticing. I'll show him what an architect from Israel can do.

With great excitement I spread the plans on the guest room floor. After a superficial glance I was convinced that they really were inadequate. I questioned Barbara's father at some length to clarify the particular problems involved in this undertaking. Then I went back to the plans and discovered many flaws (I'll omit technical details), as well as excesses contrived to increase construction costs and raise the architects' profit proportionately. (I was familiar with these devices from my work with Brumberg-Avishai-Landau.)

That evening we cloistered ourselves in the library, where, over coffee, French brandy, and a superb Cuban cigar, I listed the shortcomings and excesses I had noted in the design. Barbara's father listened attentively. "How could that be?" he said. "Impossible." We reviewed each point and then added up the sums that could be saved through my proposed revisions. The total was quite impressive. "Tomorrow morning we'll see the architects," he said, slapping my back with affection and esteem.

Mr. Miller, the head of the architectural planning firm, a man of about sixty with a high forehead and a pleasantly intellectual face, received us in his office at ten. He listened gravely to my comments, questioning me and glancing at the sketches. My exhaustive presentation was followed by a tense silence. Mr. Miller apparently agreed with me and was appalled that such elementary faults weren't spotted by his senior architects. Would I be willing to work with them on the new plans? *Wunderbar,* very good. "Young man," Miller concluded, "I like you. Your analysis was incisive. We need new blood in our office. I'd be very glad to have you join us." The next day I was installed at a spacious drafting table in his office.

Those were good days. The work was engrossing, and the four days each week away from Barbara were helpful too, I must admit. I missed her, and, lying in her girlhood bed in the long moments preceding sleep, I began to see her again as I had loved her always. One night she confessed in the darkness that she missed me very much too and thought of me incessantly, admitting that it was hard to fall asleep alone in our wide bed in Frankfurt. Our three-day weekends in her parents' home were transformed into a honeymoon, a maddeningly short one. When she went back to Frankfurt I would write her wild love letters and call her regularly to say good night to her and to Jonathan.

"Your eyes have the old glow," she remarked one morning. "Don't say it's because you love me. You love your work. And I don't mind one bit. I'm not jealous."

After about a week of work, closely supervised by Miller, he called me into his office. In the presence of Barbara's father and his two partners he offered me a permanent position, a handsome salary, and in addition (I couldn't believe my ears) an option for partnership after two years. I was utterly bewildered—Barbara's father claimed later that I actually blushed like a schoolboy. I thanked Miller and his partners (Barbara's father beamed at me proudly), saying I would consider the offer and give them my verdict in a week.

This unexpected development, which could have altered not only my immediate plans but the entire course of my life, did in fact set off quite an upheaval. My first reaction, after I left Barbara's father and returned to my desk, was negative. But that night in bed I considered the seductive offer. Why not, really, I asked myself. Why not spend a year or two in Düsseldorf? The people are congenial; they treat me well, value my work, and are open to new ideas. Miller wants me to look over some of his sketches and give him my opinion. Would I find a comparable situation in Israel? Would Brumberg ever ask me to comment on his work? Or Landau? Why not accept the proposal? (Partnership!) I could work here for two or three years and go back to Israel enriched by experience and professional know-how. Why not? Barbara's father would be very pleased, and she certainly wouldn't object. Three years pass quickly when you're involved in gratifying work.

Who knows? If it hadn't been for Max I might have succumbed to this enticing proposition. I went to Frankfurt to talk it over with Barbara. I may have even intended to impose the difficult choice on her. But she was too clever to take on the responsibility for such a serious step. "It's your decision," she said. "I wouldn't want you to blame me later on for a glittering career in Germany." The devil. She didn't express an outright opinion, yet in her characteristic way she communicated something quite clearly. A glittering career in Germany, she had said. She saw us settling there. She knew it wasn't a matter of two or three years, and she hadn't forgotten the masked ball or the pneumonia.

I went to Max for advice. Instead of telling him about the offer, I found myself attacking him and enjoying his discomfort. I suppose I wanted to put myself in the position of devil's advocate and debate with myself in his presence. I thought he would justify, or at least rationalize, his own situation. I hoped he would repel my attack, and in the course of his own defense provide compelling grounds for accepting the offer. But there he sat in his plush office, shamefaced, his eyes downcast. The conversation that followed wasn't what I had anticipated.

Can you explain what you're doing here, I challenged. You came in connection with your reparations settlement, which makes sense. You wrote me once that you would stay a year, at most two; actually, it's been about eight years. I don't get it. Did you bother to learn Arabic so you could sell refrigerators? Answer me, Max. Is this what you wanted to be . . . a German merchant? You collected reparations, settled your account with the past, made some money; why not come home? How can you stay here? You know very well what I mean when I say "here." It seems to me that you once had parents here, an entire family, and something happened to them here. How can you do business with people who . . . All right, all right, stop making faces. I won't go into the personal history of your customers, what they did—yes, your customers—to your parents, my parents, and many others. You mean to tell me you don't sell cooking ovens until the customer proves he wasn't involved in what happened here? Don't you understand? You're selling your soul every day, like a whore-in-mourning. Don't you understand this, Maxie?

I didn't hear any real defense from him, although he was trying to justify himself, that much was clear. He said he would have come home long ago were it not for . . . all sorts of things: responsibility, debts, Edna. Edna likes Europe, he said; she's comfortable in Frankfurt—besides, it's not so simple. He can't pick up and leave. Then there are the children. But he'll be back—in a year or two, at most. That's what he said, and I felt sorry for him. I saw myself in his shoes eight years later. When I left him and shook his limp hand at least I knew where I stood.

That very evening I sat down with Barbara to plan our departure. First I convinced her that I should go ahead immediately after her exams, suggesting that we send our belongings off as soon as possible, within the next two or three weeks. Only after they reached Jerusalem and the house was in good order would she set out. I'd meet her at the airport with flowers and a brass band. "There won't be anything for you to do when you arrive," I said, "no furniture moving, no books to arrange—no nothing. When you come, everything will be ready. Don't forget, by then you'll be in the eighth month." We sat up late making long lists of what was to be sent: the couch on which it all began, kitchen equipment, bedding, a new refrigerator and oven, books, rugs, a crib for Jonathan, our wedding presents, a radio, an iron—everything. ("And I'll buy a new stereo with my money. Yes, I want to. I insist," I told her.) "Also, I'll need your signature to get the things released from customs and to take the car over. I'll take it with me on the boat." "You think of everything," Barbara remarked, impressed with my talents as organizer.

When I returned to Düsseldorf I informed Mr. Miller and Barbara's parents of our decision. Miller responded with regret and suprise, and Barbara's father refused to accept the decision as final. He asked me to weigh the matter again, warning me not to be impulsive, to postpone a decision at least until after the baby was born. He tried to convince me that Miller's offer was a rare opportunity for advancement, that from every point of view it would be worthwhile to work with him for a year or two. "You can always go back to Israel," he argued, "but you won't always have such an opportunity." He talked and talked and I shook my head obstinately. "No, Mr. Stahl," I said decisively, "we've made our choice. We're going. I want my son to be born in Israel."

The next few weeks passed quickly. By the end of April, when Barbara finished her exams, all our possessions were already on their way to Israel. An experienced shipping agency, Transport (founded, ironically, in 1933), packed everything in an enormous crate and sent it to Hamburg, and from there on an Israeli freighter to Haifa.

A few days before the trip, after I said good-bye to Miller and to my other colleagues in the office, Barbara's father told me the truth. We had just finished dinner and were about to leave the table when Mr. Stahl cleared his throat and announced in a serious tone that he had a confession to make. Barbara and her mother looked up with concern. For a minute I was sure he was going to confess that he had been a Nazi, but what unfolded was entirely different. It turned out that the plans he had consulted me about, the plans I had spent more than two months revising, were concocted. It was that simple —the faults and excesses were deliberate. He had contrived this scheme to tempt me, to involve me in work so we would stay in Germany. He didn't want us to go. "Don't be angry, Uri," he said with touching tenderness, "my intentions were good. It was a test and you withstood it, every aspect of it. Not only by finding all the flaws in the design, but by discovering two further problems no one was aware of. Miller's proposal was sincere. He really wanted you to work with him. I'm very sorry you didn't fall into our trap."

Mrs. Stahl, shaking her head in wonder, said, "Ludwig, Ludwig." Seeing her father's penitent face, Barbara began to laugh merrily.

"A fine trick," I said, trying to conceal the twinkle in my eye.

"Do you forgive me?" Mr. Stahl asked humbly.

"I am unforgiving," I said sternly. "As punishment for this deception, Mr. Stahl, you must vow to visit us in Jerusalem immediately after our baby is born."

"I promise," he said, raising his hand in oath, then added meekly, "I was expecting a more severe punishment."

"You already got it," I said. He stopped in his tracks and looked at me questioningly. "I made some deliberate miscalculations in my new plan, which your architects failed to note."

"You're kidding!" he said.

"That's right," I said, linking my arm with Barbara's, "I *am* kidding. I never suspected a thing, and even if I had, I doubt if I could fool your architects. They're really first-rate. I didn't understand how they could have submitted such a plan. I was mystified for a long time but now, of course, it's clear."

We spent my last evening in Düsseldorf at an expensive restaurant, where everyone made a humorous farewell speech. As a parting gift Barbara's father gave me an antique gold pocket watch he had received from his father on his wedding day, concluding his emotionally charged words with, "Next year in Jerusalem," a phrase he had learned from his Jewish accountant. Mrs. Stahl, slightly tipsy, picked up a champagne goblet and sang a little farewell song that won prolonged applause from everyone in the restaurant. And Barbara? She stared at me all evening without a word. Her smiles were forced. Only when we were home in bed, as I reached over to turn off the light, did I notice the tears in her eyes. I lay close to her and to Jonathan all that night, whispering love and affection. She held my hand tight and said nothing.

The next day, a fine May morning, I said good-bye to her parents, asked them to look after my wife, and promised to write as soon as I reached Jerusalem. I kissed Barbara's lips and her salty eyes, placed a kiss on her belly, and set off. In the rear-view mirror I watched my wife recede into the distance.

The scenes that flashed before my eyes during the long and tiring trip from Düsseldorf to Venice were the landscape of my childhood: trees swimming in circles beyond the window, my father standing beside me on that last journey toward being an orphan. I saw him at the border station, bending over me, burying his head in my neck, his hand stroking my new coat ever so gently. "We'll all be together soon, my son," he whispered in a broken voice. "We'll join you soon, and go together to a land where the sun always shines." These were the last words I heard from his lips. I saw that his eyes were red. I remember thinking he was sick.

At the border between Austria and Italy, the scenery began to suggest Aunt Anna's home. Elm trees, apple trees, green valleys, as far as the eye could see. I heard the chatter of white geese at the roadside and whispered to myself, "*Sono stanco, Zia Anna.*" I am tired, I want to sleep in your bed, Aunt Anna. When I stopped at a little *trattoria* for Sunday spaghetti and some of the plain red wine that follows morning mass, the air was suffused with the smell of garlic which used to fill her bosom. How many years have passed, madonna! I was ten when I arrived at San Castello. Then I was eleven, twelve, thirteen, and there was a yellow cake on the wooden table in the kitchen. I dipped some cake in a dish of sweet wine. When my eyes were closed I heard Uncle Michele's coarse laughter. "*Nostro coniglio è stanco,*" he said. Our bunny is tired. In their eyes I was a little bunny, escaped from the slaughterhouse at the very last moment. Are they still alive, Uncle Michele and Aunt Anna? Why did I never write to them? Will they know me, their *coniglio*, in a new Mercedes, a boy of twenty-nine, married, almost a father?

Yes, of course I went to San Castello. How could I not go? As I stopped the car near the house, a convention of geese dispersed noisily. Three women in black eyed me with curiosity from the other side of the street. (A real street. How the village had grown!) I knocked three times before the wooden door, which was just the way I remembered it, was opened by Uncle Michele. He had aged considerably. Behind him, in the dimness of the kitchen, I saw Aunt Anna's anxious face. Though they did not recognize me, Uncle Michele's first word was "*Favorita*," which is to say: Please sit down and eat with us. I had arrived at sunset and they were in the middle of their early dinner. He invited me to the table with a welcoming gesture and repeated, "*Favorita*." Suddenly he wrinkled up his forehead and his eyes contracted. Aunt Anna gaped at me in wonder and I found myself locked in her warm embrace, kissing her sun-parched cheeks and searching in her neck for the fragrance of my childhood. "Our *coniglio* is back!" she mumbled, her eyes flooded with tears. Uncle Michele tore me away from her, placed his heavy arm around me, and kissed me, his white mustache fragrant with the smells of coarse tobacco and red wine. I spent the night in their house.

The next day on the deck of the *Moledet*, standing apart from the other passengers and watching Venice fade into the horizon, dipped in the flaming gold of sunset, I let myself be moved by the unforgettable reunion with my adopted parents. The many hours we spent together around the kitchen table engrossed in adult conversation remained with me throughout the voyage. I saw (and I see it now) Uncle Michele's furrowed face, the glass of wine in his quivering hand. I remembered (and still remember) his hoarse words which solved many riddles for me.

The man in the hunter's hat, he explained was Signor Manzone from Verona. ("He was killed, poor fellow, in a car accident two years ago. Signor Manzone, may he rest in peace, was a holy man. Only after the war did we discover he was a Communist.") In April 1941, immediately after the collapse of Yugoslavia, Signor Manzone had gone to Zagreb. ("At that time everyone was traveling to the occupied areas.") He returned with handsome spoils: three children, of whom I was one, were entrusted to him by the Jewish community council in Zagreb on the condition that he would find us shelter. The paper Uncle Michele had signed on this table in the kitchen was not a bill of sale, as I had thought all those years, but a pledge to return me to the Jewish institutions or to my relatives, if they survived, at the end of the war. ("We liked you from the very first moment. You were a handsome child and so sad. You stood here in the kitchen so fearful, like a little rabbit. From the first day we called you our *coniglio*.")

Why did they adopt me? Why did they risk it? To them it was a sign from heaven. They wanted a child. ("We tried everything—doctors, prayer, holy water. Nothing helped until you came. You were sent to us from heaven.") A few weeks after my arrival, Aunt Anna became pregnant. I remembered the baby, the tiny creature I had rocked in a wooden cradle, their son, Tonio, who was now studying in Verona. After the war, after I was taken to Milan (by a man in a white shirt from whom I first heard the word "shalom"), Francesca was born. This pretty fifteen-year-old girl sat at the table, peering at us with large black eyes. They hid me in their house a whole year. If I set foot outside the kitchen door, Aunt Anna would slap me hard. ("How you used to cry, poor *coniglio*. Your silent tears used to break my heart. We never heard you cry—we only saw. We were so afraid you would be taken away from us.") Only after I had learned Italian like a native, when I could answer questions and say I was born in Bolzano, that my father had gone into the army, my mother was dead, and Michele was my uncle, only then was I allowed to go out. ("Remember? 'If you see anyone in uniform, come right home!' Do you remember, *coniglio*?") They cried when I was taken to Milan. I kept the suitcase they had bought me for a long time. At the Technion I left it out in the rain by mistake and then had to throw it out.

What about me? What had happened to me since I left them? Did I find my parents? Did I marry?

I told them I was about to become a father and Uncle Michele filled our glasses with wine. They both drank to Barbara and to Jonathan, my son. I promised we would visit them one summer. Aunt Anna embraced me and kissed me again on both cheeks. Later, when I told them the fate of my family, she nodded sadly over and over, and tears filled her kind eyes. Crossing herself she repeated again and again, "*Santa Maria, madonna mia!*" We finally fell silent and my eyes began to droop. I heard Aunt Anna say, "*Sei stanco, coniglio.* You are tired, my little bunny. Want to sleep in Aunt Anna's bed?" They both laughed heartily.

Francesca made up Antonio's bed for me. When the door closed I threw myself on the bed and reviewed the sad, beautiful years spent in this house. I don't remember how the idea occurred to me. I was almost asleep when I suddenly asked myself (I may have been thinking that I should have brought a present) how I could compensate them for what they had done for me. I knew the answer, immediately. Of course . . . why hadn't I thought of it sooner? The perfect solution: they should receive reparations for the three years they took care of me. Someone should pay—why not me? And generously. Since the Germans are paying me five marks for every day my father spent expiring in that hell, I'll pay them ten marks for every day of shelter: 365 times three, times ten marks.

I remember getting out of bed to calculate the exact sum. My heart pounded wildly when I saw the results: 10,950 marks, the precise sum I had received for my parents' lost freedom.

The next day, after driving them through the town and being proudly introduced to many neighbors, some of whom remembered me and insisted that we drink together, I brought them home brimming with contentment and delight, and handed Uncle Michele the check I had prepared the night before. They were shocked to learn the sum in Italian lire, and refused to accept it. Only after I told them about the great inheritance that had fallen in my lap, as it were, and about my wife's rich parents, after the check passed back and forth from their hands to mine, from my hand to Uncle Michele's pocket, from there to Aunt Anna's apron, only after I threatened

that I would never see them again, nor would I write or
visit with my wife and child, only then did they yield,
showering me with thank you's and with kisses. I barely
managed to take leave of them. When the car began to
move they were still standing in front of the house,
waving and calling, "*Coniglio, coniglio.*" Their cries
echoed in my ears all the way to Venice.

I smile at myself indulgently when I remember this
parting. My dramatic gesture may have been foolish—
eight thousand Israeli pounds is a considerable sum.
I very much doubt if I would be capable of such generosity today, but that morning, for the first time since
I entered my reparations claim, I was at peace with
myself. I felt at last that I had the right to use the money
as I saw fit. My conscience was clear. When the boat
docked in Haifa, I cabled Barbara: "I AM HOME AND
I AM TOGETHER AGAIN. ALL I NEED IS YOU, MY LOVE."

It took a week to release our things from customs and
have them moved to Jerusalem. On the 23rd of May,
after the house had been put in order and painted (our
furniture crate stands at the brink of the Valley of
Hinnom to this day), Barbara arrived. We ate the
oriental dinner I had prepared in her honor and that
same night Barbara went into labor.

She gave birth in the eighth month, at five in the
morning. When I kissed her pale, tired face in the metal
hospital bed she grabbed my hand and said, "He was
born early." I leaned over her and kissed her dry lips.
"Don't worry, dear Barbara," I whispered, "he's fine.
Sleep, my love. Have a good rest."

This, in effect, is the end of the story. From here on
an entirely other story begins, one I may get to one of
these days.

Oh, yes, one further thing. When I returned from the
hospital that morning (the eastern skies already anointed
with a blazing purple sunrise), I stopped for coffee in a
little restaurant at the old bus station, which was buzzing with laborers. They were all excited about the news
that had appeared in the morning paper. I know, in fact